Praise for
A LADY OF THE WEST

"A powerful, emotionally intense, very sensual tale ... as ... untamed as the wild New Mexico landscape."

—*Romantic Times*

"Linda Howard has finally dipped her quill in historical ink. Be the first in your group to be outrageously indulged; after you've finished—sigh! —you can spread the word or you can sit in your hot tub and just dream and smile. I did all three."

—Catherine Coulter

"Filled with compelling characters, sensuous romance and loads of action."

—*Affaire de Coeur*

"*A LADY OF THE WEST* is marvelous. Textured with gritty reality, riveting action and sizzling sensuality, it still manages to capture moments of heartwarming pathos and tenderness. I read it through at one sitting because I couldn't put it down. . . . Wonderful."

—Iris Johansen

Books by Linda Howard

A Lady of the West
Angel Creek
The Touch of Fire
Heart of Fire
Dream Man
After the Night
Shades of Twilight
Son of the Morning
Kill and Tell
Now You See Her
All the Queen's Men
Mr. Perfect
Strangers in the Night
Open Season
Dream Man

Published by Pocket Books

LINDA HOWARD

the Touch of Fire

POCKET BOOKS
New York   London   Toronto   Sydney

For information regarding special discounts for bulk purchases,
please contact Simon & Schuster Special Sales at
1 800-456-6798 or business@simonandschuster.com

An *Original* Publication of POCKET BOOKS

POCKET BOOKS, a division of Simon & Schuster, Inc.
1230 Avenue of the Americas, New York 10020

ISBN: 0-671-01972-4

First Pocket Books printing October 1992

20   19   18   17   16   15

POCKET and colophon are registered trademarks of
Simon & Schuster, Inc.

Front cover illustration by Brian Bailey

Printed in the U.S.A.

Dedicated to my niece,
Brandwyn Robinson,
whom I've loved from the minute
she was born

the Touch of Fire

CHAPTER

1

1871, Arizona Territory

Someone had been on his back trail for most of the day. He had seen a telltale flash of light in the distance when he had stopped for grub around noon, just a tiny bright flicker that had lasted only a split second, but that had been enough to alert him. Maybe it had been the sun glinting off a buckle or a shiny spur. Whoever was back there had been just a little careless, and now they had lost the advantage of surprise.

Rafe McCay hadn't panicked; he had continued to ride as if he had nowhere in particular to go and all the time in the world to get there. It would be getting dark soon, and he decided he'd better find out who was tracking him before he made camp for the night. Besides, according to his calculations the tracker should be exposed on that long tree-line trail just about now. McCay got the field glass out of his saddlebag and stepped into the shadow of a big pine, making certain that no reflection could give him away, too. He trained the glass on the trail where he estimated the tracker would be and soon spotted the man: one rider on a dark brown horse with a right front stocking. The man was holding the horse to a walk and leaning over to examine the trail as they went. McCay had come that way himself an hour or so before.

Something about the rider was familiar. McCay kept the glass trained on the distant figure, trying to trigger his memory, but he couldn't get a good look at the man's face. Maybe it was the way he sat in the saddle, or maybe even the horse itself that gave McCay a gnawing sense that somewhere down the line he'd seen or met this particular man, and that he hadn't liked what he'd learned. But he just couldn't bring the man's name to mind. The rig on the horse wasn't unusual, and there was nothing about the man's clothes that was out of the ordinary, except maybe for his flat-crowned black hat trimmed with silver conchas—

Trahern.

McCay's breath hissed through his teeth.

The bounty on his head must have gotten pretty big, to attract someone like Trahern. Trahern's reputation was that he was a good tracker, a damn good shot, and that he never stopped, never gave up.

Four years of being hunted kept McCay from doing anything hasty or foolish. He had both time and surprise on his side, as well as experience. Trahern didn't know it, but the hunted had just become the hunter.

On the chance that Trahern might have a field glass, too, McCay remounted and rode deeper into the trees before circling back to the right, putting a small rise between him and his pursuer. If there was one thing the war had taught him, it was always to know the lay of the land, and he automatically chose courses that gave him, whenever possible, both cover and escape routes. He could cover his tracks and lose the bounty hunter here in the timber, but there was another thing the war had taught him: never leave an enemy on your back trail. If he didn't deal with it now, he'd have to deal with it later, when the circumstances might not be in his favor. Trahern had signed his own death warrant by trying to collect this particular bounty. McCay had long since lost any scruples about killing the men who came after him; it was a matter of his life or theirs, and he was damn tired of running.

When he had doubled back a mile, he left his horse concealed behind a rocky outcropping and made his way on foot to where he could see his original trail. By his calculations, the bounty hunter should be along within half an hour. McCay carried his rifle in a scabbard slung across his back. It was a repeater that he'd had for a couple of years now. It was plenty accurate for the distance, which was about sixty yards. He chose his cover, a big pine with a two-foot-high rock at the base of it, and settled into position to wait.

But the minutes ticked by, and Trahern didn't appear. McCay lay motionless and listened to the sounds around him. Birds were calling, undisturbed, having become accustomed to him since he hadn't moved for so long. Had something made Trahern suspicious? McCay couldn't think of anything he'd done. Maybe Trahern had just stopped to rest, cautiously putting more distance between himself and his quarry until he was ready to make his move. That was Trahern's way: biding his time until things suited him. McCay liked to operate that way himself. A lot of men had gotten themselves killed by taking the fight forward when the odds were against them.

Colonel Mosby had always said that Rafe McCay was the best he'd ever seen in ambush because he had patience and endurance. McCay could withstand discomfort, hunger, pain and boredom, divorcing his mind from it and concentrating instead on the job at hand. The growing darkness, however, opened up other possibilities. Trahern could have stopped and made camp for the night rather than try to follow a trail in the failing light. He might think it would be easier to spot a cook fire and just be lying back there biding his time; but Trahern was smart enough to know that a man on the run made do a lot of times with a cold camp, and only a damn fool slept by a fire anyway. A man stayed alive by building a small fire to cook, then putting it out and moving to another location to bed down.

McCay's own choices now were to stay right where he was and pick Trahern off whenever he *did* come down the trail, backtrack a bit more and try to find Trahern at his own camp, or use the darkness to put even more distance between them.

His horse whickered softly down by the rocks, and McCay swore violently to himself. He heard an answering whinny immediately, and the second call was right behind him. McCay reacted instantly, rolling and bringing the barrel of the rifle around. Trahern was about twenty yards behind and to his left, and it was a toss-up which of them was the most surprised. Trahern had cleared leather, but he was looking in the wrong direction, down toward McCay's horse. McCay's movement brought him swinging around, and McCay got off the first shot, but Trahern was already dodging to the side and the slug missed. Trahern's shot went wild.

The crest of the ridge was right behind McCay and he simply rolled over it, getting a mouthful of dirt and pine needles in the process, but that was better than taking a bullet. He spat the dirt out and got to his feet, bending low to keep the ridge line between him and Trahern. Silently he moved to his right, working his way back toward his horse.

He wasn't in a good mood. Damn it, what was Trahern doing wandering away from the trail like that? The bounty hunter hadn't been expecting anything, or he wouldn't have been so surprised at finding his prey right under his nose. Well, hell, sometimes even the best traps didn't work, but now Trahern was right on him and he'd lost the advantage of surprise.

He gained the shelter of another big pine and went down on one knee behind it, holding himself still and quiet while he listened. He was in a mess and he knew it. All Trahern had to do was settle down where he could watch McCay's horse, and McCay was trapped, too. His only chance was to spot Trahern before Trahern spotted him, and a lot of men had died trying to do that very thing.

Then a humorless smile lifted the corners of his hard mouth. There were only a few minutes of light left. If Trahern wanted to see who could snake around better in the dark, McCay was happy to oblige him.

He closed his eyes and let his ears catch every sound without the distraction of sight to dilute the message. He noticed a gradual increase in the chirping of insects and tree frogs, as the nighttime denizens went about their business. When he opened his eyes again, about ten minutes later, his sight had already adjusted to the darkness and he could easily make out the outlines of trees and bushes.

McCay slipped pine needles through his spurs to keep them from jingling and replaced the rifle in the scabbard on his back; the long gun would be too awkward to hold while crawling around in the dark. He removed his revolver from the holster, then eased down onto his belly and snake-crawled toward the cover of a clump of bushes.

The iciness of the ground beneath him reminded him that winter hadn't completely released its grip on the land yet. During the comparative warmth of the day he had taken off his coat and tied it to the back of his saddle. Now that the sun had set, the temperature was plunging.

He'd been cold before, and the pungent smell of pine needles reminded him that he'd crawled on his belly more than once, too. Back in '63, he'd completely circled a Yankee patrol on his belly, moving not three feet behind one guard, then returned to Mosby and reported the patrol's strength and the placement of the guards. He'd also snaked through the mud one rainy November night with a bullet in his leg and the

Yankees beating the bushes for him. Only the fact that he'd been so thoroughly coated with mud had enabled him to escape capture that time.

It took him half an hour to ease back to the crest of the ridge and slide over it as sinuously as a snake going into a river. There he paused once again, letting his eyes go unfocused while he examined the surrounding trees for a shape that didn't belong, his ears listening for the stamp of a hoof or a horse's snuffle. If Trahern was as smart as he was supposed to be, he'd have moved the horses, but maybe he'd been too wary to show himself like that.

How long could Trahern stay alert, all his senses straining? The effort exhausted most men if they weren't used to it. McCay was so used to it that he didn't even have to think about it anymore. The past four years hadn't been much different from the war, except that he was alone now, and he wasn't liberating payrolls, arms, or horseflesh from Union soldiers. And if he was caught now, he wouldn't be released in a prisoner exchange; he'd never make it to any sort of lawman alive. The bounty on his head, dead or alive, guaranteed that.

He let well over an hour lapse before, moving one muscle at a time, an inch at a time, he began working his way closer to the rocky outcropping where he'd left his horse, stopping every few feet to listen. It was slow going; it took over half an hour to cover fifty feet, and he estimated he had at least a hundred yards to go. Finally he caught the faint scrape of a horseshoe on rock as an animal shifted its weight, and the deep, sighing sound of a sleeping horse. He couldn't see either his horse or Trahern's, but the direction of the sounds told him that his horse was still where he'd left it. Trahern must have decided not to take the risk of exposing himself long enough to move the animals.

The question now was, where was Trahern? Somewhere with a clear view of McCay's horse. Somewhere that afforded cover for himself. And was he still alert, or had his senses dulled from the strain? Was he getting sleepy?

McCay calculated that it had been about five hours since Trahern had walked up on him, which would make it only about ten o'clock. Trahern was too good to let himself relax his guard this soon. The early morning hours were when the senses dulled and defenses tumbled, when the eyelids were lined with grit and weighed about forty pounds each, when the mind was numb with exhaustion.

But wouldn't Trahern, knowing that McCay would know this, expect him to wait? Wouldn't Trahern feel fairly safe in snatching an hour or so of sleep now, reasoning that any try for the horse would come right before dawn? Or that startling a dozing horse would make enough racket to awaken him?

McCay grinned, feeling the recklessness flood through him. Hell, he might as well stand up and walk right up to the horse. The odds were the same no matter what he did. When it looked as if he was damned if he did and damned if he didn't, he'd learned that the most reckless choice was the one with the best chance of succeeding.

He worked his way closer to the outcropping that sheltered the horse, then waited until the shifting sounds told him that the animal had awakened. He waited a few more minutes, then rose silently to his feet and walked up to the big bay, who caught his scent and affectionately butted him with his head. McCay rubbed the velvety soft nose, then gathered the reins and as quietly as possible swung up into the saddle. His blood was racing through his veins the way it always did at times like this, and he had to clench his teeth to keep from venting his tension in a bloodcurdling yell. The horse quivered under him, sensing his savage enjoyment of the risk he was taking.

It took iron self-control to turn the horse and calmly walk it away, but the ground was too uneven to risk even a trot. Now was the most dangerous time, when Trahern was most likely to be awakened—

He heard the snick of a hammer being thumbed back and instantly bent low over the horse's neck as he reined it sharply to the right and kicked its flanks. He felt the sharp burning in his left side a split second before he heard the shot. The muzzle flash pinpointed Trahern's position, and McCay had drawn and fired before Trahern could get another shot off. Then the big horse bolted, encouraged by another thud from McCay's bootheel, and the darkness swallowed them. He could hear Trahern's curses even over the thunder of his horse's hooves.

Concern for both their necks made him rein in the horse before they'd gone a quarter of a mile. His side was burning like hell, and wetness was seeping down the side of his pants. His horse at a walk, McCay pulled off his glove with his teeth and felt around, finding two holes in his shirt and corresponding holes in his body where the bullet had entered and exited. He yanked his bandanna from around his neck and wadded it up inside his shirt, using his elbow to keep it pressed to the wounds.

Damn, he was cold! A convulsive shudder started in his boots and rolled all the way up his body, shaking him like a wet dog and nearly making him pass out from the pain. He put his glove back on and untied his coat from the bedroll, then shrugged into the heavy fleece-lined garment. The shivers continued, and the wetness spread down his left leg. The son of a bitch hadn't hit anything vital, but he was losing a lot of blood.

The guessing game started again. Trahern would probably expect him to ride hard and fast, putting as much distance between them as he could manage by sunrise. McCay figured he'd gone about a mile when he walked the horse into a thick stand of pines and dismounted. He gave the animal a handful of feed and some water, patted his neck in appreciation of his steadiness, and untied the bedroll. He had to get the bleeding stopped, and get warm, or Trahern was going to find him lying unconscious on the trail.

Keeping the canteen of water beside him, he wrapped up in the blanket and settled down on the thick layer of pine needles, lying on his left side so his weight would put pressure on the back wound while he pressed the heel of his hand over the exit wound in front. The position made him grunt with pain, but he figured the discomfort was better than bleeding to death. Sleeping was out of the question. Even if the pain would let him, he didn't dare let himself relax.

He hadn't eaten since noon, but he wasn't hungry. He drank a little water every now and then and watched the glimmer of the stars through the heavy tree cover overhead. He listened for any sounds of pursuit, though he didn't really expect Trahern to come after him so soon. The night held only natural sounds.

Gradually he began to warm, and the hot pain in his side subsided to a dull throb. His shirt was stiffening, which meant the flow of fresh blood had stopped. It was harder now to stay awake, but he refused to give in to his growing lethargy. There would be time for sleep later, after he'd killed Trahern.

It wasn't quite dawn when he eased to his feet. A wave of dizziness threatened to topple him and he braced his hand on a tree to support himself. Damn, he must have lost more blood than he'd thought; he hadn't expected to be this weak. When he was steady, he went to the horse with a soothing murmur and got some beef jerky from his saddlebag, knowing that food and water would steady him faster than anything. He forced himself to eat, then quietly led the horse back the way they had come. It hadn't worked the first time, but it should the second. Trahern would be intent on following the blood trail.

He had been in position only a few minutes when he saw Trahern slipping up the hollow, handgun in his fist. McCay cursed silently, for the fact that Trahern was on foot meant that he was wary. The bounty hunter either had a sixth sense for danger or he was the luckiest son of a bitch McCay had ever seen.

He steadied the rifle, but Trahern used his cover well, never exposing all of himself at the same time. Rafe caught only a shoulder, part of a leg, the flat crown of that distinctive hat; he didn't have a clear shot at any time. Well, if a wounding shot was all that was offered, he'd take it. At the very least it would slow Trahern down, even the odds between them.

The next target that Trahern offered was a sliver of pants leg. A cold smile touched McCay's face as he sighted down the barrel. His hands were rock steady as he gently squeezed the trigger. Trahern's scream of pain was almost simultaneous with the sharp report of the rifle, both sounds muted by the trees.

McCay withdrew and pulled himself into the saddle, the movement more difficult than he had expected. His side began to burn again, and a damp feeling spread. Damn it, he'd opened his wounds. But now Trahern was wounded, too, and it would take him a long time to get back to his own horse, giving McCay a good head start that he couldn't afford to waste. He'd see to the wounds later.

Annis Theodora Parker calmly brewed a mild valerian tea, all the while keeping a weather eye on her patient. Eda Couey looked like a big, competent country girl, the sort you'd expect to give birth as easily as any woman could wish, but she was having trouble and was beginning to panic. Annis, known from childhood as Annie, knew that both Eda and the baby would fare a lot better if Eda was calmer.

She carried the hot tea to the bedside and held Eda's head so she could sip. "It'll help the pain," she quietly assured the girl. Eda was only seventeen, and this was her first. The valerian wouldn't really ease the pain, but it would calm the girl so she could help get her child into the world.

Eda quieted as the sedative began to work, but her face was still paper white and her eyes sunken as the labor pains continued. According to Walter Couey, Eda's husband, the girl had already been in labor for two days before he'd given in to her pleas for help and fetched Annie to their one-room lean-to shack. He'd grumbled that he hadn't been able to get any sleep with all the carryin' on, and Annie had controlled a strong urge to slap him.

The baby was turned breech, and the birth wasn't going to be easy. Annie silently prayed for the infant's survival, for sometimes the cord would get pinched during a breech birth and the baby would die in the birth canal. And she wondered if, even should it survive being born, it would live to see its first birthday. The conditions in the miserable lean-to were appalling, and Walter Couey was a mean, stupid man who would never provide anything better. He was in his forties, and Annie suspected that Eda wasn't really his wife but only an illiterate farm girl sold into virtual slavery to relieve her family of one more mouth to feed. Walter was an unsuccessful miner, even here at Silver Mesa where men were finding the precious metal in thick veins; mining was hard work and Walter wasn't inclined to work hard at anything. She couldn't allow herself to think that it would be a blessing if the baby *did* die, but she felt pity for both mother and child.

Eda moaned as her belly tightened again with a massive contraction. "Push," Annie commanded in a low tone. She could see a smooth moon of flesh crowning: the baby's buttocks. "Push!"

A guttural scream tore from Eda's throat as she bore down with all of her strength, her shoulders lifting off the pallet. Annie put her hands on the hugely swollen belly and added her strength to Eda's.

It was now or never. If Eda couldn't deliver the infant, both mother and child would die. Labor would continue, but Eda would grow progressively weaker.

The tiny buttocks protruded from Eda's body. Quickly, Annie tried to grasp them, but they were too slippery. She worked her fingers inside the stretched opening and caught the baby's legs. "Push!" she said again.

But Eda was falling back, almost paralyzed with pain. Annie waited for the next contraction, which followed within seconds, then used the natural force of Eda's internal muscles to aid her as she literally pulled the infant's lower body from the mother. It was a boy. She inserted the fingers of one hand again to keep Eda's muscles from clamping down, and with the other hand steadily pulled the baby the rest of the way out. It lay limply between Eda's thighs. Both Eda and the baby were still and quiet.

Annie picked up the little scrap, supporting it facedown on her forearm while she thumped it on the back. The tiny chest heaved, and the baby set up a mewling squall as air flooded its lungs for the first time. "There you go," Annie crooned, and turned the baby over to make certain its mouth and throat were clear. Normally she would have done that first, but getting the child to breathe had seemed more important. The little fellow jerked his legs and arms as he wailed, and a tired smile wreathed Annie's face. He sounded stronger with every squall.

The cord had stopped pulsing, so she tied it off close to his belly and clipped it, then quickly wrapped him in a blanket to protect him from the chill. After placing him next to Eda's warmth, she turned her attention to the girl, who was only half conscious.

"Here's your baby, Eda," Annie said. "It's a boy, and he looks healthy. Just listen to him cry! Both of you came through it fine. In a minute the afterbirth will come, and then I'll get you cleaned up and comfortable."

Eda's pale lips moved in silent acknowledgment, but she was too exhausted to gather the baby to her.

The afterbirth came quickly, and Annie was relieved that there was no unusually heavy bleeding. A hemorrhage now would kill the girl, for she had no reserves of strength. She cleaned Eda and restored the mean little lean-to to rights, then picked up the fretting infant, as his mother was too weak to see to him, and crooned as she rocked him in her arms. He quieted, and his fuzzy little head turned toward her.

She roused Eda and helped the girl cradle her child as she unbuttoned Eda's nightgown and guided the baby's rosebud mouth to his mother's exposed breast. For a moment he didn't seem to know what to do with the nipple brushing his lips, then instinct took over and he eagerly began sucking on it. Eda jumped, and gave a breathless little "oh!"

Annie stood back and watched those first magical moments of discovery as the young mother, exhausted as she was, looked in wonder at her child.

Tiredly she put on her coat and picked up her bag. "I'll be by tomorrow to check on you."

Eda looked up, her white, weary face lit with a glowing smile. "Thankee, Doc. Me and the baby wouldn'a made it without you."

Annie returned the smile, but she could barely wait to get outside into the fresh air, cold as it might be. It was late in the afternoon, with less than an hour of light left, and she had been with Eda all day without a bite to eat. Her back and legs ached, and she was tired. Still, the successful birth gave her an immense feeling of satisfaction.

The Coueys' lean-to was at the opposite end of Silver Mesa from the tiny two-room shack that served Annie as both office and living quarters. She treated patients in the front room, and lived in the back one. As she trudged through the mud of Silver Mesa's one winding "street," miners called out rough greetings to her. This late in the day, they were leaving their claims and crowding into Silver Mesa to fill up on raw whiskey and lose their hard-earned money to gamblers and fancy women. Silver Mesa was a boomtown, without any sort of law or social amenities, unless you counted the five saloons located in tents. Some enterprising merchants had built rough plank buildings to house their wares, but wooden structures were few and far between. Annie felt lucky to have one of them for her medical practice, and in turn the inhabitants of Silver Mesa felt lucky to have any sort of a doctor at all, even a woman.

She had been here for six—no, it was eight—months now, after failing to establish a practice in either her native Philadelphia or Denver. She had learned the bitter fact that, no matter how good a doctor she was, no one was going to come to her if there was a male doctor within a hundred miles. In Silver Mesa, there wasn't. Even so, it had taken a while for people to come to her, though like boomtowns everywhere Silver Mesa was a violent place to live. Men were always getting shot, cut, or beaten, breaking bones or crushing various limbs. The trickle of patients had slowly turned into a steady stream, until now she sometimes didn't have time to sit down from daylight to dark.

It was what she had always wanted, what she had worked years for, but every time someone called her "Doc" or she heard someone say "Doc Parker" she was filled with sadness, for she wanted to look around for her father and he would never again be there. Frederick Parker had been a wonderful man and a wonderful doctor. He had let Annie help him in little ways from the time she had been only a child, and he encouraged her interest in medicine, teaching her what he could and sending her to school when he had nothing left to teach her. He had given her his support during the hard years of earning her medical degree, for it seemed as if no one other than the two of them had wanted a woman to be learning anything at all about medicine. She had not only been shunned by her fellow medical students—they had actively tried to hinder her. But her father had taught her how to keep her sense of humor and her commitment, and he had been as excited as she when she had left to come west and find a place that needed a doctor even if she was a woman.

She had been in Denver less than a month when a letter arrived from their pastor, regretfully relaying the news that her father had passed away. He had seemed healthy enough, though he had been complaining that he wasn't a young man any longer and was beginning to feel his age. But on a quiet Sunday, just after enjoying a good meal, he had suddenly clutched his chest and died. The pastor didn't believe he had suffered.

Annie had grieved silently and alone, for there was no one to whom she could talk, no one who would understand. When she had ventured bravely out into the world she had still felt his presence in Philadelphia as an anchor to which she could return, but now she had been cast adrift. By letter she had arranged for the house to be sold and the personal possessions she wished to keep stored at an aunt's house.

She wished she could tell him all about Silver Mesa, how rough and dirty and vital it was, with humanity teeming in the mud street and fortunes being made every day. He would envy her the drama of her practice, for Annie saw everything from bullet wounds to colds to birthings.

The late-winter twilight was deepening as she opened her door and reached for the flint that always rested on a table just inside the door; she struck it and lit a thin strip of twisted paper, which she then used to light the lamp. Sighing with weariness, she put her bag on the table and rolled her shoulders to ease the kinks out of them. She had bought a horse when she'd arrived in Silver Mesa, for she frequently had to travel a fair distance to her patients, and she needed to see to the animal before it got any darker. She kept it in a small corral behind the shack, with a ramshackle three-sided shed for its shelter. She decided to go around the shack rather than through it, for she didn't want to track mud through her home.

Just as she turned to go a shadow in the far corner of the room moved, and Annie jumped, pressing her hand to her chest. She peered at the shadow and made out the form of a man. "Yes? May I help you?"

"I came to see the doctor."

She frowned, for if he was from Silver Mesa then he knew he *was* seeing the doctor. Apparently he was a stranger and was expecting a man. She lifted the lamp, trying to see him better. His voice had been deep and raspy, little more than a whisper, but with a slow, southern rhythm to the words.

"I'm Dr. Parker," she said, moving closer. "How may I help you?"

"You're a woman," the deep voice said.

"Yes, I am." She was close enough now to see fever-bright eyes and smell the particular too-sweet odor of infection. The man was propped in the corner, as if he had feared he wouldn't be able to rise again if he'd sat down in a chair. She placed the lamp on a table and turned it up so the mellow light reached into the far corners of the little room. "Where are you hurt?"

"My left side."

She went to his right side and braced her shoulder under his armpit, sliding her arm around his back to give added support. His heat shocked her, and for a moment she felt almost frightened. "Let's get you to the examining table."

He tensed under her touch. His dark hat shielded his expression but she felt the look he gave her. "I don't need help," he said, and demonstrated it by walking steadily, if a bit slowly, to the examining table.

Annie fetched the lamp and lit a second one, then

pulled the curtain that shielded the examining table should anyone else enter the room looking for medical attention. The man removed his hat, revealing thick, uncombed black hair that needed trimming, then gingerly shrugged out of his heavy shearling coat.

Annie took both hat and coat and set them aside, all the while minutely examining the man. She couldn't see any blood or other sign of injury, yet he was obviously sick and in pain. "Take off your shirt," she said. "Do you need any help?"

He looked at her with hooded eyes, then shook his head and unbuttoned his shirt as far as it would go. He pulled the fabric loose from his pants and shucked it off over his head.

A dingy strip of cloth had been tightly wound around his waist, and it was stained a yellowish, rusty color on the left side. Annie picked up a pair of scissors and neatly sliced the bandage, letting it fall to the floor. There were two wounds in the fleshy part just above his waistline, one in front and one in back. Red streaks surrounded the back wound, though both were oozing bloody pus.

A bullet wound, unless she missed her guess. She had seen enough here in Silver Mesa to give her a wide experience with them.

She realized that she hadn't removed her own coat and promptly did so, her mind on her patient. "Lie down on your right side," she instructed as she turned to her instrument tray and got out what she needed. He hesitated, and she lifted her brows inquiringly.

Silently, he leaned over to untie the thong that strapped his holster to his thigh, sweat breaking out on his face at the effort. Next he unbuckled the gun belt and placed it at the head of the examining table, within easy reach of his hand. He sat on the table, then stretched out to lie as she had instructed, on his right side and facing her. His muscles seemed to relax involuntarily as he felt the soft cushion of the mattress Annie had placed over the hard table so her patients would be more comfortable, then he shivered and tightened again.

Annie got a clean sheet and spread it over his bare torso. "That'll keep you warm while I heat some water."

She had banked the fire before leaving early that morning, and the coals glowed red when she stirred them with a poker. She added kindling and more wood, then fetched water and poured it into two iron pots that hung on a hook over the fire. The little room quickly heated as the fire grew. She placed her instruments in one of the pots to boil, then scrubbed her hands with strong soap. The tiredness that had weighed on her limbs during the trudge back from Eda's was forgotten as she considered the best treatment for her new patient.

She noticed that her hands were shaking a little, and she stopped to draw a deep breath. Normally her thoughts would be totally concentrated on the task at hand, but something about this man unsettled her. Maybe it was his pale eyes, as colorless as frost and as watchful as a wolf's. Or maybe it was his heat. Intellectually she knew it had to be fever, but the intense heat of his tall, muscular body seemed to wrap around her like a blanket every time she got close to him. Whatever the reason, her stomach had clenched into a tight knot when he'd pulled off his shirt and bared his powerful torso. Annie was accustomed to seeing men in various stages of undress, but never before had she been so acutely aware of a man's body, of the maleness that threatened her own femaleness on a very primitive level. The curly black hair on his broad, muscled chest had strongly reminded her that man's basic nature was animalistic.

Yet he had done nothing, said nothing, that was threatening. All of it was in her own mind, perhaps a product of her fatigue. The man was wounded and had come to her for help.

She stepped back behind the curtain. "I'll mix you some laudanum to ease the pain."

He pinned her with that pale, icy gaze. "No."

She hesitated. "The treatment will be painful, Mister—?"

He ignored the raised inflection that invited him to tell her his name. "I don't want any laudanum. You have any whiskey?"

"Yes."

"That'll do."

"It won't be enough, unless you drink yourself to unconsciousness, in which case it will be easier to simply take the laudanum."

"I don't want to be unconscious. Just give me a drink."

Annie got the whiskey and poured a good measure in the glass. "Have you eaten?" she asked when she returned.

"Not lately." He took the glass and carefully tilted it, then knocked the drink back with two strong swallows. He gasped and shuddered at the bite of it.

She got a basin of water and set it beside the bed, then took the glass from his hand. "I'm going to wash the wounds while the water's heating." She removed the sheet and studied the situation. The wounds were so close to his waistline that his pants presented a problem. "Can you open your pants, please? I need more room around the wounds."

For a moment he didn't move, then slowly he unbuckled his belt and began opening the buttons on his pants. When the task was completed, Annie pulled the waistband down and away, baring the sleek skin of his hip. "Lift up a little." He did, and she slid a towel under him, then folded another towel and tucked it in and over the open garment to keep it from getting wet. She tried not to notice his exposed lower abdomen, with the silky line of hair arrowing downward, but she was acutely, embarrassingly aware of this man's partial nudity. This wasn't at all the way a doctor was supposed to feel—she'd certainly never felt this way before!—and she mentally scolded herself.

He watched while she wet a cloth and soaped it, then gently applied it to the infected wounds. He drew in his breath with a hiss.

"I'm sorry," she murmured, though she didn't pause in her task. "I know it hurts, but it has to be cleaned."

Rafe McCay didn't answer; he just continued to watch her. It wasn't so much the pain that had startled him into that quick intake of breath as it was the low throb of energy that seemed to leap from her flesh to his every time she touched him. It was almost like the way the air felt charged right before a lightning strike. He'd felt it even through his clothes when she had put her arm around him to help him to the table, and it was that much stronger on his bare skin.

Maybe the fever was getting to him, or maybe he'd just been without a woman for too long. For whatever reason, every time the good doctor touched him, he got hard.

CHAPTER

2

When she touched them, the wounds began to bleed sullenly. "When did this happen?" she asked, keeping her touch as gentle as possible.

"Ten days ago."

"That's a long time for wounds to remain open."

"Yeah." He hadn't been able to rest long enough to let his flesh begin healing, not with Trahern on his trail like a goddamned bulldog. The wounds had reopened every time he'd swung into the saddle. He felt grim satisfaction in knowing that Trahern hadn't been able to give his leg the rest it needed, either.

The whiskey was making his head swim and he closed his eyes, but he found himself concentrating even more on every touch of the woman's soft hands. Dr. Parker. Dr. A. T. Parker, according to the crudely lettered sign out front of the little shack. He'd never heard of a woman doctor before.

His first impression had been that she wasn't much to look at: too thin, with the worn, weary look women often got out here. Then she had walked up to him and he'd seen the softness of her brown eyes, the sweetly untidy mess of streaked blond hair caught back in a haphazard knot, with escaped tendrils feathering all around her face. She had touched him and he'd felt the hot magic of her hands. Those hands! They made him feel relaxed and tense all at once. Hell, he *was* drunk; that was the only explanation.

"First I'm going to apply compresses of hot salty water," she explained in her cool, light voice. "They'll have to be almost scalding, so it won't be comfortable."

He didn't open his eyes. "Just get to it." He thought Trahern was at least a day behind him, but every minute he lay here was a minute Trahern gained.

Annie opened her tin of sea salt and dumped a handful in one of the pots, then used a pair of forceps to dunk a cloth in the boiling water. She held it dripping over the pot for a minute, tested the temperature with the soft skin of her forearm, then placed the steaming cloth against the entrance wound in his back.

He went rigid and his breath hissed inward between clenched teeth, but he voiced no protest. Annie found herself sympathetically patting his shoulder with her left hand while she held the hot cloth to him with the forceps in her right.

When the cloth cooled she placed it back in the boiling water. "I'm going to alternate sides," she said. "The salt helps stop infection."

"Get it over with," he growled. "Do both sides at once."

She bit her lip, then decided that she might as well. Even as sick as he was, he had an amazing tolerance for pain. She fetched another cloth and another pair of forceps, and for the next half hour applied the hot saltwater compresses, until the skin around the wounds had turned dark red and the ragged edges of the wounds themselves were white. Through it all he lay perfectly still with his eyes closed.

Then she took a pair of surgical scissors, pulled his skin tight, and quickly trimmed the white dead flesh away. The wounds bled freshly now, though the blood was still streaked with yellow. She applied pressure with her fingers around each wound, forcing out pus and old blood; a few tiny fragments of cloth emerged, as well as a thin sliver of lead from the bullet. She talked quietly all through the procedure, explaining what she was doing even though she wasn't certain he was conscious.

She washed the wounds with a tincture of marigold to stop the bleeding, then applied oil she had extracted from fresh thyme to prevent further infection. "Tomorrow I'll start using plantain bandages, but for tonight I'm going to put chickweed poultices on both wounds to draw out any pieces of your shirt that I've missed."

"I won't be here tomorrow," he said, making her jump. They were the first words he'd spoken since she had started her procedure. She had hoped that he'd fainted, had been almost certain that he had. How could he have borne that pain without sound or movement?

"You can't leave," she said gently. "I don't think you understand how serious your condition is. You'll die from the poison if those wounds remain infected."

"I walked in here, lady, so I can't be that sick."

She pursed her lips. "Yes, you walked in, and you can probably walk out, even though you're so sick a lot of other men in your condition would be flat on their backs. But in a day or so you won't even be able to crawl, much less walk. In another week, you'll probably be dead. On the other hand, if you'll give me three days, I'll have you almost well."

His pale eyes opened. He saw the earnest expression in those soft dark eyes, and felt the ache of fever all through his body. Hell, she was probably right. Even though she was a woman, she seemed to be a damn fine doctor. But Trahern was still on his back trail and he wasn't in any shape to fight the bounty hunter.

Maybe Trahern was just as sick as he was, but maybe not, and Rafe wasn't going to play those odds unless he had to.

He needed the few days of rest and care that the doc offered, but he didn't dare take them. Not here. If he could get higher into the mountains . . .

"Make your poultice," he instructed.

His low, raspy voice made her shiver. She silently went to work, picking fresh chickweed from the pots of herbs she carefully nurtured and crushing the leaves, which she then applied to the wounds. She placed damp pads over the crushed leaves and secured the poultices by binding them tightly in place. He sat up during this last part and aided her by holding the pads while she wrapped the strip of cloth around his middle.

He reached for his shirt and pulled it on over his head. Distressed, Annie caught his arm. "Don't go," she pleaded. "I don't know why you think you must, but it's very dangerous for you."

He removed the blood-soaked towels that she had tucked into his pants and slid off the examining table, ignoring her hand on his arm as if it weren't even there. Annie let her arm drop to her side, feeling helpless and angry. How *could* he risk his life like this, after she had worked so hard to help him? Why had he even come to her for help, if he wasn't going to do what she suggested?

Rafe tucked in his shirt and calmly buttoned his pants, then fastened his belt. With the same unhurried movements he buckled on his gun belt and retied the thong around his muscled thigh.

As he shrugged into his coat Annie rushed into desperate speech. "If I give you some plantain leaves will you at least try to keep them on the wounds? The bandage needs to stay fresh—"

"Bring what you need," he said.

She blinked in confusion. "What?"

"Get your coat. You're going with me."

"I can't do that. I have patients here who need me, too, and—"

He drew the big pistol and pointed it at her. She broke off, too stunned to continue, and in the silence she clearly heard the snick as he thumbed back the hammer. "I said get your coat," he said softly.

His pale eyes were unreadable, his raspy voice implacable as he issued instructions, and the heavy revolver in his hand never wavered. In numb disbelief Annie put on her coat, gathered a supply of food, and packed her medical instruments and various herbs into her black leather bag. That frosty gaze watched every move she made.

"That'll do." He took the bag of food from her and motioned with his head. "Out back. Take the lamp with you."

She realized that he must have explored her house while he'd been waiting for her, and anger seared through her. Her private quarters weren't much, just the one back room, but it was hers and she fiercely resented his intrusion. But with the barrel of his revolver pressed into the middle of her back, it seemed ridiculous to take umbrage at the invasion of her privacy. She went out the back door with him right behind her.

"Saddle your horse."

"I haven't fed him yet," she said. She knew it was a stupid protest, but somehow it didn't seem fair to expect the horse to carry her without having been fed.

"I don't want to keep repeating my orders," he warned. His voice had dropped to a whisper, making the words even more menacing.

She hung the lamp on a nail. A big bay, still saddled, stood patiently next to her mount.

"Hurry it up."

She saddled her horse with her usual brisk movements, then the man motioned her back. "Stand over there, out in the clear."

She bit her lip as she moved to obey. She had had the half-formed plan of ducking behind her horse and slipping out of the shed while he mounted, but he had foreseen that possibility. By making her stand out in the open, he had taken away her protective cover.

Keeping his eyes and revolver on her, he led the bay into the open and stepped into the saddle. If Annie hadn't been watching him so closely, she wouldn't have noticed his slight difficulty as pain hampered his motions. He stowed the bag of food in his saddlebag.

"Get on your horse now, honey, and don't get any stupid ideas. Just do what I tell you, and you'll be all right."

Annie looked around, unable to quite make herself believe that he could really kidnap her like this. It had been such a normal day, up until he had pointed his pistol at her. If she let him force her into riding out with him, would she ever be seen alive again? Even if she managed to escape, she had grave doubts about her own ability to survive in the wilderness on her own, for she had seen too much to have any naive confidence that returning to Silver Mesa would be nothing more than a simple ride. Life anywhere outside the dubious protection of a town was harrowing.

"Get on the goddamn horse." Violence and an end to his patience were starkly evident in the harsh tone of the words. Annie climbed into the saddle, hampered by her skirts, but she knew it would be useless to protest, or to ask for an opportunity to change into more practical clothing.

She had always appreciated her position at the edge of town, convenient yet private, and isolated from the noise of drunken miners as they sampled the wares of the saloons and whorehouses well into the early morning hours. Now, however, she would have given anything for the appearance of even one drunken miner. She could yell her head off and no one was likely to hear her.

"Blow out the lamp," he said, and she leaned down from the saddle to do so. The sudden absence of light was blinding, though a thin sliver of the new moon was rising.

He released his own reins and held out his gloved hand, the one that wasn't holding the pistol. The big bay didn't move, a product of good training and the control of the powerful legs wrapped around his barrel. "Give me your reins."

Again, she had no choice but to obey him. She handed him the reins and he pulled them over her horse's head, looping them around his saddle horn so her mount would have no choice but to follow him. "Don't get any ideas about jumping out of the saddle," he warned. "You won't get away, and it'll make me damn mad." His low, menacing voice made chills go down her back. "You don't want to do that."

He kept the horses to a sedate walk until they were well away from Silver Mesa, then nudged the bay into an easy canter. Annie wrapped both hands around her saddle horn and hung on. Within minutes she was wishing that she had thought to get her own gloves, for the cold night air was biting. Her face and hands were stinging already.

Now that her eyes had adjusted she could see well enough, and she realized that he was riding west, higher into the mountains. It would be even colder up there; she had seen snowcaps crowning the high peaks even in the middle of July.

"Where are we going?" she asked, striving to keep her voice level.

"Up," he said.

"Why? And why are you forcing me to go with you?"

"You're the one said I needed a doctor," he replied flatly. "You're a doctor. Now shut up."

She did, but it took all of her self-control to keep from lapsing into hysterics. Though she had never considered herself the hysterical type, this situation made her feel as if she might indulge in a well-justified loss of control. In Philadelphia, people who needed doctors did *not* kidnap them.

And it wasn't just the situation that made her afraid, it was the man himself. From the moment those cold, colorless eyes had met hers she had been very aware that this man was dangerous, the same way a cougar was dangerous. He could lash out and kill as swiftly and as casually. She had devoted her life to the care of others, to preserving life, and he was the direct antithesis of the principles she held dear. Yet her hands had trembled as she touched him, not only because of the fear, but because his strong male body had made her feel weak inside. Remembering that made her feel ashamed. As a doctor, she should have remained aloof.

By the time an hour had passed her feet were growing numb, and her fingers felt as if they would break off if she flexed them. Her legs and back were aching, and she had begun to shiver constantly. She stared at the dark shape of the man riding just in front of her and wondered how he could possibly remain in the saddle. Considering his blood loss, the fever, and the infection, he should have been flat on his back a long time ago. Such endurance and strength were intimidating, for she would have to pit herself against them in order to escape.

He had said she would be all right, but how could she believe him? She was totally at his mercy, and so far he hadn't given her any reason to believe that even a small portion of that quality was in his character. He could rape her, kill her, do anything he wanted with her, and likely her body would never even be found. Every step that the horses made carried her deeper into danger, and increased the unlikelihood that she would be able to make it back to Silver Mesa even if she managed to escape.

"P-please, can't we stop for the night and build a f-fire?" she blurted, and was startled to hear her own voice. The words seemed to have come of their own volition.

"No." Just that one word, flat and implacable.

"P-please," she said again, and was aghast to realize she was begging. "I'm so c-c-cold."

He turned his head and looked at her. She couldn't see his features under the brim of his hat, only the faint gleam of his eyes. "We can't stop yet."

"Then w-when?"

"When I say."

But he didn't say, not during those endlessly long, increasingly cold hours. The horses' breath rose in clouds of steam. The pace had necessarily slowed to a walk as the way became increasingly steep, and several times he had to unloop her reins and hold them in his hand, leading her horse directly behind him in single file. Annie tried to estimate the passage of time, but found that physical misery distorted all perception of it. She would force herself to wait until she had thought an hour had passed, then look at the moon, only to find that it had barely moved since the last time she had looked.

Her feet were so cold that every movement of her toes was agony. Her legs quivered with exertion, for caution forced her to use them to stay in the saddle since her hands were largely useless. Her throat and lungs felt raw from the cold, and each breath rasped the delicate tissues. She turned up the collar of her coat and tried to draw her head down within its protection so the air she breathed would be warmer, but the coat kept gaping open and she didn't dare turn loose of the saddle horn to hold it together.

In silent desperation she fastened her eyes on the broad back in front of her. If he could keep going, sick and wounded as he was, then she could, too. But dogged pride, she found, helped for only so long before sheer physical misery overwhelmed it. *Damn* him, why didn't he stop?

* * *

Rafe had divorced his mind from his physical discomfort, focusing all of his concentration on putting distance between himself and Trahern. The bounty hunter would be able to track him to Silver Mesa; Rafe had discovered a bent nail on the bay's right front shoe that would have left marks like signposts to a good tracker, which Trahern was. The first thing he'd done in Silver Mesa was find the blacksmith and have the bay reshod. He didn't care if Trahern discovered that, for it wouldn't make any difference; there wouldn't be any way to tell which of the myriad tracks around the smithy belonged to the bay, assuming any of the bay's tracks were left by the time Trahern got to Silver Mesa, and that was highly unlikely. It was impossible to track someone through a busy town, because tracks were constantly being smeared and overlaid with new ones.

At first Trahern would ride a wide circle around the town, looking for that telltale bent nail. When he didn't find it, he'd go into Silver Mesa and start asking questions, but he'd hit a dead end at the smithy. Rafe had rode directly out of town after having the bay reshod, back in the direction from which he'd entered. Then he had left the bay tethered and reentered the town on foot, taking care not to bring attention to himself. During the war he'd learned that the easiest way to disguise yourself was by mingling with a crowd. In a boomtown like Silver Mesa, no one paid any mind to one more stranger, especially one who didn't make eye contact or speak to anyone.

He had intended only to get bandages and carbolic wash for disinfectant, and his purpose for doing so anonymously was to keep Trahern from knowing how sick he felt. An enemy could take any small scrap of information and use it to his advantage. But caution had made him check out the entire town first, looking for alternate ways of escape if it should become necessary, and he'd seen the roughly lettered sign of Dr. A. T. Parker.

He had watched for a while, considering the risk. The doctor didn't seem to be in; a few people had knocked on the door, then gone away when the knocks went unanswered.

He had begun shivering while he watched from concealment, and this further evidence of his rising fever had decided the issue for him. He had gone back for the bay and put it in the shed with what had to have been the doctor's horse, indicating that the sawbones was somewhere in town. The doctor's office was set off by itself, a good hundred yards from the next building, and a stand of trees shielded the horse shed from view, so he felt safe in waiting there. From what he had observed, it was customary for folks to knock on the door rather than just go inside, which struck him as odd but suited his purposes. When he entered, he found that the sawbones evidently lived in the back room, which was explanation enough for the strange formality of knocking on the door of a doctor's office. Maybe the doc was a tad fussy, but Rafe allowed folks their foibles.

The neat little surgery and back room had enforced his impression of fastidiousness. There were no personal belongings left strewn around, other than a serviceable hairbrush and some books; the narrow cot was neatly made, the single dish and cup washed and dried. He hadn't looked through the physician's clothes—if he had he would have known that she was female, or at least that a female was living in the back room, maybe to take care of the doctor's needs.

There were orderly rows of small pots in all the windowsills, with a variety of plants growing in them. The air had smelled both fresh and spicy. An apothecary's cabinet had been stocked with herbs either dried or powdered, and gauze bags filled with other plants had been hung in the coolest, darkest corner. Each bag and drawer had been clearly labeled in block printing.

Waves of dizziness had kept rolling over him and at

length he had had to sit down. He thought about just taking what he needed from the doctor's supplies and leaving without anyone being the wiser, but it felt so damn good just to rest that he kept telling himself he'd sit there for just a few minutes longer.

That unusual lassitude, more than anything, was what had finally convinced him to stay and see the doctor.

Every time footsteps had sounded on the porch he had eased into a corner, but after the knock went unanswered the would-be patients had gone away. The last time, however, there hadn't been a knock; the door had opened and a thin, tired-looking woman had entered, carrying a huge black bag.

Now she was riding behind him, grimly hanging on to the saddle, her face white and pinched with cold. He knew she had to be frightened, but there was no way he could convince her he didn't mean her any harm, so he didn't try. In a few days, maybe a week, when he was well, he'd take her back to Silver Mesa. Trahern would already have left, having lost the trail with no way of picking it up again until he got news of Rafe's whereabouts. Rafe intended to make certain that didn't happen for a while. He'd change his name again, maybe get a different horse, though he hated to get rid of the bay.

Forcing her to go with him wasn't so great a risk; with her horse gone, folks would just think that she was out treating someone. Maybe they'd get curious when she didn't show up in a day or so, but there was nothing in the cabin to give alarm, no sign of struggle or violence. Since she hadn't left her black bag behind, people would logically assume that she was merely attending to some distant patient.

In the meantime, he could do with a few days' rest. He could feel the fever burning through him, feel the burning ache in his side, though the quality of that ache seemed to be changing as the burn became more of a drawing sensation. She had been right about his condition; only sheer determination had kept him going, was keeping him going now.

There was an old trapper's sod hut up here somewhere; he'd seen it a few years back, before Silver Mesa had even existed. It was damn hard to find; he only hoped he remembered its location closely enough to pinpoint it. The old geezer had partially dug out a bank and buried the back half of the hut in it, and the foliage grew so thick around it that a man had to practically walk into it before he saw it.

The hut was abandoned, or had been when he'd seen it. It wouldn't be in good shape, but it would give him a place out of the weather. At least the damn thing had a fireplace, and the trees above it would disperse the smoke so any fire he lit wouldn't be noticeable.

His head ached, and his thighbones felt as if someone was pounding them with a dull ax, sure signs of a rising fever. He had to find that hut soon or he wouldn't make it. Glancing at the moon's position, he figured it to be about one in the morning; they'd been riding for about seven hours, which by his calculation should put them close to the hut. He looked around, forcing himself to concentrate, but it was damn hard to recognize landmarks in the moonlight. There had been a huge pine, blasted by lightning, but it had probably decayed by now.

Half an hour later he realized that he wasn't going to find the hut, at least not in the dark and in his present condition. The horses were exhausted, and the doc looked as if she were going to fall out of the saddle. Reluctantly, but recognizing the necessity for it, he looked around for a sheltered spot and chose a narrow little hollow between two huge boulders. He reined the bay to a stop.

Annie was so numb that for a moment she didn't realize they had stopped. When the lack of motion finally made sense, she lifted her head to see that the man had already dismounted and was standing beside her. "Get down."

She tried, but her legs were so stiff they wouldn't work. With a small, desperate cry she simply turned loose and pitched herself down from the horse's back. She landed on the cold, hard ground with a thud that rattled every bone in her body, and tears of pain started into her eyes. She blinked them back, but she couldn't stifle a low moan as she forced herself into a sitting position.

He walked the horses away from her without saying a word, and she didn't know if she should feel grateful or indignant. She was too tired, too cold, to feel much, even gratitude that they had stopped.

She sat where she was, unable to stand or to work up much interest in doing so. She could hear him murmuring to the horses, the sound barely audible above the rustle of tree limbs in the cold wind. Then she listened to his footsteps drawing near, and even through her own physical wretchedness she noticed that his steps were uneven. He stopped right behind her.

"I can't help you," he said in a low, harsh voice. "If you can't stand, you'll have to crawl over here to these rocks. The best I can do is get us out of the wind and cover us with a blanket."

"No fire?" Her breath caught with a pang of sorrow so sharp it hurt. She had been imagining a fire all during the long, miserable hours, longing for the heat and light as if it were a lover, and now he was denying it to her.

"No. Come on, Doc, get your ass over to the rocks."

She managed. It wasn't elegant, or graceful. She crawled a few feet, then got to her knees, and finally to her feet. After a few tottering steps her legs gave way beneath her and she had to grit her teeth against the pain in her feet, but she managed to repeat the process. He walked carefully beside her, his very precision reminding her that his own strength was almost gone. She was glad that he hadn't been unscathed by the ordeal.

"All right. Here. Now scrape a big pile of these pine needles together."

She wavered back and forth as she stared at him, seeing nothing more than a big dark form standing close beside her. But she dropped back to her knees and clumsily did as he said, her frozen fingers blessedly numb to the scrapes and prickles she knew she must be getting.

"That'll do." A soft bundle dropped onto the ground beside her. "Now spread this blanket out on the needles."

She obeyed, again without comment.

"Take off your coat and lie down."

The very thought of removing her coat and exposing herself to even greater chill almost made her revolt, but at the last moment common sense told her he must mean to use their coats for cover. She began shaking convulsively as she shed the heavy garment, but he was doing the same, so she lay down in silence.

He eased down beside her, positioning himself so she was at his right side. His long legs touched hers and Annie started to scoot away, but he stopped her, his hand closing on her arm with a hard grip that made her wonder if he was truly as exhausted as he had seemed. "Get closer. We'll have to share our heat, and the blankets."

It was nothing but the stark truth. She inched closer, until she could feel the heat of his body even through their cold clothing, and the lure of the promise of comfort pulled her even closer, so that she was huddled against his side.

Moving with the care that indicated pain, he twitched the other half of the blanket they were lying on over them, then spread a second blanket on top of that. He arranged her coat over their feet, and his coat over their torsos. Finally he lay back and slipped his right arm under her head. A shudder wracked his big body from head to foot.

The fire of his fever radiated through the layers of

clothing, and as she moved even closer she wondered if he would survive the night, lying on the cold ground as he was. True, the pine needles and blanket kept some of the chill of the earth away, but in his weakened condition he might die anyway. Her hand moved to his chest and then upward, searching for his neck. She found his pulse and was relieved somewhat by the strength of the throbbing beneath her cold fingers, though it was too fast.

"I'm not going to die on you, Doc." There was faint but unmistakable amusement in his voice, overlaid with fatigue.

She wanted to make some reply, but the effort was beyond her. Her eyelids would not stay open. Her feet were tingling painfully, but not even that seemed to matter. Fever or not, the heat of his body was saving *her,* and her mind was too tired to object to the highly improper sleeping arrangement. All she could do was slide her hand down until it rested over his heart; then, reassured by the steady beat, she felt unconsciousness sweep over her like a black tide, wiping out everything.

CHAPTER

3

*R*afe came awake with a rush of panic, though only the leap of his pulse betrayed him; his muscles didn't even twitch. He didn't usually sleep so soundly, especially under these circumstances, and he was silently cursing himself even as he took stock of his surroundings. The birds were chittering without alarm, and he could hear the horses munching on some bit of greenery they'd found. Everything was secure, then, despite his lack of alertness.

The doc still lay against his right side, her head pillowed on his shoulder and her face pressed to his shirt. Glancing down, he could see that her soft blond hair had slipped from its pins and was tousled all over her head. Her skirt was tangled around both her legs and his, and he could feel the enticing softness of breast and hip and thigh. He slowly drew a deep breath, trying not to wake her. Her right hand was lying on his chest, but it might as well have been on his crotch, for the warm weight of it was making his morning erection grow that much harder. The pleasure of it spread through his body like warm honey. So he hadn't imagined the strange, tingling energy in her hands when she had touched him; he felt it now, tightening his nipples, even through his clothing and even though she was asleep.

The temptation was strong to lie there and enjoy the touch, or even to move her hand down to his loins so he could feel that strange heated energy on his shaft and balls, but he liked for his sexual pleasure to be mutual, and more than that they needed to find the trapper's hut. He closed his hand around hers and lifted it to his lips, then gently replaced it on his chest and shook her awake.

Her brown eyes opened drowsily, then her lashes fluttered back down. Dark brown doe eyes, he thought, having seen them for the first time in good light. He shook her again. "Wake up, Doc. We can't stay here."

This time her eyes opened wide and she sat bolt upright in their nest of blankets and coats, looking around in panic. He saw on her face the exact moment when she remembered the night before, saw the fear and desperation as she realized it hadn't been a dream. Then she got control of herself, and twisted around to face him. "You have to take me back."

"Not yet. Maybe in a few days." He got to his feet with some difficulty, though the sleep had done him good and he felt a little stronger. Still, as he moved his body reminded him that he needed far more than just a few hours of rest. "There's a hut close by; I couldn't find it in the dark, but we'll stay there until my side is healed."

She looked up at him, brown eyes wide with apprehension. Dark shadows still lay under her eyes, bruising the translucent skin and making her look frail. He wanted to take her in his arms and comfort her, but instead he said, "Roll up the blankets."

Annie moved to obey him and winced at the pain in her stiff, sore muscles. She wasn't accustomed to such long hours of hard riding, especially when she had been forced to use her legs to stay on the horse. Her thigh muscles trembled with the effort as she squatted to roll the blankets.

He had walked a few feet away, just enough that he was shielded by the rock but could still see her. She heard a splattering sound, like water running, and looked up in curiosity before she realized what he was doing. His pale gaze met hers without a flicker of expression, but she jerked her head down as a fiery blush burned her cheeks. Her medical training noted that at least the fever hadn't impaired his kidneys.

He came back to her side and said, "Now you. Don't try to get out of my sight. I want to see your head at all times." To make certain she didn't try to run, he unholstered his pistol.

She was appalled that he expected her to perform such a function with him standing there listening, and started to refuse, but her bladder insisted that she couldn't wait. Her face felt scorching hot as she sidled around the rock, watching where she was putting her feet.

"That's far enough."

She battled with the restrictions of her clothing, trying to reach under her skirt and petticoat to undo the tapes of her drawers without revealing either herself or her underclothing, just in case he was looking. Then she realized that of course he was looking, for how else could he know if she was in sight or not. If only she had worn drawers with an open crotch, but in fact she seldom did, for she never knew when she would be riding and she didn't care to have her bare inner thighs rubbed raw.

At last she got her clothing arranged so she could relieve herself, and she tried to do so quietly, but was forced to accept the indelicacy of nature. What did it matter anyway, when he was as likely to kill her as not? Logic made her admit that he wouldn't be going to such lengths unless he had some reason for not wanting to be seen, which meant that he was an outlaw. He'd have to be a fool to take her back to Silver Mesa as he'd promised.

And she'd have to be a fool to save his life. To save herself, she should let his condition deteriorate, or maybe even use her medical knowledge to hasten it.

Her mind reeled under the enormity of her own thoughts. She had been trained her entire life to save people, not to kill them, but killing this man was exactly what she was contemplating.

"How long are you going to squat there with your skirts hiked up?"

She stood up so suddenly that she stumbled, hampered by both the drawers twisted around her knees and her stiff muscles. The harsh intrusion of his voice had been like a dash of cold water in the face, wresting her away from her thoughts and back to reality. Her face was paper white as she turned and stared at him across the big rock.

Heavy eyelids shielded the expression in his pale eyes as he studied her, wondering what had made her turn so white and given those soft brown eyes such a stark look. Hell, she was a doctor; she shouldn't be that shocked or embarrassed by something everybody did. He could remember a time when he never would have said such a thing to a woman, but the last ten bloody years had so completely altered him from the man he had once been that the memory was a mere wisp, an echo, and he couldn't even feel regret for the change. He was what he was.

After a frozen moment she bent down to adjust her underwear, but when she straightened from the task her face still had that strangely shattered look. She came back around the rock toward him, and he held out his gloved hand to her, palm up, his fingers open.

For a moment Annie stared without recognition at the small objects in his hand, then her own hands flew to her hair and found it completely unanchored, tumbling around her shoulders and down her back.

He must have found the bone hairpins scattered on the ground.

Hastily she gathered her hair and twisted it into an untidy knot, picking the hairpins from his hand one at a time to secure the heavy mass. He was silent, watching her slender, feminine hands perform their chore, her fingers lifting each hairpin in turn from his leather-gloved palm with all the delicacy of a small bird selecting seeds. The movements were so essentially female that they made him ache deep inside. It had been too damn long since he'd had a woman, since he'd been able to luxuriate in soft flesh and sweet smell, to just look at a woman and enjoy the gracefulness of small motions that they all had, even the coarsest slattern. A woman should never let a man watch her at her toilette, he thought with sudden savagery, unless she was willing to take him into her body and let him ease the sexual hunger the sight of her at her private rituals aroused.

Then the lust seemed to drain out of him with a return of that bone-deep weariness. "Let's go," he said abruptly. If he stood there much longer, he wouldn't have the energy to find the old trapper's hut.

"Can't we eat?" Despite her best effort, there was a pleading note in her voice. She was weak with hunger and knew he had to be in much worse shape, though she couldn't tell it from his hard, expressionless face.

"When we get to the hut. It won't take long."

It took him an hour to find it, and it took her a moment longer than that to realize he had, for the mean little structure was so overgrown it was barely recognizable as being man-made. She could have cried with disappointment. She had expected a cabin, or even a rough shack, but not *this!* From what she could see through the bushes and vines growing around and over it, the "hut" was nothing more than some crudely stacked rocks and a few half-rotten timbers.

"Get down."

Annie flashed him an angry glance. She was getting

tired of those tersely worded commands. She was hungry and frightened, and she ached in every muscle of her body. But she obeyed him, and then automatically started forward to help him when he painfully dismounted. She checked the movement, and knotted her hands into fists as she watched.

"There's a lean-to for the horses."

She looked around in disbelief. She didn't see anything that remotely resembled a lean-to.

"Over here," he said, correctly reading her face. He led the bay off to the left and Annie followed with her mount, to find that he was right. There was a lean-to, constructed using the trees and slant of the earth as part of the structure; there was room for both horses, but just barely. Both ends of the lean-to were open, though the far end was partially blocked by a crudely made water trough and more bushes. A wooden pail hung from a broken tree limb that had been driven into the earthen wall. He took it down and examined it, and for a moment satisfaction registered on his drawn face.

"There's a stream running just on the other side of the hut. Unsaddle the horses, then take this bucket and fetch water for them."

Annie stared at him in disbelief. She was weak with hunger and so tired she could barely walk. "But what about us?"

"The horses get taken care of first. Our lives depend on them." His voice was implacable. "I'd do it, but other than standing here, the only thing I'm capable of right now is shooting you if you try to run."

Without another word Annie set about the work, though her muscles trembled with strain. She dumped her medical bag, the sack containing the food, both saddles, and his saddlebags on the ground. Then she grabbed up the bucket and he directed her to the stream, which was only about twenty yards from the hut on the other side but running diagonally away from the structure rather than beside it. It was only about a foot deep, less in some places and more in others. He followed her to the stream and back to the lean-to, silent and not quite steady on his feet but grimly watchful. She made two more trips to the stream, with him behind her every step of the way, before he deemed the water trough to be full enough. Both horses drank greedily.

"There's a bag of grain in my left saddlebag. Give them both a double handful. They'll have to be on short rations for a while."

That chore accomplished, he instructed her to haul their belongings into the hut. The door was a primitive affair of thin saplings tied together with a mixture of twine and vine, with two leather hinges. Cautiously she pulled it open, and had to bite back a cry of dismay. There didn't seem to be any windows, but the light spilling through the open door revealed an interior draped in cobwebs, coated with dirt, and inhabited by a variety of insects and small animals.

"There are *rats,*" she said in horror. "And spiders, and probably snakes." She whirled and faced him. "I'm not going in there."

Just for a moment, amusement played around his mouth and softened its hard lines. "If there are rats, you can bet there aren't any snakes. Snakes eat rats."

"This place is filthy."

"It has a fireplace," he said wearily. "And four walls to keep out the cold. If you don't like the way it looks, then clean it up."

She started to tell him that he could clean it up himself, but one look at his pale, drawn face stopped the words. Guilt gnawed at her insides. How could she have let herself even think about letting him die? She was a doctor, and even though he was likely to kill her when her usefulness was at an end, she would do her best to heal him. Appalled at her earlier thoughts, which were such a betrayal of both her father and herself, of her entire life, she swore that she wouldn't let him die.

But when she looked around the filthy little hut, the magnitude of the chore that faced her was so great that she let her head drop in sheer hopelessness. She took a deep breath, then gathered her strength and straightened her shoulders. First things first. She picked up a sturdy stick from the ground and gingerly stepped inside the hut. The stick did double duty in tearing down the cobwebs and in raking out the various nests she found. A squirrel scampered out, and a family of mice scurried for the four corners. Grimly she searched them out with her stick. She poked the stick up the chimney, dislodging old birds' nests and alarming some new occupant just out of reach. If there were more nests up there, a fire in the fireplace would encourage a swift evacuation.

After her eyes had adjusted to the dim light, she saw that the hut had a window on each side, the openings covered with flaps of rough boards that could be pushed up and braced open with a stick. She opened both of them, letting in an amount of light that seemed positively cheery after the gloom, though the interior of the hut looked even dirtier now that she could see it properly.

There was no furniture except for a table as roughly made as everything else, and it had two legs broken off. It lay drunkenly in a corner. The best that could be said of the hut, other than that it had a fireplace and four walls, as he had already pointed out, was that the floor was wooden. There were cracks between the boards, but at least they wouldn't be sleeping on the ground.

She carried buckets of water from the stream and sluiced the interior, since the water could drain off through the cracks in the floor and it was the fastest way to achieve a bare minimum of cleanliness. While the floor was drying, she gathered firewood and kindling, dumping both by the fireplace. Through it all, he never let her out of his sight, though she had no idea how he was remaining on his feet. He looked even more colorless every time she glanced at him.

But finally the hut was clean enough that she didn't cringe at the idea of sleeping inside it, and the other inhabitants seemed to have been routed. While she still had the strength, she dragged the saddles and their supplies inside, and made one more trip to the stream, to fill both the bucket and his canteen.

Only then did she wave him inside. Every muscle in her body was trembling and her knees were unsteady, but at least she could now sit down. She did so, on the newly clean floor, and rested her head on her updrawn knees.

The scrape of his boots on the wood made her reluctantly lift her head. He was just standing there, his eyes heavy-lidded with fever and his big body wavering slightly. She forced herself to move again, crawling over to the saddles and retrieving one of the blankets, which she folded double and spread out on the floor. "Here," she said, her voice husky with fatigue. "Lie down."

He didn't lie down so much as drop down. Annie grabbed at him to keep him from pitching over, and his weight nearly knocked her down. "Sorry," he grunted, and lay in the position in which he'd landed, breathing heavily.

She touched his face and throat, and found that his fever was, if anything, even higher. She began unbuckling his gun belt and his hard fingers closed over hers, holding them painfully tight for a minute before he said, "I'll do it." As he had before, when he removed the gun belt he placed it close to his head. She eyed the big weapon and shivered at its cold deadliness.

"Don't even think about going for it," he warned softly, and swiftly she looked up to meet his gaze. Fevered or not, he was still very much in possession of his faculties. It would be easier for her to get away if he were delirious, but she had sworn to help him if she could and that meant she couldn't leave him even if he did slide into unconsciousness. Until he was recovering, she was bound here.

"I wasn't," she said, but his eyes remained wary and she knew he didn't believe her. She wasn't inclined to argue with him over her trustworthiness, not when she was weak, hungry, and so tired it was all she could do to sit upright. And she still had to see to him before she could begin taking care of herself.

"Let's get your shirt off, and your boots, so you'll be more comfortable," she said in a practical tone, and moved to suit actions to words.

Again his hand came up to stop her. "No," he said, and for the first time she heard a fretful note in his voice. "It's too cold to take off my shirt."

Of course the exertion of cleaning out the hut had made her warm, and she had long since shed her coat, but the sun had warmed the day nicely and the air felt pleasant. She could feel him shivering under her fingers. "It isn't cold; you have a fever."

"Don't you have something in that bag of yours to bring the fever down?"

"I'll brew some willow-bark tea after I've seen to your wounds. That will make you more comfortable."

His head turned restlessly. "Brew it now. I'm so damn cold I feel like my bones are frozen."

She sighed, for she wasn't accustomed to her patients directing their treatment, but the order in which she did things really didn't make any difference and she could make a pot of coffee, too. She covered him with the other blanket and began laying a fire, kindling and rich pine chips on bottom, the larger pieces of wood on top.

"Don't build a big fire," he muttered. "Too much smoke. I have some matches in my saddlebag. Right side, wrapped in oilskin."

She found the matches and struck one on the stone hearth, turning her head away from the acrid smell of phosphorus. The pine chips caught after only a second or two. She bent over and gently blew the flames until she was satisfied that they were spreading nicely, then sat back and opened her big medical bag. It looked more like a traveling salesman's case than a doctor's bag, but she liked to have a supply of various herbs and ointments available whenever she was treating a patient, for she couldn't depend on finding what she needed in the wild. She got out the willow bark, neatly bundled in a gauze bag, and the small pot that she used for making tea.

He lay on his back, huddled under the blanket, and watched her with half-closed eyes as she poured a small amount of water from the canteen into the little pot, then set it on the fire to boil. While it was heating, she took a square of gauze, measured a bit of the willow bark into it, added a pinch of thyme and cinnamon, and tied the four corners of the gauze together to form a small, porous pouch, which she placed in the water. Finally, as a sweetener, she opened a jar and added a bit of honey.

"What was all of that?" he asked.

"Willow bark, cinnamon, honey, and thyme."

"Whatever you give me, you'll have to taste it first."

The insult made her back go rigid, but she didn't argue with him. The willow-bark tea wouldn't hurt her, and if he thought she was capable of poisoning him—well, there wasn't anything she could do about that. Her conscience was still smarting her over the horrible thought she had had that morning, and maybe he had picked up on it.

"If you slipped any laudanum into it, you'll go to sleep too," he added.

At least he was only accusing her of drugging him, not of trying to kill him! She lifted a small brown bottle from her bag and held it up for him to see. "This is the laudanum. It's almost full, if you'd like to check the level of it occasionally. Or maybe you'd feel better if you kept it." She held it out to him and he stared at her silently, his pale eyes boring into her as if he could read her mind, and perhaps he could.

Rafe stared at her, trying to decide if he could trust her. He wanted to, especially when he looked into those soft brown eyes, but he hadn't stayed alive these past four years by trusting anyone. Without a word he reached out and took the brown bottle from her, setting it on the floor beside his holster.

She turned aside without comment, but he sensed that he'd hurt her.

She unpacked the food stores, arranging them on the floor so she could see what they had. She was so hungry that nausea threatened to make her retch, and she wondered if she would be able to eat anything after all.

He had brought a coffeepot. She filled it with water and added the coffee grounds, making it stronger than she usually did because she thought she would probably need it. Then she turned back to the food, her hands shaking as she tried to decide what to prepare. There were potatoes, bacon, beans, onions, a small sack each of meal and flour, salt, canned peaches, and bread, rice, cheese, and sugar from her stores. She had been running low on food and had planned to restock, but the arrival of Eda's baby had forestalled her.

She was too hungry to cook anything. She broke off some bread and cheese, then halved the pieces and offered them to her patient.

He shook his head. "I'm not hungry."

"Eat," she insisted, and put the bread and cheese in his hand. "You need to keep your strength up. Try just a bite or two at first, and stop if you feel sick." The bread and cheese weren't the best thing for a sick man, but it was food and it was ready to eat *now*. She would make some soup for him later, when she had rested and was feeling stronger herself. She set the canteen by his hand so he could have water, then she fell on her own meager fare with barely restrained ferocity.

He ate only one bite of the cheese, but all of the bread, and he almost emptied the canteen. By the time they had finished the willow-bark tea had boiled, and Annie used a rag to lift it from the fire, then set it aside to cool.

"Why didn't you give me something for fever last night?" he asked suddenly, eyes and voice hard again.

"Fever isn't necessarily a bad thing," she explained. "It seems to help the body fight infection. You know that cauterizing a wound stops infection, so it stands to reason that the heat from a fever works in the same way. It's only when it goes on too long, or gets too high, that it's dangerous, because it weakens the body dreadfully."

He was still shivering, even covered by the blanket and with the fire going right beside him. Driven by an urge she didn't understand, she reached out and smoothed his dark hair away from his forehead. She had never seen a tougher, more dangerous man, but even so he needed care that she could provide.

"What's your name?" She had asked him before and he hadn't answered, but as isolated as they were now surely he couldn't have any reason for remaining nameless. She almost smiled at the incongruity of not knowing his name, when she had slept in his arms.

Rafe thought about giving her a fictitious name, but decided that it wasn't necessary. He would use another name after he carried her back to Silver Mesa, and there wouldn't be any connection. "McCay. Rafferty McCay. What's yours, Doc?"

"Annis," she said, and gave him a faint, soft smile. "But I've always been called Annie."

He grunted. "I've always been called Rafe. Makes me wonder why folks don't name their kids what they intend to call them." Her smile widened and he watched it, unwillingly fascinated by the movement of her lips. Her hand still lingered on his hair, fingers lightly combing through the strands at temple and forehead, and he almost sighed aloud with pleasure at that warm, tingling touch. His headache eased more with each brushing contact.

But then she moved away, and he had to restrain the urge to grab her and hold her hands to his chest. She'd probably think he had lost his mind if he did, but he felt better when she was touching him, and God knew he needed something. He felt like hell.

Annie poured the willow-bark tea into a battered tin cup and dutifully tasted it so he could see that she hadn't poisoned him. He struggled up on his elbow and took the cup, drinking the tea with four strong gulps and shuddering only a little from the bitterness. "It's not as bad as some medicine I've tasted," he commented, lying back with a stifled groan.

"The honey and cinnamon made it taste better. Both of them are good for you too. Just rest and let the tea work, while I make some soup. Liquids will be easier for you to digest for a while."

She was feeling better herself, now that she had food in her, though she was still inordinately tired. The hard work had loosened her muscles, at least for the moment. She sat on the floor beside him and peeled a few potatoes, then chopped them into fine pieces, and did the same with a small onion. There wasn't a pot big enough, so she used his skillet, adding water and salt and a bit of flour for thickening, and soon the fragrant mixture was bubbling. The fire had burned down enough that it wasn't in danger of scorching, so after adding a bit more water to make sure, she turned her attention back to her patient.

"Feeling a bit better?" she asked, placing the back of her hand against his face.

"Some." The deep ache in his thighbones had eased, as well as his headache. He felt tired and limp and a little drowsy, but warmer and—better. "Keep a pot of that stuff brewed up."

"It does better fresh," she said, though she smiled again. She folded back the blanket. "Now let's get you comfortable and see how your side is looking."

Maybe she had put something in that drink after all, because he lay there and let her undress him, stripping him of shirt and boots and even his pants, leaving him clad only in his socks and long flannel underwear, which was so soft it didn't do much of a job in disguising the outline of his loins. At her direction he eased onto his right side and she rolled his underwear down until it barely covered him. He swore under his breath as he felt his male flesh stir. Damn it, this was why women shouldn't be doctors. How was a man supposed to keep himself from getting hard with a woman's soft hands touching him all over? He watched her face, but she seemed oblivious to his lengthening erection. He reached down and twitched the blanket across his hips to hide his involuntary response.

Annie snipped through the tight cloth binding the poultice to the wounds, her attention totally absorbed by what she was doing. Carefully she eased the pads away, making a satisfied noise in her throat as she saw that the angry red color around the wounds had lessened. The pads were stained with yellow and brown; she cast them aside and leaned over to closely examine the torn flesh. There was a spot of dull metallic gleam close to the surface of the front wound, and she made another sound of satisfaction as she reached for her tweezers. Carefully she grasped the sliver of metal and drew it out. "Another piece of lead," she announced. "You're lucky you haven't already died of blood poisoning."

"So you've already told me."

"And I meant it, too." She continued with her inspection, but didn't find any other bullet fragments. The wounds looked clean. To be certain she cleaned them again with carbolic, then carefully set two sutures in each wound to close the worst of the tears but still leave them open so they could drain. He barely quivered when the needle bit into the soft flesh of his side, though a faint sheen of sweat broke out on his body. She noted the sweat, for it indicated that his fever was breaking as well as the extent of his pain.

She moistened some plantain leaves and placed them on his side, then put bandages on top of that. He gave a low murmur of relief as the soothing, healing leaves began to work their magic. "That feels good."

"I know." She drew the blanket up to his shoulders. "All you have to do now is lie there and rest, and let your body heal. Sleep if you want; I'm not going anywhere."

"I can't take that chance," he replied harshly.

She gave a small humorless laugh. "You'd wake up if I tried to take the blanket, and I'd freeze to death at night without it. I don't even know where I am. Believe me, I'm not going to leave here without you."

"Then let's just say I'll keep you from temptation." He couldn't afford to trust her, or to relax his guard for even a minute. She *said* she didn't know where she was, but how did he know if she was telling the truth or not?

"Suit yourself." She checked the soup and added more water, then settled down on the floor. She had no idea of the time. After noon, surely. It had taken her a long time to clean the hut. She stared out the open door at the long shadows cast by the trees. Why, it was late in the afternoon. "Don't the horses need more feed?" If he expected her to carry it to them, it would have to be soon, because after dark she wasn't venturing past that door.

"Yeah." His voice was weary. "Give them a little more grain." With an effort he sat up and reached for his pistol, drawing it out of the holster. Wrapped in the blanket, he struggled to his feet.

Annie was surprised by the surge of anger that shook her. It wasn't just his refusal to trust her, for she supposed she couldn't blame him for that, but because he wouldn't let himself rest. He needed to be lying down, sleeping, not following her every step. "Don't bother coming all the way out to the lean-to," she snapped. "Just stand out here in front, and you can shoot me in the back if I try to make a run for it."

For the first time, a flash of temper flared in his pale eyes. His cold control had been what had frightened her the most before, but now she wished she hadn't let her own rare anger flare, if this was what it had called up. Anger should be hot, but this man's eyes went even colder, until she felt the chill even across the width of the hut. And still he didn't lose control. He merely said, "I can shoot anything else that might be out there too," as he thumbed back the hammer and motioned for her to exit ahead of him.

She hadn't thought of that. If he was her kidnapper and an inherent danger to her, he was also her protector, for he knew how to live in these mountains, while she would have frozen to death the first night without him. He was also her only hope of getting back to Silver Mesa. On the other hand, she hadn't considered the possibility of facing danger just by stepping through the door of the hut. She hoped it was still too early in the year, and too cold, for snakes and bears to be active, but she simply didn't know. It wasn't something she had worried about in Philadelphia. She wouldn't even have known that bears hibernated if a miner hadn't mentioned it in the rambling monologue he'd been delivering to take his mind off the broken bone Annie had been setting.

Without a word she walked briskly to the lean-to, where the horses nickered at her arrival and immediately began chomping on the grain she gave them. She hauled two more buckets of water from the stream and poured them in the trough, settled the saddle blankets over the two broad backs to help keep them warm during the night, and after a pat on each nose trudged wearily back to the hut. He was still standing just in front of the door, as he had been while she performed the chores, and at her approach he stepped aside so she could enter.

"Close the door and cover the windows," he said

quietly. "It'll get cold fast now, with the sun going down."

She did as he said, though it enclosed them in a cave of darkness eased only by the small lick of flame in the fireplace. She wished for a stout bar to place across the door, but there wasn't one, though there were wooden brackets to testify that there had been at one time. McCay was easing back down onto the blanket. Annie went to the fireplace and removed the skillet of potato soup. The potatoes had cooked to mush; the soup was a little too thick, but she added water and took care of that problem. Satisfied, she poured his cup full and handed it to him.

He sipped it with the total lack of enthusiasm that told her he still had no appetite, but he did say, "That was good," when he had finished.

She ate her share right out of the skillet, smiling inwardly at how shocked all of her old acquaintances back in Philadelphia would be at her manners. But there was only one cup, one tin plate, one skillet, and one spoon, so she imagined she and her patient/captor would be doing a lot of sharing in the next few days. She cleaned the skillet, cup, and spoon afterwards, then brewed him another dose of willow-bark tea. She tasted it without comment, and he drank it down.

They both had to make a trip outside before turning in for the night, and the experience was just as humiliating for her as it had been the first time.

Her face was still red when they reentered the hut, but all of her color fled when he pointed the pistol at her and said in that flat, calm voice, "Take off your clothes."

CHAPTER

4

She stared at him in disbelief, her eyes huge. A dull roaring dimmed her hearing and for a moment she wondered if she might faint, but that escape was denied her. The barrel of the pistol looked enormous, and it was pointing right at her. Above it, his eyes were remote.

"No."

She whispered the word, because her throat was so tight she could barely speak. Several confused, fragmented thoughts skittered through her mind. He couldn't be thinking—no, surely he knew he wasn't in any shape to—he wouldn't shoot her, he needed her to take care of him—

"Don't make it any rougher on yourself than it has to be," he advised. "I don't want to have to hurt you. Just take them off and lie down."

Her hands knotted into fists. "No!" she repeated fiercely. "I won't let you do this to me."

He looked at her white face and tense body, poised as if she would flee into the night, and amusement quirked his mouth. "Honey, you must think I'm a lot stronger than I feel," he drawled. "There's no way in hell I could do what you're thinking."

She didn't relax. "Then why do you want me to take off my clothes?"

"Because I won't be able to stay awake much longer, and I don't want you sneaking out while I'm sleeping. I don't figure you'll leave without your clothes."

"I wasn't going to try to run," she assured him desperately.

"It would be dangerous for you to try to make it on your own, and that's a fact," he said. "So I'll just make sure the temptation doesn't get to be too much for you."

She couldn't even imagine taking her clothes off in front of him; her mind shied away from the idea. "Can't you t-tie me or something? You have a rope."

He sighed. "It's obvious you don't know how damn uncomfortable it is to be tied up. You wouldn't be able to rest like that."

"I don't care, I'd rather—"

"Annie. Take your clothes off. Now."

The warning was plain in his voice. She began to tremble, but she shook her head obstinately. "No."

"The only alternative is for me to shoot you. I don't want to do that."

"You won't kill me," she said, trying to sound more confident than she felt. "Not yet, anyway. You still need me."

"I didn't say anything about killing you. I'm damn good with a pistol, and I can put a bullet anywhere I want it to go. Which do you prefer, in the leg or shoulder?"

He wouldn't do it. She told herself that he wouldn't do it, that he needed her healthy so she could take care of him, but there was no hesitation at all in his face, and his hand was rock steady as he lifted the pistol.

She turned her back on him and began unbuttoning her blouse with trembling fingers.

Firelight gleamed on her satin smooth shoulders as

she removed her blouse and let it drop to the floor. Her head was bent forward, revealing the delicate furrow of the nape of her neck. Rafe felt a sudden urge to press his mouth to it, to wrap his arms around her and shelter her against him. He had had to drive her to the limit of her endurance all day long, just as he had done the night before, even though she was hollow-eyed with fatigue. And she had managed, somehow finding sufficient strength in her thin body to do the things he had demanded of her. She had fought down her natural fear of him and done her best to make him well, and he repaid her by humiliating her and terrorizing her, but he didn't dare relax his guard. He had to make certain she didn't try to run, for her sake as well as his.

She removed her sturdy half boots, then, still keeping her back turned to him, lifted the front of her skirt and fumbled with the tapes that tied her petticoat around her waist. It dropped around her feet in a froth of white, and she stepped out of it.

She was trembling visibly, even in the dim light. "Go on," he said softly. He regretted that she was so frightened, but he'd be lying to himself if he tried to deny being interested in seeing her skirt drop as well. Hell, he was more than interested, he was already hard, his erection thrusting against the flimsy covering of his longhandles. Only the blanket wrapped around him kept her from seeing his condition, if she had happened to turn around. He wondered briefly just how sick he would have to get before his cock got the message that he wasn't capable; sicker than he was now, that was for sure, and he felt like hell.

She unbuttoned the waistband of her skirt and the garment fell to the floor.

She was still covered, still wearing her stockings, knee-length drawers, and shift, but the shape of her body was revealed. Rafe inhaled deeply, fighting the sudden restriction in his chest. His loins began to throb. She wasn't thin so much as dainty, with slender, delicate bones and a sweet curve to her hips and thighs that made him break into a sweat.

She stood rigidly, as if incapable of continuing. He could let her stop now; she wasn't going to run off anywhere dressed in only her stockings and under-wear.

"The stockings."

She bent down and untied the garters above her knees, then removed the white cotton stockings. Her bare toes curled on the plank floor.

"Now your drawers." He heard the hoarseness of his voice, and wondered if she noticed it too. Damn, he didn't have to take it this far, but he couldn't seem to stop himself. He wanted to see her, wanted to feel her lying naked in his arms even though he wasn't well enough to do anything about it. He wondered if that strange hot tingle was restricted to her hands, or if he would feel it all over if he lay on top of her. Would it be more intense inside of her? The thought of feeling that unique sensation on his shaft almost made him groan aloud.

She was shaking like a leaf now, all over, from head to foot. Her shift came down to mid-thigh, but still . . . She felt utterly exposed and vulnerable as she stepped out of her drawers. The rush of cool air on her bare buttocks was shocking, and even though she knew her bottom was covered by the shift she couldn't stop herself from reaching back to make sure. Her one remaining garment was too thin for her to feel reas-sured.

He wanted that shift off. God, he wanted her naked. The sleek line of her legs almost drove him to mad-ness, but he wanted to see the curve and cleft of her bottom, the sweet fullness of her breasts, the pouty folds of her sex. He wanted to be well so he could thrust into her, spend hours between her legs and feel her release deep inside, shivering around his hardness. He wanted to make love to her every way he'd ever done it before, and try everything he'd ever heard of.

He wanted to taste her, to drive her crazy with his mouth and fingers and body. He was shaking with lust.

And she was shaking with fear.

He couldn't make her remove the shift, couldn't terrorize her any more than he already had. He dragged the blanket from around himself and draped it over her shoulders, wrapping her snugly in it. She clutched it with pitiful desperation, her head still bent forward so he couldn't see her face. Rafe ran gentle fingers through her hair, searching out all of the pins and releasing the soft, fine mass to tumble over his hands and swing forward to hide even more of her face. He pulled it back over her shoulders, where it reached almost to her waist.

Wincing against the pull in his side, he bent down and added more wood to the fire, then gathered her discarded garments, except for her petticoat, and placed them under the blanket he had been lying on, putting a bit more padding between them and the hard floor and making it damn certain she couldn't get to them without waking him up. He added his own clothing as a safeguard. Her petticoat he rolled into a pillow, and placed it at one end of the blanket.

"Lie down," he said gently, and in mortified silence she moved to obey.

She would have lain down still wrapped in the blanket, but he caught it and pulled it from her nerveless fingers. She froze, then realized that they would have to share the blanket, just as they had done the night before. She sank to her knees and held her shift close to her body as she stretched out on their crude bed, but she still felt painfully exposed. She turned on her right side, with her back to him.

He lay down beside her and also turned onto his right side. He drew the blanket up over them, then settled his left arm over her waist. The heavy weight of it made her feel pinioned. She could feel him all against her back, the hair on his naked chest brushing against her shoulder blades. He pulled her closer, nestling her buttocks to his loins, cradling her thighs to his. Annie's breath came in quick, shallow gasps. She could feel his . . . his manhood, covered only by the thin flannel of his longhandles, pushing against her bottom. Her shift might as well have not existed, for all the protection it offered. Had it ridden up, leaving her totally uncovered? She almost cried out, but she didn't dare reach down to find out.

"Shhh," he murmured against her hair. "Don't be afraid. Go to sleep."

"How—how can I?" she choked.

"Just close your eyes and relax. You've worked hard today; you need to sleep."

Even closing her eyes was out of the question. She was too aware of his partial nudity, too aware of her own bareness. She had always slept swathed in voluminous nightgowns, feeling the comforting, protective folds wrapped around her legs.

"Just so you'll know," he said softly, still so close that his lips moved her hair, "The pistol is in my right hand. Don't try to take it away from me, or I might kill you before I'm awake enough to know who you are. And the rifle isn't loaded; I took the shells out of it while you were taking care of the horses." He hadn't, because he never deliberately left himself unarmed, but she wouldn't know that. Poor little thing, she hardly knew anything at all about surviving outside a town, or even inside one. When he had looked through her cabin, he had noticed that there weren't any weapons at all, unless he considered her scalpels weapons. Silver Mesa was a boomtown, filled with rough, money-hungry, whiskey-soaked men, yet she hadn't owned the most basic means of protection. It was a thousand wonders that she hadn't been attacked and raped her first week in town.

She felt so sweet and soft in his arms. Automatically he pulled her closer and tucked his sock-clad feet under her much smaller bare ones to share his heat with her. She was trying to hold herself still, probably to keep from stirring him up even more than he was; since she was a doctor, he wryly figured that she knew what it was she was feeling pressed against her butt. But she couldn't stop the little tremors that kept shaking her, and it wasn't the cold that was making her shake. Right now, they were plenty warm. She was still terrified, and he was at a loss to know how to calm her down.

He didn't figure he'd be able to stay awake much longer, and he wanted her settled before he drifted off. She had to be tired too; if he could just get her mind off the situation, her body would take over and she'd go to sleep.

"Where're you from?" he murmured, keeping his voice low and calm. Just about everybody out West was from somewhere else.

Another shiver ran through her, but she answered, "Philadelphia."

"I've never been to Philadelphia. New York and Boston, but never Philadelphia. How long have you been out here?"

"I—I've been in Silver Mesa for eight months."

"And before that?"

"Denver. I spent a year in Denver."

"Why in hell did you leave Denver for Silver Mesa? At least Denver's a proper town."

"Denver didn't need any more doctors," she replied. "Silver Mesa did." She didn't feel like going into the particulars, because people's attitude had *hurt,* cutting her deeper than she would have thought possible.

Good. Her voice sounded calmer now. Rafe stifled a yawn. Gently he pushed her hair away from her ear and nestled closer, then tucked the blanket more securely over her shoulder. "No telling how long Silver Mesa will last," he said, letting his voice drop to nothing more than a rustle of sound. "Boomtowns die out as fast as they grow up. When the silver plays out, the miners will pull up stakes and move on, and so will everyone else."

The thought of starting all over again was depressing, even though her existence in Silver Mesa lacked any sort of luxury or even comforts. At least she was doing what she wanted to do more than anything else, which was practice medicine. Sometimes she was so frustrated that she wanted to scream. She knew so much, could *do* so much, if people would only come to her in time. So often they elected not to come at all, because she was a woman, and so they died.

But she would face the question of her future when—and if—the ore in Silver Mesa played out. She had no guarantees that she would ever even see Silver Mesa again. She should worry about that instead, but it was so difficult to form a coherent thought. For the first time in this long day, she was able to let her tired body rest. She knew she shouldn't. A tiny frisson of alarm ran through her, but it quickly faded and she didn't move. She knew she should open her eyes—when had they closed? She was warm, so warm, and her limbs felt heavy and lax. She might as well have been wrapped in a cocoon, so encompassed was she by his heat. Cocoon . . . yes, one consisting of the blanket and his arms, his legs, his very body. She could barely move, but she didn't have the energy to, anyway. For a brief lucid moment she was aware that she was going to sleep, and then she had.

Rafe felt the complete relaxation of her body and indulged in self-satisfaction. She had been so tired that she had dropped off as soon as he'd made her forget about being afraid. Now she could get some much-needed rest, and so could he, though he perversely wanted to stay awake as long as he could so he could enjoy the feel of her in his arms. A woman's body was a pure miracle of nature, the closest a man could get to heaven on earth, and it had been too damn long since he'd had the luxury of holding a woman all snuggled up to him, toasty warm, comfortable, and fairly safe. He curved his hand over her belly, and drifted to sleep with a strange sense of contentment.

He was already up when Annie woke the next morning; it was the sound he made rebuilding the fire that roused her. She scrambled to her feet in a surge of panic, then hastily grabbed the blanket to cover herself. He turned, his enigmatic eyes measuring her, and she tensed without knowing why.

"You can get dressed," he finally said. "So will I. I'll try to help you with the chores today."

She paused, but the instinct to heal was too strong. Carefully holding the blanket with one hand, she reached out the other to lay it on his unshaven cheek, a slight frown furrowing her brow as she considered his condition. He still felt too warm to her. She picked up his hand and pressed her fingers to his thick wrist, feeling his pulse, which was a little too fast and a little too shallow. "No, not today," she replied. "You need at least one more day of rest and medication before you try to do even light chores."

"Just lying around will make me even weaker."

The dismissive note in his voice made her bristle. She straightened her shoulders and gave him a stern look. "Why did you bring me here? I'm the doctor, not you. Dress if you like, it won't hurt anything, but—"

"I'll have to find some graze for the horses today," he interrupted. "And I need to set some traps, unless you want to live on potatoes and beans."

"We can do without more food for a while yet," she said stubbornly.

"Maybe we can, but the horses can't." While he was speaking, he eased down to a bending position and got his clothes from under the blanket they'd been lying on. Just as carefully he stepped into his pants and pulled them up over his hips.

Annie bit her lip, but came to the conclusion she would have to dress in front of him, just as she had undressed. Quickly, she grabbed her skirt, and after some frustrated wrestling with the blanket let it drop and jerked the garment on in exactly the same motion he had used to don his pants. She felt better once her legs were covered, but the cold air washing over her arms and shoulders was a sharp reminder that she was still far from decently clad. For the sake of modesty she put on her blouse and buttoned it before picking up her petticoat and drawers. Her clothes were sadly wrinkled, but she was so glad to have them back that she could have cried.

He pulled on his shirt but didn't attempt putting his boots on by himself; instead he walked to the door and opened it, letting in the bright, crisp early-morning sun. Annie blinked at the sudden brightness, turning away until her eyes became accustomed to it. Cold air rushed in, making her shiver. "It's supposed to be spring," she said plaintively.

"It'll probably snow up here a couple more times before the weather takes any notice of the calendar," he said, looking at the sky through the trees. It was utterly clear, meaning the weather wasn't likely to get very warm anytime soon. The temperature was comfortable enough during the day, but the nights were freezing.

While his back was turned, Annie pulled on her underwear and petticoat, then sat down to put on her stockings. Rafe looked around to find her skirts up around her knees, and his gaze lingered on the trim turn of her calves and ankles.

She wrinkled her nose at putting on clothes she had already worn for two days; both she and her garments needed a good washing, as did his, but just how she was going to accomplish such a thing baffled her. She could heat water for them to wash off with, but she couldn't see both of them sitting around naked, wrapped in only a blanket, while their clothes dried. Still, something would have to be contrived; her father had always held that cleanliness was as important to a patient's survival as any skill or knowledge a doctor possessed, and people did seem to recover better in clean surroundings.

"I wish you had thought to bring the lamp," she commented, hugging her arms. "Then we could see in here without opening the door and freezing ourselves."

"I have some candles in my saddlebags, but we're better off saving them in case the weather turns so bad we can't open the door."

She moved closer to the fire and briskly rubbed her hands together to warm them, then finger-combed her hair and pinned it up. As she put on the coffee and began making their meager breakfast, Rafe came back into the room and sat down on the blanket.

She glanced at him. "Are you hungry?"

"Not much."

"You'll know when you're really getting better, because you'll get your appetite back."

He watched her put the bacon on to fry, then stir up a batch of dough to make pan biscuits. She had a brisk, economical way of doing things that he liked, not wasting time or motion but retaining her instinctive grace. She had twisted her hair up into that knot again, he noticed. He wished she could have left it down, but long hair was dangerous over a cook fire. At least he could look forward to taking it down again when they bedded down for the night, feeling it spill over his hands. Maybe tonight she wouldn't be so frightened, not that he blamed her. Hell, a woman would have to be stupid not to feel at least a little scared in these circumstances.

"Our clothes need washing," she said crisply, not looking at him as she expertly spooned the dough into the pan. "And we both need a bath. I don't know how we'll accomplish it, but it's going to be done. I refuse to be filthy."

There had been a lot of times when he'd been a lot gamier than he was now, but women had a different set of standards for things like that. "Fine with me," he said. "I have some clean clothes in my saddlebags. I wish I'd thought to tell you to pack extra clothes, too, but I had other things on my mind." Like fighting to remain conscious; like evading Trahern and staying alive; like the fire in her hands that had both startled and aroused him. "You can wear one of my shirts, but there's no way my pants will fit you."

"Thank you," she murmured. Color mounted in her face as she bent over the fire. Pants! Her legs would be indecently outlined— She broke off her automatic thought at the realization that he had already seen more than just the outline of her legs. And she would gladly wear his pants in order to wash her own clothing. Priorities had a way of rearranging themselves when convention came head to head with necessity.

He ate enough breakfast that she was satisfied, not having expected him to eat anything at all. She brewed more willow-bark tea and he drank it without question, then lay back and let her examine his wounds. There was great improvement over the day before, and she told him so as she soaked more plantain leaves for a fresh bandage.

"So I'm going to live," he commented.

"Well, at least you won't die from *these* wounds. You'll feel much better tomorrow. I want you to eat as much as you can today, but be careful not to make yourself sick."

"Yes, ma'am." He could have sighed with pure bliss at the feel of her hands as she bandaged him.

He got completely dressed afterward, though the stitches in his side pulled when he put on his boots. Annie cleaned up after their meal, and turned to find him standing there wearing his coat and gun belt, and carrying his rifle. "Get your coat," he said. "We have to get those horses fed."

She didn't like the idea of him walking so far but refrained from wasting her breath in useless argument. He was determined not to let her out of his sight, and unless he lapsed into unconsciousness there really wasn't anything she could do about it. She got her coat without a word, and preceded him out of the cabin.

The horses were restless after having been confined in such a small space, and the big bay jostled Rafe when he led him out of the shed. Rafe's face turned white. Annie hurried to take both lead ropes from him. "I'll lead them," she said. "Don't do anything but walk. Or better still, why don't we ride the horses?"

He shook his head. "We won't be going far." To tell the truth, though he could do it if he had to, he'd just as soon not swing into the saddle yet.

He found suitable graze about half a mile away: a small, sunny meadow not fifty yards across, protected from the cold wind by the curve of the mountain rising to the north. The horses eagerly bent their heads to the winter grass while Rafe and Annie sat down and let the sun warm them. It wasn't long before both of them were taking off their coats, and a hint of color reappeared in his face.

They didn't talk much. She bent her head against her raised knees and closed her eyes, lulled by the delicious heat and the steady chomping of the horses. It was such a quiet, peaceful morning that she could have easily gone back to sleep. There were no sounds but those of nature, the rustle of wind high in the trees, the calls of birds, the horses leisurely cropping the grass. Silver Mesa was never this quiet—there always seemed to be someone in the street, and the saloons never seemed to close. She hadn't noticed the noise that much, because she was accustomed to city noises, but now she realized just how discordant those sounds were.

He shifted position, and she realized he had done so several times. She opened her eyes. "Uncomfortable?"

"Some."

"Then lie down. It's what you should be doing, anyway."

"I'm okay."

Again she refrained from useless arguing. Instead she asked, "How long are you going to let them graze? I still have a lot to do."

He looked at the sun, then at the horses. Annie's gelding had stopped grazing and was standing placidly, its head lifted and ears perked in interested attention at the sound of their voices. The bay was still grazing, but in a more desultory manner, as his appetite was satisfied. Rafe wished he could leave the horses out, but he couldn't take the chance of being caught so far away from them. Maybe tomorrow he'd feel strong enough to rig up a rough corral so they could move around rather than being cooped up in the shed. It wouldn't take much, some bushes and rope, to at least give them walking-around room.

"We might as well head back now," he finally said, though he was content to just sit in the sun. Walking reminded him of just how weak he truly was.

Annie got the horses and led them back. After she took them to the stream and let them drink their fill, they went docilely back into the shed.

The logistics of bathing almost defeated her, since there wasn't a basin or pitcher, only the one bucket for hauling water, and it was far too cold to bathe in the stream. She made do by cleaning out the coffeepot and cook pot, then putting water on to heat in both of them. When the water was boiling, she added it to the cold water in the bucket.

"You first," she told him. "I'll be right outside the door—"

"No, you won't," he interrupted, his pale eyes narrowing. "You'll be in here where I can keep an eye on you. Sit down with your back to me if you don't want to watch."

His inflexibility distressed her, but she had already

learned that she couldn't change his mind, so she didn't try. Without another word, she sat down with her back to him and rested her head on her drawn-up knees just as she had out in the meadow. She heard him undress, then the splashing of the water as he washed. After about five minutes she heard him begin dressing again, and finally he said, "I have my pants on; you can turn around now."

She scrambled to her feet and turned around. He hadn't put on a shirt yet, though a clean one was lying on the blanket. She tried not to stare at his broad, hairy chest; she had seen many bare chests without suffering any effect other than curiosity, so why did her heartbeat react so wildly to the sight of his? It was broad and muscled and dark-haired, but still only a chest, even though it had felt as solid as rock when he had held her against it during the night. "Hold the mirror so I can shave," he directed, and only then did she notice that he had laid out his razor and a small mirror.

She stepped closer and held the mirror while he soaped his face, then carefully scraped away the dark whiskers that covered his face. She couldn't prevent herself from watching him with helpless fascination. His black beard had been at least a week old when she had first met him, so she was anxious to see him clean shaven. He did some interesting contortions with his face that she remembered her own father doing, and a gentle smile touched her mouth. It comforted her to find the small similarity between her beloved father and this dangerous stranger who had her at his mercy, assuming he possessed any.

When he had finished, the revealed structure of his face made her breath catch in her chest, and she quickly turned away to hide her expression. Contrary to her expectations, the beard had actually softened him. Clean-shaven, he looked even more predatory, with his pale eyes gleaming like ice from beneath the strong ridge of black brows. His nose was high-bridged and straight, his mouth set in a hard line and bracketed on each side by a thin furrow. His jaw looked like granite, and his chin was strong and stubborn, with just a hint of a cleft that his beard had hidden until then. It was a face without a hint of softness or trust, wearing the remote expression of a man who had seen and caused so much death that it no longer touched him. In the brief moment before she had turned away she had seen bitterness in the set of his mouth, a bitterness so entrenched that it might never be erased and so intense that it had hurt her to see it. What could have happened to make a man look like that, as if he believed in nothing, trusted no one, and had nothing left of any value to himself except, perhaps, his own life—and that was only a "perhaps."

Yet he was still only a man, for all his dangerousness. He was tired and ill, and despite the things he had done that had terrified her, he had not only *not* hurt her, he had seen to her comfort and safety to the best of his ability. She didn't forget that it was to his advantage to keep her safe, or that any discomfort she suffered was purely his fault, but at the same time he hadn't been as cruel or brutal as she had feared, or as many other men would have been. He had done and said things that had terrified her, but never from sheer cruelty; it was oddly reassuring that he always had a reason for doing what he did. She was beginning to feel that she could take him at his word: when he was recovered, he would take her back, unharmed, to Silver Mesa. On the other hand, if she tried to escape from him, she was equally certain that he would stop her in any way he could, including shooting her out of the saddle.

"All right, it's your turn now."

She turned around and saw that he was completely dressed, including his gun belt. His dirty clothes lay in a pile on the floor, and he had laid out a second clean shirt for her use.

She stared at the shirt, caught in a dilemma. "Which do I wash first, myself or the clothes?"

"The clothes," he answered. "That way they'll have more time to dry."

"And what do I wear while I'm washing them?" she asked drily. "If I put on your shirt now, it'll get wet."

He shrugged. "What you do depends on how bad you want clean clothes."

She understood what he meant, and snatched up his clothes and the bar of soap without another word. She wasn't in a very good mood as she marched to the stream and knelt down on the bank. He followed, and settled down about five yards away with the rifle resting across his lap. She set to work with grim determination, for the water was icy and her hands were numb in only a few minutes.

She had wrung out his shirt and hung it over a bush to dry, and was scrubbing his pants, before she spoke. "It's too cold for snakes. And bears, too, I presume. What are you guarding me from? Wolves? Mountain lions?"

"I've seen bear out this early," he replied. "A healthy wolf isn't going to bother with you, but an injured one might. Same thing with mountain lions. You'd be in more danger if a man wandered through and stumbled on you."

She bent over and dunked his pants in the stream, watching the soap rinse away in a pale cloud. "I don't understand men," she said. "I don't understand why so many of them are so senselessly cruel, how they can abuse a woman, child, or animal without giving it a thought but get killing mad if anyone accuses them of cheating at cards. That isn't honor, that's—I don't know what it is. Stupidity, I guess."

He didn't answer. His restless eyes continued to skim their surroundings. Annie struggled to wring the water out of the heavy garment, but her hands were cold and clumsy. He got up and took the pants from her, his strong hands effortlessly twisting the water out of the material. He shook them out and spread them over another bush, then took his seat again.

She doused his underwear, then began soaping them.

"Some people are just naturally bad," he said. "Men and women. They're born mean and they die mean. Others kind of drift into it, a little at a time. And sometimes they're pushed."

She kept her head down, her attention on her chore. "What kind are you?"

He thought about it. Finally he said, "I don't reckon it matters."

It certainly didn't matter to him. He had been pushed, but the way it had happened had ceased to mean anything. He had lost everything he had believed in and fought for, lost his family, seen the reason for it all turn bitter and crumble into dust, had been hounded across the country, but finally the reasons hadn't counted for anything, only the reality. The reality was that he was constantly on the move, watching his back trail; he trusted no one, and he was willing to kill whoever came after him. Beyond that, there was nothing.

CHAPTER

5

Washing her own clothes was so much trouble that accomplishing the task was a testament to her considerable determination. Keeping her back to him, she sat down and removed her stockings, then untied the tapes of her petticoat and drawers. When she stood, both garments slid down her legs and she stepped out of them. She refused to look at him to see if he had noticed; of course he had. The blasted man didn't miss anything. Her cheeks were hot as she knelt again on the bank and began scrubbing her unmentionables. Irritated, she wished some of the heat in her face would transfer itself to her hands. How could water be this cold and still run?

To wash her shift and blouse, she had to return to the cabin and change into his shirt. He remained outside, for which she was painfully grateful, but she still felt wretchedly exposed with the window coverings propped open and the chilly air washing over her bare breasts. She jerked his shirt on over her head as quickly as possible, and sighed in relief at the comfort of the soft wool covering her.

The shirt was so huge on her that she was startled

into a soft laugh. She buttoned every button, but the neck was still so loose that it exposed her collarbones. The hem hung to her knees, and the sleeves flapped a good six inches past her fingers. She began briskly rolling them up and laughed again, for when she rolled them up to her elbow there was practically no sleeve left, as the shoulder seam drooped down almost that far. "Do you have an extra belt?" she called. "There's so much material here it'll get in my way."

He appeared in the doorway as soon as she spoke, and she shivered as she realized he had been leaning against the cabin, just out of sight. He had been only a few feet away when she had been half nude. Had he looked? She didn't want to know.

He cut a few feet of rope and she tied it around her slim waist, then snatched up her remaining clothes and marched back to the stream, where she finished her laundry. Then she had to haul more water back to the cabin and begin heating it for her own bath. She was so exhausted that she wondered if it had been worth it, but she couldn't have endured another day without washing.

She also couldn't endure bathing with the windows and door open, wondering if he were watching her. Not only that, it was too chilly, though it hadn't seemed to bother him much when he had bathed. She closed the windows and built up the fire, then faced him defiantly. "I'm not bathing with an open door."

"Fine with me."

Her cheeks got hot again. "Or with you in here."

"Don't you trust me to keep my back turned?"

Distress darkened her soft brown eyes. Rafe reached out and cupped her chin, feeling her silky texture of her flesh. "I don't turn my back on anyone," he said.

She swallowed. "Please."

He held her gaze while his thumb brushed lightly over the tender section beneath her chin. Annie felt herself begin to tremble, for he was standing far too close to her and she could feel the heat and tension of his big body. The bright, terrible clarity of his eyes made her want to shut her own to escape, but she was caught in paralyzed fascination and couldn't. This close, she could see that his eyes were gray, like winter rain, without any softening blue tinge. Black and white specks gave his irises the impression of crystalline depth. Search as she might, she could find no compassion in that clear, cold gaze.

He dropped his hand and stepped back. "I'll be outside," he said, and she nearly sagged with relief. He watched the play of expression across her face before adding, "Take off your skirt and I'll wash it for you."

She hesitated, her longing for clean clothes battling with modesty. She couldn't wear only his shirt for the length of time it would take her clothing to dry, but maybe she could fasten one of the blankets around her. Quickly, before she lost her courage, she turned her back on him and unfastened her skirt, grateful that he was such a large man and his shirt was so enveloping.

Silently he took the skirt and left the cabin, closing the door behind him. As he walked down to the stream he pictured her bathing, and he was acutely aware of her nakedness just on the other side of that door. Fever burned through him again, but it was the heat of desire rather than illness. He wanted to touch more than just her face. He wanted to lie down with her and feel her soft body in his arms as he had during the night, and he didn't want to see fear in her eyes. He wanted to see her slim thighs open for him, welcome him into their embrace.

That was what he wanted. What he needed to do was to get through the next few days, building his strength, then take her back to Silver Mesa as he'd promised and quietly disappear. He needed to keep his mind on what he was doing, rather than speculate on how she would look naked. A woman was a woman. They differed in size and color, just like men, but the basics were the same.

And the basics had been driving men mad since the beginning of time.

He laughed a little at himself as he washed her skirt, but there was no humor in the sound. She *wasn't* just like every other woman, and it was useless to try to convince himself that she was. Her hands held a strange, heated ecstasy that he couldn't forget, and he craved every little touch she gave him. He even felt some of it when *he* touched *her,* for no other woman's skin had ever felt so supple and silky to him. It had taken all of his willpower to release her and roll out of the blankets that morning, and he'd be a damn fool if he thought the temptation wasn't going to get worse with every passing hour. He'd be a double-damn fool if he let the temptation make him forget about Trahern.

He wrung out her skirt, then glanced at the sky. The sun had slid behind the mountains, and the air was already getting colder, so there wasn't any point in hanging the skirt over a bush to dry. Instead he gathered up their still-damp clothing and went back to the cabin. He could hear water splashing. "Haven't you finished yet?" he called.

"No, not yet."

He leaned against the cabin wall for support and pondered the mystery of why women took so much longer to bathe than men did, when they were smaller and had less to wash.

It was another fifteen minutes before she opened the door, her face glowing with warmth and the brisk application of soap and water. She had washed her hair, probably first thing, for the fire had already partially dried it. She wore his shirt and had wrapped one of the blankets around her like a toga. "There," she said, sighing in tired satisfaction. "I feel much better now. I'll fetch fresh water for the horses, then start supper. Are you hungry?"

He was, a little, though he wouldn't have minded if she had sat down to rest for a while. Except for when they had been sitting in the little meadow while the horses had grazed, she had been working from the moment her eyes had opened that morning. No wonder there wasn't any extra flesh on her narrow frame.

The blanket made it awkward for her to fetch water, but she refused to let him help and he wasn't certain enough of his strength to insist. All he could do was follow as she trudged back and forth, his frustration wearing his temper thin. None of what he felt was revealed in his face or actions, however, for she would be the only one to suffer if he released his anger, and none of it was her fault. Rather than whine, whimper, or complain, any of which would have been reasonable reactions from any woman who had been forced into such a situation, she had squared her shoulders and done what she could to make their circumstances easier.

But at last all of the chores were taken care of, and they could go into the cabin and close the door against the cold. Annie allowed herself perhaps thirty seconds of rest before she plunged into the preparations for supper. She was limited by their scanty provisions, but cooked some beans and bacon and made another batch of pan biscuits. She was gratified when Rafe ate with the first enthusiasm for food he had shown, a good indication of his improving physical condition. Afterward she put her hand on his forehead, and smiled at the slight dampness she found. "Your fever has broken," she said, placing her other hand against his cheek for confirmation. "You're sweating. How do you feel?"

"A lot better." He almost regretted his improvement, for that would mean she no longer had a reason to touch him. Odd, but the quality of energy from her hands had changed now that he wasn't so ill; rather than that hot, sharp tingle, the sensation was like a warm caress spreading all over his body, flooding him with pleasure so intense he almost shuddered from it.

Her smile lit up her face. "I told you I could make you well."

"You're a good doctor," he said, and her expression became so radiant that it took his breath.

"Yes, I am," she agreed without either conceit or false modesty. Her words were a simple acceptance of fact. "It's all I've ever wanted to be."

Humming, she walked to the door and stepped outside. Rafe cursed under his breath and got to his feet, his hand on the butt of his pistol as he strode after her. Annie all but collided with him as she came back in, two twigs in her hand. Her eyes widened when she saw the cold anger in his eyes. "I was just getting some toothbrush twigs," she said, holding them out for him to see. "I'm sorry. I forgot."

"Don't forget," he said sharply, grasping her arm and pulling her out of the doorway so he could close the door. She flushed and the radiance died out of her face, making him regret the edge to his voice.

She poured out some salt to clean their teeth with, and Rafe lounged back with the twig in his mouth. Her fastidiousness reminded him of times when he had taken such niceties for granted, when he had been accustomed to daily shaves and washings and had always worn clean clothes. He had taken for granted the availability of shaving soap, soda tooth powder, and fine milled soap for bathing. He had worn expensive cologne and danced many a waltz with bright-eyed young ladies. But that was a long time ago, before the war, a whole lifetime ago. He couldn't feel any kinship with the young man he had been then; he had the memories, but it was as if they were of an acquaintance rather than himself.

Annie got up and rummaged in her medical bag, taking out two small pieces of what looked like bark.

She popped one in her mouth and held the other out to him. "Here. Cinnamon."

He took the piece of bark and sniffed it; cinnamon, just as she'd said. He chewed it slowly, enjoying the taste. He could remember those long-ago young ladies chewing cinnamon or peppermint pastilles to freshen their breath, and could remember tasting that freshness in kisses.

Maybe it was the memories, or maybe it was simply because he wanted it so much. He said, "Now that our breath is kissing fresh, it'd be a shame to waste it."

She jerked her head around, her eyes wide, and Rafe slid his hand around the back of her neck, under her hair. She stiffened against the pressure that brought her head closer to his.

"No," she blurted, panicked.

"Hush. It's just a kiss, honey. Don't be afraid."

His low, drawling voice washed over her, making her go weak inside. She tried to shake her head, but his hand on her neck prevented the movement. Annie strained backward, her gaze fastened on his mouth as it came closer and closer. No, oh no, she couldn't let him kiss her, she couldn't let herself feel his mouth, not when her heart misbehaved so at the very sight of him. The temptation was too sweet, too piercing. She had felt her weakness where he was concerned on the night she had met him, and even when she had been terrified for her life she had also been aware of the dangerous attraction she felt for him. She had begun to think herself safe, for he hadn't made any sexual move toward her, not even the night before when she had slept all but naked in his arms, but now she saw the danger she was in. If she wanted to return to Silver Mesa heart-whole, she should resist, she should turn her head aside, she should scratch and claw—

Too late.

His mouth settled on hers with the slow, sure pressure of experience, cutting off her quick gasp of protest, while his hand held her still for his tasting.

Annie had been kissed before, but not like this, not with a lazily deepening intimacy that paid no attention to the useless pushing of her hands. The strong movement of his mouth opened her lips, and helplessly she felt her body quicken as a warm tide surged through her. Her hands stopped pushing and abruptly clenched his shirt. Under his guidance her mouth opened and he slanted his head to deepen the contact and take better advantage of the opportunity. His tongue moved into her mouth and Annie quivered at the shocking intrusion.

She hadn't known men kissed like this, hadn't expected him to use his tongue; she had seen a lot during medical school and in her practice as a doctor, but she hadn't known that the slow stroking of his tongue inside her mouth would make her feel weak and hot, or that her breasts would tighten and ache. She wanted him to go on kissing her like this, she wanted to press herself close against him in an effort to ease the throb in her breasts, and feel his hard arms around her. Her inexperience made her helpless against him, unable to handle her own desires or anticipate what he might do.

Rafe forced himself to release the nape of her neck and slowly withdraw his lips. He wanted to keep on kissing her; hell, he wanted to do a lot more than that! But the twinge of pain in his left side every time he moved, as well as the lingering weakness in his legs, reminded him that he wasn't in the best shape for making love. It was just as well his body had its limitations, because he'd be a fool to let this situation become complicated by sex. Returning her unharmed was one thing, but like the old saying went, hell held no fury like that of a woman who thought she'd been taken lightly and then discarded. She was less likely to tell anyone about him if she didn't feel like a scorned lover. As he eased away from her, he hoped like hell that he could take his own good advice.

She looked pale and dazed. She didn't glance at

him, but instead stared fixedly at the fire. He saw her slender throat move as she swallowed.

"It was just a kiss," he murmured, moved by an impulse to comfort her, since she seemed to need it. He scowled as he had an unwelcome thought. Though she had seemed to respond to him, it was possible she was afraid he would assault her. She had opened her mouth for him, but he couldn't say that she had returned the kiss. It infuriated him to think that maybe he'd been the only one feeling that buildup of heat and tension inside, but the possibility was there. "I'm not going to attack you."

Annie struggled to compose herself. If he thought her reaction was caused by fear, that was much better than him knowing she had wanted him to continue what he'd been doing. She looked down at her hands, but couldn't think of anything to say. Her mind felt sluggish, and her heart was still racing.

Rafe sighed and sought a more comfortable position, dragging his saddle over to lean against. It looked like he needed to get her settled down as he had the night before. "What made you want to be a doctor? It's not the usual thing for a woman."

That was the one subject guaranteed to bring her out of herself. She gave him a quick look, grateful for something to talk about. "That's certainly been impressed on me time and again!"

"I can imagine. What made you do it?"

"My father was a doctor, so I grew up around medicine. I can't remember when I wasn't fascinated by it."

"Most doctors' little girls play with dolls, not medicine."

"I suppose. Papa said it really started when I fell out of a barn loft when I was five. He was terrified that the fall had killed me; he said that I wasn't breathing, and that he couldn't find a pulse. He beat on my chest with his fist and started my heart again, or at least that's what he always told me; now that I'm older, I think I was probably only stunned. Anyway, I was very taken with the idea that he had started my heart, and from then on all I talked about was being a doctor."

"Do you remember the fall?"

"Not really." She gazed at the fire, raptly watching the small yellow tongues of flame tipped with palest blue as they wavered back and forth. "What I remember is more like a dream about falling, rather than a real fall. In the dream I had fallen, but I got up by myself, and there was a lot of light and people coming to get me. I don't remember what Papa says happened. I was only five, after all. What do you remember from when you were five?"

"Getting my ass tanned for letting chickens in the house," he said bluntly.

Annie hid a smile at the image. She wasn't shocked by his language, for after working in a boomtown for so many months, she thought there was very little that she hadn't already heard. "How many chickens?"

"Enough, I guess. I couldn't count very well at that age, but it seemed like a lot of them."

"Did you have any brothers and sisters?"

"One brother. He died during the war. How about you?"

"No, I was an only child. My mother died when I was two, so I don't remember her at all, and Papa never remarried."

"Was he happy that you wanted to be a doctor too?"

Annie had often wondered that very thing. "I don't know. I think he was proud, but worried at the same time. I didn't understand why until I entered medical school."

"Was it difficult?"

"Just getting into school was difficult! I wanted to attend Harvard, but they wouldn't accept me because I'm a woman. I finally attended medical school in Geneva, New York, where Elizabeth Blackwell got her degree."

"Who's Elizabeth Blackwell?"

"The first woman doctor in America. She got her degree in '49, but little had changed in the years since. The instructors ignored me and the other students harassed me. They accused me to my face of being nothing more than a loose woman, since any decent woman wouldn't want to see what I'd be seeing. They told me that I should get married, if anyone would have me after that, and have babies as women were supposed to do. I should leave medicine to people who were smart enough to understand it, namely men. I studied alone and ate every meal alone, and I *stayed.*"

He looked at her thin, delicate face, outlined by the glow of the fire, and could see fierce stubbornness in the set of her soft mouth. Yes, she would have stayed, even in the face of violent opposition. He didn't understand the fervor that drove her to work herself to the bone in the name of medicine, but her instructors and fellow students had certainly underestimated it. She was the only female doctor he'd ever seen, but during the war a lot of sick and wounded men would have died if it hadn't been for the women volunteering to work in the hospitals and take care of them. It was damn certain those women had seen a lot of naked men, too, and no one thought any less of them for it. More, in fact.

"Don't you want to get married and have babies? Seems to me like you could do that and still be a doctor."

She gave him a quick smile, then shyly returned her gaze to the fire. "I've never really thought about getting married. All of my time has been taken up with being a doctor, with learning everything I can learn about it. I wanted to go to England and study with Dr. Lister, but we couldn't afford it, so I've had to learn any way I could."

Rafe had heard of Dr. Lister, the famous English surgeon who had revolutionized his profession by using antiseptic methods, greatly reducing the number of deaths by infection. Rafe had seen too much battlefield surgery not to realize the importance of Dr. Lister's methods, and his own recent bout with an infected wound had impressed him with the seriousness of it.

"Well, what about now? You've learned how to be a fine doctor. Are you going to be looking for a husband now?"

"Oh, I don't think so. Not many men would be willing to have a doctor for a wife, and besides, I'm too old. I'll be thirty my next birthday, so that makes me an old maid, and men would rather have someone younger."

He gave a short laugh. "Since I'm thirty-four, twenty-nine doesn't seem so old to me." He hadn't been able to guess her age, and he was a little surprised that she had revealed it so easily, since in his experience women tended to evade the issue after they reached their twenties. Annie often looked tired and worn, with good reason, which made her seem older than she was, but at the same time her skin was as soft and smooth as a baby's and her round breasts stood upright like a young girl's. The thought of her breasts made him shift uncomfortably as his groin tightened. He'd only seen them through her shift, and he felt cheated because he hadn't felt them in his hands, hadn't seen the color of her nipples or tasted their sweetness.

"Have you ever been married?" she asked, jerking his attention back to their conversation.

"No. Never even came close." He'd been twenty-four, and just beginning to think of the security and closeness of marriage, when the war had started. The following four years of guerrilla fighting with Mosby had hardened him, and after his father had died during the winter of '64, he'd had no family left and so had drifted after the end of the war. Maybe he'd have settled down, though, if he hadn't run into Tench Tilghman in New York in '67. Poor Tench, he hadn't realized the terrible secret he'd been guarding, and it had cost him his life, but at least he'd died without knowing how they had been betrayed.

Blackness welled in him at the memory and he struggled to quell it rather than inflict the ugliness of his mood on Annie. "Let's go to sleep," he muttered, suddenly impatient to have his arms around her again, even if it was in sleep. Maybe the peculiar sweetness of her touch would lighten his dark spirit. He stood up and began banking the fire.

Annie was startled by his brusqueness, for she had been enjoying their conversation, but she obediently got to her feet. Then she remembered that she had been using one of their blankets as a dress and would now have to give it up. She froze, her pleading gaze fastened on him.

When he turned around he accurately read her expression. "I'm going to have to tie you tonight," he said as gently as he could.

She clutched the blanket to her. "Tie me?" she echoed.

He jerked his head at their damp clothing, spread out over the floor of the cabin to finish drying. "I'm not going to sleep on a pile of wet clothes. Since I can't keep the clothes away from you, I'll have to keep you away from the clothes."

She had suggested the night before that he tie her rather than make her remove her clothes, but now it seemed that she was to be both tied and largely naked. It wasn't the idea of being bound that disturbed her as much as the realization that she had to surrender the blanket. Granted, she was still wearing his shirt, and it covered more than her shift had the night before, but she was very aware of her bareness beneath it.

He untied the piece of rope she had been using to secure the blanket around her waist, and it began slipping to the floor. She grabbed it, then clenched her teeth and let it drop. The faster he got her tied, the sooner she could lie down and pull the concealing blanket over her. This humiliating exposure would be over with faster if she didn't protest.

Rafe unrolled the sleeves of the shirt until the cuffs covered her wrists, to protect her soft skin from the abrasive rope. She stood motionless, her dark eyes huge as she stared straight ahead. He pulled her hands together and looped the rope around each wrist separately, then tied a quick, efficient knot in the middle. He tested both the knot and the tightness of the rope before he let her hands drop. Automatically, she pulled at the binding to discover the strength of it herself. The rope was snug rather than uncomfortably tight, without any give in the knot.

Quickly Rafe pulled off his boots and gun belt and straightened out the blankets. "Lie down."

It was awkward with her hands tied in front of her, but not impossible. She knelt on the blanket, maneuvered to a sitting position, and managed to lie down on her side. Horrified, she felt the hem of the shirt slip upward with her movement and she made a panicked effort to pull it down behind, but her arms were so restricted that she couldn't. She felt a draft of cool air on her bare bottom. Dear God, was she totally exposed? She started to lift her head to see, but at that moment Rafe dropped to the floor beside her and spread the other blanket over them. His big body pressed close to her back and his arm settled around her waist.

"I know it's uncomfortable," he said in her ear, his voice low. "You might sleep better on your back, if lying on your side puts too much pressure on your arms."

"I'm all right," she lied, staring into the darkness. Her arms were already hurting, and she knew he'd made it as easy on her as he could.

Rafe inhaled the fresh sweet scent of her hair and skin, and a sense of well-being began to edge out his black mood. He snuggled her closer and slipped his right arm under her head. Her narrow body felt soft and wonderfully female against him, especially her rounded little bottom. He wondered if she knew the shirt had slipped up so much when she had lain down that he'd caught a glimpse of curved white buttocks. His shaft was painfully rigid, restrained as it was by his pants, but it was a good pain, the best.

Within five minutes she was subtly shifting her shoulders, trying to ease them. The second time Rafe felt her move against him, he slipped his left hand around her hip and deftly rolled her onto her back. "Stubborn."

She took a deep breath and let her shoulders relax. "Thank you for not tying me up last night," she murmured. "I hadn't realized." How strange that forcing her to take off her clothing, which had so terrified her, had in fact been an act of mercy.

"It isn't anything you'd have had any reason to know."

"But you have."

"I've been in a few tight spots. Tied others up, too, during the war."

"Did you fight for the North or the South?" There was no mistaking his southern drawl, but that didn't necessarily indicate which side he'd fought on, as the war had split states, towns and families.

"For the South, I guess, though it came down, really, to fighting for Virginia. That was my home."

"What outfit were you with?"

"I was in the cavalry." That was explanation enough, he thought, though it fell far short of describing what the companies under Mosby's command had been and done. For a relatively small group, they had tied up a hugely disproportionate number of Union troops dedicated to tracking them down, thwarting them at the least, capturing them if possible. The Union troops had failed. Mosby and his men had eluded capture time and again.

He listened to the rhythm of her breathing slow as

she relaxed and sleep edged closer. She turned her head toward him. "Good night," she murmured.

Desire slammed into his gut and he cursed his wounds, cursed the situation that made her fear him. She had said a simple good night, and he had imagined her saying it after he'd worn her out with some hard loving. Everything she said and did reminded him of sex. It would be a pure miracle if he managed to keep his hands off her for another couple of days. Right now, he'd say it was an impossibility.

"Kiss me good night." His voice was raspy with need and he felt her muscles tighten again in alarm.

"We—we shouldn't do that."

"Considering how bad I want to strip you naked, a kiss isn't much to ask for."

She quivered at his rough tone. Beside her, he was as tense as she, though for a different reason. Heat emanated from him in waves, enveloping her, but it wasn't the heat of fever. She sought reassurance, though she didn't know why she should believe a man who had kidnapped her. "A kiss is all you want?"

"Hell, no, a kiss isn't all I want!" he snapped. "But it's what I'll settle for, if you're not ready to let me between your legs."

Shock reverberated through her, making her dizzy. "I'm not a whore, Mr. McCay!"

"Fucking doesn't make a woman a whore," he replied crudely, frustration eroding his control. "Taking money for it does."

The word battered at her. She had heard it muttered as an aside once when she had been summoned to care for one of the prostitutes who had been treated roughly—assaulted would be a better description—but had never imagined that any man would say such a thing directly to her. She flinched from the crudity, and her heart began to slam against her rib cage. Men didn't talk that way to women they respected; did that mean he intended to—

He slipped his hand onto her stomach, under her

bound hands. The heat of it burned her, and her breath began coming in small pants. His fingers flexed a little, then began a delicate massaging motion. "Calm down, I'm not going to rape you."

She said on a gasp, "Then why are you saying such awful things?"

"Awful?" He considered her reaction and the possible causes. Since she was a doctor he hadn't expected her to be so missish about something he regarded as natural between men and women, and damn wonderful at that. He'd long since lost any inclination he might have had as a "gentleman" to shield women from any knowledge of sex. Her reaction made him think she either had been mistreated by some man or she was a virgin, and the best way to find out was to ask. He hoped she was virgin, because the idea of anyone mistreating her like that suddenly made him killing mad. "Are you a virgin?"

"What?" Her voice went high and almost soundless with shock.

"A virgin." Gently he rubbed her belly. "Annie, honey, has anyone ever—"

"I know what it means!" she interrupted, afraid of what he might say. "Of course I'm still a—ah—virgin."

"There's no 'of course' to it, honey. You're twenty-nine, not a silly sixteen-year-old with the dew still on. Very few women go through life without a man getting in bed with them, and a fair number aren't married at the time."

She had seen enough in her years as a doctor to admit the truth of that, but that didn't change her own situation. "I can't say about other women, but I've certainly never done—that."

"Have you ever wanted to?"

Desperately she tried to turn away from him, but his hand pressed heavily on her stomach, keeping her where she was. Lacking any other means of evasion, she turned her head away. "No. Not really."

"Not really," he repeated. "What does that mean? You either have or you haven't."

It was becoming difficult to breathe; the air seemed heavy and heated, laden with the musky scent of his skin. She was no good at dissembling, so finally she stopped trying to evade his shocking, persistent questions. "I'm a doctor. I know the facts of how people perform sexual union, and I know what men look like without their clothing, so of course I've thought about the process."

"I've thought about the process, too," he said roughly. "That's about all I've thought about since the first time I saw you. It's been hell; I was so sick I could barely stand up, but that didn't stop me from wanting to lift your skirt. My common sense tells me to leave you alone, to just take you back to Silver Mesa in a couple of days the way I said I would, but right now I'd give ten years of my life to have you under me. I've been hard for two solid days, Annie girl."

It was a bittersweet comfort to realize that he had felt some of the same helpless fascination she'd experienced since first meeting him. Touching him, even in healing, was a deep and glowing pleasure. And when he had kissed her earlier, she had thought her heart would burst. She wanted to know more. She wanted to turn into his arms and let him do the things about which she had only speculated with mild curiosity. Nothing of what she felt now was mild. Her skin felt hot and sensitive, and a low, deep throb tormented the secret places of her body. Her lack of clothing made the throbbing worse than if she had been encased in fabric, for she was tantalized by the knowledge that all he would have to do was slide the shirt up a few inches. . . .

Yes, she wanted him. But to give in to him, and to her own baser yearnings, would be the worst mistake of her life. He was an outlaw, and would soon disappear from her life; she would have to be a total fool to give herself to him and run the risk of bearing an illegitimate child, as well as the damage it would do her emotionally.

She steadied her voice, and took the route of common sense. "It would be a mistake for me to accept your advances. I think we both know that."

"Oh, I know it," he muttered. "I just don't like it worth a damn."

"That's the way it has to be."

"Then kiss me good night, honey. That's all I'm asking."

Hesitantly she turned her head, and he took her mouth in a slow, strong motion that opened her lips and left her vulnerable to the penetration of his tongue. If a kiss was all he was allowed, then he intended to make the most of it. He forced his domination on her mouth with hard, deep kisses, using his tongue in the most blatant imitation of copulation, until her bound hands came up and twisted and she was clinging to his shirt while soft little whimpers sounded in her throat. He kissed her until his entire body was throbbing with the need to empty his seed inside of her, until her mouth was swollen and tears seeped from beneath her lashes.

He wiped the moisture away with his thumb, savagely restraining himself. "Go to sleep, honey," he whispered in a hoarse voice.

Annie half stifled a moan. She closed her eyes, but it was a long time before her yearning flesh let her sleep.

CHAPTER

6

*H*e wasn't there when she woke up the next morning, and Annie panicked at the thought that he might have abandoned her there in the mountains. Her hands were unbound and that frightened her even more, for why would he have untied her unless he had planned on leaving? Still half asleep, with her hair hanging in her eyes, she stumbled to her feet and jerked the door open, then ran outside. Cold air swirled around her bare legs and rocks and twigs bruised her feet. "Rafe!"

He stepped out from the horse shed, the water bucket in one hand and the raised pistol in the other. "What is it?" he asked sharply, as his pale eyes raked over her.

She halted her headlong plunge, suddenly aware of her half-naked state and the iciness of the ground beneath her bare feet. "I thought you'd left," she said in a strained tone.

His eyes turned frosty as he stared at her, his hard face expressionless. Finally he said, "Go back inside."

She knew she should do as he said, but concern made her hesitate. "How do you feel? I don't think you should be hauling water yet."

"I said to get inside." His voice was dead level, but it carried the sharpness of a whiplash. She turned and carefully picked her way back inside, wincing as the rough ground hurt the tender soles of her feet.

She propped open one of the windows so she'd be able to see, then examined her clothing. It was stiff and wrinkled, but dry and—best of all—clean. She hurriedly dressed, shivering with cold. The chill seemed worse than it had the morning before, but maybe that was because she'd been outside with only a shirt between her and the good Lord, and Rafe hadn't built up the fire before he'd gone out.

After she had finger-combed her hair and pinned it up, she built up the fire and began cooking breakfast, but her movements were automatic. She couldn't stop thinking about Rafe, disjointed thoughts that leapt from subject to subject. He had looked much better this morning, without fever dulling his eyes and leaving his face drawn. It was probably too soon for him to be doing any physical work, but how was she supposed to stop him? She just hoped he didn't tear out the stitches in his side.

How had he gotten out of the cabin without waking her? Of course, it had taken her a long time to fall asleep and she'd been very tired, but she usually wasn't *that* hard to waken. He had lain awake for a long time, too; he hadn't tossed and turned, but she had been very aware of the tension in his arms and body as he'd held her. It would have taken only a single word or gesture of invitation from her and he would have been on top of her.

Several times she had been tempted to throw caution to the winds and say that word, and shame rose in her as she admitted to herself how close she had come to surrendering her chastity to an outlaw. She couldn't even comfort herself that she had resisted temptation because of her high moral standards, to preserve her reputation and self-respect; it was pure cowardice that had kept her from giving herself to him. She had been afraid. Part of it had been a simple fear of the unknown, and part of it had been fear that he would hurt her, emotionally as well as physically. She had treated women who had been damaged by men who were too careless or too rough, and she knew that the first time was painful for women anyway, but she had ached with lust and might have given in had it only been that. She wanted to know what it was like, to lie under a man and cradle his hard weight, to accept his body into hers.

But her deepest fear was that she was far too vulnerable to him, that by taking her body he would breach the inner walls that guarded her heart, and against all of her own self-advice and common sense she would care too much for him, and that would deal her a wound that wouldn't heal as easily as flesh did. How *could* she let herself care for him? He was an outlaw, a killer. Even now, she had no doubt that, if she tried to escape, he would shoot her. It was odd, perhaps, but she also trusted him to keep his word and return her unharmed in a few days if she didn't try to escape.

Annie had always thought of herself as a morally upright person, capable of knowing right from wrong and choosing the correct course. For her, morality had nothing to do with judgment and everything to do with compassion. But what did it say about her that she could so clearly see the violence in Rafe McCay and had still been strongly attracted to him from the beginning? He was cold and frighteningly controlled, and as dangerous as a hunting cougar, yet his kisses made her tremble and yearn for more. A little voice in her whispered that she could give herself to him, then return to Silver Mesa without anyone knowing that she had had an outlaw lover, and she was terrified she would yield to temptation.

The door opened but she kept her eyes and her attention focused on what she was cooking. Rafe set the bucket down beside the hearth. Annie glanced at it and saw that it was full of water. From experience, she knew just how heavy that bucket was, and she couldn't stop the concern she felt. Reluctantly she asked again, "How do you feel?"

"Hungry." He closed the door and dropped to the blanket. "Almost normal. Just like you said."

She gave him a quick glance. His tone had been even, without any of his former sharpness, but she knew that his voice would reveal only what he wanted it to. "I didn't say you would be almost normal. I said you'd feel better."

"And I do. Even after taking care of the horses, I'm not as weak now as I was yesterday. But the stitches are itching."

That was a good sign, an indication of healing, but she hadn't expected it so soon. Evidently he was a fast healer, as well as having the inhuman stamina he had revealed on their nightmare ride to the cabin.

"Then you're almost well." She looked at him, her eyes somber and a little pleading. "Will you take me back to Silver Mesa today?"

"No."

That single word was implacable. Annie's shoulders drooped a little. It would have been for the best, removing her from the dangerous temptation of his company, but she didn't try to argue with him. He had his own reasons for what he did and she had yet to be able to sway him from his decisions. He would return her to Silver Mesa when *he* wanted to, and not before.

Rafe watched her with hooded eyes as she poured a cup of coffee and handed it to him. He sipped the strong brew, enjoying the feel of it warming his insides and adding to the heat he already felt just from looking at her. She was uneasy around him this morning, in a way she hadn't been before even when she had been so terrified he was going to kill her. She was sexually aware of him now, and as skittish as a young mare being cornered by a stallion for the first time. Tension stretched between them like a tightly strung wire.

She was all buttoned up in her own clothes this morning, hiding behind a barricade of cloth and naively trusting that modesty would hold him at bay. He smiled into the cup as he tilted it to his mouth. Women never seemed to realize the strength of the enthrallment that drew men to them, the enchantment of soft skin and soft curves, the bone-deep, gut-wrenching need that drove men to penetrate them and get the closest to heaven a man was likely to get on this earth. Women also didn't realize the strength of their own desires, that their own bodies undermined their defenses. Annie sure as hell didn't realize it, or she wouldn't take such comfort in the useless barrier of clothing. Did she think that if he couldn't see bare skin, he wouldn't desire her?

His common sense had been pushed aside by a physical hunger so great it had become a torment. He *would* have her. Returning her to Silver Mesa without having sated himself on her was beyond him now. He could barely restrain himself from reaching out for her this instant. His life had been nothing but death and bitterness for so long that the sweet heat of her was as irresistible to him as water to a thirsty man in a desert.

Only the knowledge that he would have plenty of time for seduction, and that there was work that had to be done that day, kept him from pulling her down on the blankets. The weather had turned noticeably colder, and low, dull clouds had closed in on the mountains, snow clouds if he'd ever seen them. He would probably have time to take her back to Silver Mesa before the snow began, if he were so inclined, but he wasn't. The snow tended to be deep this high in the mountains, and the early-spring storms could be some of the worst; they might be confined to the cabin for days, even a couple of weeks. Annie wouldn't be able to hold out against him, or her own body, for that long.

But today he had to lay in a supply of firewood, a lot of it, as well as set some traps to supply them with food. He could easily hunt with the rifle, but the sound of gunfire could draw attention, and he didn't want anyone to know there were people up here. He'd have to do something about the horses, too. They couldn't be cooped up in that tiny shed, without room to move around, for days on end. He'd have to hobble them and let them graze while he came back and worked on the shed. He didn't like being so far away from the horses, in case they needed to leave in a hurry, but the animals needed to graze and he only had today, and maybe part of tomorrow, to get prepared. He decided not to tell Annie that he thought it was going to snow, because the idea of being snowed in with him might make her panic.

His hunger was wolf-sharp, and he could barely wait for the bacon and biscuits to finish cooking. Annie refilled the cup and he set it between them so they could share it. Neither of them talked during the simple meal. Rafe ate with a voracious appetite, savoring every bite of the sweet honey and hot bread.

Afterward he pulled off his shirt so she could check his wounds, and he used the opportunity to cautiously scratch the itching skin around the stitches. Annie slapped his hand away. "Stop that. You'll get the stitches irritated."

"That sounds fair. They're irritating the hell out of me."

"You're healing faster because of them, so don't complain." The wounds had closed and were healing well, with very little redness. She suspected she would be able to remove the stitches in another day or so, rather than wait the week to ten days it usually required.

She dabbed apple cider around the stitches to keep them from itching, then placed a thick pad over the wounds and bound it in place.

He was standing with his arms raised, and he frowned down at his side. "Why did you make the bandage so much thicker today?"

She neatly tied off the cloth and he lowered his arms. "To protect the wounds."

"From what?" He pulled his shirt back on over his head and tucked it into his pants.

"From you, mostly," she replied as she restored order to her medical bag.

He grunted and shrugged into his coat, then got his small hatchet out of his saddlebags.

Annie glanced at the sharp blade. "You don't need to cut firewood; there's still plenty to be picked up off the ground."

"It's not for firewood. I'm going to enlarge the horse shed." He hooked the scabbard for the rifle over his head and slid the weapon into it so it lay on his back. "Put on your coat. It's colder today, and you'll need it."

Silently she obeyed. Things went easier if she just did as he said, even though she didn't see any need in doing so much work on the shed when they would be there only a day or two. She tried to convince herself that he would take her back to Silver Mesa that soon, especially since he was doing so well. Just a few more days, and then temptation would be removed and she would be home, safe and sound, and still chaste. Surely she could remain firm for that long; after all, Penelope had guarded her chastity against zealous suitors for twenty years, waiting for Odysseus' return.

They walked the restless horses back up to the clearing, where Rafe fashioned hobbles for them and turned them loose to graze. On the walk back to the cabin, they both gathered loose firewood and stacked it just outside the door.

Next she helped him to make some simple snares,

her interest caught by the procedure. With only twine and the limber sticks that he cut with the hatchet, he fashioned several different kinds. He let her make the last one under his direction. She had deft hands, but found that trying any new skill involved a certain amount of awkwardness. He was patient with her, though he insisted that she keep redoing the snare until he was satisfied with it. Her cheeks glowed with both accomplishment and cold when she was finished.

She watched his long, muscled legs make easy work of the steep slopes as they returned to the cabin, and thought that it was beginning to feel normal to be trudging along behind him with nothing around them but the vast mountains and the silence. They were so isolated that they might as well be the only two people on earth, a man and his woman. Her stomach clenched at the thought and she hastily rejected it, because if she ever let herself think that she was his woman, she was lost. He would sense it, the way he seemed to know everything, and turn to look at her with his pale, fierce eyes. He would see her mental surrender written on her face, and he would take her, perhaps even right here on the cold forest floor.

To keep herself from wavering, she made herself think of the various crimes he could have committed. She felt a little pang of despair as she realized she had no trouble at all thinking of him as a criminal; he was hard and cold, emotionless, and even though he had treated her better than she had expected and feared, she wasn't able to delude herself about his nature. Even now he was as alert as a wild animal, his head constantly turning as he examined every detail and sought the source of every little sound.

"What did you do?" she asked, unable to stop herself even though the knowledge would be a permanent worry to her.

"When?" he murmured, halting as he studied a bird that had taken flight. After a moment he relaxed and began moving again.

"What are you wanted for?"

He glanced at her over his shoulder, cold danger glinting in his eyes. "What difference does it make?"

"Did you rob someone?" she persisted.

"I'll steal if I have to, but that isn't why I'm wanted."

His tone was flat and casual. Annie shivered, and she reached out to catch his gloved hand. "Then why?"

He stopped and looked down at her. A humorless quirk tugged at his mouth. "Murder," he said.

Her throat went dry, and she dropped his hand. Oh, she had known it from the beginning, recognized his capacity for violence, but hearing him say it as casually as he would have pointed out an interesting bird made her heart almost stop. She swallowed, and forced herself to ask, "Did you do it?"

He seemed surprised by the question. His eyebrows lifted briefly. "Not the one I'm accused of." No, he hadn't killed poor Tench, but he'd killed plenty of the ones who had come after him, so he guessed it didn't matter at this point.

His phrasing didn't go unnoticed. She turned and walked past him, and he fell into step behind her.

She walked almost blindly. She was a doctor, not a judge. She wasn't supposed to ask the whys and wherefores when someone was ill or hurt, she wasn't supposed to weigh their worth as human beings before giving them the benefit of her skill and knowledge. She was simply supposed to heal, to the best of her ability. But this was the first time she had had to face the fact that she had saved the life of an admitted killer, and her nerves twisted with anguish. How many more people would die because this man had lived? He might have lived anyway, without her help, but she would never know that.

And yet . . . and yet even if she had known, that first night, could she have refused him treatment? In all conscience, no. Her oath as a physician bound her to do what she could, in all circumstances, to heal.

But even without the oath, she couldn't have let him die. Not once she had touched him, trembled from his animal magnetism, felt his low, raspy voice weave a sensuous spell around her. Why try to lie to herself? Even though she had been truly terrified those first two nights, lying in his arms had made her entire body heat with instinctive pleasure.

Come the night, she would be lying in his arms again.

She shivered and pulled her coat tightly around her. Maybe it was better that she knew him for what he was. It would give her the strength to resist him.

But even now, as she thought of the coming night, her breasts started aching and heat built in her loins, and she knew shame.

The hard work necessary to enlarge the horse shed came as a relief, for she was able to concentrate on the simple physical labor. He knocked the lean-to down and put the wood, which had been planed and roughly finished, aside to be reused, then began cutting down saplings and securing them on top of each other. He braced them against the bank and the standing trees and notched them so they would interlock. At his direction, she began mixing mud to daub between the saplings and seal the rough walls against the wind. She did so with a fastidiousness that made him hide a grin; getting her hands dirty was unavoidable, but she took care that her clean clothes didn't suffer.

He more than doubled the length of the original shelter. He dragged the water trough into the middle so each horse had equal access to it, then used two saplings as rails to equally divide the space. Annie saw him stop and rub his side occasionally after he had exerted himself, but he looked like he was massaging a sore muscle rather than suffering sharp pain.

When they had first begun she had assumed it

would take them all day, if not part of the next day, to finish the project, but within four hours he was using the original wood to build a door and frame. She filled in the cracks with mud, with him helping finish this final touch, then she stepped back to look at the fruit of their efforts. It was rough and not very appealing, but functional. She hoped the horses appreciated their new quarters.

She checked the sun after they had washed their hands in the icy stream. "I need to put the beans and rice on to cook now. Those beans didn't get quite done enough last night."

He was sweating despite the cold, and she guessed he would welcome a rest. He had to be feeling the effects of doing hard physical work so soon after being as ill as he had been. He went inside with her and dropped down onto the blankets with a sigh. Within minutes, though, he was frowning as he poked a callused finger into the wide cracks in the floor.

"What's wrong?" she asked, looking up from the meal preparations and seeing the scowl.

"You can feel the cold coming through these cracks."

She leaned over and held her hand over the floor. Sure enough, there was a distinct chill. "Why worry about it now? We've managed so far, and you can't put down another floor."

"Because it's gotten colder already, and my guess is it's going to get worse. We won't be able to stay warm enough to sleep." He got to his feet and started toward the door.

Annie looked at him in surprise. "Where are you going?"

"To cut some more saplings."

He had to go only about ten feet, and she listened to the sound of wood being chopped. He returned shortly with four saplings, two over six feet long and two only about half that length. He made a rectangular frame with them, lashing the ends together. Then he carried in big armloads of pine needles and spread them inside the frame to create a soft, thick barrier between them and the floor. The frame kept the pine needles together. He spread one of the blankets over the frame, then stretched out on his roughly made bed to test its comfort. "Better than the floor," he announced.

She wondered what else he intended to do that day. She found out when he insisted on gathering more firewood. "But why do we have to do it now?" she protested.

"I told you, it's getting colder. We'll need the extra firewood."

"Why can't we get it as we need it?"

"Why make extra trips out into the cold when we can already have the wood at hand?" he retorted.

She was tired, and getting snappish. "We won't be here long enough to use all of this."

"I've been in the mountains before, and I know what I'm talking about. Do as you're told."

She did, but with ill grace. She had worked harder during the past three days than she ever had before, so she wouldn't have minded resting a bit. Even before she had met him, she had been exhausted from delivering Eda's baby. And she hadn't slept well the night before, which was all his fault. She had an even temper and was seldom fretful, but fatigue was eroding her normal good humor.

Finally they had collected enough firewood to satisfy him, but even then there was no rest. They had to walk up to the clearing to collect the horses. When they reached the clearing it was empty, and Annie's heart plunged. "They're gone!"

"They won't be far. That's why I hobbled them."

It took him perhaps ten minutes to locate them; they had smelled water and picked their way down to a stream, probably the same one that ran so close by the cabin. The horses' morning restlessness had been worked off by the day's leisurely grazing, and they didn't resist his hand on their halters. Annie took charge of her gelding and silently they led the animals back.

Even then he wouldn't let her rest. He wanted to check all of his snares before nightfall, and he made her walk with him. He defied everything she knew about human strength and stamina; he should have been exhausted by noon, but instead he had worked a full day that would have worn out even a healthy man.

The snares were empty, but he didn't seem surprised or disappointed. It was twilight as they returned to the cabin, and the failing light combined with Annie's tiredness to make her stumble a little on a protruding root. She caught herself and wasn't in any danger of falling, but Rafe's hand shot out and gripped her upper arm with a strength that startled her into crying out.

"Are you all right?" He caught her other arm and steadied her in front of him.

She took a deep breath. "I'm fine. You startled me when you grabbed my arm."

"I didn't want you to fall. If you broke an ankle, you'd find out right quick I'm not as good a doctor as you are."

"I'm fine," she repeated. "Just tired."

He didn't release her, but kept a steadying hand on her arm the rest of the way. She wished he wouldn't touch her. The touch of that hard, powerful hand was too hot, its warmth too penetrating. It undermined her rational resolve to keep a distance between them. But of course he hadn't made any such decision, so he wasn't acknowledging the shield of indifference she kept trying to erect.

He closed up the cabin for the night while she finished their supper. It was a relief to finally be able to sit down, even if it was on a rough wooden floor with cold air seeping through the cracks. She cooked a slice of bacon and crumbled it in with the beans and rice for flavoring, then added a bit of onion. The tantalizing aroma filled the small room, and Rafe sat forward with an avid glint in his eyes as she spooned it out for him. Annie was so tired that she didn't eat much, which was just as well, because Rafe finished every bite.

She still had one thing she wanted to do before she collapsed for the night. After their dishes were cleaned, she picked up the second blanket and looked around, trying to decide how best to arrange it.

"What are you doing?"

"Trying to figure out how to hang this blanket."

"Why?"

"Because I want to wash off."

"Then do it."

"Not in front of you."

He gave her a hard look, then without another protest he took the blanket from her hand. He was tall enough to reach the ceiling beams, and easily snagged two corners of the blanket on the rough wood, curtaining off a small section of the room. Annie took the water bucket behind it and removed her blouse. After a moment's hesitation, she slid the straps of her shift down her arms and let it fall to her waist. Carefully she washed as best she could, keeping a weather eye on the curtain, but he made no move to interrupt her privacy. When she was dressed again she emerged from behind the blanket with a quiet thank-you.

He took the bucket from her hand. "You might want to go back behind that blanket. I've sweated like a horse today, and could use a wash myself."

She whisked herself behind the blanket almost without pausing. Rafe's eyes gleamed as he removed his shirt. The fact that he had worked hard wasn't the only reason he wanted to wash. Had he been alone he wouldn't have bothered, but they would be turning in soon, and a woman as dainty about her personal habits as Annie would more likely welcome a man who didn't stink of sweat. He tossed his dirty shirt aside, then as an afterthought stripped completely naked. Thanks to Annie, he had clean clothes to put on. He squatted by the bucket and washed, then put on clean socks, underwear, and pants, but decided to leave off his shirt.

He reached up and unhooked the blanket, and in the dim firelight Annie blinked at him like a sleepy owl. He surveyed her sharply and realized that she was almost asleep on her feet. He had been making seduction plans, but in all of them he had counted on her being awake. Frustration rose in him as he realized he was going to have to wait.

Doctor that she was, she checked the snugness of the bandage around his waist. "Did it bother you much today?"

"Just a bit sore. That stuff you put on it helped the itching."

"Apple cider," she said, and yawned.

He hesitated, then reached out and began unpinning her hair. "You're almost asleep where you stand, honey. Let's get your clothes off so you can get some sleep."

She was so tired that she actually stood there like a docile child until he began unbuttoning her blouse. Then her eyes widened as she realized what he was doing and she jerked back, her hands flying protectively to pull the edges of cloth together.

"Take them off," he said, his tone and words implacable. "Down to your shift."

Even though she knew it was useless, she still couldn't stop the single, desperate word. "Please."

"No. Come on, now. The sooner you get undressed, the sooner you can go to sleep."

It was even more difficult to give up the protection of her clothing than it had been the first time, because now she realized how truly vulnerable she was. She knew she could resist him; it would be difficult, but she could do it. But how did she resist herself? She thought of fighting, then discarded that idea as useless, for he was a great deal stronger than she and the struggle would only result in torn clothing—hers. She thought of asking him for his word that he wouldn't touch her, but knew that that too would be a useless effort. He would only look at her with that unyielding gaze and refuse.

He took a step toward her, and Annie quickly turned her back. He caught her shoulders and she gasped, "I'll do it."

"Then get it done."

She bent her head and obeyed. He stood right behind her and took each item of clothing from her shaking hands, except for her shoes and stockings. She thought she would burn up, with the heat of the fire in front of her and the heat of his body behind. She stood with her back to him, staring blindly into the fire, while he spread her clothes under the blanket. Then he took her hand and gently guided her to the bed he had made for them.

CHAPTER

7

*R*afe stirred and drowsily snuggled her closer. Her soft bottom nestled against his loins, bringing him fully erect. The discomfort awakened him enough for his eyes to slowly open. An automatic glance at the fire told him that he couldn't have been asleep long, half an hour at the most. He sighed and inhaled the sweet warm scent of her skin. As soon as she had realized he didn't intend to force himself on her, she had relaxed and gone almost immediately to sleep. She lay curled in his arms as limply as a child, with his bigger, stronger body curved to shield and warm her.

Still half asleep, he put his hand under her shift, on her hip, and slowly stroked upward. God, how smooth and soft she was. He slipped his hand around to her belly and pressed backward, and she muttered a little in her sleep as she shifted her buttocks to a more comfortable position against the ridge of his shaft.

His pants were in the way. He unbuttoned them and shoved them down, along with his underwear, and took a deep breath of relief at the exquisite freedom. He rolled his hips against her again, shuddering at the pleasure of her naked flesh touching his. He'd never before wanted any woman this intensely, until it was all he thought about, until the smallest touch from her made his male flesh rise hard and urgent. Sweet Annie. She should have let him die, but she hadn't. There wasn't any meanness in her, just that special, magical heat that she refused to share with him. She was still a little afraid of him; she didn't know how good he could make it for her, and he would, he knew the sensual capability of her body much better than she did. He imagined her inner tightness and warmth, and how her little sheath would clench and shiver around him in climax, and he almost moaned aloud.

He was sweating, and his heart was pounding. His erection throbbed.

"Annie." His voice was low and strained. He moved his hand across her bare belly to grip the curve of her hip. "Turn over, sweetheart."

Her eyes half opened and she murmured sleepily but turned in his arms, urged on by his hand. He reached down and lifted her right thigh over his hip, opening the notch of her legs and bringing her full against him. He pressed his sex boldly against the soft folds thus exposed to him, and sought her mouth with his.

The pleasure was overwhelming. Annie almost drowned beneath it, sleep-dulled reason slipping away from her. He was touching her between her legs, touching her with something thick and hot and smooth, and he was kissing her so deeply she could hardly breathe. The shift slipped downward from her shoulder and his hand closed over her breast, cupping and kneading, his rough thumb rasping across her tender nipple and setting it on fire. Blindly she caught at his shoulders, her fingers digging into the sleek, heavy muscles. He angled his hips inward, and the thick shaft between her legs pressed urgently against her. It was his penis, she thought dimly, her mind drugged with both sleep and pleasure, but surely it was too big. She hadn't expected it to be that big. He pulled her leg higher and suddenly the pressure was more intense and instinctively she tried to draw back. He halted the movement, his hard hand clenching on her bare buttock, and he groaned aloud. "Annie!"

Her soft flesh was yielding to that dominant pressure and her eyes flew open as real pain threatened. She convulsed, fighting and twisting, sobbing with the abrupt and terrifying realization of what was really happening. Rafe tried to catch her thrashing legs and Annie threw herself from the crude bed, landing on her hands and knees beside it. Her shift was hanging off her shoulder, baring one breast, and the hem of it was twisted around her waist. Frantically she tugged at it, trying to cover her hips and breast. Dry sobs shook her as she stared at him. She didn't dare take her eyes off him.

"God *damn* it!" Rafe rolled onto his back with a gutteral curse, his hands clenched as he tried to control both his loins and the almost unbearable need to have her back in his arms. His naked shaft thrust into the air, so painfully swollen he thought he might explode at any second. And there was Annie, on her hands and knees on the rough planks, her hair falling in her face and her entire body shaking with sobs, but her eyes were dry, and she was staring at his loins with unconcealed terror and confusion.

Gingerly he pulled up his pants and with some difficulty got to his feet. Annie whimpered and shifted away from him. Swearing again, the curses almost soundless as he forced them between his clenched teeth, he leaned down and grabbed up both his gun belt and rifle. He could barely stand to glance at her cowering, shaking form. "Put on your clothes," he barked, and slammed violently out of the cabin.

The cold bit into his overheated flesh. He was half naked, without shirt or boots, and steam rose off of his chest. He welcomed the cold, needing ease from the fever that burned him alive, far worse than the fever from his wounds had been.

He leaned against a tree in the darkness, the cold, rough bark scraping his back. Dear God, had he nearly *raped* her? He had awakened already aroused, and she had been soft and nearly naked in his arms, and he hadn't had any other thought in his mind except taking her. She had responded at first, he knew she had; he'd felt her hands clutching him, felt the answering pressure of her hips, but something had frightened her and she had panicked. For one savage moment he hadn't cared that she was frightened, that she had begun fighting him; he had been on the verge of penetration and blind instinct had been driving him. He'd never forced a woman in his life, but he'd come damn close to it with Annie.

He didn't dare go back in there. Not like this, not with lust raging through him like a ruthless fever, demanding release. He couldn't lie beside her and not take her.

He swore long and inventively, the vicious stream of words slicing through the blackness. The cold was like a knife on his bare flesh; he'd freeze to death out here.

He knew what he had to do but he didn't like it. He jerked his pants open and closed his fist around his straining shaft. His eyes closed, and his shoulders ground against the bark of the tree. Curses jerked from between his tightly ground teeth, but finally he found, if not pleasure, at least a definite relief, and a necessary one before he could go back inside.

The cold was rapidly becoming unbearable. He straightened away from the tree and went back to the cabin. His face was unreadable as he closed the door with icy control.

Annie stood rigidly by the fireplace. She was still barefoot, though she had gratefully obeyed his last order and scrambled into her clothing so hastily she had torn one of the tapes on her petticoat. She tried to control her breathing, but it shuddered in and out of her lungs.

She clutched his big knife in her right hand.

Rafe saw it immediately, and something flared in his pale eyes. He moved across the cabin like an attacking panther; Annie cried out and lifted the knife, but she had barely begun to move when he caught her wrist and twisted it, and the heavy weapon clattered across the floor.

He didn't release her wrist and didn't retrieve the knife. He just stared down at her, seeing the panic in her wide dark eyes.

"You're safe," he said harshly. "I'm not a rapist. Do you understand me? I'm not going to hurt you. You're safe."

She didn't answer. He let her go and grabbed up his shirt, pulling it on over his head. He was shivering, and even the relative warmth of the cabin wasn't enough. He added more wood to the fire, making it blaze brightly, then caught her wrist and pulled her down to sit beside him on the floor.

His face was grim. "We're going to talk about it."

She shook her head in a quick negative movement, then glanced away.

"We have to, or neither one of us will be able to sleep tonight."

Her gaze strayed toward the rumpled bed, then darted away. "No."

He didn't know if she was agreeing with his assessment or rejecting the very thought of lying down with him again.

Deliberately he released her and braced himself on his right hand, drawing his left knee up and letting his wrist dangle over it. He could sense her acute attention to every move he made, even though she wasn't looking directly at him, and she let herself relax a little as his casual posture reassured her.

"I had dozed off," he said, keeping his voice low

and even. "When I woke up I was hard, and half asleep. I just reached out and pulled you to me without thinking. Then by the time I woke up, I wasn't thinking about anything except getting inside of you. I was on the edge. Do you understand what I'm saying?" he demanded, putting his finger under her chin and forcing her to look at him. "I was almost ready to climax. I was that hungry for you, sweetheart."

She didn't want to hear his endearments, but the gentleness in that last word almost undid her. The expression in his gray eyes was piercing, turbulent.

"I won't rape you," he continued. "Things wouldn't have gone as far as they did if I'd been good awake. But you were responding to me, damn it. *Look at me!*" His voice cracked like a whip as her eyes shifted uneasily away. She swallowed and returned her gaze to meet his.

"You wanted me too, Annie. It wasn't all on my part."

Honesty was a burdensome thing, she found, a goad that wouldn't let her take refuge behind lies. It would be better if she could keep such knowledge to herself, but he deserved the truth. "Yes," she admitted raggedly. "I wanted you."

An expression of combined bewilderment and frustration crossed his face. "Then what happened? What scared you?"

She bit her lip and looked away, and this time he permitted it. She struggled with how much to tell him and how to phrase it. Her thoughts were shattered by the enormity of what she had just admitted to him, and the power of the weapon it gave him. Had he been a little slower, a little more careful—had he been *awake*—he would likely have accomplished her seduction, and now he had to know that was all that was required for success, for she had confessed her vulnerability.

"What happened?" he prompted.

"It hurt."

His face softened and a little smile curled his mouth. "I'm sorry," he murmured, reaching out to brush her hair back from her face. He smoothed the strand over her shoulder, his touch lingering, caressing. "I know it's your first time, honey. I should have been more careful."

"I think it would have to hurt under any circumstances." She bent her head on her drawn-up knees. "I treated one of the prostitutes in Silver Mesa once. She had been brutalized by one of her customers. I couldn't help remembering."

It occurred to Rafe that an inexperienced woman whose exposure to sex had been limited to the seamier, rougher aspects of it could be excused for being wary of the act. "It wouldn't be like that. I won't lie to you and tell you it won't hurt, because it probably will, but any man who would deliberately tear a woman apart like that is a bastard and should be shot. I'll take it easy with you," he promised. With a shiver she realized that to him the outcome wasn't in any doubt. He had taken note of the weakness she had exposed and doubtless planned to take full advantage of it. If he got her back on that bed. . . . She couldn't allow it to happen.

"Please," she said. "Just take me back to Silver Mesa without doing that. Take me back untouched. I have to live with myself. If you have any mercy at all—"

"I don't," he interrupted. "You won't wake up branded. For a little while we'll be as close as two people can get, and I swear I'll make it good for you. Then I'll get out of your life and you'll go on as before."

"And what if I ever want to get married?" she challenged. "I know it's unlikely, but it isn't impossible. What would I tell my husband?"

Rafe's hand fisted with a deep-burning rage at the thought of some other man having the right to touch her, make love to her. "Tell him you rode horses astride," he said roughly.

She blushed, her face turning fiery red. "I do. But I won't lie to the man I've married. I'd have to tell him that I'd given myself to a killer."

The words hovered between them, as sharp-edged as a razor. Rafe's face went cold, and he got to his feet. "Get in the bed. I'm not going to stay awake all night because you're a coward."

Annie regretted her last sentence, but arousing his anger had been the only defense she could find. Her virginal fear hadn't been any protection at all, against either him or herself; he had known it, and had been slowly wearing her down. Only her shock, combined with the threat of pain, had enabled her to fend off his seduction the first time. When he had returned to the cabin she had been in despair that she would give in to him when next he touched her; he had mistaken the cause and labeled it fear, but she could still feel the throbbing need he had aroused deep inside her, and she knew better.

At her hesitation, he leaned down and grabbed her arm, then hauled her to her feet. Quickly she put up her hands to ward him off. "At least let me keep on my clothes! Please, Rafe. Don't make me take them off."

He wanted to shake her and tell her that a pair of cotton drawers wouldn't protect her from him if he decided to take her. But maybe his unruly loins would behave better if she was encased in cloth, if he couldn't feel her soft skin against him. "Lie down," he snapped.

Gratefully she crawled between the blankets, and curled up on her side away from him.

Rafe lay down and stared at the shadowed ceiling. She thought of him as a killer. A lot of other people did too, and there was a huge price on his head. Hell, yes, he'd killed; he'd long ago lost count of how many men had fallen from lead he'd put into them, way before he'd started running for his life, but that had been war. The men he'd killed since then had all been after him, and when given the choice between the other man's life and his own the other man had always come up a distant second.

He wasn't an upstanding citizen, the type a woman could dream about marrying and settling down with. Since he'd been on the run he had lied, stolen, and killed, and would do so again if necessary. His future looked pretty damn grim, even if he did manage to stay ahead of the law. He had kidnapped Annie and dragged her up here into these mountains, scaring her half to death. Looking at it like that, why would any woman want to bed down with him? Why should it sting so bad that she had hurled the word "killer" in his face?

Because it was Annie. Because he wanted her with every bone, every ounce of blood in his body.

Annie lay awake too, long after the fire had burned down, long after she had finally felt his tense body relax and his breathing deepen with sleep. She stared into the darkness with dry, burning eyes.

She had to get away. She had thought she could resist him, and protect herself, for another few days, but now she knew that even one more day would be too long. The only safeguard around her heart now was the fact that she hadn't fully belonged to him; once he took her, the heated intimacy would erode even that feeble shield. She didn't want to love him. She wanted to pick up the threads of her life where they had fallen, and find everything unchanged.

But if he took away that last tiny protection, nothing would be the same. She would go back to Silver Mesa, and she would spend long days trying to heal the sick and wounded, but inside she would be nothing but raw pain. She would never see him again, never know if he was safe and unharmed, or if the law had finally caught up with him and he had ended his life on a gallows with a noose around his neck. He might lie dead of a bullet wound, unburied and unmourned, while she spent her life waiting to hear from him, eagerly looking at every tired and dirty stranger who rode into town before turning away in disappointment when it wasn't him. It would never be him, and she wouldn't know it.

If she stayed, if she succumbed to the weakness, the fever of desire in her, she might bear his child. She would have to leave Silver Mesa, find some other place where she could practice medicine, and she would have to pretend to be a widow so her child, his child, wouldn't bear the stigma of illegitimacy. Even if Rafe did survive and come looking for her, he wouldn't find her because she would have left town and changed her name.

She had thrown all sorts of excuses at him, all except the real one, that she didn't want to love him. She was afraid to love him. He had been more right than he knew when he had called her a coward.

So she had to leave. She was too terrified to sleep, for if she dared close her eyes she wouldn't awaken until it was too late, and she wouldn't have another chance to get away.

She made herself wait, to minimize the length of time she would have to travel in the cold and darkness. She would try to leave about half an hour before dawn, when Rafe should be sleeping the soundest.

She tried not to let herself think of the dangers, for she didn't know how to get back to Silver Mesa. Had she been less desperate, she would never even have considered leaving on her own. All she knew was that he had headed west out of Silver Mesa, so she would go east. Should she get lost, and she knew she would, all she had to do was keep traveling east and she would eventually get out of the mountains. She would have to travel without a weapon, and would have to leave her big medical bag behind; the thought of it wrung her heart, but she accepted its loss. The instruments and medicines and herbs it carried could be replaced.

She caught herself dozing and forced her eyes to open.

How long had it been? She had lost all sense of time. She panicked, then realized that she would have to leave now or take the risk of staying too long. It might be the middle of the night rather than close to dawn, but she had to take the chance.

With excruciating care she inched away from him, pausing for a long time between each movement. He slept on, undisturbed. It seemed to take an hour, but was probably only about fifteen minutes before she had maneuvered herself off the pine-needle bed and crouched on the floor. The chill went through her bare feet. Dismayed at the delay, she nevertheless took the time to crawl over to the fireplace and feel around in the dark until she found her shoes and stockings. It wouldn't do her any good to lose her toes to frostbite.

She only hoped it would soon be daylight and grow warmer, for she didn't dare get her coat. It was lying close by his head, and his rifle was lying across it. There was no way she could get it without awakening him.

The most difficult part was getting the door open. She eased to her feet and groped for the roughly whittled handle.

Her chest was so tight with anxiety that she could barely breathe. She closed her eyes and prayed as she pulled the door open with agonizing care, cold sweat dripping down her spine as she waited in terror for a scrape, a creak, a noise that would bring him up from the blankets with that big pistol in his hand.

The cold air rushing in was bitter and stung her eyes. Dear God, she hadn't expected it to be this bad.

Finally she had the door open enough that she could

squeeze through, and then she faced the equally difficult task of closing it without disturbing him. A freezing wind blew through the trees, rattling the naked limbs like the bones of a skeleton, but except for that the night was utterly silent.

She almost sobbed aloud with relief when the door finally rested in its frame again. There was a faint lightening of the sky overhead that made her think she had estimated the time right, after all, and dawn was only a few moments away.

Picking her way in the dark so she wouldn't stumble, she made it to the horse shed. She was already shuddering convulsively with the cold by the time she opened the door. Her gelding, roused from a doze, recognized her scent and blew a soft welcome that wakened Rafe's bay stallion. Both animals turned toward her with curious snorts.

It was warmer in the horse shed, almost comfortable with the heat given off by their great bodies. Too late she remembered that her saddle, like Rafe's, was in the cabin, and tears stung her eyes as she leaned her head against the gelding's side. It didn't matter. She tried to tell herself that it truly didn't matter, that she rode well enough to make it bareback. Under normal circumstances she wouldn't have had any trouble, but these circumstances were far from normal. It was cold and dark, and she didn't know where she was going.

At least he'd left the saddle blankets on the animals to help them ward off the cold. Going strictly by feel, and murmuring softly to the gelding to keep it calm, she slipped the bridle and bit in place. He took the bit easily and stood still under her soothing hands. As quietly as possible she led the gelding out of the shed and closed the door behind her. The stallion blew a protest at losing his companion.

She paused in indecision. Should she mount the horse now or lead him until there was enough light to see? She would feel safer on his back, but horses didn't see all that well in the dark and often depended on the rider to know where they were going. She would be totally lost if the gelding stumbled and came up lame, so she decided to lead him.

The cold was almost paralyzing. She leaned closer to the animal's heat as she led him slowly away from the cabin.

A hard arm swept around her waist and lifted her off her feet. Annie screamed; the sound was high and shrill and was abruptly smothered by a big hand covering her mouth. The gelding shied, startled by her scream, and the reins in her hand were suddenly tugged hard. The hand left her mouth to grab at the bridle, pulling the horse down and calming him. "You goddamned little fool," Rafe said in a low, harsh voice.

After returning the horse to the shed, he carried her into the cabin as if she were a sack of flour slung under his arm and roughly deposited her on the blankets. Swearing steadily under his breath, he stirred up the fire and threw wood on. Annie couldn't stop shaking. She huddled on the blankets, her arms wrapped around her torso and her teeth chattering.

Suddenly his control broke. He flung a stick of wood across the cabin and wheeled on her. "What's wrong with you?" he roared. "Would you rather die than have me inside you? It'd be different if you didn't want me, but you do. Tell me you don't want me, by God, and I'll leave you alone. Do you hear me? Tell me you don't want me!"

She couldn't. She flinched from his rage, but she was too numb with despair to manage a lie. All she could do was helplessly shake her head, and shiver.

He stood over her huddled body, his tall frame

blotting out the fire. His broad chest was heaving like a blacksmith's bellows. With a violence born of frustration he pulled off his coat and threw it, too. Annie noticed that he was completely dressed, which meant that he had been aware she had gone from the moment she had crept out the door, otherwise he wouldn't have had time to have dressed. She hadn't had a chance to escape.

"It's the middle of the night and you didn't even take a coat." His voice was harsh with restrained violence. "You'd have been dead within a couple of hours."

She lifted her head. Her eyes were dark pools of despair. "Isn't it nearly dawn?"

"Hell, no, it isn't dawn! It's about two in the morning. It doesn't make any difference what time it is, daylight or dark, you'd have died out there. Can't you tell how much colder it is? It's going to snow, probably by morning. You'd never have made it out of the mountains."

She thought of being alone out there for hours, unable to see, getting colder by the minute. As short a time as she had been outside, she still felt frozen to the bone. She probably wouldn't have lived even until morning.

Rafe squatted down in front of her and she had to fight the urge to draw back. His pale eyes were savage in expression. His voice dropped until it was an almost soundless rasp. "Were you so afraid I'd rape you that you'd rather die?"

Shock rippled down her spine. He had saved her life. She stared at him as if she had never seen him before, her eyes searching out each detail of his face. It was a hard, uncompromising face, the face of a man who had nothing to lose, a man who lacked everything that by her standards was needed to make life worthwhile. He had no home, no friends, nothing good or warm or secure. If she had frozen to death it would have been less trouble for him, more food for him, yet he had come after her, and it wasn't because he had feared she would make it back to Silver Mesa and tell someone—who?—where he was. He had *known* she wouldn't make it. He had brought her back because he didn't want her to die.

In that silent instant she felt her last fragile defense crumble into dust.

Hesitantly she reached out and placed her cold hand on his face. His beard rasped against her sensitive palm. "No," she whispered. "I was afraid that you wouldn't have to."

The expression in his eyes changed, became more intent, as he registered her meaning.

"It was a losing battle against myself," she continued. "I've always thought of myself as a virtuous woman, with standards and ideals, but how can I be virtuous if I feel such shocking things?"

"How could you be a woman," he countered, "if you didn't?"

She looked at him with a tiny smile on her lips. That was the heart of the matter, she supposed. She had devoted her entire life to being a doctor, to the exclusion of everything else, including the normal female roles of wife and mother. Despite the arguments she had used earlier, she doubted she would ever marry, for she would never give up her work and she doubted any man would want a wife who was a doctor. Now she was finding, to her astonishment, that her body had desires of its own, very womanly desires.

She took a deep breath to steady herself. If she took the forbidden step she would have turned a corner in her life, and there would be no going back.

The truth was there had been no going back from the moment she had felt her resistance dissolve. She faced the truth that she was already half in love with him, for good or ill. Perhaps she loved him completely; she was inexperienced in these matters and couldn't say for certain exactly what she was feeling, only that she wanted to be a woman, *his* woman.

"Rafe," she said in a small, scared voice, "would you please make love to me?"

CHAPTER

8

She could see his pupils expand until the black nearly eclipsed the pale crystal irises. His mouth tightened and for a moment she thought he was going to refuse. Then he put his hands on her shoulders and gently forced her to lie down on the tangled blankets. Her heart was pounding so forcefully against her ribs that she found it difficult to breathe. Even though she had given him permission, indeed, had *asked* him to do this, she found that it wasn't easy to relinquish the control over and privacy of her body. Moreover, from the size of his sexual organ as she had seen it earlier, she expected the denouement to be uncomfortable at the least. She didn't think she could gladly embrace pain.

Rafe saw the tension in her white face, but he wasn't capable of doing anything to relieve it. From the moment she had spoken his attention had focused on possessing her. He was painfully hard, his loins heavy and tight. If it hadn't been for the earlier episode outside he thought he would probably climax even before entering her, and even so his sexual control, so customary that he took it for granted, felt almost nonexistent.

He forced himself to concentrate on not ripping her clothes off, and that was all he was capable of doing. Just one thing at a time. If he tried to do more, it would shatter the precarious control he maintained on his body. He focused in turn on each button on her blouse, the waistband of her skirt, the tapes of her petticoat.

By the time he had stripped her down to her drawers and white cotton stockings, his hands were shaking and it was all he could do to keep from groaning out loud. He removed the drawers and did make a low, animal sound. Her narrow body was soft and white, her breasts so pretty and round he almost couldn't stand it, her slim thighs curving upward in sleek columns to a neat little patch of light brown hair. He stood up and threw off his own clothing, his eyes never leaving the apex of her tightly clenched legs.

Even though she had asked him for this he knew she had to be frightened, never having done it before, but he couldn't find either the words or the patience to reassure her. He pried her knees apart and mounted her, using his muscled thighs to force her legs wide open. She gave a thin, startled cry as his shaft butted hard against her tender cleft.

Rafe felt her trembling beneath him. It cost him pain, effort, and sweat to refrain from shoving himself into her, but he held on. He touched her chin, and her fearful dark gaze met his. "It's going to hurt," he said grimly.

"I know." Her voice was a mere thread of sound.

"I won't be able to stop."

She knew that, could feel the straining desperation of his body, see it in his eyes. "I . . . I don't want you to."

He was lost, drowning, as the last shred of control unraveled. The wonderful, heated energy of her was pouring into him all along their naked bodies and he couldn't think, couldn't talk. He thought he heard her say, "Rafe?" but there was a roaring in his ears that was growing louder and almost blocked out everything else, and he wasn't certain she had spoken. He was gripped by the primitive need to possess, to brand her as his with the seal of flesh. He couldn't wait a second longer. He reached between her legs and opened the soft folds, then guided the head of his shaft to the exposed little opening and pushed inward, squeezing himself inside. He was aware of the resistance of her small virginal channel as he stretched it, felt the fragile barrier of her maidenhead as it gave way beneath his onslaught, then he was lodged deep inside her and the ecstasy was as strong and strangely wonderful as he had known it would be, a tingling heat that spread throughout his genitals like wildfire and made him feel as if he would explode, before traveling on to every nerve ending in his body.

He slid his hands under her buttocks and lifted her up as he began thrusting. He clenched his teeth at the difficulty of it, for she was very tight, her flesh resisting him. Oh, damn, damn, it was over too soon, but he couldn't stop it. His lower spine prickled and his testicles tightened almost unbearably, and with a gutteral cry he arched back as his seed erupted into her in an explosive climax that left him hollowed out and empty, sprawled on top of her without the strength to move.

Maybe he immediately drifted into an exhausted doze, or maybe he was dazed, but reality lost its sharp edge. He was acutely aware of Annie, of the female scent, texture, and shape of her soft body beneath him, while everything else around him lost its focus and meaning. Eventually he realized that he was crushing her, that the small, jerky movements of her chest meant she was struggling to breathe, and he managed to ease his weight onto his elbows. Sweat ran into his eyes, stinging them, and he became aware then of the burning wood snapping in the fireplace, of the heat on his naked skin. He became aware, also, of her desperate silence and the stark pain mirrored in her eyes as she stared, unblinking, at the ceiling.

He didn't have to be a mind reader to know that he had hurt her, and that she would resist going through the experience again. Regretfully he eased out of her body with a comforting murmur which she appeared not to hear. Since she had been a virgin, she had no idea of the pleasure the act could give, but thank God he was far more experienced and knew how to both reassure her and give her the delight she deserved.

He washed himself, a pang hitting his heart when he saw her blood on his flesh. Damn, why couldn't he have controlled himself better? He'd never been that aroused before, so frenzied that he couldn't stop. It embarrassed him, and at the same time the excitement of it made his heart thunder in his chest. He was already impatient to take her again, to feel the ecstasy of her heat tingling all through him. He wet the cloth again and went back to go down on one knee beside her.

Annie had flinched when he had withdrawn from her; part of her had simply been grateful that it was over, but part of her wanted to scream and beat him with her fists. She felt battered and too weak to move. The private area between her legs throbbed, and she ached inside. She didn't want him to ever touch her again.

Had the promise of physical pleasure been nothing more than a chimera designed by nature to draw women into the mating process? She felt cheated and ashamed. She didn't think she would ever forget the shock of nakedness, both hers and his, or the way her entire body had jolted when she had felt his shaft pressing inexorably into her. The pain had been acute, jabbing deep within; the sense of invasion had been almost unbearable. Yet she hadn't tried to push him away, because he had said he might do this; some dim sense of honor had made her endure in silence, with her teeth clenched against the pain and her hands gripping the blanket.

She felt his hands on her legs and instinctively closed them together, protecting herself from another invasion.

"I'm just going to clean you up, honey," he said in a soothing tone. "C'mon, darlin', let me take care of you."

She bit her lip, oddly disturbed by some other note she could hear in his voice. The "darlin'" had been more pronouncedly southern than his usual accent, and underlaid with a possessiveness that hadn't been there before.

His strong hands were opening her legs and she tried to bolt upright, flushing with shame at her exposure. She saw the streaks of blood and semen on her thighs and thought she would die of mortification. "I'll do it," she said hoarsely, reaching for the cloth.

He caught her shoulders and forced her down on the blankets. "Lie still. This is one case, Doc, that I know more about than you do."

She closed her eyes, resigned to having to endure yet again. He spread her legs and gently but thoroughly washed between them. "Do you have any slippery-elm ointment?"

Her eyes sprang open as she realized he had opened her medical bag and was rummaging through it. "What?"

"Slippery-elm ointment. We used it during the war," he said.

She had to struggle to keep from slapping his hands away from her precious bag. "In the dark blue jar, in the bottom of the bag, right corner."

He brought out the small jar, opened it, and sniffed. "That's it." He dipped his finger into it and came out with a liberal amount. Before she knew what he was about he slid his hand between her legs and his finger slipped into her sore passageway, eased by the slickness of the ointment. Her body jerked and she grabbed his wrist with both hands, trying to force his hand away from her body. Her face burned with embarrassment.

"Easy," he murmured, ignoring her ineffectual struggles. He put his other arm around her and held her against him while his finger worked deep in her tender body. "Stop fighting, honey; you know this'll make you feel better."

She did, but she didn't want his attention, or his concern. She wanted to nurse her bitter anger. Annie had never felt petty before, but she did now and was loath to relinquish her grudge.

Finally he withdrew his hand and once more eased her down and drew the blanket up over her. She drew a shaky breath at the relief of having her nakedness shielded, and closed her eyes rather than watch him as he moved around the cabin. Why didn't he put on some clothes? she wondered violently, and thought about putting on her own clothing. Only the idea of leaving the protection of the blanket to do it kept her where she was.

She stiffened when he got under the blanket with her but left her protest unspoken. The only alternative to sharing their body heat was for each to take a blanket and roll up in it, which wasn't as efficient. Remembering how cold it had been outside, she knew that the cabin was going to be much colder than usual in the morning and they would need all the heat they could muster. That didn't, however, mean that she liked it.

Rafe put his arm under her head and rolled her into his embrace. She resisted, her hands pushing against him. He nuzzled his lips against her hair. "Would you like to slap me?"

She swallowed hard. "Yes."

"Would you feel better if you did?"

She thought about it, and finally said, "No. I just want you to leave me alone."

The despair in her voice made his heart catch a little, even though he knew the remedy. "It won't hurt like that again, darlin'."

She didn't answer, and with sudden intuition he knew she was thinking that she wouldn't take the chance, that as far as she was concerned her first time had been her last. Very gently, because gentleness was what she needed now, he cupped her chin and turned her face up, and his kiss on her mouth was as light as a breeze.

"I'm sorry," he whispered. "I should have gone a lot slower, but I lost control." He should have had plenty of control, but almost from the first he had known that making love to Annie wouldn't be like having any other woman. She was unique, and so was his response to her. There wasn't any way he could explain it to her without sounding crazy, because he would swear she didn't know about or would understand the strange, heated ecstasy of her touch. When he had entered her, the sensation had been so intense that he had thought his entire body would explode. Just the memory of it now was enough to make his loins tighten with beginning arousal.

"So did I," she replied dully. "I lost control of my common sense."

"Annie, darlin'," he began, then paused, for he couldn't think of any words that would comfort her. She had been both hurt and disappointed; he couldn't demonstrate to her just yet that it wouldn't be painful again, but it was time to take care of that disappointment rather than try to soothe her first.

He kissed her again, keeping the contact warm and gentle. She didn't open her mouth to him, but he hadn't expected her to yet and he wasn't ready to force her response. He kissed her again and again, not just on the lips but on her cheeks, her temples, her eyes, the tender underside of her chin. He whispered how pretty he thought she was, how he loved to take her hair down, how soft and silky her skin was. Despite herself she listened, and he felt some of the tension ease out of her body.

Very gently he slid his hand over her breast, kneading with a slow, hypnotic motion. She tensed again, but he kept up the tender, distracting kisses and lover's whispers until she softened against him once more. Only then did he rasp his callused thumb over and around her exquisitely sensitive little nipple, feeling it instantly tighten and thrust upward. She shivered, then went very still in his arms. Was it fear, he wondered, or was she feeling the first lash of arousal? He fondled the satiny mound, then slid his hand to her other breast and caressed it to the same ripe turgidity. Annie was still holding herself almost motionless, but he was so attuned to her that he heard her breathing change to swift, shallow little gasps.

Now he set his mouth on hers with sensual determination, and after a moment's hesitation she yielded, her lips softly parting and allowing him entry. He took it with discretion; rather than simply thrusting his tongue inside her mouth he used light caressing strokes that gradually penetrated until he was taking her mouth with the deep, arousing kisses that both of them needed. His own breathing grew ragged but he firmly clamped down on his response. No matter what it cost him, this time was purely hers. He was abruptly terrified that if he wasn't able to show her the pleasure she might turn away from him forever, and he didn't think he could bear it.

The changes in her body were small but delicious. He felt the increased pliancy of her flesh, the way her skin grew warmer and more moist. Her heart was beating a light tattoo that throbbed against his palm as he continued to stroke her breasts. Her nipples felt like ripe berries rolling between his fingers, and suddenly he was overwhelmed by the need to taste her, to draw her nipple deep into his mouth. He had taken her, but he hadn't made love to her, and he wanted all of the intimacies there could be between a man and his woman. And she *was* his, he thought fiercely. Every soft inch of her.

Her arms curled around his shoulders, and her fingers stroked his neck before sliding into his hair. Heat flowed through him and his shaft hardened into a full erection. If her hesitant response had that kind of effect on him, he wondered if he'd be able to survive if she were fully aroused. He couldn't think of a better way to die.

He arched her back across his arm and trailed his kisses down her throat. He paused to feel the wild flutter of her pulse in the small hollow at the base, pressing his tongue against the translucent skin. From there his mouth followed the fragile arch of her collarbone, which led him to the sensitive joining of shoulder and neck. He heard the low, vibrant murmur she made and a thrill ran over his skin, roughening it.

He couldn't deny the temptation any longer. He tossed the blanket back and bent his head to her breast, circling her nipple with his tongue, making it tightly bud, before drawing it into his mouth with a strong, uncomplicated suckling. The taste of her was intoxicating, as hot and sweet as wild honey, and she was crying out, sharp, breathless sounds of pleasure. Her slender body twisted against him, and he slid his hand between her legs.

Annie cried out again, a sound of helpless desire. A small voice of reason wailed in despair, but the inner protest was useless against the whirlpool of desire he had set spinning inside her, drawing her further and further into the dark vortex. She felt on fire, her entire body flushed, her breasts aching from his gentle torture. It *was* torture, she was sure of it, for why else would he be driving her, under the fierce lash of increasing pleasure, to the point of madness where she begged him to take her again in an act that had given her only pain and remorse? The worst of it was that she had no defense, no weapons with which to fight him. He had lulled her with gentle kisses, tamed her to accept his touch on her breast, and then used the pleasures of her own body against her. She had dimly realized it when he had begun kissing her with those deep, drugging, violently possessive kisses, but already it had been too late for her. When his mouth had closed on her breast in that shocking way she hadn't been able to resist, had even reveled in the heated intimacy of it.

He was touching her private flesh now in a way he hadn't done before, slowly circling his rough fingertip around the small nub at the top of her sex, and she would have screamed if she'd had enough breath. Wildfire leaped through her as her entire being seemed to focus in that single spot. She could feel her legs stretching indecently wide, feel the tiny nubbin throb and strain as if begging for each touch. It was agony, and his finger circled maddeningly, both easing the tension and making it worse. Then he pressed his thumb down on her, almost roughly, while with a butterfly touch of his middle finger he rimmed the soft, sore entrance to her body. She flinched, but felt her hips begin to slowly rock, and she couldn't stop the motion or the wild sounds coming from her throat. It was too much, with his mouth on her breast and his hand between her legs and a river of heated sensation flooding through her.

Then his mouth left her breast and slid slowly, maddeningly down her belly. His hand shifted to her thigh and opened her legs even more, and before she even had an inkling about his intentions his mouth was hot on her exposed female flesh. She went rigid from an unbearable surge of pleasure, her mind emptied of thought or reason, or even shock. He put his hand under her buttocks and lifted her up to give himself better access, and his tongue swirled and licked and stabbed her with fire.

She heard herself sobbing. She felt his warm hair brush against her thighs in a silky caress. She felt the rough texture of the blanket beneath her, the heat from the fireplace dancing on her bare skin. She still tasted his lips. She existed only through her senses, a purely physical being, and he controlled her.

She was dying. She felt her consciousness fading until the only awareness left to her was of his ravaging mouth, lips and teeth and tongue killing her with such sweet torment. Her entire body clenched unbearably, the tension coiling tighter and tighter, the heat engulfing her. She couldn't breathe, and her heart was pounding so fast it was sure to explode. A high, thin cry pierced the silence, a cry for mercy, but he had none. Deliberately he pushed one of his big fingers into her, and the nerve endings in her painfully sensitive opening rioted at the sensation of being invaded. The hot coil of tension pulled even tighter and abruptly snapped. She heard herself screaming, but those hoarse cries didn't sound like her voice. Great waves of sensation flooded through her, wiping out everything in their path and totally consuming her. He held her surging body down and his mouth pressed hard to her, and gradually the tidal waves subsided into gently swirling eddies that caught her unawares with an occasional throb of pleasure.

She was too limp, too exhausted to move. Her eyelashes lay heavily on her cheeks, and she couldn't lift them. Her heartbeat slowed and her thought processes resumed, but they were oddly chaotic.

She didn't know what to think. What he had just done to her, given to her, had been outside her realm of imagination. She had known the basic facts of sex, of penetration and his release of semen, but she hadn't realized any of . . . *this* existed, or was even possible. The things he had done, the way she had felt. . . . Had that been the way he had felt, when he had been thrusting inside her and had suddenly stiffened and given that deep, gutteral cry? He had lain atop her afterward as if he had been utterly exhausted, as if he had no energy to move.

He lay down beside her and took her in his arms,

then pulled the blanket over them. Her head was nestled on his shoulder, their naked bodies pressed intimately together. His muscled thigh pushed between hers and she sighed as the movement forced her quivering muscles to relax from their vain effort to hold herself from him.

His mouth brushed her temple, and his big hand stroked her back and buttocks. "Go to sleep, darlin'," he murmured, and she did.

CHAPTER

9

He rolled out of the blankets and Annie lifted her heavy eyelids, desperately needing a few more hours of sleep for, after all, she had been awake most of the night. "Is it morning?" she asked, hoping that it wasn't. Without his warmth beside her, the cold crept through the blanket and made her shiver.

"Yeah."

She wondered how he could tell, when it was as dark as night inside the cabin with the door closed and the window coverings down. She could barely make out the outline of his form in the dull glow of the coals in the fireplace. For a moment she wondered why the coals hadn't been banked, then memory crashed through her and she not only remembered why the fire had been rebuilt during the night, she remembered why she hadn't been able to get much sleep. Rafe's tall body was totally naked, as was hers. She huddled under the blanket, feeling the stiffness in her thighs and the tenderness between her legs. She remembered everything he had done to her, and the blinding upheaval of her senses, and she wished she could remain hidden beneath the blanket for the rest of her life. How could she possibly carry on as normal, when every time she looked at him she would remember the shattering intimacy of the night? He had seen her naked and exposed his own body to her; he had penetrated her, suckled at her breast and—dear God —he had put his mouth on her in the most shocking way possible. She didn't think she could face him at all.

He added wood to the fire, and as the flames leaped up she was able to see him more clearly. She hurriedly closed her eyes, but not before the image of his naked, muscular frame was imprinted on her consciousness.

"C'mon, honey, get up."

"In a minute. It's too cold right now."

She heard the rustle of his clothing as he dressed, then silence for a moment. Her skin prickled with unease, and she quickly opened her eyes.

She didn't know what she had expected to see, but it certainly wasn't Rafe holding her shift close to the fire, warming it. He turned both sides to the growing flames, chasing the chill from the fabric, then crushed it in his hands to hold the heat as he thrust it under the blanket. The toasty warm cloth felt heavenly against her skin. She stared at him, a little stunned, a little breathless, as he picked up her drawers to perform the courtesy again.

She struggled into her shift with the blanket still shielding her, but her mind was no longer on the embarrassment of facing him, or even being nude in front of him. He slid the warm drawers under the blanket and immediately turned to her blouse, his expression absorbed as he held it out to the flames. Her heart surged painfully, and she almost burst into tears as she pulled on her undergarment. She had known terror at his hands, but he had also shown a rough sort of concern for her well-being. He had possessed her, hurt her, then cared for her afterward and taken her into the dark whirlpool of passion Despite everything she had been half in love with him but no longer. The unselfconscious care he took in warming her clothes for her took her unawares, and forever changed something fundamental in her. She felt the inner shifting and settling, and stared at him with dazed, stricken eyes, fully recognizing the moment for what it was. She loved him, irrevocably, and in doing so had undergone a sea change that had in a few seconds completely altered her life.

"Here you go." He brought the warmed blouse to her and she sat up, slipping her arms into the sleeves as he held it for her. He rubbed her arms and shoulders, then brushed her tangled hair out of her face. "I'm going to get a bucket of fresh water while you finish dressing."

He put on his coat and picked up the bucket. A frigid blast of air rushed in when he opened the door and Annie hugged the blanket around her, shivering. She couldn't believe how cold it was. If Rafe hadn't caught her last night, she would already be dead. The thought of it made her shiver even more.

She donned the rest of her clothes and was painstakingly working the tangles out of her hair when Rafe reentered with another freezing rush of air. "Is it snowing?" she asked. She hadn't looked out either time he had opened the door, preferring to hide her face from the cold.

"Not yet, but it's as cold as a witch's tit." He squatted down and began making a pot of coffee.

She wondered how he could be so matter of fact after the night they had just spent, then a pang hit her as she realized he had made love to other women and none of that was new to him. She made herself face the fact that making love with her didn't necessarily mean he returned her feelings.

Suddenly he turned and hauled her into his arms, opening his coat and wrapping her inside the warmth with him. "Don't ever try to run from me again," he said fiercely, his raspy voice low.

She put her arms around his waist, taking care not

to put pressure on his wounds. "No," she said in agreement, the words muffled against his chest.

He brushed his mouth over her hair. The thought that she might have been caught out in that bitter cold, without even a coat, made him want to simultaneously spank her and crush her against him. God, he'd come so close to losing her.

Her hands were gently wandering over his back, leaving a trail of glowing heat behind. His manhood stirred, and with faint disbelief he wondered if her effect on him would ever lessen or if her touch would always induce an immediate sexual reaction.

He cuddled her closer. "Are you all right?"

She knew what he was asking and her face heated. "I'm fine," she said gruffly.

He tilted her head back, his pale gray eyes sternly searching the dark liquid depths of hers. "You're not sore?"

Her blush deepened. "A little. Not as much as I'd expected." Of course, his treatment with the slippery-elm salve had done a lot to lessen her discomfort. The memory of how he had administered it to her made her squirm.

His thoughts were running with hers. "I should have seen to you before you got dressed." His voice deepened. "Do you need more salve?"

"No!"

"I think you do. Let me see."

"Rafe!" she wailed, her face so hot she thought it would catch fire.

A slow smile curved his mouth and wrinkled his eyes at her reaction to his teasing. "I'm going to look at you a lot, honey. If I hadn't been worried that you'd be too sore, I'd have been on top of you before you were good awake this morning."

Her heart thumped in her chest and she stared up at him with wide eyes. Did she want him to do it again? Those things he had done to her afterward had been so marvelous she didn't know if she could survive another onslaught, but she was wary of the actual sex act. What if the next time was just as painful?

He frowned at her expression. "You did know," he said deliberately, "that last night wouldn't be the only time." His tone of voice made it a statement rather than a question.

She bit her lip. "Yes, I knew." The hard fact was that, if he wanted her, she would oblige and trust that it would grow easier. There was no going back, no returning to virginity, and despite everything she didn't want to. She was still dealing with the shock of realizing that she loved him, but she *did* love him and that meant giving herself to him.

He bent his head and kissed her, and his big hand covered her breast with unhesitating possessiveness. "I'm going to see to the horses and check the traps while you cook breakfast." He kissed her again and released her, setting his hat on his head as he turned toward the door.

"Wait!" Annie stared at him. Despite the way he had worked the day before, and the way he had made love to her, he had been very ill only a couple of days earlier. She didn't know that she wanted him to check the traps by himself.

He paused, giving her a questioning look.

She suddenly felt foolish, though she didn't know why. "Don't you want a cup of coffee first?"

He glanced at the fireplace. "It isn't ready."

"It will be soon. You need something hot inside you before you go out again. Wait until after breakfast and I'll go with you."

"Your coat isn't heavy enough for staying out in this kind of weather for that long."

"Wait until after breakfast anyway."

"Why? I can have it all taken care of by the time you've finished cooking."

She said in a rush, "Because I don't want you to check the traps by yourself."

He looked startled. "Why not?"

She put her hands on her hips, suddenly irritated with him beyond all reason. "Three days ago you were burning up with fever and could barely walk, that's why! I don't think you've recovered enough to tramp all over the mountains. What if you fall, or become too weak to get back?"

He grinned and grabbed her, kissing her hard. "That was three days ago," he said. "I'm fine now. You healed me."

He released her and left the cabin before she could stop him again. Probably she didn't know how true his statement was. Oh, her skill at doctoring had helped, what with her poultices and herb teas, the stitches and bandages and fussing concern, but she had healed him with the heat of her touch. He had felt the force of it moving through his body that first night. He didn't understand it, didn't know how to ask her about it, but he had no doubt that she could have healed him even without her store of knowledge.

He watered and fed the horses, then with a weather eye on the low, gray clouds he began checking the various snares he had arranged. A rabbit was in the third one, and he felt a surge of relief. A nice pot of rabbit stew would stretch out their meager food supplies. He still felt that snow was coming; it might be only a couple of inches, but it could be a couple of feet, keeping them inside at least while the snow was falling, and that could last several days. He thought of being stranded in the cabin with Annie and found himself smiling like an idiot. If their food situation was okay, he wouldn't mind that at all.

He knocked the rabbit in the head and reset the snare, then hurriedly checked the remainder of the traps, but the rabbit was the only yield. He chose a spot well away from the cabin to skin and dress the animal, then carried the carcass to the creek to wash it and remove the blood from his hands. Figuring breakfast should be just about ready, he gladly returned to the warmth of the cabin.

Annie whirled anxiously when he opened the door, but her expression relaxed when she saw that he was okay. Her gaze moved to the carcass in his hand. "Oh, good, you got a . . . whatever it is."

"Rabbit."

He shed his jacket and hat and gratefully took the cup of hot coffee she poured for him, sipping it while she cooked and dished up their simple breakfast. They sat down on the floor to eat and he put his hand on the nape of her neck, holding her for a hard, hungry kiss. When he released her she was pink and a little flustered. He wondered wryly how he had held off for as long as he had, because he sure as hell couldn't keep his hands off her now.

They ate, and then Rafe helped her clean their few dishes. When he started out for more water he paused with the door open, despite the frigid air, and said, "Come look at the snow."

Hugging her arms against the cold, she went to stand beside him. Huge white flakes were swirling noiselessly downward. The forest was as silent as a cathedral. In the short time it had taken them to eat, the ground had become covered with white and still the snow drifted down in a ghostly dance. He put his arm around her and she let her head rest on his chest.

"You knew all day yesterday that it was going to snow," she said. "That's why you insisted on gathering so much wood and making the horses more comfortable."

She felt his steely muscles tense. "Yes."

"You're recovered enough, and had enough time. You could have taken me back to Silver Mesa."

Again he said, "Yes."

"Why didn't you?"

He was silent for a while, and they both watched the snow. Finally he spoke. "I couldn't let you go just yet." Then he took the bucket and walked through the snow to the creek.

Annie quickly shut the door and stood close to the fire, rubbing warmth back into her arms. *I couldn't let you go just yet.* She felt both sad and exhilarated, for by his words he still planned to return her to her home and ride away, just as she had feared would happen. And yet . . . no one else had ever thought she was special, except for her father, and he had naturally been prejudiced. When she had looked in the mirror she had seen a rather thin woman, past the first blush of youth, with tired but pleasant features. Her coloring was unremarkable, though sometimes she had been startled to see that her eyes could appear almost black, and dominate her face. She had certainly never before stirred anyone to passion.

But Rafe had looked at her with passion right from the beginning. She had felt it herself, though she had been too ignorant of the subject to recognize it for what it was. Rafe had known, though, and that was what had given his crystalline eyes such a dangerous glitter. He had wanted her then and he wanted her now with the same savage hunger, though he was restraining himself out of consideration for her.

By the time he returned from the creek she had busied herself cutting up the rabbit for stew. As a precaution he strung the rope from the cabin to the horse shed so he would be able to take care of the animals should the wind pick up and turn the silent snow into a blizzard. Then he brought in more wood. Since the cold prevented them from opening the window coverings it was dark in the cabin; the fire was the only illumination. Because of that, and because the bitter weather made the cabin colder than usual, he disregarded his normal caution and kept the fire high. No one was likely to brave the weather to investigate a curl of smoke even should one be visible in the white curtain of snow, which wasn't likely.

Annie added potatoes and onions to the stew, then opened her black bag and threw in pinches of various herbs. She had always found it convenient that so many of the cooking herbs, such as sage, rosemary, and tarragon, also had healing properties.

Rafe was carefully cleaning his weapons and checking his ammunition by the light of the fire, but nothing truly escaped his attention. He gave her proof of that when he asked, "How did you learn so much about plants? I doubt they taught it to you in medical school."

"Well, no. A lot of it is general knowledge, of course, and has been used for centuries in Europe. But some of the European plants can't be found here, so I had to find out which American plants were also useful. Old country people are the best ones to talk to, for they've had to do their own doctoring and they know what works and what doesn't."

"What got you so interested in it?"

She smiled. "I'm interested in anything that helps people get well," she said simply.

"Where do you get them?"

"Fields, flower gardens." She shrugged. "Some I grow myself, like mint and rosemary and thyme. Plantains are really just common weeds, but I can't get them out here. What I have left is what I brought with me from home. Aloe seems to work almost like plantains, but you need a fresh plant. I have several back in Silver Mesa."

She put the stew on to simmer and then looked fretfully around the dark cabin. "I don't know how long I'll be able to stand staying in the dark all day long. Now I know why people pay a fortune to have glass shipped out here."

"I have some candles," he reminded her.

She sighed. "But what if it snows for days? I doubt you have *that* many candles."

"No, just a few."

"Then we'd better save them."

He thought of all the various means of providing light he'd seen over the years. Oil lamps were best, of course, but they didn't have one. There were also pine-tar torches, but they smoked like a son of a bitch. The dimness didn't bother him, as it wasn't complete, but he'd learned both patience and endurance and his nerves were like iron. Annie, however, had probably never spent a day without sunlight, and it would understandably wear on her nerves.

Carefully, he put his weapons aside. "Maybe," he said, watching her with acute attention, "you need to find something about the dark to appreciate."

A quick reply sprang to her lips but died unsaid as she saw his pale eyes glittering in the firelight. She swallowed and her eyes widened, then she was in his arms and he was laying her down on their pine needle bed.

She trembled and eyed him uncertainly. Rafe kissed her, leaning over her with her head cradled on his arm. "It won't hurt, darlin'," he said in that deep, slow, southern tone she recognized as his lovemaking voice. "You'll see."

In the end, all she could do was trust him and give him the response he insisted on. She was helpless to do otherwise. The night before he had shown her the pleasure her body was capable of knowing, and the need to find it again sprang up strong and hot under his kisses. He wooed her again with light touches of his mouth that gradually deepened, with firm caresses through her clothing that soon made her impatient with the barriers between his skin and hers. He didn't strip her all at once, but would remove one garment and then return to his patient kisses and stroking. It seemed forever before he finally slid his hand inside her shift and cupped her bare breast, and she gave a quick, sharp sigh of relief.

His hard mouth curved into a smile, but it was one of purely male satisfaction rather than amusement. "You like that, don't you?"

She moved her legs restlessly, and her head turned toward him. "Yes."

He tugged the strap down off her shoulder and the shift drooped, baring her. Hc thought he'd never seen more delectable breasts, firm and round and proudly upright. They weren't big, but they filled his hand nicely. Her nipples looked like dark pink berries, flushed and extended from his touch. He bent his head and leisurely suckled her, determinedly ignoring his thrusting erection in order to seduce her with her own pleasure.

Her hands plucked at his shirt in frustration and he paused long enough to hook it off over his head.

The heat and power of his naked chest pressed down on her, and her breasts tightened at the contact. Fire was burning through her, the same fire he had ignited before, and she moved urgently against him in search of relief. Some time later she became aware that his hands were under her skirt, releasing the tapes of her undergarment, and she lifted her hips to aid him in removing it. Her thighs opened eagerly to his touch.

It was light at first, no more than a gentle rubbing, but soon his fingers sought out and concentrated on the most sensitive spot. That awful, wonderful tension began building in her, and she whimpered.

Then his fingers slid into her and she cried out, her hips lifting from the bed. She felt the wetness between her legs and didn't care. Rafe forced her head back with a kiss so hard and deep it bruised her lips, and she didn't care about that either. She clutched his bare, damp shoulders and moved against him.

Stifling a curse of agonized arousal, Rafe unbuttoned his pants and pushed them down. He spread her legs wider and slid his hips into the cradle, gritting his teeth against the surge of heat through his loins as he touched her. Annie went still, fear edging into her desire. He positioned the thick head of his shaft against her and then held her head framed between his hands, their gazes locked as he slowly, inexorably pushed into her.

Her pupils expanded until her eyes were enormous black pools, and she sucked in a deep breath. Dimly she realized that it wasn't painful as it had been before, but the sense of invasion, of being stretched, was almost unbearable. Her flesh was still tender and a little raw, and the nerve endings screamed a protest as his thick length forced her open. Her loins clenched around him in a futile effort to halt the alien intrusion and he groaned aloud, sagging weakly against her.

And still he pushed, sheathing himself to the hilt. She felt him deep inside, touching the entrance to her womb, and wild pleasure exploded through her.

He began thrusting, slowly at first, then with increasing speed and power. Her inner muscles clung to him, slick and hot.

She couldn't bear it. It was too much, too frightening. She tried to slide backward away from him, but he hooked his hands under her shoulders and held her.

"Don't fight it," he crooned, his breath hot against her temple. "It's too good to fight. Is it hurting?"

She would have sobbed if she had had the breath. All she could do was say, "No," on a hard gasp.

His hips recoiled and advanced, thrusting him deep within her. Her own hips were rocking back and forth and she couldn't control them. Desperately she began fighting, and Rafe caught her arms. "It's all right," he soothed. "You're almost there." He moved higher on her, so that with each thrust and withdrawal the base of his shaft rubbed against her. "Lift up against me, honey," he commanded with a deep groan.

She didn't. She couldn't. She felt as if she were fighting for her life as she desperately tried to shrink from him, pressing her hips down hard against the blanket. The force he was arousing in her was so strong she didn't dare let it explode. She heard herself sobbing now, harsh sounds that burned in her throat.

His hair was dripping wet with sweat, and his face was stark with the effort his control was costing him. He slid his hands under her buttocks, pushing his fingers into the soft cleft to grip her hard. She screamed in shock and her hips jerked upward, away from the startling touch. Sensation jolted through her and she felt her sanity sliding away as the dark whirlpool grabbed her again, flinging her up and then pulling her down, drowning her. He was still gripping her buttocks, working her up and down in rhythm with his thrusts, then his hoarse groans mingled with her cries as his big body convulsed against her.

Afterward he held her head and kissed her as if he couldn't get enough of her, kisses as deep and hard as if their passion hadn't just been expended. Tears seeped from beneath her lashes, but they weren't tears of pain. She didn't know why she was crying. Exhaustion, perhaps, or maybe it was a natural reaction to having survived a cataclysmic upheaval of her senses that had shaken her to her marrow. Why hadn't she died? Why hadn't her heart exploded from the strain, why hadn't the heat boiled her blood in her veins? She felt as if all of that had happened, as if she should be no more than ashes in his arms. So it hadn't been a chimera after all, but a force that welded them together with chains she would never be able to break.

He wiped the tears away with his thumbs. "Look at me, darlin'," he urged. "Open your eyes."

She did, staring at him through a shimmering veil of moisture.

"Did I hurt you again? Is that why you're crying?"

"No," she managed to whisper. "You didn't hurt me. It's just . . . too much. I don't know how I lived through it."

He rested his forehead on hers. "I know," he murmured. What happened every time he touched her was outside his experience too, and out of his control.

CHAPTER

10

They spent most of the day lying entwined on their rough bed. They both slept, feeling the effects of the long night just passed and the exhaustion of their lovemaking. Annie got up once to sleepily check the stew and add more water, and to replenish the fire. By the time she returned to the blankets, Rafe was awake and aroused by her seminudity. The remainder of their clothes were shed, and he made love to her with a slow, lingering power that was no less shattering than before. It was afternoon when they woke again, and the chill of the air made them shiver.

"I need to check on the horses," he said regretfully, and put on his clothes. He'd have liked nothing better than to spend a few more days lying naked with her. He only wished they had a proper bed, with thick covers to keep them warm. Funny, he'd never before missed the creature comforts.

Annie dressed too. She felt boneless, and incredibly languid. She had forgotten about the snow until he opened the door and a landscape of white greeted them along with a rush of frigid air. A pale, unearthly light filled the cabin. It was still snowing, and during the hours they had spent making love over half a foot had accumulated, covering the forest floor and draping the trees in an icy white mantle.

It was only a few minutes before he returned, stamping snow from his boots and brushing it off his hat and coat. Annie handed him a cup of the coffee left over from breakfast, strong and bitter by now, but he drank it without even a grimace.

"How are the horses?"

"Restless, but they'll be fine."

She stirred the stew; it was ready to eat, the rabbit tender after simmering all day, but she wasn't hungry. She desperately needed some fresh air to clear her head, but as Rafe had pointed out, her coat wasn't heavy enough for this type of weather. After a few moments she decided it didn't matter.

Rafe watched her put on her coat. "Where're you going?"

"I'm going to step out for a few minutes. I need some fresh air."

He began pulling his own coat back on.

She gave him a surprised look. "You don't have to go with me. I'm just going to stand outside the door. Stay in and get warm."

"I'm warm enough." He leaned down, picked up one of the blankets, and wrapped it around her Indian style, pulling one of the folds up to protect her head. Then he stepped out into the eerie white world with her and held her firmly in his arms.

It was so cold that it hurt to breathe, but the icy air cleared her head. She nestled securely against Rafe's big body and in silence watched the snow fall. It was almost twilight, and the weak winter sunlight that had penetrated the thick layer of clouds had waned. The ghostly illumination came more from the snow than from the sun. The tree trunks were stark black sentinels. She had never known it to be so quiet; there were no insects buzzing, no birds calling, not even the rustle of bare tree limbs. They were so isolated that they might as well have been the only two living creatures on earth, for the blanket of snow so muffled sound that she couldn't even hear the horses.

The cold cut through her skirt and petticoat and seeped up through the soles of her shoes, but still she clung to him and endlessly drank in the cruel, beautiful splendor surrounding them. Somehow it gave her a base of reality, as if the dark, heated intimacy of the cabin were a dream that existed only in her emotions. Too much had happened in too little time, turning her life upside down. How long had it been? It felt like a lifetime, but it had only been four—or was it five?—days since she had delivered Eda's baby and trudged wearily back to her cabin to find a wounded stranger waiting for her.

She shivered and Rafe said, "That's enough. Come on back inside now, it's getting dark anyway."

The comparative warmth of the cabin enfolded them, though it took a moment for her eyes to adjust to the gloom. She felt more awake now, the cobwebs gone from her brain. She made fresh coffee, and when it was ready they ate the stew, delighting in the change of menu.

The trouble with being cooped up, she decided, was that there was nothing to do. The first few days she had worn herself out working and had been ready to go to sleep not long after sundown. But having spent most of the day in bed, now she wasn't tired. Had she been at home she would have worked with her herbs, drying some, mixing others. Or she could have read, or written to her old friends in Philadelphia. Here, there were no books and no light to read them by even if there had been. She had no sewing, no cleaning to do. Considering all he had done the past two days, she couldn't pretend that Rafe needed her medical help any longer. It felt very odd, having nothing to do, and she said as much out loud.

Rafe understood how quickly cabin fever could

affect some people, and though his inclination was to take her to bed he accepted that even with liberal applications of the slippery-elm salve she would be too sore for the long hours of repeated lovemaking that he wanted. "I've got a pack of cards in my saddlebags," he suggested instead. "Do you know how to play poker?"

"No, of course not," she said automatically, but he saw the quick flare of interest in her brown eyes. "You'd really show me how?"

"Why not?"

"Well, some men wouldn't."

"I'm not some men." He tried to remember if there had been a time when he would have been shocked by a poker-playing lady, but those days wouldn't come to mind. Their ashes were far too cold.

His deck of cards was dog-eared and stained; Annie eyed them as if they were the symbol of everything dangerous and forbidden. He positioned their saddles in front of the fire to give them something to lean against, which would be more comfortable than sitting tailor fashion, and explained the suits and hands to her. She caught on quickly, though she didn't have enough experience to be able to figure the odds on filling a hand. He moved on to blackjack, which was better suited to being played with just two people, and the game interested her enough that they played for a couple of hours.

Finally the game palled, and Rafe suggested going to bed. He was amused to see the quick look of alarm she gave him. "It's all right," he said. "I know you're sore; we'll wait until tomorrow."

She blushed, and he wondered how she still could.

He gave her his shirt to wear to bed, not because he didn't want her naked—he did—but because it would keep her arms and shoulders warm and would be more comfortable than her high-necked blouse. She slid under the blanket and into his arms with a shy sweetness that made him sigh with regret.

Neither of them was really sleepy, but he was content—almost—to just lie there with her. Idly he picked up her hand and carried her fingers to his lips. The heat made his mouth tingle.

She nestled her head more securely on his shoulder. She would have loved to live only in the moment, but unfortunately that wasn't possible. Though she loved him, there was no way to forget that they had no future together, that perhaps he had no future at all. Her heart squeezed painfully at the thought of a bullet extinguishing the hot vitality in his powerful body, of him lying cold and still and forever gone from her.

"This man they think you killed," she said hesitantly, knowing he wouldn't like her bringing up the subject. "Do you know who did it?"

He was still for a fraction of a second, then he touched her fingers to his lips again. "Yeah."

"Isn't there any way you can prove it?"

He'd tried, back when he had been so angry that he'd wanted to make them all pay, and nearly lost his life, only to realize that all of the proof pointed to him. He knew who had killed Tench, or at least who had arranged it, but there was no way in hell to prove that his finger hadn't pulled the trigger. He didn't tell her that, though, just said, "No," in a soft tone and held her hand to his face.

"I can't accept that," she said in a low, fierce voice. "There has to be a way. What happened? Tell me about it."

"No," he said again. "The less you know the safer you'll be. They're not after me because of what I did, honey. They're after me because of what I know, and they'll kill anyone they think I've told." That was one reason he'd finally given up trying to exonerate himself; after two people who had tried to help him had turned up dead, Rafe had stopped trying. The only people who were likely to believe him were his friends, and he couldn't get his friends killed. Besides, what the hell did it matter anyway? He'd had his illusions destroyed, but other people had a right to theirs. Sometimes it was the only comfort they had.

"But what can be that dangerous?" she argued, lifting her head from his shoulder.

"This. I won't risk your life by telling you."

"Then you should have thought of that before dragging me up here. If anyone finds out, won't it be assumed that you talked to me?"

"No one in town saw me at your place," he assured her.

She tried another tack. "Someone is hunting you, aren't they? Right now, I mean."

"A bounty hunter named Trahern. A lot of other people too, but Trahern's the one I'm most concerned about right now."

"Will he be able to track you to Silver Mesa?"

"I figure he's already done that, but I had my horse reshod there and there's no way he could have picked up the trail."

"Does he know you were wounded?"

"I reckon. He's the one who put lead in me."

"Then won't he think to check if there's a doctor in town?"

"He might, because I got lead in him, too. But as far as he knows I wasn't hurt that bad, and it had been ten days since he'd shot me, after all, so he probably figured I was okay." He moved her hand back to his lips. "And from what you said, you rode out a lot to see sick folks, so no one would think it was unusual that you were gone."

That was certainly true enough. She had even thought the same thing herself. She smiled as she saw a flaw in his logic. "If no one will know I've been with you, then how can it be dangerous for me if you tell me anything? I'm certainly not going to run around Silver Mesa blabbing about it."

"Just in case," he said gently. "I won't take the chance."

She sighed in frustration, but sensed how implaca-

ble he was. That seemed to be one of his main
characteristics: when he made up his mind, he didn't
relent. He made a mule seem reasonable.

"What did you do before the war?"

The question startled him, because he had to think
about it for a moment. "Studied law."

"What?" Of all the things he could have said,
nothing would have surprised her more. He seemed so
naturally dangerous, everything about him perfectly
bred to be the predator he was, that she couldn't
imagine him dressed in a suit and pontificating before
a judge and jury.

"I didn't say I was any good at it. My father was a
judge and for a while it seemed like the thing to do."
Mosby had been a lawyer, and the two of them had
whiled away many an hour arguing obscure points of
law. At the same time, Rafe knew he'd never have
been interested enough in the law to have been a
success at it. He had simply absorbed a lot of it by
being his father's son. Absently he carried Annie's
hand down to his chest and brushed her fingers over
his nipple. That sharp, sweet tingle made it tighten
immediately.

With interest Annie felt his hard, flat nipple pucker
just the way hers did, and she wondered if he enjoyed
the sensation. He moved her hand to his other nipple
and it reacted the same as the other. He brushed her
fingers back and forth over his chest in a slow, absent
motion.

She sighed. "I can't imagine you as a lawyer."

"I can't either. When the war started, I found out I
was much better at something else."

"What was that?"

"Fighting," he said simply. "I was a damn good
soldier."

Yes, he would be. "You said you were in the
cavalry?"

"In the First Virginia, with Jeb Stuart, for a while.
Until '63."

"What happened then?"

"I joined the Rangers."

The word puzzled her for a moment, for the only context she could put it in was the Texas Rangers, and of course that wouldn't be right. She had heard the word "rangers" bandied about during the war, but it had been over for six years and she couldn't bring the memory into focus. "What rangers?"

"Mosby's Rangers."

Shock reverberated through her. Mosby! His reputation had been legendary, and the gossip about him had been frightening. Even as absorbed as she had been in medical school, she had heard about Mosby and his devil rangers. They hadn't fought like normal soldiers; they had been masters at deceit, at hit-and-run fighting that had made it almost impossible to capture them. She hadn't been able to picture Rafe as a staid lawyer, but it was so terribly easy to see him as a guerrilla fighter.

"What did you do after the war?"

He shrugged. "Drifted. My father and brother had both died during the war, and I didn't have any other family." He shut out the surge of bitterness and concentrated instead on the erotic thrill of Annie's hand as he brushed her fingertips back and forth over his nipples in lazy caresses. His nipples were so tight and throbbing that he could barely stand it. She had never touched him intimately, and he closed his eyes as he imagined her hand closing around his shaft. God! He'd probably go mad with frustration.

"If you could, would you go back?"

He thought about it. Back East it was just too civilized, and he'd lived too long observing no rules except his own, grown too used to the vast expanses around him. He had reverted to the wild, and had no desire to be tamed again. "No," he finally said. "There's nothing for me there. What about you? Do you miss the big cities?"

"Not exactly. I miss the convenience of a regular

town, but being able to practice medicine is really what's important to me, and I couldn't do it back East."

The temptation was killing him. He said, "There's something else you couldn't do back East."

She looked intrigued. "Oh? What?"

"This." He moved her hand under the blanket and folded her fingers around his manhood. A wild electricity shot through him, the pang so strong that he drew in his breath with a sharp hiss and his entire body tensed.

Annie had gone very still. He could barely feel her breathing.

She was both shocked and enthralled. The thick length surged in her hand; to her delight, she could feel it actually increasing in size. After she got over her shock, she realized that it felt marvelous, so hot and strong and pulsing with independent life, so hard under the smooth skin. She explored the thick bulbous tip, then trailed her fingers downward to his loose, heavy testicles. She cupped them, enjoying the soft, cool feel of them in her palm. They tightened almost immediately, drawing up toward his body. Her fascination made her forget that she should be shocked.

Rafe arched on the blanket, his blood pounding through his veins. He could barely think. He should have resisted temptation, he should have known that the hot thrill of her touch would be unbearable on his genitals. His vision clouded with a dark mist as his climax surged ever closer to eruption. With a harsh sound he jerked away from her. "Stop!"

The violence of his desire caught her by surprise, then the knowledge of her own feminine power flooded through her. She looked up at him, a very female smile touching her lips. She smoothed her hands up his torso, and he quivered like a stallion. "Make love to me," she invited in a soft murmur, and that was all the invitation he needed. He shot up from the blankets and was mounting her all in one motion. Annie lifted her hips for his possessive inward thrust, accepting him with a wince at the discomfort but a great inner joy at the pleasure she knew she was giving him. He pumped deep inside her and shuddered as his seed emptied with a great rush that left him lying limply atop her.

Desperately he sucked air into his heaving lungs. God, it had to ease up soon or he was going to kill himself making love to her. He'd thought that the intensity of it would fade to manageable levels, but so far it hadn't. Every time the desire had been just as urgent, riding him hard.

The danger was that he would let his lust for her cloud his thinking. Hell, he'd already done that. He should have returned her to Silver Mesa and gotten as far away from the place as he could, but instead he had deliberately delayed until they were snowed in. He'd planned her seduction well, but in the feeding of his sexual hunger he had himself been seduced. He couldn't think beyond the next few days, secluded with her in this warm, dark cabin, greedily taking all of her special heat for himself.

The days passed in a sensual blur. Sometimes it seemed to Annie that they spent more time naked than clothed; even during the day they were often entwined on the blankets, having just made love or about to make love again. Day and night blended for her, and sometimes when she woke from a doze she wasn't certain which it was. She became so accustomed to his penetration that it felt more normal than being apart from him.

When she thought of the future she was terrified, so she blocked it out. There was only now, these dark, sensual days together. On the day she watched him ride away from her—on that day, she promised herself, she would start thinking of the future again, of the long, endless trickle of time without him.

For now she let herself be submerged by the physical. She'd never dreamed lovemaking could be so intense, so intoxicating. He made love to her in all the ways a man could use a woman, guiding her to pleasures undreamed of, completing his stamp of possession. The voluptuousness of it enthralled her, and her sexual self-confidence bloomed.

It was a shock to get up on the eighth day of the snow to the sound of dripping water and realize the snow was melting. She had become so accustomed to the bitter cold that when the temperature surged above freezing it felt almost balmy, and indeed the first unmistakable signs of spring began to appear while snow still covered the ground. Over the next several days the little creek swelled with runoff, and Rafe took the horses to the small hidden meadow to let them work out their fidgets from being cooped up for so long and to paw the snow aside to find the tender green shoots of new grass.

She knew they would soon have to leave, indeed could already have left, though the melting snow did make travel hazardous. She sensed that Rafe was using it as an excuse, but she didn't mind. Every minute she could spend with him was infinitely precious because there were so few of them left.

He had taken the horses to graze one morning and she was using the opportunity to heat water for washing. He had given her his spare pistol as a precaution while he was gone, even though he was only a few minutes away, and she kept it in her skirt pocket on her trips back and forth to the creek. The weapon was heavy and dragged at her skirt, irritating her, but common sense kept her from leaving it at the cabin. Bears were emerging from their winter dens, hungry and irritable; Rafe had said a bear wasn't likely to bother her, but she wasn't about to take any chances. She might not be able to hit what she shot at, but at least the sound would bring Rafe at a run.

On her second trip back from the creek she was

watching where she stepped, for the melting snow had left the ground muddy and slippery. A horse whickered and she looked up, startled, at the strange man sitting his horse in front of the cabin. The bucket of water slipped from her hand as panic shot through her.

"I beg your pardon, ma'am," the man said. "I didn't mean to scare you."

She couldn't think of anything to say. Her mind had gone blank, her lips were numb.

He eased back into his saddle. "I saw your smoke," he offered. "Didn't know anybody had settled in up here, and thought it might be a camp."

Who was he? Just a drifter, or someone who would be a threat to Rafe? He didn't seem to be threatening, in fact was being careful not to make any moves that she could call aggressive, but the shock of an intruder on their private world had her reeling. Where was Rafe? Oh God, don't let him come back now!

"I don't mean you no harm," the man said. His eyes were calm, his voice almost gentle. "Is your man around?"

She didn't know what to say. If she said yes, then he would know she wasn't alone. If she said no, who knew what he would do? Annie had treated too many wounds over the years to automatically believe in the goodness of her fellow man. Some of her fellow men had no goodness in them at all. But he wasn't likely to believe she was living up here in the mountains by herself anyway, so finally she nodded.

"Reckon I could speak with him? If you'd just point me in his direction, I'll stop botherin' you and let you go on about your work."

Another quandary; did she dare let him approach Rafe without warning? Rafe was likely to shoot first and ask questions later, which could result in an innocent man's death, but on the other hand if this man wasn't so innocent she could be risking Rafe's life. Her mind sped. "He'll be back shortly," she finally said, the first words she had spoken. "Would you like to have a cup of coffee while you wait?"

The stranger smiled. "Yes ma'am, I surely would." He stepped down from his horse and waited for her to approach. She picked up the empty bucket and carefully held it so it hid her sagging pocket. If she could just get the man inside, then Rafe would see his horse and know to be cautious, and with the pistol hidden in her pocket she could make certain Rafe wasn't in any danger.

The man left his rifle in its scabbard on the saddle, but she noticed that he wore a big pistol strapped low on his hip, the holster tied around his thigh just as Rafe wore his. That wasn't uncommon, but it did make her even more wary. He had a slight limp, but didn't seem to be in any pain or hampered by it very much.

She led the way into the cabin and set the bucket down by the fireplace, then poured the man a cup of their breakfast coffee. He removed his flat-brimmed black hat and thanked her in a polite voice for the coffee.

The window coverings were open, letting the sunlight in along with the brisk fresh air, and he looked around interestedly as he sipped the coffee. His gaze lingered on the rough-framed pine-needle bed that took up most of the left side of the cabin and Annie felt her face heat, but he didn't say anything. He took in the neatness of the mean little cabin, the total lack of furniture, the two saddles on the floor, and drew his own conclusions.

"Guess you were lucky to find the cabin when you did," he said. "Before the snow came."

He thought they were travelers who had been stranded by the snow. Relief flooded through her but before she could agree with him his gaze lit on her big black medical bag and his eyebrows drew together in a puzzled frown. Her bag! Annie gave it an agonized glance. It didn't look like anything but what it was; doctors all over the country carried similar ones. It wasn't the usual piece of luggage for either home-steaders or travelers.

"You must be that doctor," he said slowly. "The one from Silver Mesa who's been missing for a couple of weeks. I'd never heard tell of no female doctor before, but I guess they weren't lying."

Annie wanted to tell him that it was her husband who was the doctor; it was the most logical thing to say, and the most believable, but she had always been a horrible liar and now she couldn't manage it at all. Her mouth was too dry, and her heart was thundering in her chest.

He looked at her, and her white face and wide, panicked eyes would have made him suspicious even if he hadn't already been. He looked back at the saddles, stared hard at them, and suddenly the big revolver was in his hand and pointed straight at her.

"That's McCay's rig," he snapped. The friendly tone was gone; his voice was heavy and menacing now. "I must have hit him worse than I thought if he needed a doctor. Where is he?"

She couldn't send him up to the meadow. "H-hunting," she stammered.

"On horseback? Or on foot?"

"O-on foot. The horses are g-grazing." Her voice wavered out of control. The barrel of the pistol was huge and black, unwavering.

"When's he due back? C'mon, lady, don't make me hurt you! When's he gonna be back?"

"I don't know!" She wet her lips. "When he gets something, I suppose."

"How long has he been gone?"

She panicked again, because she had no idea what to say. "An h-hour?" she said, making it a question. "I don't know. I've been heating water to wash clothes and I haven't been paying attention—"

"Yeah, yeah," he interrupted impatiently. "All right. I haven't heard any shots."

"He—he has some traps out, too. If there's anything in one of them he wouldn't have to shoot anything."

The man looked around, his sharp gaze roaming over the cabin and looking out the open door at his horse tethered in plain sight. He jerked his head toward the door. "Outside, lady. I've got to get my horse put up. If he shows up while we're out there, I'd advise you to hit the ground, because lead's gonna be flyin'. And don't try to scream or nothin' to warn him. I don't want to hurt you, but I aim to get McCay any way I can. Ten thousand's a lot of money."

Ten thousand; dear God. No wonder he was on the run. For that kind of money, every bounty hunter in the country must be looking for him.

The man kept the pistol trained on her as she walked woodenly to the empty horse shed, where he put his horse in one of the stalls. This was the bounty hunter who had been chasing Rafe, the one who had shot him, but she couldn't remember what Rafe had said his name was. Her mind felt frozen with fear, unable to think or plan. In all her bleak imaginings of the future, she had never dreamed she would see Rafe gunned down in front of her. It was a nightmare too horrible to contemplate, yet it was going to happen unless she could think of something to stop it. All she could do, however, was try to hold her skirt in such a way as to disguise the weight of the pistol in her pocket.

The pistol was her only chance, but she didn't know how to seize the opportunity; she had no delusions about being able to draw it, cock the hammer, and actually hit what she fired at, especially since the man was watching her so closely. She would have to do it when his attention was elsewhere, and that meant when Rafe was approaching. She wouldn't have to actually hit him; just firing the gun would splinter his attention and warn Rafe, so Rafe would have a chance. She didn't dare think about what chance she would have.

The man directed her back into the cabin, and Annie stood rigidly beside the fireplace with her back to the wall.

He let down both of the window coverings, preventing Rafe from seeing inside the cabin should he approach from the side. Rafe would have to come in the door, and he would be perfectly outlined against the brilliant light reflected off the melting snow. He would be blinded, unable to see into the dimness of the cabin, while the bounty hunter waiting for him would have a perfect shot. Rafe wouldn't have a chance.

Unless he noticed that the window coverings were down; he would wonder about that, knowing how Annie disliked sitting in the dark cabin. And he might notice the hoofprints out front. Rafe was as wary and alert as a wild animal, never taking chances. She thought he would notice those things. But what could he do? Come in firing blindly? The smartest thing would be for him to silently retreat to the horses and get away while he could. She closed her eyes and began praying that he would do that, for if she could just believe he was alive and safe somewhere she'd be able to bear never seeing him again. What she couldn't bear was to see him killed.

"What's your name?" she asked shakily.

The man gave her a hard look. "Trahern. Not that it matters. You just stand there where he can see you when he comes in."

She was the goat to bait the tiger into the trap. Trahern was standing to the left, lost in the shadows. Her eyes had adjusted and she could see him just fine, but Rafe wouldn't see him at all.

She started to say something else but Trahern motioned her into silence. She stood frozen with fear, her eyes huge and despairing, her gaze fixed on the open door as they listened for Rafe's approach. Minutes ticked by, and her locked knees began to shake. The trembling traveled upward until she was quaking as if she had palsy. The silence made her want to scream.

One second there was nothing there, and the next she could see him. She was too petrified even to scream a warning, but none was needed. Rafe held a finger to his lips. He was just barely in her field of vision through the open door, some thirty feet away from the cabin. Annie felt pinned to the wall and totally exposed by the stream of light coming through the doorway. She sensed Trahern watching her, so she couldn't even roll her eyes in his direction. Her heart was pounding so hard it was jarring the material of her blouse, and her hands felt both sweaty and ice-cold. Her lungs felt restricted and it hurt to breathe.

Then Rafe was gone again, vanishing from her sight as if he'd been a ghost.

Her hand was hidden in the folds of her skirt. She began inching it toward her pocket, and her wet hand closed over the huge butt of the pistol. She put her thumb on the hammer to test how difficult it would be to cock it; to her horror, she couldn't budge it. She would need both hands just to cock the damn thing! An odd rage seared through her. *Damn* Rafe! Why hadn't he given her a weapon she could handle?

She rolled her head against the wall and looked at Trahern. He must have sensed something; his attention was riveted on the doorway.

Trahern thumbed back the hammer of his gun, the small click rasping on her nerves like an explosion.

She could see Rafe again, sliding silently toward the open door. His own pistol was in his hand, ready to fire, but the advantage of surprise wouldn't be enough. Trahern would be able to see him perfectly, while he would have to guess at Trahern's location.

Trahern moved slightly, all of his instincts alert. Like a wolf he sensed that his prey was near. He would fire as soon as Rafe appeared. And Rafe would die in front of her, the light in those fierce eyes fading away to blankness.

From the corner of her eye she saw Rafe move, attacking like a panther in a smooth, silent explosion of power and speed. She began screaming, but her throat locked and no sound came out. Trahern's hand came up and so did hers. Her hand never left her pocket. Somehow she fired through the material of her skirt.

CHAPTER

11

Explosions of gunfire rocked the tiny room, deafening her. Smoke filled the air and the stench of cordite burned her nostrils. She stood frozen, the pistol still clutched in her hand, the barrel protruding from the burnt, tattered remains of her pocket. Rafe was there somehow, she didn't know how. She couldn't remember seeing him come through the door. Someone was screaming.

Rafe was yelling something, but she didn't know what. She could barely hear him over the ringing in her ears. He slapped her leg and hip and she began sobbing, trying to push him away. It took her a moment to realize that her skirt was on fire.

Then, with a jolt, splintered reality settled into place again.

Rafe crossed the room to kick the pistol away from Trahern's outstretched hand, and the screaming ebbed to moans. On trembling legs Annie managed to move a few steps and then stood frozen again, staring at the man lying crumpled on the floor.

Blood soaked his lower abdomen, turning his shirt and pants black in the shadowed depths of the room.

It pooled around and under him, soaking through the cracks in the floor. His eyes were open and his face was absolutely colorless.

"Why didn't you shoot me?" Rafe asked harshly, going down on one knee beside the bounty hunter. He knew he'd given Trahern the perfect opportunity, but when he had seen Annie's skirt flaming nothing else had seemed to matter except getting to her before the fire licked upwards. He had literally turned his back on the bounty hunter—and Trahern had held his fire.

"No point in it," Trahern rasped. He cleared his throat. "I'm not going to be able to collect the money. Hell with it." He moaned again and then said, "Damn. I never thought to see if she had a gun."

Horror licked through Annie. *She had shot a man.* She had heard other shots, but somehow she knew that Trahern had been falling even before Rafe had come through the door. She hadn't aimed, she didn't even know how she had managed to pull back the hammer. But the bullet had found its mark, and Trahern lay bleeding to death on the floor.

Suddenly she could move, and she whirled to grab her bag, dragging it across the floor to the bounty hunter. "I've got to get that bleeding stopped," she said frantically, going down on her knees beside Rafe. She flinched from the horrible wound. Trahern was gut shot, and her medical training told her that he was a dead man even though her instincts were screaming at her to do something to help him.

She reached out and Rafe's hands shot forward, catching hers and holding them. His gray eyes had a stark look in them. "No," he said. "You can't do anything for him, honey. Don't break your heart trying." He didn't think even Annie's healing touch could work against a wound of such magnitude, but she would exhaust herself in the effort.

She jerked futilely at her hands, trying to free them.

Tears welled in her eyes. "I can stop the bleeding. I know I can stop the bleeding."

"If it's all the same to you, ma'am, I'd rather bleed to death than have the poison set up in my gut and take a couple of hard days to die," Trahern said drowsily. "At least it don't hurt so much now."

She sucked in her breath. Her chest hurt with the effort. She tried to think clinically. The wound was bleeding far more than most abdominal wounds. From the location of it, and from the amount of blood, the bullet must have severed or at least nicked the huge vein that ran along the spine. Rafe was right; there was no way she could save him. Trahern would be dead in another minute or so.

"Just pure luck," Trahern muttered. "I lost your trail in Silver Mesa so I decided to rest up while my leg healed. I headed out yesterday, and saw your smoke this morning. Pure damn luck, and all of it bad." He closed his eyes and seemed to be resting for a moment. It took a great deal of effort for him to open them again.

"It's known you're in the area," he said. "Other bounty hunters . . . got a U.S. marshal on your trail, too. Name of Atwater. Damn bulldog. You're the best I've ever tracked, McCay, but Atwater don't give up."

Rafe had heard of the lawman. Noah Atwater, even more than Trahern, didn't know the meaning of the word quit. He had to get out of this area, and fast. He looked at Annie and something punched him in the chest, hard.

Trahern coughed. He looked confused. "Got any whiskey? I could use a drink."

"No, no whiskey," Rafe replied.

"I have some laudanum," Annie said, and tried again to free her hands. Rafe still refused to let her go. He pulled her closer to him. "Rafe, let me go. I know there isn't much I can do, but the laudanum will help ease the pain—"

"He doesn't need it, honey," Rafe said gently, and tucked her head against his shoulder.

Annie pushed at him, then she saw Trahern's face. It was utterly still. Rafe reached out and closed the bounty hunter's eyelids.

She sat in frozen shock. Her seat was a rock outside the cabin where Rafe had led her and gently pushed her down. She clutched a blanket around her, because she couldn't seem to get warm.

She had killed a man. She went over and over it in her mind, and each time she accepted that she hadn't had a choice, that she had had to shoot. There hadn't been time to think, only to act. It had been pure chance that the bullet had hit its target, but she couldn't excuse herself on those grounds, for even if she had *known* the shot would kill Trahern she would still have fired. In a choice between Rafe's life or Trahern's, there was no choice at all. To save Rafe, she would do whatever had to be done. And none of that changed the fact that she had violated her oath, the physician's creed, and her own values by taking a life rather than doing everything in her power to save it. The betrayal of herself was numbing. The knowledge that she would do it again, if faced with the same circumstances, was shattering.

Rafe was swiftly, efficiently getting their gear together. The ground was still too frozen for him to bury Trahern, so the body still lay in the cabin. Annie knew she couldn't go back in there.

Rafe was considering his next move. He had Trahern's weapons and supplies; his own horse was well rested and well fed. He wouldn't need to stock up on grub for a while. He had to get Annie back to Silver Mesa, then he would cut south through the Arizona desert and head for Mexico. That wouldn't stop the bounty hunters, but it would get Atwater off his trail.

Annie—no, he couldn't let himself think about Annie. He'd known from the beginning that they wouldn't have much time together. He'd return her to her home and her work, and let her get on with her life.

But he was worried about her. She hadn't said a word since Trahern had died. Her face was white and still, her eyes huge and black with shock. He remembered the first time he'd killed a man, back during the war; he'd retched until his throat was raw and his stomach muscles sore. Annie hadn't vomited. He'd have felt better if she had.

He got the horses saddled and went over to her, crouching down and taking her cold hands in his, rubbing them to give her some of his warmth. "We have to go, honey. We can make it out of here by sundown, and you can sleep in your own bed tonight."

Annie looked at him as if he were crazy. "I can't go back to Silver Mesa," she said. Those were the first words she'd said in an hour.

"Of course you can. You have to. You'll feel better once you're home."

"I killed a man. I'll be arrested." She spoke very precisely.

"No, honey, listen." He'd already thought about that. It was probably well known that Trahern had been on his trail, and with Atwater following close behind it probably wouldn't be long before Trahern's body was found. "They'll think I did it. No one knows you've been with me, so we can do as we originally planned."

But she was shaking her head. "I won't let you take the blame for something I did."

He stared at her in disbelief. "What?"

"I said I won't let you be blamed for something you didn't do."

"Annie, honey, don't you understand?" He smoothed a strand of hair back from her face. "I'm already wanted for murder. Do you think Trahern is going to make any difference to what happens to me?"

She looked at him steadily. "I know you're already

blamed for someone else's crime. I won't let you be blamed for mine too."

"Shit." He rose to his feet and restlessly ran his hand through his hair. There had to be some way he could make her see reason, but offhand he couldn't think of it. She might still be in shock, but she'd made up her mind and there wasn't a damn thing he could do about it. He forced himself to consider what would happen. She wasn't likely to hang or even go to jail for killing Trahern; she was, after all, a woman and a respected doctor, while Trahern had been a bounty hunter. Lawmen didn't think much of bounty hunters. But once the circumstances of Trahern's death became known, that Annie had spent almost two weeks in Rafe's company, he knew that her life wouldn't be worth two red cents. She would be killed by the same man who had had him on the run for four years; rather, the man's minions would do it. Rafe's nemesis had enough money that he never had to dirty his hands with any of the details, and a lot of that money had been earned with other men's blood.

He had to take her with him.

The solution was both simple and terrible. He didn't know if she could survive a life on the run. He knew for certain she wouldn't survive if he took her back to Silver Mesa. Damn her morals; she wouldn't budge from her stand, and it would cost her her life. The cost was too high, at least for him.

But what would it do to her to have to give up everything she'd worked so hard to accomplish? Being a doctor meant so much to her. There wasn't any way she could follow her calling while she was on the hoot-owl trail with him.

Useless regrets, because he had no choice. She wouldn't have a practice if she returned to Silver Mesa; all too soon she would only have a grave.

Maybe it had been fever that had clouded his thinking when he had taken her from her house, but maybe it had been his own arrogance. He knew he was good; he had been certain he'd eluded Trahern, and equally certain he could use Annie's healing skills, enjoy her soft body, and return her to Silver Mesa undetected. He hadn't allowed for chance, for the twists of fate that turned the best of plans upside down, and now Annie was caught in the same nightmare web that had bound him for four years.

The only thing in their favor was that no one knew they were together. Atwater was looking for a lone man, not a man and a woman traveling together. It could be a useful disguise.

Annie hadn't thought of it, she was still too much in shock, but it would be assumed that he'd killed Trahern anyway. No one knew she was with him, so how could she be suspected? She was in danger only if she confessed. It made no difference to their situation: she had to go with him.

The thought of it made him dizzy, and after a moment he realized it was relief. He had steeled himself to take her back to Silver Mesa, to say good-bye and ride away, but now he wouldn't have to. She was *his*.

He crouched down in front of her again and framed her face with his big hands, forcing her to give him her attention. Her big brown eyes looked so lost and bewildered that he couldn't stop himself from kissing her, hard. *That* got her attention. She blinked and tried to pull her head away, as if she couldn't understand why he was doing that now when they had more important things to think about.

Just to show her, and because he couldn't stand for her to pull away, he kissed her again. "I'm not taking you back to Silver Mesa," he said. "You'll have to stay with me."

He didn't know if he'd expected an argument or not. He didn't get one. She simply studied him for a minute, then nodded.

"All right." She paused, and worry darkened her face. "I hope I don't slow you down."

She would, but it didn't matter. He couldn't leave her behind. He pulled her to her feet. "Let's go. We need to get away from here."

She obediently climbed into the saddle. "Why aren't we taking Trahern's horse?"

"Because someone might recognize it."

"Will it be all right?"

"I unsaddled it. When it gets hungry enough, it'll start looking for grass. Either someone will find it or it'll go wild."

She looked at the cabin and thought of Trahern lying dead inside it. She hated to leave without burying him, but she accepted that it wasn't possible.

"Stop thinking about it," Rafe ordered. "There's nothing you could have done that would have made any difference, and nothing you can do now."

It was an extremely pragmatic piece of advice; she just hoped she was strong-minded enough to take it.

The bright sunlight was almost blinding on the snow, and the sky was so blue it made her ache inside. There was a fresh, sweet scent that heralded the explosion of new life beneath the snow as spring finally made its appearance. A life had ended, but time moved on. Two weeks ago she had been forced into the mountains on a nightmare ride in the darkness, cold and terrified, pushed to the limits of her strength and beyond. Winter had still held the land in its bleak grip. Now she was leaving these same mountains with something like regret, willingly following the man who had kidnapped her, and this time she was surrounded by a beauty so wild and intense that she almost couldn't take it in. In those two weeks she had healed a wounded outlaw and fallen in love with him. He was her lover now, this tall, hard man with the frosty eyes, and to protect him she had killed another human being. Just two weeks, but in that length of time the land and her life had changed beyond recognition.

Rafe kept the horses in the snow as much as he could. It made the going slower than necessary and also left an extremely visible trail; she started to point this out to him and then realized that the snow was melting and would destroy all traces of their passage. Anyone trailing them would have to find the cabin and pick up their trail almost immediately, or the tracks would be gone.

"Where are we going?" she asked when they had been riding for a couple of hours.

"Silver Mesa."

She reined in her horse. "No," she said, going pale. "You said I could stay with you."

"Don't fall behind," he snapped. "You are staying with me. I didn't say I was leaving you in Silver Mesa, I said we're going to Silver Mesa."

"But why?"

"You need more clothes, for one thing. I wouldn't normally chance it, but your place is far enough away from the rest of the town that I can get in and out without being seen."

She looked down at her skirt, with a big hole burned in the side where the pocket had been. She had come so close to burning alive that it made her quake to think about it, and yet at the time she hadn't even been aware of the danger.

"I want to go with you."

"No."

His voice had that tone that said he'd made up his mind and wasn't going to be swayed, but she tried anyway. "Why, if no one is likely to see us?"

"Chance," he said. He'd disregarded it once; he wouldn't again. "If by chance I'm seen, I don't want anyone to be able to connect you with me. It's for your own safety. Just tell me what you need, and I'll try to find it."

She thought of all the herbs she had growing in their little pots and knew she would have to leave them behind. All of her books, some of them her father's, were incredibly precious to her and most of them could never be replaced, yet neither could she carry them with her. If she went back, if she saw her familiar possessions in the place that had become home to her, if she were forced to decide what she took and what was left behind, it would hurt far more than simply never seeing them again and accepting that they were gone. Rafe would pack a few clothes for her and that would be the end of it. At least she still had her medical bag, which was her most precious possession of all.

Even with the slowness of their progress, they reached the base of the mountains well before nightfall. Rafe insisted that they stop while they were still sheltered by the trees and wait until dark. She was glad for the rest. The day's events had left her exhausted, and her mind was still trying to grapple with the changed circumstances of her life. Of all the scenarios she had imagined, this hadn't been one of them.

Sundown painted the sky, then purple shadows crept over the land. Beneath the trees it was almost totally dark. "I'm going now," Rafe said, his deep voice barely audible. He placed a blanket around her shoulders. "Stay right here."

"I will." She was a bit uneasy about remaining there by herself in the dark, but she would manage. "When will you be back?"

"It depends on what I find." He paused. "If I'm not back by morning, assume that I've been caught."

Her heart squeezed painfully. "Then don't go!"

He knelt down and kissed her. "I think it'll be fine, but there's always a chance that it won't be. Just in case, if I get caught—"

"I won't let you hang for something I did," she said, her voice trembling.

He touched her cheek. "They don't hang dead

men," he said, and swung into the saddle. Annie listened to the muffled hoofbeats as they faded away into silence.

Wearily she closed her eyes. He wasn't worried about being hanged. A bounty hunter wouldn't worry about keeping him alive for trial; he would be killed immediately. Only if a lawman caught him would there be a chance of him living to see a trial, and she knew he would choose a fast bullet over months in jail that ended with a rope.

She stared into the night, so tired her eyes were burning, yet she couldn't sleep. What could she have done differently that would have changed the morning's events? She could think of nothing, and yet she kept seeing Trahern's open, unseeing eyes. He had been a killer, hunting men for money, but he hadn't seemed particularly mean. He had been polite to her, had at first tried to reassure her, had even, within the realm of possibility, tried to make certain she wouldn't be hurt. Morals, or had he simply been disinterested because there was no profit to be had in her death? She wished he had been a filthy, brute, but life never seemed to be that clear-cut.

And yet it had been that clear-cut for Trahern. He hadn't shot Rafe when he'd had the chance because he had known he was dying and thus wouldn't be able to collect the bounty money. As Trahern himself had said, there was no point in it. For him, it had simply been a question of money and nothing else.

The stars came out and she stared at them through the trees, wishing that she knew how to tell time by their position. She had no idea how long Rafe had been gone, but it didn't matter. He would either be back by morning, or he wouldn't.

If he didn't return, what would she do? Ride back to Silver Mesa and pick up her life where she had left it?

Say that she had been summoned to treat someone a good distance away? She didn't think she could calmly ride back into town and carry off a charade like that, knowing that Rafe was dead.

She was acutely aware that he could just keep on going, that he might have had no intention of returning for her, but her heart didn't believe it. With no real evidence to sustain her, only the love she bore him, she knew that he wouldn't abandon her like that. Rafe had said he would be back. As long as he was alive, he would keep his word.

It seemed as if hours had passed and dawn had to be on the horizon before she heard the sound of a horse being walked toward her. She scrambled to her feet and almost fell, for she had been sitting so long that her legs were cold and numb. Rafe dismounted and immediately put his arms around her. "Was there any trouble?" he asked into her hair. "Did anything frighten you?"

"No," she stammered, burying her face against his chest and inhaling the wonderful hot male scent of him. Nothing had frightened her except the horrifying possibility of never seeing him again. She wanted to cling to him and never let go.

"I got fresh clothes for you, and some other things."

"Such as?"

"Another cup, for one thing." She heard the amusement in his voice. "And another cook pot. Soap and matches. Things like that."

"No oil lamp?"

"Tell you what. If we find another cabin to stay in, I promise I'll find an oil lamp for you."

"I'll hold you to that," she said.

He spread a blanket on the ground. "We might as well bed down here," he said. "Come morning, we'll head south."

They had Trahern's blankets now, and were below the snow line, so she knew they would be warm enough. The question was whether or not she could sleep. She curled up on her side and pillowed her head on her arm, but as soon as she closed her eyes she saw Trahern's body and she quickly opened them again.

Rafe lay down beside her and pulled the blankets over them. His hand was heavy on her stomach. "Annie," he said, that special note in his voice that said he wanted her.

She tensed. After everything that had happened that day, she didn't think she could lose herself in lovemaking. "I can't," she said, her voice breaking a little.

"Why not?"

"I killed a man today."

After a moment of silence he leaned up on his elbow. "Accidentally. You didn't mean to kill him."

"Does that make any difference to him?"

Another silence. "Would you hold your fire if you could do it over again?"

"No," she whispered. "Even if I knew I was going to kill him, I would still have to shoot. In that regard, it wasn't an accident at all."

"The men I've killed were during war or to prevent them from killing me. I learned not to worry about their decision in coming after me; they made it, so they took the consequences. I can't live my life regretting that I'm the one alive, instead of them."

She knew that. Her mind accepted it. Her heart, though, was sick with combined shock and sadness.

His hand became more insistent, turning her onto her back. "Rafe, no," she said. "It wouldn't be right."

He tried to see her face through the darkness. All day long he had been aware of her suffering, and though he couldn't put himself in her place to the extent that he could feel her pain, he had understood the reasons and worried because she was hurting. He

179

had hoped that the sudden action forced on them would keep her from brooding, but it hadn't.

Doctors spent their lives trying to help others. The calling had been even stronger for Annie, for she had had to fight just for the chance to learn. His little darling hadn't even been able to bring herself to hurt him even when she had been terrified for her life, yet she had shot without hesitation to protect him, and now her soul was hurting.

She had no idea how to handle it. When he had been forced to face death he hadn't had the luxury of time to reflect on it; the battle had moved too swiftly. Afterward he had vomited and wondered if he could ever face another dawn, but the sun had risen after all and there had been other battles. He had learned how frail human life was, how easily snuffed, and how little difference it made.

Annie would never be able to accept that. Life was precious to her, and it humbled him that she had killed to defend him. She was mired in remorse, and he couldn't leave her there. He didn't know what else to do but refuse to leave her alone with death filling her memories. He leaned over her. "Annie. *Our* lives didn't stop."

His strong hands were under her skirt, opening her drawers and pulling them down, then he flipped her skirt up and rolled on top of her. His heavy weight held her down, his thighs forced hers open.

His penetration hurt, because she wasn't ready for him, but her hands dug into his powerful back as she clung to him. His powerful thrusts moved her back and forth on the blanket. His heat comforted her, inside and out. She caught her breath on a sob, but she was glad he hadn't stopped. She sensed that he knew what she was feeling, just as he knew that the celebration of life is keenest when faced with the specter of death. He wouldn't let her wallow in guilt. *This is life,* he was telling her. With the force of his body he was drawing her away from the death scene being played over and over in her mind.

She did sleep, eventually, worn out from the demands he had made on her and the explosive reaction of her own body. Rafe held her in his arms and felt her finally relax, and only then did he allow himself to sleep.

CHAPTER
12

"**W**here are we going?" she asked when they stopped at noon to eat and rest the horses.

"Mexico. That'll get Atwater off my trail."

"But not the bounty hunters."

He shrugged.

"Trahern said that the bounty on you is ten thousand dollars."

Rafe's eyebrows went up and he whistled. He looked a little pleased. Annie had never struck a person in her life, but she was sorely tempted to slap him. Men!

"It's gone up," he said. "Last I heard, it was six thousand."

"Who was it you were supposed to have killed?" she asked in bewilderment. "Who was that important?"

"Tench Tilghman." Rafe paused, his eyes on the horizon. In his mind he saw Tench's young, earnest face.

"I've never heard of him."

"No, I suppose not. He wasn't anyone important."

"Then why is there so much money offered for a reward? Was his family rich? Is that what it is?"

"It isn't Tench's family," Rafe muttered. "And Tench was just an excuse. If it hadn't been him, they would have pinned someone else's murder on me. Killing me is the whole point of it, not justice. It doesn't have a damn thing to do with justice."

She said, "You didn't want to tell me before because you said it would be dangerous for me to know. What difference does it make now? I can't go back to Silver Mesa and pretend I've never heard of you."

She was right about that. Rafe looked at her, sitting as erect as if she were in a drawing room back East, her blouse buttoned right up to her throat, and he hurt inside. What had he done to her? He had forced her from the life she had forged for herself and now she was on the run with him. But he couldn't have left her behind or she would have confessed to killing Trahern, and then the men following him would have known, or guessed, that she might know him, might know his secrets, and they wouldn't take a chance; she would be killed. Maybe it was time that she knew about the others; the bounty hunters and the lawmen weren't the only ones after him. It was only fair that she knew what they were up against.

"All right. I guess you have a right to know now."

She gave him a disgruntled look. "I'd say so, yes."

He stood up and looked around, taking his time, studying the horizon. They were well concealed by trees and rocks, and the only things moving were some birds wheeling lazily overhead, black against the cobalt sky. The white-capped mountains towered overhead.

"I met Tench during the war. He was from Maryland, a few years younger than me. A good man. Level-headed."

Annie waited as she saw Rafe trying to work out how to frame the story.

"When Richmond fell, President Davis moved the government by train to Greensboro. The treasury was moved too. On the same day Lincoln was assassinated, President Davis, in a wagon caravan, slipped past the Yankee patrols, and headed south. Another wagon caravan carried the treasury, but it went by a different route."

Her eyes widened suddenly. "Are you talking about the missing Confederate treasure?" she asked in a choked voice. "Rafe, is all of this about gold? You know where it is?" Her voice rose in a squeak.

"No. In a way."

"What do you mean, 'in a way'? Do you know where the gold is or don't you?"

"I don't," he said flatly.

She exhaled, feeling weak. She didn't know if she was relieved or disappointed. All of the newspapers had been full of the mystery of the vanished Confederate gold; some had advanced the theory that the ex-Confederate president had secreted it away, others that remnants of the defeated Confederate armies had taken it to Mexico in an effort to raise more troops. Some Southerners had charged that the gold had been stolen by Yankee troops. She had read of theory after theory, but all of them had seemed to her to be nothing more than guesses. Six years after the war had ended, the lost Confederate gold was still lost.

Rafe was staring at the horizon again, his expression hard and bitter. "Tench was part of President Davis's escort. He said that they went to Washington, Georgia, and found out that the money was in Abbeville, not very far away. The treasure wagons joined up with President Davis. He ordered part of the money, about a hundred thousand dollars in silver, to be paid to some cavalry troops in back pay they were owed. About half of the treasury was sent back to Richmond to the banks, and President Davis took the rest to use to escape and set up another government."

She was stunned. "What do you mean, it was returned to Richmond? Are you telling me the banks have had the gold all this time and didn't tell anyone?"

"No, it never made it back to Richmond. The wagon train was robbed about twelve miles out of Washington—Georgia, not D.C.—probably by some of the locals. Forget about the gold. It isn't important."

She had never heard anyone dismiss a lost fortune as "unimportant" before, but his expression hadn't lightened, so she bit back any other questions.

"President Davis and his escort, with the remainder of the treasury, split up in Sandersville, Georgia. The treasure wagon slowed them down too much, so President Davis and his party went on ahead, trying to get to Texas. Tench was with the group that stayed with the treasure wagon, and they headed down into Florida to keep from being captured. They were supposed to meet up with President Davis at a prearranged place when it was safer."

Rafe paused. She realized that he hadn't looked at her once since he'd started talking. "Money isn't all they were carrying. They had some government papers, and some of President Davis's personal belongings.

"They were close to Gainesville, Florida, when they heard that President Davis had been captured. Since there wasn't any point in going on, they didn't know what to do with the money, but finally they decided to divide it equally among them. It didn't amount to a huge fortune, about two thousand dollars each, but two thousand meant a lot after the war.

"Tench somehow ended up with the government papers and President Davis's personal papers as well as his share of the money. He expected to be stopped and searched—all disbanded Confederate troops were if the Yankees could find them—so he buried the money and the papers, figuring he'd get back to them."

"Did he?"

Rafe shook his head. "I met up with Tench in '67, in New York, just by accident. He was there to attend some sort of convention. I was there with—well, never mind why I was there."

A woman, she thought, and was surprised by a surge of furious jealousy. She glared at him, a wasted effort since he still wasn't looking at her.

"Tench met another friend there, Billy Stone. The three of us went to a club, drank too much, talked over old times. Another man, by the name of Parker Winslow, joined us. He worked for the Commodore, Cornelius Vanderbilt, and Billy Stone seemed impressed by him, introduced him around, bought him drinks.

"We got drunk, got to talking about the war. Tench told them that I'd ridden with Mosby and they asked a lot of questions. I didn't tell them much; most people wouldn't believe how it was anyway. And Tench told them about what had happened with their part of the treasury, how he had buried his part of it with President Davis's personal papers and just never gotten back to it. He said he guessed it was about time to go back to Florida. Winslow asked how many people knew about the money and papers, and if anyone else knew where they were buried. Like I said, Tench was drunk; he threw his arm around my shoulders and said that his ol' friend McCay was the only other person on earth who knew where he'd buried his share of the treasury. I was drunk too, so it didn't make any difference to me if he thought he'd told me where the money was buried; I just went along with it.

"The next day, when he was sober, Tench got worried about maybe talking too much. A smart man doesn't let many people know he has money buried somewhere, and this Parker Winslow was a stranger. He felt uneasy about it for some reason. Since he'd already told the other two that I knew the location, he drew a map showing where the money and papers were buried and gave it to me. Three days later he was dead."

She had forgotten about the flare of jealousy. "Dead?" she echoed. "What happened to him?"

"I think it was poison," he said tiredly. "You're a doctor; what will kill a young healthy man within a matter of minutes?"

She thought about it. "Any number of poisons. Prussic acid can kill in as little as fifteen minutes. Arsenic, foxglove, wolfbane, nightshade; they can kill about that fast if enough is used. I've heard there's a poison in South American that kills immediately. But why do you think he was poisoned? People do get sick and die."

"I don't know that it was poison, I only think it was. He was already dead when I found him. I hadn't gone back to my hotel room the night before—"

"Why?" she interrupted, glaring at him again.

Something in her voice got through to him. He turned his head and saw her expression, and for a moment he looked both disconcerted and sheepish. He cleared his throat and said, "Never mind. I went to Tench's room and found him dead. Something didn't feel right, or maybe I was suspicious because he'd been so uneasy and then died like that. Anyway, I left his hotel room. Parker Winslow was in the lobby of the hotel when I went down; he lived in New York, so I knew he didn't have a room there. He saw me, but didn't speak. I went back to my own hotel and it looked like someone else had been there, but nothing had been taken."

"Then how do you know someone had been in your room?"

He shrugged. "Just a few little things that weren't exactly as I'd left them. I packed in a hurry, but before I could finish there were a couple of policemen beating on the door. I went out the window with what I had. The next morning I read in a newspaper that I was wanted for the *shooting* murder of Tench F. Tilghman. Tench hadn't been shot when I saw him."

"But why would anyone shoot a dead man?" Annie asked in bewilderment.

He glanced at her. His eyes were wintry. "If someone had had half of their head shot off, would you suspect they'd died of poison?"

Understanding dawned. "Poison does take a certain expertise. Not everyone knows what to use, or how much."

"Right. Like a doctor." He shrugged again. "I haven't had any medical training, so if it were known that Tench died of poisoning, then I wouldn't be the most logical suspect. I figure someone broke into my hotel room to kill me, too, but I wasn't there; then I saw Parker Winslow at the hotel, which means I could have implicated him, so Tench's death was rigged to look like a shooting death and I was charged with it. Since the attempt to kill me hadn't worked, a murder conviction would have me swinging. I'm not a likely poisoner, but I *am* damn handy with a gun. Of course, it doesn't make any difference to me if I'm wanted for murder by poisoning or murder by shooting; either one would have me hunted down."

"Why go to that much trouble for just two thousand dollars? I assume you think that was the reason why Tench was killed. As you said, it isn't a huge fortune, and it's buried somewhere in Florida. That isn't the same as robbing someone who has two thousand dollars in their possession."

"That's what I thought. So I went to Florida to see exactly what it was Tench had buried. The train stations were watched; I had to go by horse, but I had the advantage of knowing where I was going. They just knew the general area."

"It wasn't the money, was it?" she asked slowly. His pale, frosty eyes met hers, waiting. "It was the papers."

He nodded. He seemed very remote to her, his mind gone back four years in time. "It was the papers."

"You found where Tench had buried them?"

"Yes. Everything was wrapped in oilcloth."

She waited, not saying anything. Rafe was looking at the horizon again. "The government papers," he said deliberately, "were documentation of Commodore Vanderbilt's financial aid to the Confederacy."

Annie went cold. Those papers were documentation of nothing less than the treason of the wealthiest man, or at least one of the wealthiest men, in the nation.

"Railroads are the backbone of an army," Rafe was continuing, still in that calm, remote voice. "The longer the war lasted, the more profits the railroads made and the more important they were. Vanderbilt made a fortune during the war. President Davis's personal papers included a diary in which he speculated about Vanderbilt's motives and the results of prolonging a war that he already had accepted was *a losing effort*. Davis knew the war was lost but with Vanderbilt's money he was deliberately prolonging it anyway."

"Vanderbilt knew about the documentation," she whispered.

"Obviously. No government would destroy that kind of evidence when it could be used later, regardless of the outcome of the war. Certainly Vanderbilt never would have destroyed anything that gave him that much influence over anything."

"He must have thought it had disappeared during Mr. Davis's escape, or even that Mr. Davis himself had destroyed it."

"When President Davis was captured and imprisoned, he was . . ." Rafe paused, frowning as he searched for the correct description. ". . . subjected to torture, both mental and physical. Perhaps it was encouraged to find out if President Davis knew where those papers were. Perhaps not. If the president hadn't used them as a leverage to get himself out of prison, it was likely he didn't have them. Vanderbilt must have felt safe in assuming them lost forever."

"Until Tench mentioned the papers he had in the hearing of Mr. Winslow, who was an employee of Vanderbilt."

"And someone, obviously, who knew the importance of the papers."

"Someone who could have also participated in the treason, and been implicated."

"Yes."

She stared around them at the glorious spring day. The horses were contentedly cropping the tender new grass, and the world felt fresh. A sense of unreality jarred her. "What did you do with the papers?"

"I sent the silver to Tench's family, anonymously. The papers are in a bank vault in New Orleans."

She jumped to her feet. "Why haven't you used those papers to clear your name?" she yelled, suddenly furious. "Why haven't you turned them over to the government so Vanderbilt can be punished? My God, the lives he cost—"

"I know." He turned to face her. She fell silent at the bleakness of his face. "My brother died at Cold Harbor in June of '64. My father died in March of '65, defending Richmond."

There was no way to tell how long the war would have lasted without Vanderbilt's aid; perhaps the battles at Cold Harbor would still have been fought, but almost certainly it wouldn't have dragged on until April of '65, and his father would still be alive. It had cost him his family.

"All the more reason to make him pay," she finally said.

"I was killing mad at first; I couldn't think. They had picked up my trail in Florida and weren't far behind. I put the papers in the bank vault under a false name and ran. I've been running ever since."

"In God's name, *why?* Why haven't you used them to clear your name?"

"Because they wouldn't. I'm wanted for Tench's murder. I can't prove that Tench was killed because of the papers; I can't prove that I didn't do it."

"But Vanderbilt is obviously behind it. He's the one who had put such a large bounty on your head. At the very least you can use those papers to force him to cancel the bounty and . . . and maybe use his influence to have the murder charge dropped."

"Blackmail. I thought of it. I tried, a couple of times, but I needed help. I've been hunted without letup; I couldn't get back to New Orleans. The people I told," he said slowly, "were all killed."

"So you stopped trying." She stared at him with dry, burning eyes. Her chest was hurting. He had been forced to run like a wild animal for four years. What he was saying was that it wasn't only bounty hunters and lawmen after him; Vanderbilt must have a private army searching for him too, perhaps using the bounty hunters and following close behind to eliminate anyone who they thought Rafe might have talked to. It was hideous. She didn't know how he had survived. Yes, she did. Most men would have been caught and killed a long time ago, but Rafe wasn't most men. He had been one of Mosby's rangers, trained in stealth and evasion. He was tough and smart and cold-minded.

He gave evidence of that now when he turned and said emotionlessly, "We need to be moving."

The pace he set was as fast as he could maintain and still be reasonably careful about their tracks. He wanted to put more distance between them and Silver Mesa, where it was possible that anyone who happened to see them would recognize Annie. He could have traveled faster had he been alone; he had to carefully watch both Annie and her gelding, for neither of them was used to the long hours of travel. His bay was hard and muscled from years on the trail, but the gelding had had only occasional use, and it would take time to build up his stamina.

He wished he knew how close Atwater was, and if any other bounty hunters were in the area. He figured he could bet on the latter; Trahern was too well known for his presence to go unnoticed, and the other vultures would flock around him hoping to get the prey. It would be safer to avoid meeting anyone on the trail for several days, at least.

He tried to shake off his morose mood, but it had settled on his shoulders like a blanket. It had been years since he'd told anyone about Tench and the Confederate papers, years since he'd even let himself think about it that much. All of his attention had been on staying alive, not rehashing the events that had made him an outlaw. He was a little surprised by the intensity of the sense of betrayal he felt even now. He had met Jefferson Davis several times in Richmond and had been impressed, as was almost everyone who had ever met the man, by his almost otherworldly combination of intelligence and integrity. Rafe hadn't believed in slavery, his family hadn't owned any slaves, but he had firmly believed in the concept of states' rights over the authority of a central government and in the protection of his home, Virginia. Mr. Davis had made him feel as the American Revolutionists must have felt a century earlier, as if he were involved in a greater purpose, that of creating a new and sovereign nation. It had been a kick in the teeth to discover that Mr. Davis had given up the cause as lost and yet had still accepted money to keep the war going so a rich man could become even richer.

How many people had died during the last year of the war? Thousands, including the two who had meant the most to him, his father and his brother. It was more than betrayal, it was murder.

Annie's questions, as she tried to understand all the ramifications, had brought it all back to him. In the beginning he had compulsively reexamined every detail, every possibility, in an effort to find some way of stopping Vanderbilt. He hadn't been able to think of one.

Turning the papers over to the authorities would result in Vanderbilt's arrest—or maybe not; the man was enormously rich—but it wouldn't get the murder charges dropped. Rafe would have revenge, but he had to be alive to enjoy it. Revenge didn't do a dead man a whole hell of a lot of good.

Annie had thought of the blackmail gambit too. When he had first thought of it, four years ago, it had seemed simple: he had written a letter to Vanderbilt threatening to send the papers to the president unless the murder charges were dropped. The first problem was that he obviously hadn't been able to tell Vanderbilt how to get in touch with him. He would never have survived to hear Vanderbilt's reply. The second problem was that Vanderbilt seemed to have ignored the threat and continued with his all-out effort to have Rafe killed. It was difficult to blackmail someone who thought he could stop you without bowing to your demands.

That was when he had tried enlisting other people to help him implement the plan. After two of his old friends had been killed, he had given it up. It was obvious Vanderbilt would stop at nothing. But now things had changed; he had Annie to think of. If it would allow them to live in peace, he was willing to try again, if only they could find someone they could trust and who had the means of implementing the threat. It had to be someone whose murder couldn't easily be passed off, someone with authority. The trouble was that not many outlaws knew people like that.

He glanced at Annie, her posture determinedly erect despite her obvious fatigue. He realized that he was thinking in terms of *us* now rather than *him*. All of his decisions affected her now.

Right before sunset he signaled a stop and made a

small smokeless fire; after they had eaten, he put out the fire and destroyed all sign of it, then they rode another couple of miles in the rapidly deepening twilight to make camp for the night. He estimated they were still too close to Silver Mesa to relax, so they crawled between the blankets completely dressed. He didn't even remove his boots, nor Annie her shoes. He sighed, remembering the nights in the cabin when they had slept naked.

She turned into his arms, winding her own arms around his muscled neck. "Where in Mexico are we going?" she asked sleepily.

He'd been thinking about that too, and it was a difficult question. "Maybe Juarez," he said. Getting there would be the problem. They would have to go through desert and Apaches to get there. On the other hand, it would make anyone on their trail think twice about following them.

CHAPTER

13

"Why haven't you just changed your name and disappeared?" she asked one day about a week after they had left the cabin. She thought it had been a week, but she wasn't certain. Out here, surrounded by nothing but the sheer majesty of the land, she had lost track of such mundane, human things as names on a calendar.

"I've changed my name several times," he replied. "And grown a beard."

"Then how would anyone know you?"

He shrugged. "I rode with Mosby. There were a lot of photographs taken of the ranger companies, so anyone with money would have been able to come up with some of those and find out what I look like. In some of them I had a beard, because it isn't always convenient to shave. For whatever reason, I seem to be easily recognized."

His eyes, she thought. No one, having once seen those pale, crystalline eyes, would ever forget them. Changing his name and growing a beard wouldn't change his eyes.

He had shot a small deer and they had spent two

days at the same camp while he smoked the tender meat. Annie was grateful for the respite; though she knew he had set the pace as slow as he had dared, she had been in agony for the first few days. The soreness in her muscles had eased as she became accustomed to the long hours in the saddle, but spending two entire days without having to even get on a horse had been pure luxury.

Their camp was under an overhang of rock, about ten feet deep and just high enough at the opening for him to stand erect. The farther south they had gone the more sparse the vegetation had become, but there was still some timber to provide cover, and grass for the horses. A jumble of boulders at the mouth of the overhang kept their fire from being visible, and there was a small stream nearby. Lying in Rafe's arms with the semblance of a roof overhead, she felt almost as secure as she had in the cabin.

He had been considerate of her while she had been so sore, holding her at night without even mentioning making love, but during the two days they had spent in camp he had seemed to be making up for his temporary celibacy. As she cooked their supper over the small fire she watched him curing the deer hide. His dark hair had grown so long it curled down over his shirt collar, and he was so darkly tanned that she thought he could pass as one of the Apaches he had been telling her about. She loved him. It seemed to grow more powerful every day, crowding out everything else until it was difficult to remember how her life in Silver Mesa had been.

The bonds of the flesh. She had known from the beginning that if she allowed him to make love to her he would possess a part of her that she would never be able to reclaim, but not even instinct had prepared her for the strength of the ties. And perhaps his lovemaking had resulted in even more.

She stared pensively into the fire. Since she didn't know the exact day of the month she wasn't certain if her menstrual courses should have begun, but certainly it was almost time. It had been perhaps three weeks since Rafe had taken her from Silver Mesa, and her last course had ended a few days before that. She was fairly regular in her cycle, but not so regular that she could know to the day when it should begin.

She wasn't certain how she would feel if she were indeed pregnant. Was it possible to be both terrified and happy at the same time? The thought of having his baby made her dizzy with delight, but a pregnant woman would slow him down. He would have to leave her somewhere when she became unable to travel, and she couldn't bear the thought of that. Desperately she hoped that her body hadn't proven immediately fertile.

She had taken a human life. It would be ironic justice if the bearing of another human life resulted in the loss of the man she loved. Sermons from her childhood boomed through her head, dire threats of divine retribution and the scales of fate.

Rafe looked up from the hide he was working and saw the desolation in her dark eyes as she stared blindly at the fire. He had hoped she would be able to forget the shock of Trahern's death, but she hadn't, not completely. For the most part, during the day while she was busy, she could put it out of her mind, but when it grew quiet he could see the sadness growing in her.

After the first time, during the war, he had always been able to accept the deaths he had caused. Reduced to the simplest terms, it had been his life or theirs, and that was still how he looked at it. He was a warrior. Annie wasn't. The tenderness of her emotions, that deep wellspring of compassion, was part of what drew him to her. With bemused disbelief he remembered that when he had first seen her he had thought her to be thin, tired, and rather plain. He didn't know how he could have been so blind, because when he looked at her now he saw a kind of beauty that took his breath. She was softness, and warmth, and an all-encompassing caring that wrapped around him with the tenderest of bonds. He saw intelligence and honor, and God, yes, a physical beauty that gave him an erection just from looking at her. Removing her clothes was like unwrapping a treasure that had been concealed under the drabbest of covers.

She would never be able to calmly dismiss the loss of human life. And he would never be able to watch her suffer without feeling the need to comfort. He just wasn't certain he knew how.

"You saved my life," he said into the silence. She looked up, a little startled, and he realized he hadn't put it into words before.

"Actually, you've saved me twice. Once with your doctoring and then again from Trahern. He wasn't going to even try to take me back alive." He went back to working the deer hide. "Trahern once went after a seventeen-year-old kid who had a dead-or-alive bounty on him. The kid had killed the son of some rich man in San Francisco. When Trahern caught up with him, the kid was on his knees in the dirt begging Trahern not to kill him. He was crying, his nose running. He swore he wouldn't try to escape, that he'd go back peacefully. Guess he'd heard Trahern's reputation. It didn't do him any good. Trahern shot him between the eyes."

She heard his unspoken message, that Trahern wasn't any great loss to the human race. She also saw something else, something she had been too preoccupied before to notice. "I don't regret killing *Trahern,*" she said with slow deliberation, making him look at her. "I regret that it was necessary to kill anyone. But even if it had been that marshal, Atwater, I would have done the same thing." *I chose you,* she silently told him.

After a moment he gave a brief nod and returned his attention to working the hide.

Annie stirred their supper. Rafe's story had helped

dispel her melancholy, though she knew part of her would never be the same. It couldn't be.

Night fell in a silent explosion of color, the sky overhead changing from pink to gold to red to purple in a matter of minutes, then fading away and leaving only a hush behind, as if the world had caught its breath at the spectacle. Only the faintest remnant of light lingered in the sky when he took her to their blankets.

"Hello the camp! We're friendly an' sure would appreciate a cup of coffee if you got any to spare. We ran out a couple days ago. All right if we come in?"

They had just finished breakfast. Rafe was on his feet with his rifle in his hand before the first word had finished sounding. He motioned for Annie to stay where she was. The shout had come from a stand of piñon pine about a hundred and fifty yards away, far enough that the horses, grazing off to the left in a pocket that wasn't visible from the trees, hadn't warned him of anyone's approach. He could see two men on horseback in the shadows under the pines. He looked at the fire. Only a thin haze was floating upward; someone either had to have damn sharp eyes to have spotted it, or they had to be deliberately looking. He suspected it was the latter.

"We're out of coffee ourselves," he shouted in reply. When no invitation to approach the camp was issued, anyone without an ulterior motive would ride on.

"We'd be glad to share a meal with you, if you're low on food," came the answering shout. "No coffee, of course, but we'd be right glad of the company."

Rafe glanced at the horses, but discarded the idea of running for it. Their situation was pretty good; they had food and water, and were protected on three sides. And the country, though mountainous, was too open, without the thick forest that would have enabled them to slip away. "You'd best ride on," he replied, knowing they wouldn't.

"That's not a very friendly attitude, mister."

He didn't answer again. It would be a distraction, and he wanted all of his attention on the two men. They had separated, to keep from presenting a single target. They definitely didn't have a neighborly visit in mind.

The first shot struck sparks about two feet over his head. Behind him he heard Annie gasp. "Bounty hunters," he said.

"How many?"

He didn't look at her, but she had sounded calm. "Two." If there had been a third one working his way closer, the horses would have heard that. "We'll be all right. Just stay down."

He didn't return fire. He didn't believe in wasting ammunition, and he didn't have a clear shot at either one of them.

Annie withdrew to the deepest corner of the overhang. Her heart pounded, making her feel nauseated, but she forced herself to sit quietly. She could help Rafe best by staying out of his way. For the first time she regretted her lack of expertise with a firearm. Out here, it seemed, ineptitude could be suicidal.

Another shot, this one ricocheting off the rocks that guarded the mouth of the overhang. Rafe didn't even flinch. He was well protected and he knew it.

He waited. Most men got impatient, or they got too self-confident. Sooner or later they would expose themselves to fire. He settled in with deadly patience.

The minutes ticked past. Occasionally one or the other of the two men would fire a shot as if they weren't certain of Rafe's position and were trying to draw him out. Unluckily for them, he had long ago learned the difference between acting and merely reacting; he would fire only when he felt he had a good shot.

It was over half an hour before the man on the left shifted position. Maybe he was just making himself comfortable, but for a couple of seconds his entire upper body was exposed. Rafe gently squeezed the trigger and made the bounty hunter comfortable permanently.

He was moving before the sound of the shot had died away, slipping past the rocks and away from the overhang with a low-voiced command to Annie not to move a muscle. The other bounty hunter might try to wait him out and collect all of the ten thousand for himself, but it was possible he'd just leave his partner's body behind and ride for reinforcements. Rafe's mind was cold and clear; he couldn't let the other bounty hunter ride away.

There was too much open ground between him and the remaining hunter, preventing him from getting to the trees just as it had prevented them from getting to the overhang. They hadn't chosen their place of attack well. Rafe studied it with a strategist's eye and decided they were fools. A smarter move would have been to hang back until the lay of the land let them get closer, or try to swing around and set up an ambush. Well, now one of them was a dead fool and the other one would be shortly.

More shots were fired from the trees, evidently in a burst of rage that wasted ammunition and didn't accomplish a thing. Rafe glanced back at the overhang. The only thing Annie was in danger from was a freak ricochet, and the way she had squeezed back into that low corner made it unlikely. If only she stayed there; he'd told her not to move and he'd meant it literally, but it would be nerve-racking for her to sit there without being able to see or knowing what was going on.

Cautiously he worked his way around to a better angle, since he couldn't do much about the distance. He couldn't see the other bounty hunter, but there were still two horses back among the trees.

Then he caught a bit of movement and saw a flash of blue, probably a sleeve. Rafe concentrated on the spot, letting his gaze go unfocused so he could pick up even the slightest movement. Yeah, there he was, fidgeting behind that tree. He didn't have a clear shot at him, though.

The morning sun was heating up fast, shining down on his bare head. He wished he'd gotten his hat, then shrugged. It was probably just as well. It would only have given him a bigger silhouette.

He found a good place to set up, in a split boulder with a small juniper growing out of the split. It made a fine rest for the rifle. He eased into position and set his sights on the tree where the bounty hunter was trying to make up his mind what to do. He hoped it didn't take long.

The bounty hunter fired a few more shots in a futile effort at provoking a response. The best shot Rafe had was at an arm, so he waited. If he just winged the man and he was able to ride off, they'd be in a lot of trouble. An entire army of bounty hunters would converge on the area.

Suddenly the bounty hunter seemed to lose his nerve and started edging backwards, toward the horses. Rafe lined up the sights and tracked his movement with the barrel. "Come on, you son of a bitch," he muttered. "Give me a target for just two seconds. Two seconds, that's all I need."

He actually needed less. The man moved into view, carefully keeping the trees between him and the overhang, but Rafe wasn't at the overhang. It wasn't a clean shot, just his shoulder and part of his chest, but it was enough. Rafe squeezed the trigger and the bullet knocked the man off his feet.

Screams of pain came from the trees, evidence that the shot hadn't been a killing one. "Annie!" Rafe roared.

"I'm here."

He heard the fear in her voice. "It's okay. I got both of them. Just stay there, I'll be back in a few minutes."

Then he began working his way toward the trees,

not taking it for granted that the man he'd wounded wasn't able to shoot. A lot of men had gotten killed by incautiously approaching a "dead" man or one hurt so bad he was supposedly unable to shoot. Even men who were literally drawing their last breaths were able to shoot.

He could hear the groans of the wounded man as he slipped into the trees. The man was sitting propped against a tree, his rifle on the ground a few feet away. Keeping both his attention and his rifle aimed at the man, Rafe kicked the weapon away, then relieved him of his pistol.

"You should have ridden on," he said evenly.

The bounty hunter glared up at him with pain- and hate-filled eyes. "You son of a bitch, you done killed Orvel."

"You and Orvel fired the first shot. I just fired the last one." Rafe rolled Orvel over with the toe of his boot. Heart-shot. He collected Orvel's weapons.

"We didn't mean you no harm, just thought we'd set a spell. Gets lonesome out here."

"Yeah. You were so hungry for company, you lost your head and started shooting." Rafe didn't believe his show of innocence. The man was filthy and unshaven and smelled to high heaven. Pure, stupid meanness glared out of his eyes.

"That's right. We just wanted some comp'ny."

"How did you know we were up there?" The more he thought about it, the less likely it was they had seen any smoke. Nor did he think this pair had picked up their trail; for one thing, they had already been camped under the overhang for two days, and for another, this pair didn't seem smart enough to follow a trail as elusive as the one he'd been leaving.

"We were just passin' by, seen your smoke."

"Why didn't you ride on when you had the chance?" Rafe regarded him dispassionately. Blood was spreading down the man's chest but he didn't think it was a mortal wound. From the looks of it, the bullet had shattered his collarbone. Rafe wondered what he was going to do with him.

"You didn't have no call tellin' us to ride on, instead of askin' us into camp. Orvel said you just wanted to keep the woman to yourself—" He broke off, wondering if he'd said too much.

Rafe's eyes narrowed with cold rage. No, they hadn't seen any smoke. They had seen Annie when she had gone for water. These two pieces of shit hadn't had bounty on their minds, but rape.

He now had a dilemma on his hands. If he were smart, he'd put a bullet in this bastard's head and rid the world of some trash. On the other hand, killing him now would be cold-blooded murder, and Rafe wasn't willing to sink down to their level.

"Tell you what I'm going to do," he said, walking toward the horses and gathering their reins. "I'm going to give you some time to think about the error of your ways. A lot of time."

"Where you going with them horses? That's stealing!"

"I'm not taking the horses, I'm turning them loose."

Despite his pain, the man's dirty jaw sagged. "You can't do that!"

"The hell I can't."

"How'm I supposed to get to a doctor without a horse? You done busted up my shoulder."

"I don't care if you get to a doctor or not. If I'd had a better shot, you wouldn't have to worry about your shoulder."

"Damn, man, you can't just leave me out here like this."

Rafe turned his cold, pale eyes on the man and didn't say anything. He started to lead the horses off.

"Hey, wait a minute." The man was staring hard at him. "I know who you are. I'll be damned. I'll just be goddamned. This close to you and we didn't even know—ten thousand dollars!"

"Which you won't be collecting."

The man grinned at him. "I'll dance a jig and buy a drink for whoever does collect it, you bastard."

Rafe shrugged and led the horses past the man, who was struggling to get to his knees. Without the horses, without a weapon, it was unlikely he'd make it to any sort of town. Even if he did it would take him days, perhaps weeks. By then, Rafe figured, he and Annie would be far away. He didn't like the possibility of anyone knowing he was traveling with a woman now, but it was a chance he had to take. At least the bounty hunter hadn't been able to see Annie well enough to be able to give a description of her.

It was the sudden motion, the faint scrabbling noise, that alerted him. He dropped the reins and spun, automatically going down on one knee even as he reached for his pistol. The bounty hunter must have had a spare pistol tucked in his belt against his back; the shot went high, where Rafe had been only a split second before, merely burning a graze on top of his shoulder. Rafe's shot wasn't high.

The bounty hunter collapsed back against the tree, his mouth and eyes opening in an expression of stupid astonishment. The light died out of his eyes and he fell sideways, burying his face in the dirt.

Rafe got to his feet and calmed the skittish horses. He stared at the dead bounty hunter and was suddenly weary. Damn, would it never end?

He examined the dead men's weapons, which were dirty and in bad shape. He discarded them but took the ammunition. He searched the saddlebags for supplies and found coffee. The lying bastards. He unsaddled the horses and slapped them on the rump, sending them flying. They weren't exactly prime examples of horseflesh, but they couldn't do worse with freedom than they had at the hands of these two. Then he took what supplies he and Annie could use and walked back up to the overhang.

She was still sitting in the corner, hugging her knees.

Her face was pale and strained. She didn't move even when Rafe walked under the sheltering ledge and dropped the bag of supplies, but her big eyes asked questions.

He squatted down in front of her and took her hands, sharply examining her to make certain no flying splinters of rock had hit her. "Are you all right?"

She swallowed. "Yes, but you aren't."

He stared at her. "Why?"

"Your shoulder."

Her words made him aware of the stinging on his left shoulder. He barely glanced at it. "It's nothing, just a graze."

"It's bleeding."

"Not much."

Moving slowly, stiffly, she crawled out of the corner and went over to her medical bag. "Take off your shirt."

He obeyed, though the wound truly was only a burn and was merely seeping a little watery blood. He watched Annie closely. She hadn't asked about the two bounty hunters.

"One of them was already dead," he said. "The other was just wounded. He drew a second pistol from his belt when I was leading the horses away. I killed him too."

She knelt on the ground and carefully washed the graze with witch hazel, making him flinch from the stinging. Her hands were shaking, but she drew a deep breath and forced herself to steady. "I was just so frightened you'd be hurt," she said.

"I'm fine."

"There's always the chance that you won't be." With a tiny separate part of her brain she wondered why a man who hadn't twitched a muscle when she had treated wounds far worse than this would make such a face at a little stinging. She smeared some of the slippery-elm ointment on the oozing wound and lightly bandaged it. As he had said, it wasn't serious.

Rafe wondered if he should tell her that, though the two had been bounty hunters, it hadn't been bounty on their minds. He decided not to. Instead he waited until she had finished and then drew her up into his arms, kissing her hard and holding her against him, absorbing her special warmth into his bones to chase away the chill of death.

"It's time to leave," he said.

"Yes, I know." She sighed. She had enjoyed the rest, but he had planned for them to move on that day anyway. She just wished they had been able to slip away without seeing anyone.

How had he kept his sanity these past four years, continually hunted like a wild animal and unable to trust anyone he met? He'd had to be on constant guard.

"I'm a burden to you, aren't I?" she asked, keeping her face buried against his chest so she wouldn't have to see the truth in his eyes. "You could move faster without me, and anytime there's trouble you'll have to watch out for me."

"I could travel faster," he said truthfully, and stroked her hair. "On the other hand, no one is looking for a man and a woman traveling together, so it evens out. But you aren't a burden, honey, and I'd rather have you close to hand so I *can* look out for you. It'd worry the hell out of me if I didn't know what you were doing and if you were all right."

She lifted her head and managed a smile. "Are you trying to sweet-talk me with that southern charm?"

"I don't know, am I?"

"I think so."

"Then you're probably right. So you think I'm charming?"

"You have your moments," she allowed. "They don't come real close together."

He leaned his forehead against hers and chuckled, and with a start she realized it was the first time she had ever heard him laugh, even that small sound. God knew there hadn't been a lot in his life that he could laugh about.

He released her after a moment, his mind already on breaking camp. "We're going to cut more toward the east now," he said. "Straight into Apache country. Maybe it'll make anyone else who cuts our trail think twice about following us."

CHAPTER

14

The land opened up even more, with wider expanses of plains broken by raw, jagged mountains. Varied cactus plants began to appear among the thinning grasses. The huge bowl of sky overhead was so impossibly blue that sometimes she felt lost in it, reduced to total insignificance. She didn't mind. In a way, it was even comforting.

She had spent all of her life in various cities and towns, surrounded by people. Even Silver Mesa, crude as it was, teemed with humanity. Until Rafe had taken her up into the mountains she had never known true solitude, but a part of her, some distant primitive instinct, seemed to recognize it and embrace it like an old friend. The myriad rules of life that had always surrounded her, and which she had followed without question, had no place out here. No one would say anything if she elected not to wear a petticoat, or think her rude if she didn't make small talk. Actually, Rafe was likely to give her unabashed male approval for leaving off her petticoat. The freedom of it sank slowly into her mind, and then into her pores. She felt as unfettered as a child.

The third day after they had left the overhang camp brought evidence that she wasn't pregnant. She had thought she would be relieved, and was startled by a fleeting sense of regret. Evidently the desire to bear his child was another primitive instinct that exerted itself regardless of circumstance and logic.

Her entire life had changed within the space of a few short weeks, and despite the danger dogging their trail she felt wonderful, reborn. If it hadn't been for the threat to Rafe she would have been content with life as it was, just the two of them, alone under a sky so impressive she could understand why simple people had prayed to the sun as a god, why one always had an impression of heaven as being upward, somewhere in that great blue bowl.

There was still a lingering pain at having been forced to kill, but Rafe's tale of the kind of man Trahern had been had helped her. She could put it aside, and focus outward as warriors had always done. She couldn't see herself as a warrior, but the situations were roughly the same and so she did as warriors do: she moved on, mentally and emotionally.

"I like it out here," she told Rafe late one afternoon when the purple twilight began creeping down the mountain slopes toward them. For the moment they were still wrapped in golden sunlight, but the advancing shadows whispered that night would soon arrive.

He smiled a little as he studied her. She no longer seemed to bother much with hairpins; her long, streaked blond hair was plaited into a single loose braid that hung down her back. The spring sun had bleached out the strands around her face so that they looked like a halo. He had trouble making her wear her hat; she would put it on during the middle of the day, but in the morning or afternoon she was just as likely to be bareheaded as not whenever he looked at her. She hadn't tanned much, though, and he suspected she never would. The only difference was a slightly warmer hue to her fine-grained skin. And petticoats seemed to be a thing of the past for her; she had opted for coolness and more freedom of movement. The long sleeves of her blouse were habitually rolled up, except when he made her roll them down for protection from the sun, and the top two buttons at her throat were never fastened.

There was still that feminine fastidiousness about her that made her always look neat and fresh, but she was infinitely more relaxed, and even seemed happy. He wondered about that, because he had thought the loss of her medical practice would constantly chafe at her. But all of this was still new; the fascination of it would wear off, and that was when she would miss the career for which she had trained her entire life.

"What do you like most about it?" he asked lazily.

"The freedom." She smiled at him.

"We're on the run. Does that feel free to you?"

"All of this feels free to me." She waved her hand at the enormous landscape surrounding them. "Everything is bigger than life. And there are no rules; we can do whatever we want."

"There are always rules. It's just that they're a different set of rules. Back in Philadelphia you couldn't go without your petticoat; here, you don't go without your weapons."

"In Philadelphia, I would have to bathe behind a locked door." She pointed to where the small stream they had camped beside widened into a pool just big enough for bathing. "Here, there are no doors to lock."

The expression in his pale eyes changed at the mention of bathing. The past several days, since her menses had started, had been increasingly frustrating. If she stripped off naked, as he suspected she intended, he would be reduced to beating his head against a rock somewhere to take his mind off his clamoring needs. A man on the trail got used to long periods without a woman, but damn if having one wasn't the easiest thing in the world to get accustomed to again. The tyrant in his pants had come to expect frequent loving attention, and had been making Rafe miserable.

She smiled at him, slowly and sweetly. "Why don't you take a bath with me." It wasn't a question. She began unbuttoning her blouse as she walked down to the curve in the stream where it deepened and widened.

Rafe found himself on his feet, his heart beating hard. "Are you all right now?" he asked in a hoarse voice. "Because if you take off your clothes in front of me I'm going to be inside you, honey, whether you are or not."

She smiled over her shoulder. Her dark eyes looked soft and sleepy. The seductiveness of it slammed into his gut. Damn, how had a woman who had been so innocent such a short time ago learned how to do that?

"I'm fine," she said.

The answer, of course, was that he had made damn certain she lost that innocence. He had made love to her so many times and so many ways over the past weeks that sometimes he had felt drugged with sex. And women were natural seductresses, even when they didn't know what they were doing. Just being female made them seductive, nature's lodestone that drew men like flies to honey.

Not even his surging lust could make him forget the need for caution. He doused the fire so it couldn't be spotted in the deepening shadows, even though he hadn't seen any signs of their being followed, and carried both rifle and pistol with him down to the stream, where he placed them within easy reach. He didn't take his eyes off Annie as he began stripping.

She had removed her blouse, then paused to work her hair free from the braid. Her raised arms lifted and exposed her breasts, barely covered as they were by the thin shift. Her nipples, already erect, pressed against the cloth. Rafe felt dizzy from the rush of blood through his body.

He forced himself to look away, and inhaled deeply to steady himself. He took a slow, careful look around to make certain no danger was threatening, and returned to the task of undressing just as Annie was wading naked into the pool, carrying her clothes. Her round, dimpled buttocks made him dizzy all over again.

The little pool at its deepest was only knee high, and it felt freezing after the spring heat of the sun. Annie bit back a squeal and with her foot found a smooth area in which to sit. She caught her breath and did so. It was a good thing she had taken a deep breath, because the coldness of the water temporarily deprived her of the ability.

Cold or not, she couldn't pass up the opportunity to bathe and wash her clothes. She lathered up the bar of soap in her hand and began the laundry.

She looked up as Rafe waded into the pool. He didn't seem to even notice the temperature of the water. His eyes were intent, and he was fully aroused. Annie's breath caught again at the power of his muscled body. She began to have doubts about finishing the chore first.

"Bring your clothes," she said. "They need washing."

"Later." His voice was guttural.

"Clothes first."

"Why?" He sat down in the water and reached for her. Then suddenly the temperature of the water got through to him and his eyes widened as he said, *"Shit!"* explosively.

She tried to control her shivers by scrubbing harder. "It'll probably take that long to get used to the water, for one thing. For another, if I don't wash the clothes first, they won't get done. Do you honestly expect me to have the energy to wash clothes *afterward?"*

"I don't think I can get that used to the water," he muttered. "Hell, we might as well do laundry."

She hid her smile as he stood up and reached for his clothes, dragging them into the water. He was shivering, too. He was scowling as he took the soap and began scrubbing his own garments.

After a few minutes, though, the water didn't seem as cold, and the warmth of the setting sun on her bare shoulders was a delicious contrast. As she finished rinsing each garment she wrung it out and tossed it onto a bush growing alongside the stream. Rafe did the same, and soon the bush was almost flattened beneath the weight of wet clothing. She began soaping herself, and the friction of her hands sliding over her skin added to the warmth.

She wasn't surprised when Rafe's hands joined hers, or at the places he elected to wash. She turned into his arms and his mouth came down hard on hers. The familiar taste of him was like heaven. The restrictions of the past few days had been frustrating for her, too. Without preliminaries he pulled her astride his thighs and onto his thrusting erection.

It had been only a few days, but she was shocked anew at the almost unbearable fullness. How had she forgotten? She couldn't move; she felt as if he stretched her to the limit, that any motion would result in pain. But his hands were on her buttocks, moving her, and there was no pain, only the overwhelming sense of being penetrated and filled. She collapsed weakly against him, her face buried in the warm flesh of his throat.

"I thought the water was too cold," she managed to murmur.

His reply was deep and rough. "What water?"

Afterward she walked on trembling legs back to the camp, shivering again as the cooling air washed over her wet flesh. She wished she had thought to carry a blanket to the stream so she wouldn't have had to make the short trip while naked. She dried off and hurried into clean clothing.

It was later than when Rafe normally insisted they move camp after having eaten, but she didn't suggest remaining where they were. He'd taught her the value of always being cautious. Without protest she began gathering up their wet clothing and various other articles while he resaddled the horses. Twilight was rapidly fading into true darkness as he led them to a secure place to bed down for the night.

Before she got between the blankets that night, she reached under her skirt and untied her drawers, then stepped daintily out of them. Rafe joined her under the blankets and twice during the night demonstrated his appreciation of the convenience.

He had hoped, since there were only two of them, that they would be able to slip through the Apache lands without seeing or being seen by anyone. It would have been much more difficult for a larger party to travel undetected, but entirely possible for one or two people to do so. It required caution, but Rafe was a cautious man.

The Apache were nomads, wandering wherever the food supply led them. The bands were never large, seldom over two hundred people, since that many would have made fast movement impossible. But the Apache didn't have to be a large band to be dangerous to white people. Cochise, chief of the Chiricahua, had been fighting for his land against the white man for as long as Rafe could remember hearing about it. Before Cochise, it had been Mangas Coloradas, his father-in-law. Geronimo led his own band. Anyone with a brain in their heads would go out of their way to avoid the Apache.

With that in mind, he had developed the habit of going ahead to check out the water sources before he allowed Annie anywhere near. The roaming bands of

Apache also had to have water, so the most logical place for them to set up their temporary camps was near a stream. The next day, he was glad of his caution when, lying flat on his belly just at the rise of a hill, he eased his head around a rock just enough to see and found himself looking down at an Apache camp. For a moment sheer terror held him paralyzed, for it was almost impossible for a man to get this close, and slip away again, without being detected. The dogs would bark, the horses would shy, the ever-alert warriors would see him. He began swearing silently as he eased back behind the rock.

There were no shouts of alarm, though, and he forced himself to lie completely still until the tremors in his legs had calmed. If he managed to get back to Annie, he'd take her and ride as hard and fast in the opposite direction as the horses would go. If he got back to Annie . . . God, what would happen to her if he were captured? She was alone out there, well hidden and protected for the moment, but she would never be able to find her way back to civilization.

The camp was one of the smaller ones. He tried to fix in his mind how many wickiups there had been, but panic had blotted out everything but the overall impression. And come to think of it, there hadn't been many people around; did that mean that the warriors were out hunting, or perhaps on a war party?

Taking even more care this time, he took another look. He counted nineteen wickiups, a small band even if he figured five people for each dwelling. There was almost no activity, in itself unusual because the women always had work to do even if the warriors were gone. There should be children playing, but he saw only two small boys and they seemed to be doing nothing more than quietly sitting. Behind the camp, in a bend where the grasses grew sweeter, were the band's horses. Rafe estimated the number of the remuda and a frown drew his brows together. Unless this band was unusually rich in horses, the warriors were in camp. It didn't make sense.

An old woman, bent and gray, hobbled to a wickiup carrying a wooden bowl. Now Rafe noticed a black spot where a wickiup had been burned. There had been a death in the camp. Then he saw another black spot. And another one.

There were likely to be more. There was sickness in that camp.

He felt a cold knot in the pit of his stomach as he thought of the possible diseases. Smallpox was what came to mind first, for it had decimated every Indian band it had touched. Plague, cholera . . . it could be anything.

He bellied down from the rise and carefully worked his way back to where he had left his horse. He and Annie would give the camp a wide berth.

She was waiting exactly where he had left her, concealed from the sun by rocks and trees. She was half-dozing in the noon heat, languidly fanning herself with her hat, but she sat up as he approached.

"There's a band of Apache about five miles east. We'll head due south for about ten, fifteen miles, then cut east."

"Apache." Her cheeks paled a little. Like everyone out West, she had heard tales of how the Apache tortured their captives.

"Don't worry," he said, wanting to reassure her. "I saw their camp. I think most of them are sick with something. There were only a couple of kids and one old woman moving around, and there were several burned wickiups. That's what the Apache do when there's been a death; everyone else in the family moves out of the wickiup and they burn it to the ground."

"Sickness?" Annie felt herself go even whiter as she felt a horrible decision yawning at her feet like an abyss. She was a physician. The oath she had taken hadn't made any distinction between white, black, yellow, or red. Her duty was to help the sick and injured in any way she could, but she had never imagined that that duty would take her into an Apache camp knowing that she might never leave it.

"Forget it," Rafe said sharply as he read her mind. "You're not going in there. There's nothing you can do anyway; disease seems to go through Indians like a hot knife through butter. And you don't know what it is. What if it's cholera, or the plague?"

"What if it isn't?"

"Then it's most likely smallpox."

She gave him a wry little smile. "I'm the daughter of a physician, remember; I've been vaccinated against smallpox. My father was a firm believer in Dr. Jenner's methods."

Rafe didn't know if he trusted Dr. Jenner's vaccination theories, especially where Annie's life was concerned. "We aren't going in there, Annie."

"We weren't going anyway. I don't see any need for you to be exposed to whatever illness it is."

"No," he said firmly. "It's too dangerous."

"I'm a doctor. Do you think I haven't done this before?"

"Not with Apache, you haven't."

"True, but they're sick. You said so yourself. And there are children in that camp, children who might die if I don't do what I can."

"If it's cholera or plague, there isn't anything to be done."

"But it might not be that. And I'm very healthy; I never get sick. I haven't even had a cold since . . . why, I don't remember the last time."

"I'm not talking about a cold, damn it." He caught her chin and turned her face up to his. "This is serious. I won't let you risk your life."

His eyes had gone so cold that she almost shivered, but she couldn't back down. "I have to," she replied softly. "I can't pick and choose those I'll aid; that would make a mockery of my training, my oath. I'm either a doctor or I'm . . . nothing."

His mental rejection of her intention was so violent that he had to clench his fists to keep from grabbing her. By God, he wouldn't let her enter that camp if he had to tie her on that horse and not let her loose until they reached Juarez.

"I have to go," she repeated. Her dark eyes were bottomless, drawing him down into her soul.

He didn't know how it happened. Knowing that it was stupid, knowing that he shouldn't let her get within a mile of that camp, he gave in.

"Then we'll both go."

She touched his face. "There's no need."

"I'll decide what the need is. If you ride into that camp, I'll be riding right beside you. The only way to keep me out is if you stay out too."

"But what if it *is* smallpox?"

"I had it when I was five; a very mild case. No scars. I'm a lot safer from it than you are with your pin scratches."

Knowing that he had had smallpox was a relief, if he insisted in going into the camp with her as she knew he would. "You can stay back while I go in and see what it is."

He shook his head. "You aren't riding in alone."

They stared at each other, equally stubborn. Because he had given in on the first issue, Annie gave in on the second.

The dogs did come running, barking furiously, when they rode into the camp. The two little boys looked terrified and ran. The old woman Rafe had seen earlier came out of a wickiup, a different one from the one he had seen her enter before, and she too ran as fast as she could.

No one else came out of the wickiups.

Annie was terrified of what they would find when they entered the dwellings. Visions of bloated bodies lying in black vomit floated in her mind, and she knew that sometimes it wasn't a good thing to know so much, for her imagination could conjure up all the hideous symptoms.

The first wickiup they came to was as good a place as any to start. Rafe reined in and she followed suit, sliding out of the saddle. She started for the flap of hide that covered the entrance and he reached out, halting her with a firm grip. He tucked her behind him, then opened the flap himself and looked inside. Two people lay on the blankets. They were covered with spots.

"It looks like smallpox," he reported grimly. If it was, they were wasting their time and Annie was wasting her energy. Unlike the white man, who had built up a certain resistance to the disease after thousands of years of exposure, the Indian hadn't come into contact with it until the white man brought it, and he had no resistance at all.

Annie ducked under his arm and into the wickiup before he could grab her. She knelt beside one of the still figures, a woman, and carefully examined the spots that dotted her skin. She sniffed the air. "It isn't smallpox," she said absently. Smallpox had a distinctive odor that was missing.

"Then what is it?"

The spots on the woman's skin had turned black, indicating hemorrhaging. Annie put her hand to the woman's forehead and felt the fever burning there. Black eyes slowly opened and stared at her, but they were dull and uncomprehending.

"Black measles," she said. "They have measles."

It wasn't as deadly as smallpox, but it was serious enough. The complications from measles killed a lot of people. She wheeled on Rafe. "Have you had measles too?"

"Yeah. Have you?"

"Yes, I'll be fine." She stepped out of that wickiup and began going from one to another, lifting the flaps and looking inside all of them. There were two, three, four people inside each of them, most of them in various stages of the disease. The old woman they had seen earlier cowered in one. A few people were tending the sick, but with a hopelessness that prevented them from even showing alarm at the sudden appearance of two of the white devils, or perhaps those still on their feet were in the first stages and felt ill too. The two little boys they had seen seemed to be all right, and there were two toddlers and a baby who didn't have the telltale spots. The baby was wailing, an unusual thing in an Apache camp. She stepped inside and lifted the infant, who immediately stopped squalling and stared up at her with innocent, solemn eyes. The baby's mother was so listless with fever that she could barely lift her eyelids.

"I'll need my bag," Annie said briskly, her mind already on the monumental job ahead of her even as she rocked the baby in her arms.

CHAPTER

15

"*T*here's nothing you can do," Rafe said with slow menace. "It's measles. It's the same as smallpox: they'll either die or they won't."

"I can give them something to bring the fever down. I can make them more comfortable." They had been arguing for ten minutes. She still held the baby, who had smiled at her to reveal two tiny white teeth and was now noisily sucking on a plump fist.

"What will you do when some of the warriors get well and decide to kill me and make you a slave? That's if the medicine man doesn't get jealous and decide you should die, too."

"Rafe, I'm sorry, I know it's against your better judgment, but I can't leave any more than I could not have come here in the first place. Please understand. Most of them are already broken out in spots, so it will only be a few days before they'll begin getting well. Just a few days."

Rafe wondered when his brain had begun turning to mush where she was concerned. "You know I can make you go."

"Yes, I know," she admitted. He was strong enough

to make her do anything he wanted. She could even understand his position, and knowing the validity of his arguments made her doubly appreciate his restraint, especially since he was usually so implacable.

"It's dangerous for us to stay so long in one place."

"But on the other hand, an Apache camp is probably the safest place for us to be if we *aren't* moving. How many bounty hunters are likely to look for us here?"

None, he had to admit.

He found himself giving in again. "All right. Will four days be enough?"

She thought about it. "It should be."

"Whether it is or not, four days is the outside limit. When a few of the bucks start moving around, we leave."

"All right." She saw the wisdom of his qualification. Just because she would be working to help the Apache didn't mean they would appreciate it.

She had counted sixty-eight people. She had never had so many patients at one time before and hardly knew how to begin. The first thing she did was go from wickiup to wickiup and check on the condition of each person. Some people seemed to have mild cases of the disease, some severe. The old woman who had evidently been trying to care for the entire band worked up enough courage to fly screeching at Annie when she knelt beside the sick people in the wickiup where she had hidden. Rafe quickly caught the old woman's arms and made her sit down. "Stop it," he said sharply, hoping his tone of voice would keep her quiet even though she wouldn't understand what he was saying. He wished he spoke at least a few words of the Apache tongue, but he didn't, and it wasn't likely anyone here would speak any English. The old woman, however, cowered back into her corner and contented herself with glaring at the intruders.

Annie didn't have much hope for the ones with black measles, though she had seen people recover.

The greatest danger, to all of them, was the fever that could soar so high it caused convulsions. She had seen that often people who survived such a high fever weren't right in the head afterward. There was also the possibility of pneumonia and other complications. If she let herself stop to think, common sense would force her to admit it was hopeless to expect much. Rather than do that, Annie didn't let herself stop. Even if she saved just one person, that was one person, an atonement for Trahern.

She hoped her supply of willow bark held out. She fetched water and put it on to boil, all the while deciding on her course of action. She would make the tea weak; it would lower the fever even if it didn't break it, and her supply would last longer that way. She was sure the Indians themselves would know which local plants could be used to fight fever, but the language barrier prevented her from asking.

While the tea was steeping she began another search of the wickiups, this time looking for any of the herbs the Indians normally used. Perhaps she would be able to use some of them. Rafe followed her every step, as alert as a hunting wolf.

The baby was howling again. It was probably hungry. She went into the wickiup where it lay screaming and picked it up. Evidently it was more frightened than hungry, for again it cuddled contentedly in her arms. She couldn't bear listening to it cry continuously like that, so she carried the infant with her, reasoning that it couldn't be exposed to the disease more than it already had been.

She did find bundles of dried plants but didn't recognize most of them. She wished she had spent more time in the area so she could have explored the healing properties of the local plants. Nevertheless she gathered them up; maybe the old woman would be able to indicate how some of them were used.

The two young boys had crept out of their wickiup to stare at her and Rafe with huge, frightened eyes.

One of the youngsters carried a bow that was as long as he was but made no effort to use it. Annie smiled at them as she rushed past in an effort to reassure them, but they hid their eyes.

"Let me have the baby," Rafe muttered as she held it with one arm and tried to measure honey and cinnamon into the willow-bark tea with her free hand. She looked at him in surprise; somehow the idea of a baby being cradled in those steely arms seemed ludicrous, but she gladly gave up her burden.

The baby began to cry again. Rafe cradled the fuzzy little head in his big hand as he held the child to his chest, but it wasn't soothed. Annie gave it a worried look. "I hope it isn't getting sick," she said. "Measles is so hard on tiny babies. Maybe it's just hungry."

More than likely it was crying because Annie wasn't holding it, Rafe thought. It was undoubtedly hungry too, but Annie's touch had calmed it despite that. He dipped his finger into the jar of honey and slipped it into the little mouth. The baby squalled around his finger for a minute, then the sweet taste registered and it clamped down on his finger with a frantic sucking. He winced as two sharp little teeth dug into his flesh. "Hey! Damn it, you little cannibal, turn loose!"

The honey was gone and his finger wasn't very productive. The baby began wailing again. Rafe started to dip his finger in the honey again but Annie stopped him. "You have to be careful giving honey to babies. Sometimes it makes them really sick. Maybe the mother is still nursing; why don't you check and see? If not, I wrapped up a biscuit left over from breakfast. Soak it in water and give it to the baby in tiny bites. And see if the baby needs drying."

She was gone in a flurry of skirts. Rafe looked down with alarm at the little carnivore in his arms. How had he wound up as mammy? How was he supposed to see if the mother was still nursing the baby? The woman was almost unconscious, and he didn't speak Apache anyway. And what did Annie mean, see if it needs drying? So what if it did? He had no idea what to do about it.

Feeding it, though, seemed like a good idea. He could handle that. He searched the saddlebags until he found the leftover biscuit. The kid was squalling again, and kicking in outrage. He'd thought all Apache babies were kept bound in cradleboards, but maybe that was only when the mother was carrying it around.

He did as Annie had directed and soaked the biscuit in water, then broke off small bits of the soggy bread and poked it into the baby's mouth, taking care to avoid those two small teeth. Evidently the baby had already learned the mechanics of eating, because it knew what to do. Blessed silence fell again.

Rafe kept his attention on Annie as she moved from wickiup to wickiup with the pot of willow-bark tea. The two little boys were staring at him as if he had two heads. Probably Apache warriors didn't tend to babies. He could understand why.

The baby did feel decidedly damp. Sighing in resignation, Rafe began unwrapping it. After all, he couldn't keep thinking of it as "it." Time to find out if it was a he or a she.

It was a she. To his relief, being wet was her only problem. The naked baby in his lap seemed to enjoy the cool freedom, and kicked energetically while she made cooing sounds. He smiled as he looked at her, and the round little face smiled back. She was funny-looking, with her soft fuzzy hair sticking straight up on her head like a brush. Her dark skin was as smooth as honey, and her slanted black eyes wrinkled up every time she smiled, which was every time he looked at her.

He tucked her into the cradle of his arm and set off for the wickiup where Annie had found her. There should be some clean cloths in there to wrap her in. When he opened the flap, the young woman who was the baby's mother tried to roll onto her side so she could get up. Her fever-dulled eyes were fixed desperately on the infant. Rafe squatted beside the woman and gently pushed her onto her back again.

"It's all right," he said as soothingly as he could, hoping his tone of voice would calm her even though she couldn't understand the words. He patted her shoulder, then touched his hand to her face. Her skin was scorching hot. "We'll take care of your baby. See, she's fine. I just finished feeding her."

The woman didn't seem comforted, but she was too ill to struggle. She closed her eyes and seemed to sink into a stupor. Beside her lay a warrior who was breathing heavily and hadn't stirred at all. His round face and bristly hair looked exactly like the baby's.

Rafe found the cradleboard and binding cloths, but he didn't want to wrap the kid up to where it couldn't move. He improvised a hip wrapping and was just tying it off when Annie entered the wickiup with her pot of willow-bark tea.

"It's a girl," Rafe said. "I don't know if the mother's still nursing her or not. The kid ate the biscuit like she knew what she was doing."

Annie couldn't help smiling at the plump brown infant resting so calmly in the crook of his muscled arm. She had always liked babies; helping a woman give birth had always been her favorite part of being a doctor. When she had picked up the Indian baby earlier it had felt—right, somehow. Maybe it was because she had been thinking about having Rafe's child, and for the first time she had pictured herself as a mother.

Gently, she opened the front of the woman's dress. Rafe turned his back, jiggling the baby and talking to her. The mother's breasts were normal, not swollen with milk, so Annie knew that, for whatever reason, the infant had already been weaned. It was unusual for a baby so young not to still be nursing, but sometimes the mother either didn't have milk to begin with or something happened that stopped her milk. Annie had even seen a few cases where the infants had weaned themselves as soon as they started cutting teeth. She closed the woman's dress. "You can turn around now. The baby has already been weaned; we'll have to feed her."

She lifted the woman's head and patiently spooned the tea into her mouth, coaxing her to swallow. It was more difficult with the warrior, for she couldn't rouse him. Looking at him, Annie felt her stomach clench; she didn't think he would live. She didn't give up, though. She talked to him and stroked his throat, making him swallow a little bit of tea at a time. His body heaved with coughing, another symptom of the disease. She put her hand on his chest, feeling the congestion rattle in his lungs.

Rafe watched her with enigmatic eyes. She healed wounds with her hot touch, calmed babies and horses, drove him crazy when they were making love, but could her special gift do anything against a disease? He realized that he hadn't considered that before, and wouldn't really be able to tell now. Some of the Indians would recover from the measles and some of them wouldn't; there was no way to tell which of the survivors would have died without Annie. And would it be her herbs, or her touch? Unless, of course, *all* of them survived. The thought made his heart jump into his mouth, and he fought to keep the panic out of his eyes. God, if she could do *that,* how could he justify keeping her to himself? Something that special wasn't meant to be hidden away. It would be criminal to do so.

His mouth twisted wryly. He was a fine person to be worrying about anything being criminal or not.

No longer hungry, the baby began yawning. Rafe put her down on a blanket and did what he could to help Annie.

There were two women and one man, besides the old woman, who were still on their feet, but they were feverish and alarmed by the intrusion of white people into their camp. The man had tried to get his weapons, but had calmed down when Annie had spoken softly to him and tried to show that she meant no harm and was trying to help. Annie mentioned this to Rafe as they worked, and he swore to stay by her side from now on. If the Apache warrior had been a little less sick, he might have killed her. He was furious with himself for being so careless.

The old woman crept out again. She watched as Rafe held one big warrior up so Annie could coax him to drink the bark tea. The warrior tried to struggle and Rafe effortlessly subdued him. The old woman spoke to the warrior, perhaps reassuring him; he relaxed, and drank the tea.

The old woman's face was lined with wrinkles like the arroyos scoring the land, and she was thin and bent. She studied these two whites who were the enemies of her people, carefully watching the big man who wore his weapons with such ease, but even the great Cochise admitted that not all white people were bad. At least these two seemed to want to help—well, the woman wanted to help, and the white warrior with the fierce pale eyes let her have her way. The old woman had seen it before in her long life: even the boldest, strongest warrior became oddly helpless around a certain woman.

The woman was interesting. She had the strange pale hair, but her eyes were dark like those of the People. She knew healing, so perhaps she was a medicine woman. The band's medicine man had been one of the first to succumb to the spotted disease, and everyone had been terrified. Perhaps this white woman knew how to cure the white man's disease.

The old woman shuffled forward. She indicated herself and said, "Jacali," which Annie took to be her name, then gestured toward the pot of tea Annie was holding. Annie gave it to her. The old woman sniffed it, then tasted it. She gave it back to Annie with some words and nods, and by gestures gave them to understand that she would aid in the care of her people.

Annie touched herself and then Rafe, repeating their names. The old woman said each name in turn, the syllables harsh and distinct, but Annie smiled and nodded and the introductions were considered finished.

She was glad of an extra pair of hands. Of the entire band, only this old woman and the two boys showed no signs of measles. Everyone would have to be fed, and now that Annie had dispensed the willow-bark tea she set about making a weak broth from the Apaches' stores of dried jerky. It would have helped had there been one big pot, but if there was such an item in the camp she hadn't seen it. Rafe built up the cook fires and she turned the chore over to Jacali, showing the old woman how weak she wanted it. Jacali signaled her understanding.

"What now?" Rafe asked.

She tiredly rubbed her forehead. "I need to make a horehound cough syrup, to help relieve the congestion in their lungs. I think several of them have pneumonia already. And they need to be bathed in cool water to help lower the fevers."

He pulled her to him and held her for a long minute, wishing he could make her rest, but he knew they would both be much more tired before the crisis had passed. He kissed her hair. "I'll wash them down while you make the cough medicine."

He had chosen to undertake a monumental task. By his reckoning there were almost seventy of the Indians, with only three of them healthy, four if he counted the baby girl with the spiky hair. There were old people, young people, middle-aged people, the strong ones afflicted as well as the weak. He stripped muscled warriors down to their breechcloths, fighting some of them, so he could ease the aches of fever with cool water. Knowing the Apache notions and rules of modesty were as strong as, though somewhat different from, those of the white man, he took care not to expose the women any more than necessary, merely pushing their dresses up so he could bathe their legs and arms.

The children were the easiest, but they were also the most frightened. Some of them cried when he touched them. He handled them gently as he removed their clothes, and held one terrified four-year-old on his lap as he cooled down the sturdy little limbs. The little boy couldn't stop crying in his misery. Rafe cuddled him, talking softly to him, until the child lapsed into a fretful sleep. Then Rafe removed the body of the child's mother, who had died in the short time since Annie had administered the willow-bark tea. Jacali, the old woman, broke into wails when she saw Rafe's blanket-wrapped burden, and the two little boys ran and hid.

It was the grief in Annie's eyes that hit him hardest. He knew some of the Apache customs dealing with death, but he didn't know how they were going to manage. Apaches wouldn't live in a wickiup where someone had died, but he couldn't bring the sick people outside or be continually moving them from one wickiup to another whenever someone died. Nor did he know the Apache custom for burial. Finally he decided to leave it to Jacali, for she would do as much as she was able within their customs.

Cooling the fevers was a never-ending job. If someone had slipped into a doze he left them alone, but those who were restless, or whose fevers had gone so high that they were insensible, had to be continually bathed. The three who had been trying to help Jacali had evidently been in the beginning stages of the disease; by that night, they were as sick as the others.

Annie moved from one patient to the other, dispensing the horehound cough syrup to those whose lungs sounded congested. To others, who were coughing but whose lungs sounded clear, she gave a hyssop and honey mixture.

It went on all night. She didn't dare sleep, for she was terrified that someone would go into convulsions from the fever. She boiled more willow-bark tea and spent hours coaxing fretful, violent, or unconscious patients to swallow. Some of the younger children cried most of the night, and their misery wrung her heart. Those whose spots seemed to be itching were washed with apple-cider vinegar. The baby girl howled vigorously whenever she became hungry or needed cleaning, or was frightened by the absence of her mother. The young woman tried several times to respond to her baby's cries, but she was too weak.

By dawn, five more people had died.

Doggedly Annie made the round with yet more tea, her eyes dark-circled with fatigue. She entered one wickiup to find a warrior trying to roll to his side, his hand reaching out for the woman who lay beside him. Her heart catching, Annie rushed to the woman and found that she was merely sleeping. As this was one of the Indians whose lungs had been congested, she went almost limp with relief, and gave the warrior a blinding smile. His slanted, enigmatic black eyes studied her, then with a groan he collapsed onto his back again.

She slipped her arm under his shoulders and eased him up so he could sip the tea, which he did without fuss. When she let him back down, he seemed to be a little dazed, but he muttered something to her in his guttural language. She placed her cool hand on his forehead and indicated that he should go to sleep. Still looking puzzled, he did so.

She stumbled as she left the wickiup. Rafe was immediately beside her, his hard arm around her waist. "That's enough," he said. "You need some sleep." He guided her to the blankets he had spread in the shade of a tree, and Annie gratefully sank down. She should have argued with him, she thought tiredly, but she had sensed that he wasn't going to give in this time. She was asleep by the time her head touched the blanket.

The two little boys had crept curiously near. Rafe put his finger to his lips in a hushing motion. Solemn black eyes looked back.

He was tired himself, but rest could come later, when Annie was awake. He wanted to hold her in his arms while she slept, feel the warmth of her slight body and absorb some of her magic. It was enough, though, to guard her as she slept.

By the third day, Annie didn't know how she was going to make it. She had slept only in snatches, as had Rafe. A total of seventeen people had died since she and Rafe had entered the camp, eight of them children. It was the loss of the children that hurt her the most.

Whenever she could, she would sit and hold the plump baby girl who glowed with health like an oasis in the midst of the desert. The infant cooed and squealed and waved her dimpled hands about, smiling indiscriminately at whoever held her. The weight of that small, wriggling body in her arms was infinitely soothing.

The baby's mother seemed to be recovering, as did her father. The young woman had smiled wanly at her daughter's imperious wails. The round-faced warrior still slept a lot, but his fever seemed to have abated and his lungs were clear.

Then, within a matter of hours, one of the little boys who had seemed so healthy began running a high fever and went into convulsions. Despite the willow-bark tea Annie spooned down him, he died that night

233

without ever breaking out into spots. Only the circles on his gums indicated the disease that had burned through his young body. Annie cried in Rafe's arms.

"I couldn't do anything," she sobbed. "I try, but sometimes it doesn't seem to matter. No matter what I do, they still die."

"Hush, sweetheart," he murmured. "You've done more than anyone else could."

"But it wasn't enough for him. He was only about seven years old!"

"Some younger than he was have already died. They don't have any resistance to the disease, honey; you know that. You knew from the first that a lot of them would die."

"I thought I could help," she said. Her voice was thin and desolate.

He lifted her hand and kissed it. "You have helped. Every time you touch them, you help."

She still couldn't feel as if she were doing enough. Her supply of willow bark had all been used. What she wouldn't have given for more, or for meadowsweet, which was even better at lowering fevers but didn't grow in the Southwest. Jacali had shown her some bark and indicated it came from a tree Rafe called a quaking aspen, but it seemed the women in the band had gathered it during a forage to the north and there was only a small supply of it. She boiled it much as she had the willow bark, and the resulting tea had helped the fevers, but it didn't seem to be as efficient, or perhaps she was simply making it too weak. She was too tired to decide.

Jacali shuffled around with the endless cups of jerky broth, coaxing nourishment down sore throats. The little boy whose friend had died began shadowing Rafe, often peering at Annie from behind the shelter of Rafe's long, muscled legs.

When some of the warriors began showing distinct signs of recovery on the fourth day, staring at her with their unreadable gazes, Annie expected Rafe to throw her on a horse and start riding.

Instead, late that day, he came to her with the baby in his arms. She was crying ceaselessly, her tiny arms and legs jerking, and her dark skin was flushed even darker with fever. Black spots had begun breaking out on her stomach.

CHAPTER

16

"*N*o," Annie said hoarsely. "No. She was fine this morning." Even as she said it, she knew what a useless protest it was. Illnesses didn't always follow the same timetable or have the same symptoms, especially in infants.

His face was grim. Only one of the Indians who had broken out in the black spots that signaled hemorrhaging had lived, and that one was a warrior, with a warrior's strength. The man was still very ill and weak. Rafe knew as well as Annie that the baby's chances weren't good.

Annie took the baby. The little thing stopped crying, but moved fretfully in her hands as if trying to escape the pain of fever.

It was dangerous to give medication to a baby this little, yet Annie didn't think she had a choice. Perhaps it was just as well that the tea from the quaking aspen was weaker than the willow-bark tea. She dribbled a small amount of it down the baby's throat, then spent an hour gently washing her in cool water. Finally the baby slept, and Annie forced herself to carry her back to her mother's side.

The young woman was awake, her dark eyes huge with anxiety. She turned onto her side and touched her daughter with a trembling hand, then tucked the hot little body close to hers. Annie patted her shoulder, then had to leave before she began crying.

There were still too many very sick people for her to allow herself to break down. She had to see to them.

Rafe had noticed that a few of the warriors were recovered enough to sit up and feed themselves. He was right behind her every time she entered one of those wickiups, the thong slipped off his revolver, and his icy gaze saw every movement while she was there.

The warriors, for their part, stared just as fiercely at the white man who had invaded their camp.

"Do you really think this is necessary?" she asked when they left the second wickiup where the performance had been repeated.

"It's either that or we leave right now," Rafe flatly replied. They should have left anyway, and he knew it, but he would have to tie her over the saddle to make her leave the baby, and something in him didn't want to leave, either. The baby didn't have much of a chance as it was; if Annie left, she wouldn't have any.

"I don't think they'll try to hurt us. They've seen that we're only trying to help."

"We may have violated some of their customs without knowing it. White people are their hated enemies, honey, and don't forget it. When Mangas Coloradas was tricked into a meeting under a guarantee of safety, then killed and his head cut off and boiled, the Apache swore eternal vengeance. Hell, who can blame them? But I won't trust your safety with them for one minute, and for your own sake don't ever forget about Mangas Coloradas, because they won't."

So much pain, on both sides. It weighed down on her as she went from patient to patient, dispensing tea and cough medication, trying to soothe both fever and grief, for there wasn't a family in the little band that hadn't been touched by death. Jacali too made the rounds, talking to her people, so everyone knew the magnitude of the tragedy that had befallen them. Annie heard the soft, stricken wailing within the privacy of the wickiups, though they never displayed their grief in her presence. They were both proud and shy, and naturally wary of her anyway. All of the goodwill on her part wasn't going to wipe out the years of warfare between their people.

When she checked on the baby she found her lying listlessly, no longer even fretting. Again she spoon-fed the tea to the baby and sponged her with cool water, hoping to bring her some relief. The little chest sounded so congested it was as if there were barely room for air in her lungs.

The mother forced herself to sit up, and she held her child on her lap, crooning weakly in an effort to rouse the baby. Rafe entered the wickiup and sat down just inside the entrance. "How is she?"

Annie looked at him with agony in her eyes and gave a tiny shake of her head. The young mother saw it and uttered a sharp protest, snatching the child to her breast. The round, fuzzy head lolled back on the doll-like neck.

Jacali too came into the wickiup, and sat waiting.

When the mother grew tired, Annie took the baby and rocked her while she hummed the lullabyes she remembered from childhood. The peaceful, infinitely tender sounds filled the quiet wickiup. The baby's breath grew more labored. Jacali leaned forward, her old eyes sharp.

Rafe lifted the baby from Annie's exhausted arms and put her to his shoulder. She had been plump and energetic only that morning, but already the heat of the disease was wasting her. He thought of the round cheeks and spiky hair, and the two gleaming little teeth that nipped so sharply.

If it were his child, he thought, to lose her would be

unbearable. He had known her only four days, and spent only an hour or so playing with her, yet he had such a heavy weight on his chest he felt almost smothered.

Annie took her again, and coaxed more tea down her. Most of it dribbled from the small, slack mouth. She was still holding her when the tiny body began to stiffen and shudder.

Jacali snatched the baby and carried her outside, despite the mother's sharp cry of anguish. Annie jumped to her feet and surged through the open flap, propelled by a burst of fury that banished her exhaustion. "Where are you going with her?" she demanded, even though she knew the old woman couldn't understand her. She could barely make out Jacali's departing figure in the darkness and she ran after her.

But Jacali only went to the edge of the camp and sank down on her knees. She laid the baby on the ground in front of her, then began a low, mournful chanting that sent shivers down Annie's spine.

Yet when Annie reached for the baby again, Jacali snatched her up with a hissed warning.

Rafe put his hand on Annie's shoulder, holding her in place, his face like stone as he stared at the tiny form in Jacali's hands.

"What is she doing?" Annie cried, tugging against his grip.

"She didn't want the baby to die in the wickiup," he said absently. Perhaps the baby was already dead; it was too dark to tell if she was breathing or not. He felt Annie's warm vibrancy under his hand, and it pierced all the way to his heart.

He hadn't asked her about her special gift, hadn't alluded to it in any way. He was almost certain she didn't realize the power she had and he had kept his awareness of it to himself, probably out of pure selfishness, for he had wanted something of her that no one else knew existed. What was it like for other people when she touched them? Did they feel the same hot rush of passion that she always evoked in him? Surely not, for he had noticed that her touch had calmed the fevered Indians rather than rousing them. And females wouldn't be stirred to lust by her touch anyway. He had puzzled over the quality of it even as he kept the knowledge to himself.

It had been almost a relief to realize that she couldn't work miracles; people still died, despite her healing touch. But if she realized the power of her gift, she would feel an almost crushing responsibility to use it even when it was hopeless, and for that reason, too, he had kept silent. She worked herself to exhaustion now; what extremes would she push herself to if she knew? How much more deeply would her failures hurt her? Because she would consider them personal failures, and would try all the harder. How much strength did it cost her, this gift, and how much could she bear to lose before her heart or her spirit gave out under the burden of it?

All of his natural instincts shouted for him to protect his woman. He would fight to the death to protect her from harm. Yet how could he stand here and watch the baby die when it was possible Annie could save her? It might not work; the child might die within the next minute, but Annie was the only chance she had.

He moved like lightning striking, scooping the limp little body from Jacali's arms before the old woman could even cry out. He turned and thrust the baby into Annie's arms. "Hold her," he said between his teeth. "Put her against your breast and hold her. Rub her back with your hands. And concentrate."

Stunned, Annie automatically cradled the infant to her. The baby was still alive, she realized dimly, though essentially lifeless with fever. "What?" she asked in confusion.

Jacali was screeching in fury and trying to get around him. Rafe put his hand on her chest and pushed her back. "No," he said in such a deep, crackling tone that the old woman stopped still. His pale eyes glowed with a rage that burned through the darkness, like a demon's, and she screeched again, but this time in terror. She didn't dare move.

Rafe turned back to Annie. "Sit down," he barked. "Sit down and do what I told you."

She did. She sank down onto the dirt, feeling the grit shifting beneath her. The cool night wind fluttered in her hair.

Rafe squatted in front of her and arranged the baby so that she lay against Annie's breast, Annie's strong heart thudding beneath the tiny, failing one. He took her hands and placed them against the baby's back. "Concentrate," he said fiercely. "Feel the heat. Make *her* feel it."

She felt totally confused; had both Rafe and Jacali run mad? She stared at him, eyes wide. "What heat?" she stammered.

He put his hands on hers, forcing them to flatten against the little form. "Your heat," he said. "Concentrate, Annie. Fight the fever with it."

She had no idea what he was talking about; how could you fight a fever with heat? But his eyes were glittering like ice in the moonlight and she couldn't look away from him; something in those pale, crystalline depths pulled her in, sent the night swirling away. "Concentrate," he said again.

She felt a deep throbbing. His eyes still held her, filling her vision until she could see nothing else. It wasn't possible, she thought, to see so clearly in the dark. There was no moon, only a faint starlight. Yet his eyes were a colorless fire, pulling her out of herself. The throbbing intensified.

It was the baby's heart, she thought, that she could feel throbbing. Or perhaps it was her own. It filled her entire body, surging like the tide. Yes, it was a tide, lifting her up and sweeping her away. She sensed the deep rhythmic surge of it, surrounding her with liquid warmth. She heard the roaring of it, muted and far away. And what she had thought was the moon was really the sun, burning brightly. Her hands were burning too, and now the throbbing was concentrated in her hands. Her fingertips pulsed, her palms thrummed with the energy of it. She thought her skin must surely dissolve under the pressure of it.

And then peace began to edge in as the tide became gentle breakers, lapping lazily against some unknown shore. The light was even brighter than before, but it was also softer, and incredibly clear. She wasn't drifting, she was floating, and she could see forever. The land spread out before her, great expanses of green and brown, and the deepest blue of the oceans, bluer than she had known anything could be, and she could see the misty, glowing curve of the earth, and it humbled her to think that everyone she had known and would ever know lived on this small, lovely place.

The throbbing had subsided to a steady hum, and she felt both incredibly heavy with exhaustion and weightless, as if she were indeed floating. The great light began dimming, and gradually she became aware of the warm little body she held to her breast, wriggling under her hands, crying fretfully.

She opened her heavy eyelids, or perhaps they had been open anyway and only now could she see. A sense of unreality seized her, as if she had awakened in a strange place and didn't know where she was.

But it was the same place. She was sitting in the dirt at the edge of the camp, and Rafe was kneeling in front of her. Jacali was squatting on her haunches a few feet away, her slanted black eyes filled with a sort of wonder.

It was daylight. Somehow the day had come and she hadn't noticed. Perhaps she had slept, and dreamed, but she was so very tired she didn't see how she could have slept. The sun was high; it was late in the morning.

"Rafe?" she asked, bewildered fear making her voice desperate.

He reached out and took the baby, who was squirming and wailing. The fever was down, though not broken, and the spots weren't as dark. She was awake and fretful, and her mother would be totally frantic. He kissed the silky, spiky hair and passed the infant on to Jacali, who accepted her in silence and hugged her to her own sagging bosom. Then he took Annie in his arms.

He was so stiff he could barely move, and he felt disoriented. How had so much time passed? He had been lost in the dark pools of Annie's eyes and . . . and something had happened. He didn't know what. All he knew was that she needed him, and he was burning for her with a frenzy that was almost uncontrollable. He lifted her high in his arms and bore her away, pausing only long enough to snatch one of their blankets.

He followed the stream until they were out of sight of the camp, and hidden from any casual view by a small copse of trees. There he spread the blanket and placed her on it, and stripped away all of the clothing that had been keeping him from contact with her skin. "Annie," he said in a rough, shaking voice as he spread her thighs, his hard, callused hands dark against the paleness of her skin. His shaft was so engorged he could scarcely breathe or move from the throbbing pressure of it. Her slim arms came up to wrap around his muscled shoulders, and he pushed deep into the tight, wet welcoming of her body. Her soft sheath embraced him with a rhythmic clenching as she adjusted to his width, and her legs came up to lock around his hips.

He wasn't aware of the hard thrusting of his body. He knew only the vibrant energy pouring out of her, more intense than ever, tingling through him like a great underground current. He had never before felt so alive, so fierce, so purified. He heard her cry out, felt the violence of her completion, and his seed spewed out of him in a white-hot eruption of his senses. He thrust deep in a primal search for her womb at the pinnacle of sensation, and even before the last spasms had faded he knew he had made her pregnant.

He sank weakly to the blanket beside her, still holding her to him with fierce possessiveness. She gave a little sigh and closed her eyes, and was asleep even before her breath had washed over his shoulder where she lay. He felt as if he had taken a huge blow to the chest, robbing him of breath, but for the first time in years he was seeing clearly.

The four years he had been hunted had almost turned him into a pure killing animal; he had lived by his instincts, his reflexes cat-quick, his sole object to stay alive. But now he didn't have just himself to consider, he had Annie to protect, and probably their child. Yes, he was sure there would be a child, and he had to plan for the future. He had lived in the present for so long that it felt strange to think of the future; hell, for four years he hadn't *had* a future.

Somehow he had to clear his name. They couldn't just keep running, and even if they did find some remote spot and settle down, they would always be looking over their shoulders, living with the fear that some bounty hunter or lawman, smarter than most, had managed to track them. The running had to end.

Knowing it and planning it were two different things. He was so tired, and the incredible clarity of vision was already fading. He couldn't even think now, his eyes were closing despite himself. And, damn it, he was already hard again, though the urgency was gone. Half asleep, he shifted onto his side and lifted her thigh over his hip, then slipped gently into her sweet warmth. The perfection of it soothed him, and he slept.

The noon sun penetrated the shade of the trees and was burning his bare leg. He opened his eyes and absorbed the details of reality. They had slept only a little over an hour, but he felt as rested as if it had been an entire night. Damn, what had he been thinking of, going to sleep like that with both of them naked and so close to the Apache camp? Not that they hadn't needed the sleep, but he should have been more cautious.

He gently shook her, and her eyes opened sleepily. "Hello," she murmured, and snuggled closer to him as her lashes drooped again.

"Hello yourself. We need to get dressed."

He watched as her eyes popped open. Then she was sitting up and grabbing her shift to cover her naked breasts. She blinked owlishly at him. "Did I dream?" she asked in bewilderment. "What time is it? Have we slept out here all night?"

He pulled on his pants, wondering what she remembered of the night. He wasn't certain he remembered that much of it himself. He eyed the sun. "It's a little after noon, and no, we didn't sleep out here all night. We made love here about an hour ago. Do you remember?"

She looked at the tangled blanket and her face was radiant. "Yes."

He said cautiously, "Do you remember the baby?"

"The baby." She went very still. "The baby was very sick, wasn't she? She was dying. Was that last night?"

"She was dying," he agreed. "And yes, that was last night."

Annie spread her empty hands and looked down at them with a faintly puzzled expression, as if she expected to see the baby in them and couldn't understand why she wasn't. "But what happened?" Suddenly she began jerking on her clothes, her movements frantic. "I've got to see about her. She could have died while we were out here. I can't believe I just totally forgot about her, that I—"

"The baby's all right." Rafe caught her hands and held them, forcing her to look at him. "She's all right. Do you remember what happened last night?"

She was still again, staring into his light gray eyes. An echo stirred through her, as if she were looking into a deep well where she had once fallen. The familiarity of it stirred other memories. "Jacali grabbed her, and ran outside," she said slowly. "I went after her . . . no, *we* went after her. Jacali wouldn't let me have her, and I remember being so angry that I felt like slapping her. Then you . . . you took her away from Jacali and gave her to me . . . and you told me to concentrate."

The memories swirled around her, and her hands throbbed with the remnants of energy. She lifted her hands and found herself staring at them without knowing why. "What happened?" she asked blankly.

He was silent while he pulled her shift on over her head, covering her in case anyone intruded on their privacy. "It's your hands," he finally said.

Still she looked at him with a total lack of understanding.

He took her hands and held them to his mouth, kissing her fingertips before folding them warmly in his hard palms and carrying them to his chest. "You have healing hands," he said simply. "I noticed it the first time you touched me, back in Silver Mesa."

"What do you mean? I'm a doctor, so of course you can say I have healing hands, but then so does every doctor—"

"No," he interrupted. "No. Not like yours. It isn't knowledge or training, it's something you have inside you. Your hands are hot, and they make me tingle when you touch me."

She blushed fiery red. "Yours make me tingle, too," she mumbled.

Despite himself he chuckled. "Not like that. Well, yes, like that too. It's your whole body, and it drives me wild when I'm inside you. But you have healing hands, true healing hands. I've heard of it, mostly from old folks, but I didn't believe it until you touched me and I felt it."

"Felt *what?*" she asked desperately. "My hands are just ordinary."

He shook his head. "No. They aren't. You have a special gift, sweetheart; you can heal where others can't, and it isn't medicine, it's you." He looked away from her, toward the distant purple mountains, but he was seeing deep inside himself. "Last night . . . last night, your hands were so hot I could barely stand to hold them. Remember? I was pressing them to the baby's back. And I felt as if I were holding a hot poker, as if the skin was being burned off my palms."

"You're lying," she said. The harsh tone of her own voice shocked her. "You have to be lying. I can't do that. If I could, none of them would have died."

He rubbed his face, feeling the rasp of his beard against his palm. God, how long had it been since he'd shaved? He couldn't even remember. "I didn't say you were Jesus," he snapped. "You can't raise the dead. I've watched you, and sometimes the person is too sick for even you to help. You couldn't have helped Trahern, because whatever it is you have doesn't stop bleeding, it didn't even stop the bleeding when my shoulder was grazed. But when I was so sick, when we first met, just your slightest touch made me feel better. You cooled me, took the pain away, made the wounds heal faster. Damn it, Annie, I could *feel* the skin pulling together. That's what you can do."

She was speechless, and suddenly panic stricken. She didn't want to be able to do any of that, it was too much. She just wanted to be a doctor, the best doctor she could be. She wanted to help people, not—not perform some kind of miracle. If it were true, how could she not have known?

She shouted that question at him, as angry as she was afraid, and he jerked her into his arms. The hard face that bent over hers was just as angry. "Maybe you've never wanted to save anyone as much as you wanted to save that baby!" he yelled. "Maybe you've never concentrated like that before. Maybe you were too young, maybe it's something that grows stronger with age."

Tears burned her eyes and she hit at his chest. "I don't want it!" Even to herself she sounded like a child protesting having to eat vegetables, but she didn't care. How could she live with such a burden? She had visions of herself being locked away, with an endless procession of ill and wounded being brought to her, of her life never being her own again.

His anger died as swiftly as it had flared up. "I know, honey. I know."

She pulled away and in silence finished dressing. The sensible part of her scoffed at what he had told her; things like that just didn't exist. She had been trained to trust in her skill, her knowledge, and in luck, because being a good doctor definitely took luck. None of her instructors had ever said anything about her having "healing hands."

But would they even have noticed? She had been largely ignored, and definitely resented. And if they had seen something that made her superior to her classmates, would they have told her? The answer was no.

And common sense didn't explain what had happened last night. There was no explanation. Even if she accepted that she had healing hands, the events of the night, the total immersion of herself in . . . something . . . went far beyond that. She remembered the throbbing in her hands, in her entire body and in the baby's body, as if their heartbeats were linked. She remembered being lost in the crystal depths of Rafe's eyes.

And she remembered his frenzied lovemaking, as if he couldn't get inside her quickly enough, or go deep enough. She remembered clinging to him, her hips rocking and reaching up to him like the beat of a primal drum. An instinctive knowledge crept into her mind, and she knew that he had made her pregnant.

A deep sense of peace spread through her even as she gave him a quick, guarded glance. She couldn't imagine it would be welcome news to him.

She looked at her hands again, finally accepting. Logic wasn't always necessary, or even possible. "I don't know what I'm going to do," she said in a low voice.

His jaw was rigid as they walked back to the camp, his arm heavy and possessive around her waist. "Pretty much as you did before," he answered. "Nothing's changed, except now you know."

CHAPTER

17

The camp was still quiet when they returned to it, but the quiet had a different quality to it. It was more restful, as if the crisis had passed. Annie ducked into the wickiup belonging to the baby's parents and found the young Apache woman sitting up, holding her child on her lap and crooning to her as she coaxed the fretful infant to drink some of the bark tea. The baby was still feverish and spotty, but even the quickest glance told her that the child was going to live. She examined the mother, and smiled her pleasure, for she expected her to be on her feet in another day. The baby's father, the round-faced warrior, was also awake and without fever, though still very weak. Both parents stared at Annie and the tall white man who stood behind her like a fierce guardian angel, but they didn't seem fearful. The warrior even said something, weakly, and gestured with his hand toward the baby. Even without knowing the language, Annie could tell he was thanking them.

They left the wickiup together, with Annie passing through the flap first. A white man stood some fifteen feet away, a shotgun in his hands. She straightened abruptly, blood rushing from her face and leaving her deathly pale. Behind her, she felt Rafe slowly straighten, then move her gently to the side.

The man's face was as lined and weathered as old leather, and his hair was graying, even though Annie would have guessed his age as in the mid-forties. He was a little over medium height, and as lean and hard as a mustang. His left eyelid drooped a bit, making it look as if he were winking. There was a badge pinned to his vest.

"Atwater," he said in a dry, cracking voice. "U. S. marshal. You're Rafferty McCay, and you're under arrest. Drop that pistol real slow, son, because I'm a mite nervous about bein' in the middle of an Apache camp, and this here Greener will cut you in two if it goes off."

Rafe sat on the ground, his hands tied securely behind his back. Atwater had threatened to tie Annie too if she made any move to help Rafe, so Rafe had sharply ordered her to leave him alone. She sat down nearby, her face as white as paper and her heart beating heavily in her chest.

Jacali circled at a cautious distance, hissing and muttering, and Atwater eyed her warily. The old woman was definitely hostile. Two warriors managed to step outside their wickiups, though they were too weak to walk even to where Rafe sat tied. One of them was holding a rifle, but he didn't lift it in a threatening gesture. It was as if, as long as this situation remained between the White Eyes, they were content to leave it alone. Still, Atwater kept an eye on him, too.

Atwater was pondering how he was going to get his captive to jail, and he admitted to himself it was going to be a mite tricky. Like he'd said, they were not only in the middle of Apache country, but right smack-dab in the middle of an Apache camp. And there was the woman to consider. Little thing, but Atwater didn't discount her. He'd known women to go to some hellacious lengths for the men they thought they loved.

Tracking McCay had been the damnedest job he'd ever undertaken. If he hadn't been trained by some Injuns himself, he never would have managed it. Even so, part of it had been luck. Following a hunch and hanging around to see what the bounty hunter Trahern had done, for one thing. Going after McCay had been the last job Trahern would ever take. Couldn't say he regretted the bastard's death.

But the tracks around the cabin in the mountains, only a few, had made him think there were two horses. Either McCay now had him a packhorse or someone was with him, someone who didn't weigh much. At first Atwater had thought it was a packhorse, because McCay wasn't likely to take up with any kids or women, he was too smart for that, too much of a lobo. But then he remembered hearing that the doctor in Silver Mesa was a woman, and that she hadn't been seen at her cabin for a week or so. It wasn't unusual, no one seemed to think, since she was sometimes called away to an area ranch, but Atwater had the knack of taking odd pieces of information and making a picture out of them.

So, just for the hell of it, figure McCay had a woman with him now, maybe the doctor. Why would he take up with a woman after all these years? It wasn't likely unless the woman had somehow come to mean something to him. Where would he go with a woman he cared for? North, up the outlaw trail? Maybe. Some good hiding places up in that damn wilderness. North would have been where most men would have gone, where it was logical to go, but McCay wasn't most men. No, McCay would take the least-expected route. South, toward Mexico. Through Indian territory.

Tracking him was slow going. He didn't leave much

of a trail even where he could be expected to. But those two dead bounty hunters in the stand of trees, with the buzzards circling overhead, had been a pretty good signpost.

It took continuous circling to find a track, and he'd come across only a couple of camps, so well hidden were they. Atwater was proud of his tracking, but he had to admit it would have taken him a lot longer to catch McCay—he refused to think that he might *never* have caught him—if the outlaw hadn't stopped at the Apache camp.

Now, there was a puzzle. Atwater didn't like puzzles. He was a naturally curious man, and when a puzzle came along he couldn't rest until he'd solved it. It didn't make sense for McCay to stop for so long at one place, but he had. Atwater knew he'd been at least three days behind the couple, and he had watched from up in the hills for two days before coming down. He'd kept expecting the two to ride out, and it sure as hell would've been easier on his nerves not to have to come down into an Apache camp.

What he had seen just didn't fit with what he knew of McCay. A cold-blooded killer didn't spend five days taking care of a bunch of sick Apaches. Now, he'd have expected the doctor to want to try to help, maybe; at least that wasn't out of the realm of possibilities. But he also would have expected McCay to either override her and force her to ride on, or callously leave her behind. He had done neither.

Instead, for two days Atwater had watched the outlaw carrying water and helping the old woman with the dead, playing with a baby, taking time with that young Injun kid, and watching over the doctor like a hawk. Through his spyglass he had even seen, through an open flap, McCay sponging off a sick warrior. Nope, that just wasn't normal behavior at all.

And then that thing with the sick baby last night. He hadn't been able to tell what was going on in the dark, but come morning he'd seen something he purely didn't understand. The two of them, the outlaw and the doc, had been sitting for hours in the dirt facing each other, motionless. It had looked like they were in some sort of trance or something. Damn spooky. The doc had been holding the baby to her, and McCay had had his hands pressed over hers. The old woman had sort of watched over them, but it had been plain she'd been kinda unnerved, too.

And then the baby had started crying, and they'd woke up from their trance or whatever, and McCay had grabbed his woman and a blanket and taken her off for a while. Atwater hadn't followed. McCay wouldn't be going anywhere without the horses, and he believed in giving folks their privacy at certain times.

So here he had him a dilemma, sure enough. A cold-blooded killer ought to act like a cold-blooded killer, keep things simple. When the little pieces didn't fit, it made Atwater wonder. He was wondering now.

"Gettin' you to a jail somewhere is goin' to be a bitch," he mused aloud. "Pardon me, ma'am. I've been worryin' about it some. What if these here Apaches take it in their heads they don't like you being tied up and all? After you helpin' them when they was sick like you did. Can't tell what an Injun will think. I speak some Apache, and I don't like the things that old woman's been saying, I'll tell you that."

"He won't make it to a jail alive," Annie said desperately. "He'll be killed before you can get him there."

"I don't 'spect no bounty hunter to give me any trouble, ma'am." Atwater stared at her with his odd, half-winking gaze.

"It isn't just the bounty hunters, there are—"

"Annie, no." Rafe's voice cut across hers like a whiplash. "You'll just get him killed too."

The marshal considered that. Another damn puzzle. "Now, why should that matter to you?"

"It doesn't," Rafe said grimly. He shrugged his wide shoulders, trying to ease the pressure on the joints. The rope was tight, and securely knotted. There was no way he could slip out of it.

Atwater continued as if he hadn't spoken. "You've killed so many men, what would one more matter to a bastard like you? Pardon me, ma'am. You've left quite a string of dead men behind you, startin' with that poor Tilghman feller back in New York. Supposed to be a friend of yours, at that."

"He didn't kill Tench," Annie protested. Her mind felt paralyzed. She thought she should be doing something, but she didn't know what. Atwater had sat down about fifteen feet from Rafe, still holding that shotgun with both hammers jacked back, ready to shoot. He seemed to be considering killing Rafe right now and saving himself the trouble of taking him back to jail. He wouldn't receive a bounty, of course, since he was a marshal, but by his lights justice would have been served. Why go to the trouble of a trial? "He was framed. This isn't about Tench at all."

"Don't matter," Atwater said. "He's killed enough since then. Reckon I could add Trahern to your list, too, McCay, but I didn't much like the bastard. Pardon me, ma'am."

"Rafe didn't kill Trahern, either," Annie said. She was totally without color, even her lips were white.

"Annie, shut up!" Rafe snapped, but he might as well have saved his breath.

"I killed him," she said softly.

Atwater's eyebrows rose. "Do tell."

She was twisting her hands, and suddenly wished violently that she had Rafe's spare pistol in her skirt pocket right now. "He was going to ambush Rafe," she said in an agonized tone. "I had a pistol in my pocket . . . I'd never fired a weapon before. I couldn't pull the hammer back when I tried . . . but then he was going to shoot and somehow I did shoot it, I don't know how, while it was still in my pocket. It caught my skirt on fire. I killed him," she said again.

"She didn't do it," Rafe said sharply. "She's just trying to take the blame for me. I did it."

Atwater was getting damn tired of this. He didn't like it when outlaws turned out to have noble streaks. Tarnished his image of them.

Not that he hadn't known women to try to take the blame for something their men had done; the law was going to treat a woman different than it would a man in most cases. Few women ever actually went to prison. But in this case he didn't think the doc was trying to take the blame for something McCay had done, because that tale of her skirt catching fire just wasn't something anyone would make up. No, McCay was the one trying to take the blame, because he was afraid for the doc.

But now the doc had confessed to killing a man, and that annoyed him, because as an officer of the law he was expected to do something about it. He considered it for a minute, then shrugged. "Sounds like an accident to me. Like I said, I didn't think much of the bastard. Pardon me, ma'am."

Rafe closed his eyes with relief. Atwater scowled.

Annie scrambled closer, her eyes both earnest and desperate. Atwater cocked his head warningly, and lifted the shotgun. Off to the side, Jacali muttered a dire threat if he harmed the white magic woman.

"None of this is about Tench," Annie said. "Tench was just an excuse." Atwater turned his full attention on her, and she ignored the way Rafe was glaring at her. She suspected he thought it was useless to try to persuade Atwater, though perhaps he did feel the knowledge would endanger the marshal's life too. Rafe's streak of gallantry could take her by surprise, running side by side as it did with his steely implacability when he'd made up his mind to do something.

She started at the beginning. As she told how it had

all happened, the improbability of it struck her and she almost faltered. How could anyone believe such a tale? Even the most trusting of persons would need to see the documents Rafe had locked away in a bank vault, and Atwater didn't look trusting at all. He was glaring at Annie, then at Rafe, as if even listening was an insult to his intelligence. His drooping eyelid drooped even more.

When she finished he stared at her in silence for a full minute, then grunted. The gaze he turned on Rafe was baleful. "I hate to have to listen to bullshit like that," he barked. "Pardon me, ma'am."

Rafe merely glared back, his jaw set and his mouth a thin, grim line.

"The reason I hate to listen to it," Atwater continued, "is that liars try to sound reasonable. No point in lying if no one's goin' to believe you. So when somebody tells me something that no self-respectin' liar would ever come up with, that makes me curious. I purely hate to be curious about somethin'. Interferes with my sleep. Now, there ain't no doubt you done killed yourself a bunch of men in the last four years, but if what the doc here says is true then I'd have to consider it self-defense. And I did wonder just who this Tench feller was that he'd be worth the ten thousand dollar price on your head, seein' as how I'd never heard of him if he was supposed to be so all-fired important. That's a mite curious in itself."

Annie swallowed hard, not daring to look at Rafe. The marshal seemed to be thinking out loud, and she didn't want to interrupt him. Hope surged wildly through her, making her dizzy. Dear God, please let him believe her!

"So now I've got all these curious things naggin' at me. What in hell am I supposed to do about it? Pardon me, ma'am. The law says you're a murderer, McCay, and as a lawman I'm supposed to bring you in. The doc says there's some people after you paid to make sure you don't ever make it to trial. Now, I figure

I'm paid to make sure justice is served, but now I'm not so sure I'd be servin' justice if I bring you in. Not to say that I could do it," he said dryly, eyeing the big Apache warrior who was standing outside again, still holding the rifle and glaring at them with black basilisk eyes. It looked like the Indians weren't taking too kindly to McCay being tied up. He turned back to Rafe. "Why'd you spend so long helpin' these Indians? I wouldn't've caught you if you hadn't stopped."

Annie drew in an agonized breath. Rafe wanted to stomp Atwater for distressing her. "They needed help," he said curtly.

Atwater rubbed his jaw. Probably the doctor had persuaded him, and now she was all tore up about it. He looked at the black-bearded outlaw again and saw the anger in those funny-looking eyes. Well, he'd seen it before. Something about women could sweeten the hardest man, and this rough gunslick was definitely sweet on the doc. She was pleasant on the eye, for certain, but it was more than that. Those big dark eyes of hers made him feel funny in the pit of his stomach, an old trail hound like him. If he were twenty years younger, he might get all testy on her behalf too, especially if she ever looked at him the way she'd been looking at McCay.

Well, hell, here he was faced with a dilemma. Not only did that tale of hers intrigue him, but when added to the other little things that had bothered him, like there being such an unusually large bounty and the evidence of his own eyes that McCay wasn't the cold-blooded killer his reputation made him out to be, he had to consider the possibility that the wild story just might be true. He'd give it even odds, which meant that to serve justice he had to check it out, something easier said than done. He sighed; just as well he hadn't signed on as a marshal because it was an easy job.

Even getting out of this camp could prove to be a

mite tetchy. That big warrior was scowling, and brandishing his rifle. It wouldn't do to get him riled.

Atwater made his decision. He sighed wearily as he got to his feet. Now his life was all complicated again, and he suspected it was going to get even worse.

He stalked over to Rafe and slipped his knife from his belt. Annie struggled to her feet, biting back a protest. "These Apaches look a bit testy," Atwater said. "Maybe they don't like you bein' tied up, but maybe they don't like whites, period. Hard to tell. On the chance that what they're objecting to is the rope around your hands, I'm going to risk it and untie you. I'm not going to take my eyes off of you for one minute. Don't even look like you're thinkin' of making a run for it," the lawman said sourly. "It sure gets my water hot when somebody makes me out a fool. Pardon me, ma'am. But I'll cut you down and not lose a minute's sleep over it if you try to give me the slip. Now, I'm willing to take you to New Orleans to check out this wild tale of yours. I'd feel foolish asking for your word that you won't run, so I'm not asking. I'm just going to keep the doc right beside me, 'cause I don't think you'll leave without her. Now, do you reckon these Apaches are going to get ornery when we leave?"

Rafe's eyes were bright and hard. "I guess we'll find out, won't we?"

There was no point in waiting until the next day to leave the camp. Their horses were well rested, and truth to tell, Rafe was just as glad to get away before any more of the warriors recovered. Several of them were well enough anyway to gather outside as Rafe saddled the horses, and all of them were armed. A few of the squaws also came outside, but most of them remained in the wickiups with the invalids who still needed care. Under Atwater's eagle eye, Annie slipped in to see the baby for a moment, and was rewarded by a smile that revealed the two little teeth. She was still feverish, but chewing energetically on a piece of leather. The mother shyly laid her hand on Annie's arm and said something, a rather long speech that conveyed her thanks by tone and wasn't dependent on the understanding of words.

The warriors watched enigmatically. The biggest of them, a man who was almost as tall as Rafe, wondered if he would ever understand the white eyes. There was enmity between their peoples, yet the white warrior and his woman, the magic woman, had worked hard to save the band. The warrior even remembered lying almost naked while the white warrior cooled him with water, which was a thing that was beyond believing. And the magic woman . . . never had he known such a touch. Her hands had been cool, yet hot underneath, and so soothing he could almost feel the peace spreading through him. She had given him rest, and eased his struggle against the fever burning him alive. And she had saved Lozun's baby, when Jacali had said the child was so near to the spirit world there had been no breath left in her body. The white woman's magic was true, and the white warrior knew her worth, guarding her well. That was good.

Then this other white man had come, and pointed his weapon at the white warrior, and tied him with rope like a captive. Jacali had been enraged, and had tried to get him to shoot the new intruder, but he had waited, wanting to see what would happen. The three white people had sat down and made many of their strange-sounding words, and then the old one had cut the ropes from about the white warrior and now they were riding out together. Yes, the white eyes were truly strange people. As grateful as he was to the magic woman, he was glad to see them go.

But they would be traveling east, through the land of his people, and perhaps they would need his protection. There were few white eyes the People could call "friend"; it would be a dishonor to him if he allowed them to be killed. So he gave the beaded amulet and his words to Jacali, and she carried them to the magic woman whose pale hair framed her face like the sun. The old white eyes knew some of the words of the People, and he gave them to the magic woman as Jacali spoke them. And the magic woman smiled. Beside her, the white warrior watched everything with his sharp eyes, guarding his woman as he should.

The warrior was glad to see them ride out of his camp.

Annie turned the beaded amulet over and over in her hands, tracing the intricate pattern. It was an exquisite piece of work, and Atwater had explained that it was the equivalent of a safe-conduct pass. That wasn't it literally, but it was as close as he could come. The explanation satisfied her.

It would take them weeks to get to New Orleans; they had to cross the whole of New Mexico, Texas, and Louisiana. Atwater had mentioned taking the train, but Rafe had sharply vetoed the idea, which had completely soured the lawman's mood.

When they were out of sight of the Apache camp, Atwater abruptly swung the shotgun on Rafe. As he hadn't returned Rafe's weapons, there wasn't a damn thing Rafe could do about it except face the marshal with cold fury in his eyes. "Don't reckon I need to worry about getting to New Orleans," he said.

"Oh, we're still goin'," Atwater said. "It's just that I don't quite trust you to stay put. Now, I did warn you that I don't take kindly to bein' made a fool of, but people have been known not to take my warnings. I'm goin' to remove temptation from your path, so to speak. Put your hands behind your back."

Rafe did, his face set. Annie wheeled her gelding close by and Atwater gave her a warning look. "Keep your distance, ma'am. This is the way it has to be."

"But there's no need," she protested. "We want to get this settled a lot more than you do. Why would we run?"

He shook his head. "No use arguin'. Don't reckon I'd be much of a lawman if I took every outlaw at his word when he swore not to run."

"Let it drop, Annie," Rafe said tiredly. "It won't kill me."

She knew that, but she also knew from experience just how uncomfortable it was, and Rafe had tied her hands in front of her rather than behind. She thought of trying to ambush Atwater herself, but they *needed* him; he had the authority to get things accomplished, and surely even the people who were after Rafe would think twice before shooting a U.S. marshal.

When they made camp that night, Atwater didn't even release Rafe so he could eat; Annie had to feed him. She was exhausted after the long days of taking care of the Apaches, and could barely stay awake long enough to eat her own meal. As soon as the dishes were cleaned she got a blanket and rolled up in it between the two men. Rafe's hard face told her that he didn't like the new sleeping arrangements at all, but she could hardly snuggle up against him with Atwater there. She held her breath, but he didn't say anything. Instead he chose to bed down within arm's reach of her, and she gave a little sigh of relief that he would be so close.

He lay down on his side, facing her, his bound hands behind his back.

"Will you be able to sleep?" she asked with soft concern in her drowsy voice.

"I'm so tired I could sleep standing up," he replied. She wasn't certain she could believe him, but she was too tired to make certain. She wished she was closer to him. After these weeks of being with him, she felt lost without those hard arms wrapped around her while they slept. It helped that he was at least close enough to touch if she should reach out her hand.

She went to sleep easily, but Rafe lay awake for a while, thinking, trying to ignore the ache in his arms and shoulders. He wondered if she was pregnant. He thought she was, but would have to wait impatiently until nature confirmed it. The conviction that she carried his baby only intensified the twin instincts of possessiveness and protectiveness. If he had his way, she would never sleep more than an arm's length from him again. Taking care of Annie was the most important job he'd ever had in his life.

They were going to New Orleans. The reality of it was a little hard to take. He had spent so many years running, consumed by bitterness and his sense of betrayal, that the sudden reversal was disorienting. Of course, the ropes biting into his wrists and the uncomfortable strain on his shoulders reminded him that not everything had changed, after all. As far as Atwater was concerned, there was something here that needed investigating, but he still considered Rafe an outlaw. Atwater was a funny man, hard to figure. He had a reputation as a real hard case, as willing to bring his man in dead as alive, as long as he brought him in, but the marshal had simply listened to Annie's explanation and decided, just like that, to see if maybe it was all true. It felt strange, after those years on the run, but for the first time Rafe had a sense of real hope. When Atwater saw those papers in New Orleans, he'd know that Rafe was telling the truth, and since the marshal had federal connections he could probably do something to get the murder charges dropped.

Providence sure manifested itself in some strange shapes, but Rafe had to admit that the lean, cantankerous, droopy-eyed marshal was the answer to his prayers.

Atwater lay awake, watching the stars overhead and thinking. What in hell had he gotten himself into, agreeing to take McCay to New Orleans to check out that story of his? This was Rafe McCay, not some farm boy; sheer practicality told him that he'd have to untie the man occasionally, and if McCay took it in his head to escape Atwater had no doubt he'd find a way to do it. Damn it, why didn't he just take the outlaw to the nearest town and lock him up? He could manage to get McCay a hundred miles or so, but hell, New Orleans had to be around a thousand miles away. This was definitely not one of his better ideas.

But he'd committed himself and he knew he wouldn't change his mind, even though he also knew he couldn't, by himself, keep McCay from escaping somewhere during those thousand miles. After all, he had the doc to help him, and the only way Atwater could prevent that was to tie her up too, and that would bring up more problems than he thought he could handle. Besides, she wasn't a criminal, even though she'd been riding with McCay, so it wouldn't be right to treat her like one.

Why not just accept that somewhere down the line he was going to have to trust McCay and untie him? They sure as hell couldn't ride through a town with the man trussed up like that; people took notice of things like that, and attracting notice was something Atwater didn't want to do. Well, he'd think on it some. Right now he didn't feel certain enough in his mind to let McCay loose.

It wasn't the most comfortable thought for a lawman to have, but Atwater had learned years ago that the law and justice weren't always the same thing. He remembered a woman who had died a few years back when some drunk cowboys, hoorahing a town, had raced a freight wagon down a street in El Paso and run over her. The law had said it was an accident, and let the cowboys go. The grief-stricken husband had taken his rifle and killed several of the cowboys. The man had obviously been deranged with grief and hadn't known what he was doing. Atwater figured that was justice.

His own wife had died back in '49, caught in a

shoot-out between a couple of drunk miners in California. In that case, justice and the law had marched together, and he'd been able to see both of them swinging from a rope. It hadn't brought Maggie back, but knowing that justice had been served had kept him from going crazy with grief himself. To Atwater's way of thinking, everything had to balance out; that was justice. He figured his job as a lawman was to keep the scales balanced. Sometimes it wasn't easy, and sometimes it was a damn pain in the ass, like now.

He wished he hadn't noticed that McCay looked at Annie the way he himself used to look at his own sweet Maggie.

CHAPTER

18

"We're getting married," Rafe said grimly.

Annie lowered her eyes. They were in a hotel room in El Paso; Rafe had stepped inside with her, but the door was still open and she was acutely aware of Atwater standing in the hall, keeping his eye on Rafe. They had been on the trail for six weeks and Atwater had only untied Rafe that morning, muttering a cantankerous warning that he'd shoot first and find out his intentions later if Rafe made any sudden movements. She doubted they would have come into town at all, but they desperately needed supplies and Atwater hadn't been about to leave them while he rode in alone. Rafe had somehow convinced him to check into the hotel so Annie could have a good night's sleep. She knew why he was worried about her.

"Because I'm pregnant." She said it as a statement, because she knew it wasn't a question. She had known for certain for almost a month, since her menses hadn't come, though she had suspected from the very day Rafe had made love to her at the Apache camp. Evidently he had suspected too, for those sharp eyes had noted even the smallest symptom.

She didn't know how she felt, or even how she should feel. Supposedly she should feel relief that he wanted to marry her and give the baby legitimacy, but now she had to wonder, hollowly, if he would have wanted to marry her if she hadn't been pregnant. It was probably silly of her, under the circumstances, but she would have liked to have been wanted for herself.

Rafe saw the hurt in her eyes and instinct led him to the answer she needed to hear. He had paid such close attention to her, looking for the signs, or lack of them, that would signal a pregnancy, that it had become habit for him to study her for the nuances of expression. He took her roughly in his arms and pressed her head against his shoulder, cradling her while he ignored Atwater standing in the hall watching them. "We're getting married *now* because you're pregnant," he clarified. "If you weren't, I'd want to wait until this mess is cleared up so we could have a proper church wedding—with Atwater giving you away."

She smiled at that last bit. The assurance helped her feelings some, though she couldn't help but think that the subject of marriage had never even come up before. With his arms around her, though, all she could do was close her eyes and relax. It seemed like an eternity since the last time he had held her; all of these weeks on the road they had been constrained by both Atwater's presence and Rafe's bound hands, though Atwater had eventually started tying his hands in front of him. The last two of those weeks she had been burdened by an ever-increasing fatigue, one of the symptoms of early pregnancy, and she had craved his support. It had taken almost more than she could do to stay in the saddle all day.

But now at last she could sleep in a real bed, and she could have a hot bath in a real tub. The luxury of it was almost overwhelming. She did feel a little stifled by having four walls around her and a roof overhead, but that was a tolerable price to pay for the bed and bath.

Rafe felt her relax and rest her weight against him; he slipped his arm under her knees and lifted her. "Why don't you take a nap?" he suggested softly, seeing her eyes already closing. "Atwater and I have something to do."

"I want a bath," she murmured.

"Later. After your nap." He placed her on the bed and she made a sound of pleasure in her throat as she felt the mattress beneath her. He leaned down and kissed her forehead; a little smile fluttered on her lips, then faded as she dropped off to sleep. He regretted that they weren't putting the mattress to better use after those frustrating weeks on the trail, but maybe that would change soon.

He stepped out of the room, closing and locking the door behind him. Atwater scowled at him. "Is she all right?"

"Just tired. You could have given us a minute of privacy," Rafe said, glaring at the lawman.

"I'm paid to see justice done," Atwater replied grouchily. "I ain't paid to trust people." His gaze traveled past Rafe to the closed door. "She needs the rest, poor little thing. I knew we were settin' too hard a pace for her, but you can't just wander through Injun country takin' your time and sniffin' the flowers."

"Come with me," Rafe said. "I've got something to do."

"Like what? We're here to get supplies, not traipse all over town. And you can damn sure bet that if you go anywhere, I'm going to be right there behind you."

"I have to find a preacher. We want to get married while we're here."

Atwater scratched his chin, frowning. "I don't advise it, son. You'd have to use your real name, and it ain't exactly unknown."

"I know. I'll just have to take the chance."

"Any particular reason?"

"From here on out, there's more of a chance I'll be recognized, maybe even killed. I want Annie to be my legal wife just in case."

The marshal still wasn't convinced. "Seems to me that gettin' married would just increase those chances. You'd better think it over."

"She's pregnant."

Atwater glared at him for a few seconds, then gestured down the hall toward the stairs. "I guess you're gettin' married, then," he said, and stalked down the hall beside Rafe.

They got lucky with the preacher they found, a tenderfoot newly arrived from Rhode Island who had no idea about the notoriety of the man standing not two feet from him. He gladly agreed to perform the marriage ceremony at six o'clock that evening. Then Rafe insisted on stopping in a dress shop, hoping there would be something already made that Annie could wear for her wedding. There were a few dresses to choose from, and the only one that looked small enough to fit Annie's narrow frame was more serviceable than decorative, but he bought it anyway. It was clean and new, and the blue color was nice.

They started back to the hotel, with Atwater walking just a little behind Rafe so he could keep an eye on him. The marshal's suspicious nature was getting on Rafe's nerves, but he reckoned he could put up with it until they reached New Orleans. It was a small enough price to pay for his freedom.

El Paso was a dirty, bustling, wide-open town, the streets filled with a mixture of humanity from both sides of the border. Rafe kept his hat pulled low over his eyes, hoping he wouldn't be spotted. He didn't see anyone he knew, but there was always a possibility that someone he'd never met would recognize him.

They walked by an alley; Rafe was already half a step past it when he heard the scraping of sudden movement and he whirled instinctively, already going down in a crouch. A pistol barrel was just protruding beyond the wall, and it was aimed at Atwater. In slow motion he saw the marshal grabbing for his pistol, but Rafe knew that he wouldn't get to it in time; Atwater had wasted a precious split second when he had looked first at Rafe. The man's damn suspicious nature would likely get him killed, because he had been so set on keeping Rafe from escaping when he should have been paying attention to what was going on around him.

If Atwater got killed, Rafe wouldn't have a snowball's chance in hell of getting those charges taken care of before someone put a bullet in his back.

Everything was still moving like molasses. He saw the pistol, saw Atwater turning, realized the marshal wouldn't be able to shoot in time—and in the next instant his big, muscled body collided with the marshal, bowling him over as the sound of the shot exploded close to his head. He heard Atwater's grunt of pain, then they hit the sidewalk hard and rolled off it onto the dusty street. He heard men yelling, heard a woman scream, was aware of people scattering. He caught a glimpse of a face in the shadow of the alley and then he had Atwater's pistol in his hand and he was firing, and the man in the alley flopped backward.

Rafe rolled off Atwater and sat up, cocking the hammer again as he scanned the gathering crowd for another threat. He slanted a quick glance at Atwater, who was gingerly sitting up and holding his hand to his head. Blood streaked through the marshal's fingers. "You okay?" he asked.

"Yeah," Atwater replied, sounding disgusted. "As okay as a man can be who let himself be blindsided like a dumb greenhorn. Parted my hair for me, but I deserve it." He pulled his bandanna from around his neck and pressed it to the wound.

"You sure as hell do," Rafe agreed. He was totally

without sympathy. If Atwater had been paying attention, it wouldn't have happened. He stood and extended his hand to the marshal to help him up, then pushed his way through the crowd gathering around the bushwhacker to kneel by the man's head. Bloody spittle dripped from his mouth. Lung-shot, Rafe saw. He wouldn't last more than a minute or two.

"Does anyone know who he is?" he asked.

"Don't recognize him right off," someone said. "He might have friends in town, but he's probably just a drifter. We got a lot of strangers riding through."

The man's eyes were open and he was staring at Rafe. His lips moved. "What's he sayin'?" Atwater asked irritably, going down on one knee on the man's other side. "What did I ever do to him? Can't say as I've ever seen him before."

But the man didn't even glance at Atwater. His lips moved again, and though no sound emerged Rafe could see that his mouth formed the word "McCay." Then he coughed, and a gurgling sound bubbled up from his throat. His legs twitched spasmodically and he died.

Rafe's mouth tightened and he stood up, gripping Atwater's arm to pull him up, too. "Let's go," he said, and practically dragged Atwater out of the alley, leaning down to grab the package containing Annie's dress from the dirt where it had fallen.

"Let go of my arm," Atwater said irritably. "Damn it, you got a grip like a vise. And I'm an injured man, I don't need to be hurryin' along like this. What set your tail on fire?"

"He might have a partner with him." Rafe's voice sounded remote, and his pale eyes were glittering like ice as he examined every face, every shadow they passed.

"Then I'll handle it. I won't be caught by surprise again." Atwater scowled. "You've got my damn pistol."

Silently Rafe tucked it back into the marshal's holster.

Atwater scowled. "Why didn't you use it to escape?"

"I don't want to escape. I want to get to New Orleans and get those papers. You're the only chance I've got of getting my name cleared."

Atwater's frown deepened. Well, he'd known all along that he'd have to trust McCay at some point, but he had still halfway thought that the outlaw would bolt at the first opportunity and he'd have to hunt him down again. McCay had not only just saved his life, he hadn't escaped when he'd had the perfect opportunity. The only reason he wouldn't have done so would be if he'd been telling the truth. What had been a possibility, something that needed checking out, became for Atwater in that instant a definite fact. McCay wasn't lying. He had been framed for murder, and he was being hunted like a wild animal because of these papers. What had been going on for four years sure as hell wasn't justice, and Atwater was bound and determined to shift the balance.

"I guess I might as well start trusting you," he grumbled.

"Might as well," Rafe agreed.

They had reached the hotel and climbed the stairs to their room, tiptoeing past the room where Annie slept so their footsteps wouldn't awaken her. Atwater poured some water in a bowl and wet his bandanna, then gingerly began washing the crease in his skull. "My head hurts like a son of a bitch," he observed. A minute later he added, "That bushwacker knew who you were. He said your name. So why'd he go after me instead of you?"

"He probably wanted you out of the way so he could collect the bounty. He must have recognized you; you're not exactly unknown in these parts."

Atwater snorted. "I'm just glad he didn't say your

name out loud." He peered into the mirror. "Guess the bleedin's stopped. My head's still pounding, though."

"I'll get Annie," Rafe said.

"No need to, unless she can do something about this headache."

His eyes were enigmatic. "She can." He paused with his hand on the doorknob. "I'm going down to the front desk to have water sent up for our baths. I'm not about to get married covered with dust and smelling like a horse. You want to follow me down to make sure I don't run?"

Atwater sighed and waved his hand in dismissal. "I don't reckon," he said, and their gazes met, a look passing between them in which the two men understood each other perfectly.

Rafe arranged for the bathwater first, then returned upstairs. Annie was still sleeping when he let himself back into the room, and he stood beside the bed looking down at her for a moment. God. His baby was growing inside that slim body, already sapping her strength. If he could, he'd carry her around on a cushion for the next eight months. About seven and a half months, actually, because it had been six weeks since that time in the Apache camp. Six weeks since he'd made love to her.

He thought about the changes in her body that the coming months would bring, and felt desperate at the thought that he might not be there to see them. Her belly would round out, and her breasts would grow heavy. His shaft lengthened and grew hard at the mental image, and a fleeting grin touched his mouth. Decent men were expected to leave their wives alone during such a delicate time; guess this proved he wasn't a decent man.

The tub and hot water would be coming up soon and she needed to tend to Atwater before then, so he leaned down and gently shook her awake. She muttered and pushed his hand away. He shook her again. "Wake up, honey. Atwater's had a little accident and needs you."

Her drowsy eyes flew open and she scrambled from the bed. Rafe grabbed her as she swayed, and was almost swamped by the pleasure of holding her again. "Slow down," he murmured. "He isn't hurt bad, just a crease, it left him with a headache."

"What happened?" She pushed her hair away from her face as she reached for her bag. Rafe forestalled her and picked it up himself.

"He got in the way of a stray shot. Nothing serious." No point in worrying her.

In the room next door, she made Atwater sit in a chair while she carefully examined the scalp wound. As Rafe had said, it wasn't serious.

"Sorry to bother you, ma'am," Atwater said apologetically. "It's just a headache. I guess a shot of whiskey would do just as well."

"No, it won't," Rafe said. "Annie, put your hands on his head."

The look she shot him was a little distressed, because she felt both uneasy and unsure about what he'd said about her healing. But she obeyed and gently set her hands on Atwater's skull.

Rafe was watching the marshal's face. At first he looked merely puzzled, then interested, and finally an expression of almost blissful relief spread across his features. "Well, I declare," he sighed. "I don't know what you did, but it sure stopped my headache."

Annie lifted her hands and absently rubbed them together. So it was true. She did have some unexplained power to heal.

Rafe put his arm around her waist. "The wedding's at six o'clock this evening," he said. "I bought you a new dress for the ceremony, and a tub and hot water for a bath are on the way up."

The distraction worked. Her lips parted with pleasure. "A bath? A real bath?"

"A real bath. In a real tub."

He leaned down to get his saddlebags and Annie's dress; Atwater didn't voice a protest at his obvious intentions. Instead the marshal was almost beaming at them as he absently touched the raw place on his scalp, which somehow wasn't all that sore now.

Annie looked at the saddlebags as he dumped them on the floor in her room. She hadn't missed the implication of his action, either. "What happened?" she asked.

"When Atwater was shot, I didn't try to run," Rafe said in simple explanation. "He decided he might as well trust me."

"He won't tie you up anymore?" Her expression told him how much it had distressed her for him to be bound.

"No." He reached out to touch her hair just as the expected knock sounded on the door. Rafe opened it to admit two half-grown boys, straining under the weight of the tub. Two more boys followed, each carrying two buckets of water that they poured in the tub. They left, and returned a few minutes later with four more buckets of water, this time steaming hot, which were added to the tub. "That'll be four bits, mister," the oldest boy said, and Rafe paid him.

Annie's fingers were flying over her buttons as soon as the door closed behind them. Rafe watched her avidly, his hungry gaze slipping over the pale curves of breast and thigh, the soft curls on her mound. Then she stepped into the water with a voluptuous sigh. She closed her eyes and leaned back against the high lip of the tub.

She hadn't even thought to get the soap. Rafe got it from their saddlebags and dropped it into the water with a small splash. She opened her eyes to smile at him.

"This is heaven," she purred. "Much better than cold streams."

He had some mighty fond memories of a couple of

those cold streams. He was growing harder by the second. He began pulling off his clothes, thinking of the fond memories he could have of that tub.

She glanced at the bed as he stepped into the tub. "We'll get to the bed tonight," he promised.

Noah Atwater, U.S. marshal, stood rigidly by her side, all cleaned up and slicked down, and gave her into the protection and care of her new husband. Annie was a little bemused by it. Rafe had mentioned marriage once, she had lain down to take a nap, and woke a couple of hours later to the news that the wedding would take place in only a couple of more hours. She was wearing a new blue dress, plainly made but it fit well enough. Beneath it, her body still throbbed from his lovemaking. Six weeks' abstinence had made him . . . hungry.

His close-cropped black beard suited him. She stole admiring glances at him all during the short ceremony. She wished that her father were alive for this moment, wished that Rafe didn't have a murder charge hanging over his head and an army of assassins looking for him, but even so she was happy. She remembered her terror when Rafe had kidnapped her from Silver Mesa, and marveled at how much the situation had changed during the few short months since then.

Then the ceremony was over, the preacher and his wife were beaming at them, Atwater was surreptitiously wiping his eyes, and Rafe was turning her face up for a warm, hard kiss. She was briefly astonished: why, she was a married woman now! How remarkably simple it had been.

When they reached Austin two weeks later, they checked into another hotel under assumed names. Rafe put Annie to bed again and immediately sought out Atwater. The two weeks since their marriage had seen her strength fade rapidly as morning sickness began to plague her. The trouble was it wasn't limited to the mornings, with the result that she was managing to keep very little food down, and not even the ground ginger powder she'd been taking could settle her stomach.

"We'll have to go the rest of the way by train," he told Atwater. "She can't make it on horseback."

"I know. I been right worried about her myself. She's a doctor; what does she say?"

"She says that she's never again going to pat an expectant mother and tell her that being sick is just part of having a baby." Annie had kept a sense of humor about it. Rafe hadn't. She had been growing thinner by the day.

Atwater scratched his head. "You could leave her here, you know, and we could go on to New Orleans by ourselves."

"No." Rafe was adamant about that. "If anyone heard that I got married and investigates, she'll be in as much danger as I am. More, because she doesn't know how to protect herself."

Atwater glanced down at the gun belt buckled low on Rafe's hips. He had returned Rafe's weapons to him on the theory that two armed men were twice as good as one. If anyone could protect Annie, it was this man.

"Okay," he said. "We'll go by train."

Perhaps it had been the physical exertion of riding that had made Annie so ill, for she began to feel better the next day despite the rocking motion of the train. She had protested the new mode of travel, knowing that Rafe had elected to continue by train because of her, but as usual he'd been as unmovable as a granite wall. Atwater bought some face powder ("Damn humiliatin' thing for a man to be buyin'. Pardon me, ma'am.") and Rafe used it to make his beard gray.

With a bit of the powder dabbed at his temples, he looked very distinguished. Annie was much taken with his appearance, for she thought that was how he would look in twenty years' time.

She had never been to New Orleans before, but she was too tense to appreciate the varied charms of the Crescent City. They checked into another hotel, but it was too late for Rafe to go to the bank and retrieve the documents. Even train travel was tiring, so they ate dinner in the hotel and then retired to their rooms.

"Is Atwater going with you tomorrow?" she asked when they were lying in bed. She had been worrying about it all day.

"No, I'm going alone."

"You'll be careful, won't you?"

He lifted her hand and kissed it. "I'm the most careful man you've ever known."

"Maybe we should make your hair completely gray tomorrow."

"If you want." He was willing to have his entire body powdered if it would relieve her anxiety any. He kissed her fingertips again, and felt the warm tingle that was evidently for him and him alone. No one else felt this from Annie. He figured it was from *her* response to *him*. "I'm glad we're married."

"Are you? I seem to be nothing but a nuisance lately."

"You're my wife, and you're pregnant. You aren't a nuisance."

"I've been scared to even think about the baby," she confessed. "So much depends on what happens the next few days. What if something happens to you? What if the papers are gone?"

"I'll be all right. They haven't caught me in four years, they aren't going to catch me now. And if the papers are gone . . . well, I don't know what we'll do about Atwater, and I don't know what we can do even if the papers are there. Atwater might balk at blackmail."

"I won't," she said, and Rafe heard the determination in her voice.

He left his gun belt at the hotel, though he did carry his spare tucked into his belt at the small of his back. Atwater had come up with a coat of more eastern cut for him to wear, as well as another hat. Annie powdered his hair and beard. Deciding he was as disguised as it was possible for him to be, he walked the seven blocks to the bank where he had left the documents. It wasn't likely that anyone would notice him, but he carefully watched everyone around him. No one seemed to be displaying any interest in the tall, gray-haired man who moved with pantherish grace.

He knew that it wasn't likely Vanderbilt's men had any inkling of where he'd left the papers; if it had been suspected the documents were in New Orleans, Vanderbilt would have had an army searching the city, including the bank vaults, which weren't proof against influence. And if the documents had been found, the hunt for Rafe wouldn't have been so intense. After all, without the documents to back him up, he had no proof of anything, and who was likely to take his word? Vanderbilt certainly didn't seem to be worrying about Mr. Davis confessing. The ex-Confederate president's word wouldn't carry any weight outside the South, where it might cause a lynching; no, Vanderbilt had nothing to worry about from Mr. Davis.

The easy way out would be to arrange for the documents to be given to Vanderbilt in exchange for the murder charges being dropped, but Rafe didn't like that idea. He didn't want Vanderbilt to walk away unscathed. He wanted the man to pay. He wanted Jefferson Davis to pay. The only thing that bothered him about making certain Mr. Davis suffered for his betrayal was that, all over the South, hundreds of thousands of people had survived because, despite defeat, they had kept their pride intact. He knew his fellow Southerners, knew that fiercely independent pride, and knew also that news of Mr. Davis's betrayal would shatter the pride that was both regional and personal. It wasn't just Mr. Davis who would suffer, it was every man who had fought in the war, every family who had lost a loved one. The folks in the North would have a revenge, for Vanderbilt would be tried for treason and probably shot, but for the Southerners there would be nothing.

When he reached the bank he took out the key to the vault and turned it in his hand. He had kept that key with him for four years, inside his boot. He hoped he would never have to see it again.

He had the key, and he had the name on the bank-vault records. There wasn't any trouble in retrieving the package. He didn't unwrap the oilskin there in the bank, just tucked it under his coat and walked back to the hotel.

He knocked on Atwater's door when he passed it. It opened immediately, and Atwater entered their room with him. Annie was standing rigidly at the foot of the bed, her face white. She relaxed visibly when she saw him, and flew into his arms.

"Any trouble?" Atwater asked.

"Nothing." Rafe took the package from beneath his coat and gave it to the marshal.

Atwater sat down on the bed and carefully unwrapped the oilskin. The sheaf of papers inside was several inches thick, and it took some time to go through them. Rafe waited quietly, just holding Annie. Most of the documents Atwater discarded to the side, but several of them he kept to look over again. When he was finished, he looked at Rafe and let out a long whistle. "Son, I don't know why the bounty on your head isn't ten times what it is. You must be the most wanted man on the face of the earth. You can wreck an empire with this."

Rafe looked cynical. "If the bounty had been much higher, it might have made too many people curious. Someone might have asked questions, the same questions you asked about who Tench was that he was so important."

"And the answer would be that he wasn't, that he was just a nice young feller. Well, it sure made *me* curious." Atwater looked at the documents again. "That son of a bitch betrayed his country, and caused thousands of people on both sides to be killed. Hanging would be too good for him." For once, he didn't beg Annie's pardon for cursing.

"What do we do now?" Annie asked.

Atwater scratched his head. "I don't rightly know. I'm a lawman, not a politician, and I got a feeling it's gonna take a politician to handle this, damn their slippery souls. Pardon me, ma'am. I don't know the people who have enough power to handle this. For all we know, some of the sons of bitches in Washington, pardon me, ma'am, could have been getting some of the money Vanderbilt made in extra profits. If these papers are used before the murder charges are dropped, then Vanderbilt sure ain't going to use his influence to *get* them dropped. He'd probably enjoy seein' you hang alongside him. The charges have to be dropped first."

"Wouldn't the existence of these papers make a difference in whether or not Rafe is found guilty?" Annie asked desperately. "You believed us; why wouldn't a jury?"

"I can't say as to that. From what I heard, the case against him is pretty much black and white. He was seen leaving Tilghman's room. Tilghman was then found dead. Some folks might think he murdered Tilghman so he could have those papers and the money all to himself, maybe even to try blackmail. A smart lawyer can turn things around so a man don't even know hisself."

She hadn't thought of that. No, letting Rafe go to trial was too much of a risk.

Atwater was still thinking. "I don't know any politicians," he repeated. "Never wanted to."

Annie picked up some of the papers and began reading. It made her nervous to realize that she was holding history in her hands. She scanned through them and a picture formed in her mind of the man who had written them. Jefferson Davis had been portrayed in the northern papers as a despicable person, but the facts of his life prior to the outbreak of war said differently. He was a graduate of West Point and the son-in-law of Zachary Taylor. He had been a United States senator, and secretary of war under President Pierce. He had been said to possess the finest intellect and most sterling integrity of his age, despite these documents that said otherwise.

"Where is Mr. Davis now?" she asked, without knowing that the question had been forming. It just came out.

Rafe looked blank. The last he'd heard, the ex-Confederate president had been released from prison and had gone to Europe.

Atwater pursed his lips. "Let me see. Seems like I heard tell he's settled in Memphis, with an insurance company or something."

Annie looked back at Rafe. "You know Mr. Davis," she said. "He's a politician."

"For the losing side," he pointed out ironically.

"Before the war, he was a senator, and on the cabinet. He knows people."

"Why should he help? If anything, he'd turn me in so these papers could be kept private."

"Not," she said carefully, "if he has any integrity."

Rafe was enraged. "Are you asking me to trust in the integrity of the man who sold out his country, who caused thousands of people to die needlessly, including my father and brother?"

"Strictly speaking, he didn't do that," Annie argued. "He didn't betray his country, not if you consider his country to be the Confederacy. He took funds to keep fighting the war so the Confederacy could be preserved."

"And if you'll read those papers again you'll see, in his own handwriting, that he knew it was a useless effort!"

"But he was honor bound to make the effort anyway. That was his job, until the Confederate government dissolved itself and the states rejoined the Union."

"Are you defending him?" Rafe asked, his voice dangerously soft.

"No. I'm saying he's our only chance, the only politician you know who has a vested interest in these papers."

"She has a point," Atwater said. "We could take a steamboat ride up the river to Memphis. Never been on a steamboat before. I heard tell it's a nice way to travel."

Rafe strode to the window and stood looking out at the busy New Orleans street. In four years he'd never been able to get over his anger at and sense of betrayal by President Davis. Maybe that had warped his thinking, maybe not. Going to the man wasn't an option he would ever have considered. But Annie thought it was a viable one, and so did Atwater. Atwater was a shrewd bastard, but the argument that carried the most weight with him was Annie's.

She was his wife and carried his child. That alone made her special, but she wasn't like other people. He hadn't seen a shred of malice in her, not even when he could reasonably have expected it. She had seen ugliness in her life and in her profession, but it hadn't touched the pure inner core of her. Maybe she saw things more clearly than he did right now. Because he trusted her, because he loved her, he sighed and turned from the window. "We go to Memphis," he said.

"We'll have to be careful," Atwater said. "Ain't no sign that Davis is in on this with Vanderbilt, but he won't want these papers made public either."

Rafe sighed, but remembered Davis's reputation.

Except for this one instance, his integrity had been unblemished. And given the way he had been treated after the war, Mr. Davis couldn't be very sympathetic toward the North. It didn't make any difference anyway.

"We don't have a choice. We have to trust him."

CHAPTER

19

*I*t wasn't difficult to find Mr. Davis's house in Memphis, for the ex-Confederate president was a famous personage. He was indeed working with an insurance company, a job provided for him by supporters so the proud man wouldn't be reduced to accepting charity, but quite a comedown for a man who had, for four years, headed a nation.

Rafe and Annie remained secluded in yet another hotel room while Atwater contacted Mr. Davis at his place of business, which seemed the simplest way. Rafe was glad to have Annie all to himself for a while, for even though they had had their own stateroom on the steamboat, Atwater had always been nearby. He wanted to make love to his wife in the daylight, so he could clearly see the subtle changes wrought by pregnancy. As yet her belly was still flat, though it felt taut and her breasts were heavier, the nipples darker. He was entranced, and for a time forgot about Atwater and Mr. Davis, about everything but the magic they had together.

When Atwater returned he was in a disgusted mood. "Refused to even talk to you," he said. "Now, I didn't come right out and say what we had, because there were some folks in the office who could've overheard. But Mr. Davis said he was trying to recover from the war, not relive it, and he didn't think anything could be gained from discussing it yet again. That's his words, not mine. I don't talk like that."

"He'll have to change his mind," Rafe said. His eyes said that he didn't care about Mr. Davis's sensitivity.

Atwater sighed. "He's worn out, true enough. He don't look all that healthy."

"I won't either, at the end of a rope." Then he wished he hadn't said it, because Annie flinched. He patted her knee in apology.

"Well, I'll go back tomorrow," Atwater said. "Maybe I can catch him when there ain't a whole gaggle of folks with one ear cocked toward his office."

The next day Atwater carried a note with him. The note informed Mr. Davis that the people who wished to see him had some of his old papers with them, papers that had been lost during the flight to Texas, right before he was captured.

Mr. Davis read the note and his fine, intelligent eyes went unfocused as he looked back in time to those frantic days six years ago. He carefully folded the note and returned it to Atwater. "Kindly inform these people that I would be pleased to meet with them at my home for dinner tonight, at eight o'clock. You are included in the invitation, sir."

Atwater nodded, satisfied. "I'll do that," he said.

Annie was so nervous she could barely fasten the blue dress she had worn to be married, and Rafe brushed her hands aside to finish the job himself. "The dress is getting snug," she said, indicating her waist and bosom. In another month she wouldn't be able to get into it at all.

"Then we'll get you some new dresses," he said, leaning down to kiss her neck. "Or you can just wear my shirts. I'd like that."

She hugged him in sudden panic, as if she could keep him safe within the shelter of her arms. "Why haven't we had any trouble?" she asked. "It worries me."

"Maybe no one expected us to come east—and remember that we traveled through Apache territory. Not only that, they were looking for one man, not two men and a woman."

"Atwater's been a blessing."

"Yeah," he said. "Though I didn't think so when I was sitting in the dirt with my hands tied behind me and that shotgun pointed at my belly." He released her and stepped back. He wasn't nervous, but he was as tense as coiled wire. He didn't look forward to seeing Mr. Davis. It was a meeting he could gladly have foregone the rest of his life.

Mr. Davis's house was modest, as were his means. He was still sought out by all the people of influence, social and otherwise, and the modest house saw a steady stream of visitors, but that night his only company was a U.S. marshal, a tall man, and a rather slight woman.

Mr. Davis examined Rafe's face carefully, before Atwater could introduce him, and then held out his hand. "Ah, yes, Captain McCay. How have you been, sir? It has been several years since last I saw you, I believe early in '65."

The phenomenal memory didn't take Rafe by surprise. He forced himself to shake the ex-president's hand. "I am well, sir." He introduced Annie, who also shook hands with Mr. Davis. The ex-president's hand was thin and dry, and she held it a moment longer than necessary. Mr. Davis's extraordinarily fine eyes looked thoughtful, and he glanced at their clasped hands.

Rafe's eyelids lowered as he felt a surge of ridiculous jealousy. Had Annie been sending a message with her touch? Mr. Davis's expression had visibly softened.

"Marshal Atwater didn't give me your name when he requested this meeting. Please, won't you sit down? Would you care for something to drink before dinner?"

"No, thank you," Rafe said. "Marshal Atwater didn't tell you who I am because of the chance that my name might have been overheard. I'm wanted for murder, sir, and the reason is these papers."

Annie watched the thin, ascetic face of the ex-president as Rafe told him everything that had happened in the past four years. It was the most intelligent face she had ever seen, with a high, wide forehead and a certain nobility that transcended the flesh. He had been labeled a traitor to the nation by northern newspapers and she supposed she had to consider him so, but she could also see how he had been chosen to lead the government of the breakaway states. There was a certain frailty about him, no doubt caused by two years of imprisonment, and a sadness deep in those fine eyes.

When Rafe had finished Mr. Davis didn't speak, but held out his thin hand. Rafe gave him the documents. He leafed through them in silence for several minutes, then leaned back in his chair and closed his eyes. He looked unutterably weary.

"I had thought these destroyed," he said after a moment. "Would that they had been; Mr. Tilghman would still be alive, and your own life wouldn't have been ruined."

"Disclosure wouldn't make Vanderbilt's life very comfortable, either."

"No, I can see that it wouldn't."

"Vanderbilt was stupid," Rafe said. "Surely he foresaw that these documents could be used against him, to obtain money."

"I would not have done so," Mr. Davis said. "They must be used, however, to obtain justice for you."

"Why did you do it?" Rafe suddenly asked, bitterness apparent in his tone. "Why did you take the money, knowing it was useless? Why prolong the war?"

"I had wondered if you'd read my private notes." Mr. Davis sighed. "My job, sir, was to keep the Confederacy alive. The thoughts I put down in my private notes were my deepest fears, yet there was always the chance that the North would have grown tired of war and demanded an end to it. So long as the Confederacy existed, I served it. It was not a complicated decision, though it is one I bitterly regret. If foresight were as sharp as hindsight, think what tragedies could have been avoided. Hindsight is, unfortunately, a useless commodity, good only for regrets."

"My father and brother died the last year of the war," Rafe said.

"Ah." Mr. Davis's eyes darkened with sorrow. "You have just cause for your anger. I apologize to you, sir, and offer you my sincere condolences, though I am certain you don't desire them. If I may make amends to you in any way, I will do so."

Atwater broke in. "You can help us think of a way to get those murder charges dropped. Just revealing Vanderbilt as a traitor won't do it."

"No, I can see that it wouldn't," Mr. Davis said. "Let me think on it."

"You must go back to New York," he said the next day. "Contact Mr. J. P. Morgan; he's a banker. I have written a letter to him." He passed the folded letter to Rafe. "Take the relevant documents pertaining to Mr. Vanderbilt's donations to the Confederacy to the meeting with you. I would like to keep the remaining documents, if you don't mind."

Rafe glanced down at the letter. "What's in it?" he asked bluntly.

"Mr. Vanderbilt has a great deal of money, Captain McCay. The only way to fight him is with more money. Mr. Morgan can do this. He is a young man of rather stringent morals, but an extremely astute businessman. He is building a banking empire that can, I believe, contain Mr. Vanderbilt's influence. I have outlined the situation to Mr. Morgan and asked for his assistance, which I have reason to believe he will give."

Annie sighed when Rafe told her they had to go to New York. "Do you think the baby will be born on a train somewhere?" she asked whimsically. "Or perhaps on a steamboat?"

He kissed her and stroked her stomach. He hadn't been a very good husband so far, dragging her all over the country just at the time when she most needed peace and quiet. "I love you," he said.

She jerked back to stare at him, her dark eyes widening with shock. Her heart leaped and she put a hand to her chest. "What?" she whispered.

Rafe cleared his throat. He hadn't planned to say what he had, the words had come out all by themselves. He hadn't realized how naked and vulnerable that short sentence would make him feel, or how uncertain of himself. She had married him, but she hadn't had a lot of choice, since she was having a baby. "I love you," he said again, and held his breath.

She was pale, but a radiant smile broke over her face. "I—I didn't know," she whispered. She flung herself into his arms, clinging as if she would never let go.

The constriction in his chest eased, and he could breathe again. He carried her to the bed and placed her on it, then stretched out beside her. "You can say the words, too, you know," he prompted. "You never have."

The smile grew even more radiant. "I love you."

There were no extravagant declarations, no analysis, just the simple words, and they were the right ones for both of them. They lay together for a long time, absorbing each other's nearness. He smiled as his chin rested on top of her head. He should have known, that very first time when he had forced her to lie down on the blanket and share her body heat with him on a cold night, and he had wanted her then despite his illness, that she would come to mean more to him than anything else in his life ever had or ever would.

A week later the three of them sat in J. P. Morgan's richly paneled office in New York City, the place where it all had started for Rafe, four years before. Morgan tapped the letter from Jefferson Davis in his hand, thinking how curiosity could motivate men to do unusual things. It had been obvious to Morgan from the start that these people wanted a favor from him and he usually refused to see such people, but his secretary had said they had a letter from Jefferson Davis, the former president of the Confederacy, and sheer curiosity had led him to grant an interview. Why would Mr. Davis write to him? He had never met the man, had strongly disapproved of Southern politics, but Mr. Davis's reputation was intriguing. J. P. Morgan was a man who held integrity to be the most important virtue.

The banker listened to Marshal Atwater outline the circumstances, and only then did he open the letter from Jefferson Davis. He was thirty-four years old, Rafe's age, but already laying the groundwork for a banking empire that he fully intended to control. He was the son of a banker, and understood the subtleties of the business from top to bottom. He even looked like a banker, his form already showing signs of a prosperous stoutness. His intensity shown in his eyes.

"This is incredible," he finally said, laying the letter aside and picking up the documents to study them. He looked at Rafe with the sort of wary respect one gives a dangerous animal. "You've managed to elude what amounts to an army for four years. I think you must be a formidable man in your own right, Mr. McCay."

"We all have our special battlegrounds, Mr. Morgan. Yours are in boardrooms."

"Mr. Davis thinks the boardroom is the way to control Mr. Vanderbilt. I think he is right; money is the one thing Mr. Vanderbilt understands, the one thing he respects. I will be honored to assist you, Mr. McCay. The evidence here is . . . sickening. I trust you will be able to evade the hunters for another few days?"

It took J. P. Morgan eight days to arrange the kind of backing he needed, but he didn't intend to make a move without it. The way to win battles was not to fight them until you had the weapons needed to win. J. P. Morgan had those weapons when he made an appointment to meet with Vanderbilt, and he already had the idea of another battle forming in his mind, one that would take years to win, but these papers had given him the edge he needed.

Annie was almost ill with tension. Everything hinged on this meeting; the next half hour would decide if she and Rafe could ever live a normal life or would forever be on the run. Rafe had wanted her to remain behind, but she had too much at stake to be able to do so and in the end he relented, perhaps realizing that the apprehension of waiting would be worse on her than knowing what was happening.

Rafe's pistol rested comfortably in the small of his back. On the way into Commodore Vanderbilt's office, he noted every employee, every room. Atwater did the same. "Do you see that Winslow feller?" he hissed, and Rafe shook his head.

Vanderbilt's office was luxuriously furnished, in a far more elaborate style than J. P. Morgan's. The banker's office was intended to convey prosperity and trust; Cornelius Vanderbilt's was intended to showcase his wealth. There was a silk carpet on the floor and a crystal chandelier overhead; the chairs were of the finest leather, the paneling of the richest mahogany. Annie had almost expected to see a cruelly leering devil sitting in the big chair behind the enormous desk, but instead it was occupied by a white-haired old man, growing increasingly frail with age. Only his eyes still hinted of the ruthlessness he had used in building his empire.

Mr. Vanderbilt had looked in surprise at the four people who had entered his office, for he had been under the impression that he would be seeing only Mr. Morgan, a banker of sufficient power that he had deigned to receive him. Nevertheless he offered them the amenities of a host before the conversation turned to business. It always turned to business, and for what other reason would a banker have requested an appointment with him? It was a matter of pride to him that Mr. Morgan had come to him, rather than expecting that he visit the banker's offices. It revealed exactly who had the most power. He took out his watch and glanced at it, a hint that his time was valuable.

Mr. Morgan noticed the action. "We won't use much of your time, sir. May I introduce U.S. Marshal Noah Atwater, and Mr. and Mrs. Rafferty McCay."

A federal marshal? Vanderbilt scrutinized the older man, a rather unprepossessing individual. He dismissed him as unimportant. "Yes, yes, get on with it," he said impatiently.

All four of them had been watching him closely, and Annie was bewildered by his total lack of response to Rafe's name. Surely a man who had spent a sizable fortune trying to find someone and kill him would remember his quarry's name.

Silently Mr. Morgan placed the documents on Vanderbilt's desk. These were not the originals, but faithful copies. What mattered was that the Commodore knew they had the information.

Vanderbilt picked up the first page with a slightly bored manner. It took him only a few seconds to realize what he was reading and his gaze jumped back to Mr. Morgan, then to Atwater. He sat up very straight. "I see. How much do you want?"

"This isn't blackmail," Mr. Morgan said. "At least not for money. Am I correct in assuming that you didn't recognize Mr. McCay's name?"

"Of course not," Vanderbilt snapped. "Why should I?"

"Because you've been trying to have him killed for four years."

"I've never heard of him. Why should I want to have him killed? And what does he have to do with these papers?"

Mr. Morgan studied the older man for a moment. Vanderbilt hadn't even made an effort to deny the information contained in those papers. "You're a traitor," he said softly. "This information would have you in front of a firing squad."

"I'm a businessman. I make a profit. This"—he indicated the papers—"was a paltry sum compared to the profits it generated. The North was in no danger of losing the war, Mr. Morgan."

Vanderbilt's reasoning made Rafe tense; he wanted very much to slam his fist into the man's face.

Very concisely, Mr. Morgan related the events of four years ago. Vanderbilt's eyes flicked to Rafe, then to Atwater again. Annie realized that he expected to be arrested. When Mr. Morgan had finished, Vanderbilt said impatiently, "I don't know what you're talking about. I didn't have anything to do with all that."

"You didn't know that the papers had survived, and that young Mr. Tilghman knew where they were?"

Vanderbilt glared at him. "Winslow informed me of that, yes. I told him to take care of it. I assumed he had, as that was the last I heard of it."

"Winslow. That would be Parker Winslow, I take it?"

"Yes. He's my assistant."

"We'd like to speak with him, please."

Vanderbilt rang a bell, and his secretary opened the door. "Fetch Winslow," the Commodore barked, and the man withdrew.

The door opened some five minutes later. The inhabitants of the room had been sitting in thick silence, waiting for the new arrival. Rafe deliberately didn't turn around when he heard footsteps approaching. He pictured Winslow as he had been four years ago: slim, impeccably groomed, his blond hair just going gray. The perfect businessman. Who would ever have thought Parker Winslow was a murderer?

"You sent for me, sir?"

"I did. Do you know any of these gentlemen, Winslow?"

Rafe looked up just as Parker Winslow's bored gaze touched him. The other man looked startled, then afraid. "McCay," he said.

"You killed Tench Tilghman, didn't you?" Atwater asked softly, leaning forward as all his hunting instincts were awakened. "So he could never dig up those papers. You tried to kill McCay too, but when that failed you made it look as if McCay had killed him. It would have been a perfect plan, yessir, perfect, except McCay escaped. The men you hired couldn't catch him. You put a bounty on his head, and kept raisin' it until every bounty hunter in the country was after him, and they still couldn't catch him."

"Winslow, you're a goddamned idiot," Vanderbilt snapped.

Parker Winslow looked wildly around the room, then back to his employer. "You told me to take care of it."

"I wanted you to get those papers, you stupid son of a bitch, not commit murder!"

Rafe was smiling as he came out of his chair. It wasn't a pleasant smile. The Commodore shrank from it; J. P. Morgan was shocked by it. Parker Winslow was frankly terrified. Atwater settled back in his chair, content to watch.

At first Winslow tried to evade the punishing fists, then he tried to fight back. Both were futile efforts. Calmly, deliberately, Rafe broke the man's nose and knocked out his teeth, shut both of his eyes, then began working on his ribs. Each blow was as precise as a surgeon's scapel. The sound of ribs cracking was audible to everyone in the room. The secretary had opened the door at the first sound of a body thumping to the floor, then hastily closed it again at Vanderbilt's barked order.

Rafe stopped only when Winslow was lying unconscious on the floor. Annie got to her feet, and Rafe whirled with the savage grace of a predator. "No," he said flatly. "You aren't going to help him."

"Of course I'm not," Annie agreed, reaching for her husband's fists and holding them in her own. She lifted them to her lips and kissed the bruised knuckles. There were limits to her oath as a physician, she had found. It hadn't been very civilized of her, but she had enjoyed every blow Rafe had landed. Rafe shivered at her touch and his eyes darkened.

Winslow began to moan, but after an appalled look at him not even Mr. Morgan paid him any attention. "I don't suppose this settled the matter," Vanderbilt said. "I repeat my original question: how much?"

J. P. Morgan's demands were short. Any further action against Rafferty McCay would result in the Confederate papers being made public, and the Commodore would face a charge of treason. The cooperation of the banks in any future Vanderbilt enterprise depended on McCay's name being cleared of all charges, immediately. Whether the Commodore had had any knowledge of Parker Winslow's actions was irrelevant; it was Vanderbilt money that had been behind it, and his own dishonorable actions that had precipitated it. In return, the papers would remain private, in a location unknown to Vanderbilt. Any action taken against any of the people in the room would result in immediate disclosure.

Vanderbilt's eyes were hooded as he listened to the demands and conditions. He was boxed in and he knew it. "All right," he said abruptly. "The charges will be dropped within twenty-four hours."

"There's also the problem of getting the word out to the men Winslow has hunting Mr. McCay."

"It will be taken care of."

"By you, personally."

Vanderbilt hesitated, then nodded. "Anything else?"

Mr. Morgan considered the question. "Yes, I believe there is. I don't think it would be unreasonable for some sort of restitution to be made to Mr. McCay. A hundred thousand dollars, in fact, seems very reasonable."

"A hundred thousand!" Vanderbilt glared at the younger man.

"As opposed to a firing squad."

Behind them, Atwater chuckled. The sound was loud in the silence of the room.

Vanderbilt swelled with impotent fury. "Very well," he finally said.

"He didn't have any regret or shame at all for betraying his country," Annie said. She couldn't understand someone like that. "All he cared about was his profit."

"That's his god," Rafe said. He still felt dazed. It had been not quite one day, but J. P. Morgan had called at the hotel less than an hour before with the news that Vanderbilt had made good on his promise and that the murder charges against him had been dropped. Mr. Morgan suggested that they remain in New York for a time so the word would have time to spread. He had also said that a hundred thousand dollars had been deposited in Rafe's name, at his own bank, of course.

"Do you mind?" Annie asked quietly. "That he isn't going to be brought to justice?"

"Hell, yes, I mind," he growled, then went to sit down beside her on the bed where she was resting. "For prolonging the war, I'd not only like to see him shot, I'd want to pull the trigger myself."

"I'm not certain I believe he didn't know what Winslow had done."

"It's possible that he sacrificed Winslow without even blinking, but on the other hand Winslow didn't start yelling that Vanderbilt had been behind the entire scheme, so the odds are he really didn't know. It doesn't make much difference. He was at the root of the entire situation."

"No one will ever know what he did, and he'll just continue to get richer and richer. It makes me so angry when I think what they did to you."

He rubbed his hand slowly over her belly. "I never would have met you if it hadn't been for Vanderbilt's treason. Maybe fate evens things out." Thousands of men dead, all for one man's greed. But if things had been different, he wouldn't have Annie now. Maybe things just happened, maybe there was no great cosmic scale in which evil and good were carefully balanced. He had to live in the present rather than waste any more time with regrets and bitterness. He not only had Annie, he would be a father soon, an event that was already looming large in his mind. But thanks to Atwater, and Jefferson Davis, and J. P. Morgan, and most of all thanks to Annie, he was not only a free man, he was well off financially and could take care of Annie the way he wanted.

"What will happen to Parker Winslow?" she asked.

"I don't know," Rafe said, but he had a good idea. Atwater had left the hotel without saying where he was going. Sometimes justice worked best in the dark.

* * *

Atwater slipped into Winslow's residence with the stealth of a man who had a great deal of practice in getting around without attracting attention. He could make out the rich furnishings as he moved from room to room; the damn varmint had been living well while Rafe McCay had been forced to live like an animal.

The marshal couldn't think of the last time he'd had a friend. Not since sweet Maggie had died, probably. He'd lived a solitary life, in his support of law and order and his own pursuit of justice. But, damn it, Rafe and Annie had become his friends. They had spent long hours talking around campfires, watching each other's backs, planning and worrying together. Things like that tended to bond people together. As a friend and as a lawman, and by his own personal code, he needed to see that justice was served.

He found Winslow's bedroom and entered it as silently as a shadow. It was a hard thing he had to do, and for a moment he hesitated, staring at the sleeping man in the bed. Winslow wasn't married, so there wasn't a missus there to be terrified out of her wits, and Atwater was glad. He thought about waking Winslow, but discarded the idea. Justice didn't demand that the man know of his own death, only that the deed be done. Very calmly, Noah Atwater drew his pistol and evened the scales of justice.

He was gone from the house before the servants sleeping in the attics could rouse themselves and scramble into their clothing, not certain what it was they had heard. Atwater's face was curiously blank as he walked through the night-darkened streets, his thoughts turned inward. His execution of Winslow had been nothing less than justice, but maybe his own motivation had been more complicated than that; maybe, because of the way he felt about Rafe and Annie, there had been a bit of revenge in him, too. And maybe it was time he turned in his badge, because when other things began to matter, then he couldn't consider himself a pure servant of the law any longer. And after what had happened to Rafe, and seeing how money and power had so successfully manipulated the system to ruin the life of an innocent man branded "outlaw," Atwater couldn't say he believed in the law the way he used to, even if he would always be a man of justice in his heart.

But he was satisfied. The scales were balanced.

CHAPTER

20

Atwater slammed into the ranch house, his face pale with anxiety. Rafe stepped into the hall to meet him. His own face was tense, and his shirt sleeves were rolled up.

"Can't find him nowheres," Atwater growled. "What good's a doctor if he ain't never around when a body needs him? He's probably curled up somewhere with a damn bottle."

Atwater's assessment was probably true. The citizens of Phoenix, whose population had exploded since the first house had been built a year before, were rapidly coming to the same conclusion and turning more and more to Annie with their medical problems. That wasn't much help to Annie, though, who was now herself in need of a doctor.

"Keep looking," he said. He didn't know what else to do. Even a drunk doctor had to be better than no doctor.

"Rafe," Annie called from inside the bedroom. "Noah? Come in here, please."

Atwater looked uneasy at entering a room where a woman was in labor, but the two men went into the

301

room Rafe had just left. Rafe went to the bed and took her hand. How could she look so normal when he was frankly terrified? But she smiled at him, and adjusted her bulk more comfortably on the mattress.

"Forget the doctor," she told Atwater. "Just fetch Mrs. Wickenburg. She's had five of her own and has a good head on her shoulders; she'll know what to do. And even if she doesn't, I do." She smiled at Rafe. "It'll be all right."

Atwater was already leaving the ranch house at a run. Another contraction began low in Annie's belly and she grabbed Rafe's hands, placing them flat on her tightening abdomen so he could feel the power of his child's efforts to be born. He turned absolutely white, but when the contraction eased Annie lay back with a smile. "Isn't it wonderful?" she breathed.

"Hell, no, it isn't wonderful!" he barked. He looked sick. "You're in pain!"

"But our baby will be here soon. I've delivered babies, but obviously I've never experienced it from this position before. It's really interesting; I'm learning a lot."

Rafe felt like tearing his hair out. "Annie, damn it, this isn't a class in medical school."

"I know, darling." She stroked his hand. "I'm sorry you're upset, but truly, everything is perfectly fine." She was surprised at how upset he was, but she realized she should have expected it. No expectant mother in history could have been more cosseted than she had been on the long trip across the country to Phoenix, a brand-new city with brand-new attitudes, not only by Rafe but by Atwater, too, who had resigned his job as marshal and, at Rafe's invitation, joined them as a partner in the sprawling ranch they now owned in the Salt River Valley.

He hadn't wanted her to begin her medical practice until after the baby was born, but time passed slowly for her with nothing to occupy her but the increasing ripeness of her body. So far it was only women who had come to her, women with personal medical problems or their own pregnancies, and sometimes they brought their children. Most people still went to Dr. Hodges, who had an unfortunate fondness for the bottle, but several women had told her that, after her baby was born and she was able to begin a full-time practice, they intended to make certain their entire families came to her.

She was glad it was winter, so she wasn't having to go through labor during the intense heat. During late summer they had had to sleep out on the veranda, though the adobe ranch house was built along Spanish lines, with arches and clean open spaces, and high ceilings to alleviate the heat. She loved her new home. Everything about her new life seemed perfect. Most of all, there was Rafe. He was still impossibly stubborn and autocratic, still the lean, dangerous man with pale crystal eyes who could make most people shiver with just a look, but she knew the passion and sensuality in him, and had no doubts of the strength of his love. There had been days during the autumn when he had carried her out to a certain place where they could lie unseen, with only the great blue sky overhead and the warm earth beneath them, and they had made love naked on a blanket spread on the ground. Her pregnancy had made her skin acutely sensitive and he had reveled in her increased sensuality. She had at first been shy of revealing her body as her abdomen swelled larger, but Rafe had loved feeling the movements of his child within her.

Her contractions had begun during the night, very mild twinges that had kept her awake but weren't really uncomfortable, and progressed slowly. She had expected that, since it was her first baby. By noon the contractions had begun to feel sharper, and she had told Rafe she thought the baby would be born that day. To her surprise, he had immediately panicked, and so had Atwater, who had rushed off in search of Dr. Hodges.

"My water hasn't even broken yet," she said. "There's plenty of time."

He looked grim. "You mean this is going to go on a lot longer?"

She bit her lip, knowing that he would find it unforgivable if she smiled. "I hope not *too* much longer, but it will probably be tonight before it's born." She wasn't looking forward to the next several hours either, but she was anxious to get it over with and actually hold her baby in her arms. She felt an incredible bond with the little creature who had been growing inside her, this child of Rafe's.

The next contraction felt stronger and came sooner than she had expected it. She breathed carefully until it was over, pleased that things were progressing. Part of her was still a doctor, and academically she found it interesting. She suspected, however, that before it was over she would totally forget about how interesting it was and be just another woman submerged in the struggle to give birth.

It was another two hours before Atwater returned with Mrs. Wickenburg, a sturdy woman with a pleasant face, and during those two hours Annie's labor had rapidly become stronger. Rafe hadn't left her side.

Water was boiled, at Annie's instructions, and the scissors for cutting the cord dropped in the boiling water. Mrs. Wickenburg was calm and capable. Rafe carefully lifted Annie so that thick towels could be placed under her.

She managed a smile at him. "I think it's time you left now, darling. It won't be much longer."

He shook his head. "I was there when the baby got started," he said. "I'll be here when it's born. I'm not leaving you to do this alone."

"Just don't faint or get in the way," Mrs. Wickenburg said comfortably.

He didn't. When the contractions came hard and fast, Annie clung to his hands with a grip that left them bruised and swollen the next day. He ground his teeth whenever she groaned aloud, and he held her shoulders when the great final pain seized her in its grip and didn't relent until a tiny, blood-smeared infant slid out of her body and into Mrs. Wickenburg's waiting hands.

"My goodness, that was a good birth," Mrs. Wickenburg said. "It's a girl, and what a sweet little thing she is. Look how tiny! My last one was twice this size."

Annie relaxed, sucking in air with great gulps. Her child was already crying, a ridiculous mewing sound like a kitten. Rafe looked dazed as he stared at the baby. He was still holding Annie, and suddenly his grip tightened as he leaned his head down against hers. "God," he said in a ragged voice.

Mrs. Wickenburg tied off the cord and cut it, then quickly cleaned the baby and gave her to Rafe to hold while the afterbirth came and she took care of Annie.

Rafe was entranced. He couldn't take his eyes off his daughter. His two hands were bigger than she was. She wriggled and jerked her legs and her arms waved erratically. She wasn't crying now, but he was fascinated by the expressions fleeting across the tiny face as she frowned and puckered her mouth and yawned. "I'll be damned," he said tightly. Annie's daughter. He felt as if he'd been punched in the chest, much the same sensation he got at times when he looked at Annie.

"Let me see her," Annie breathed, and with exquisite care he placed the baby in her arms.

Raptly, Annie examined the minute features, loving the downy curve of cheek and perfect rosebud mouth. The baby yawned again, and for a minute her vague, unfocused eyes opened. Annie drew in her breath at the light grayish blue color. "She's going to have your eyes! Look, they're already grayish."

To him the baby looked like Annie, with the same delicately formed features already detectable. She did have black hair, though; her tiny head was covered with it. His coloring, Annie's features. A blending of them, formed during a moment of such intense ecstasy it had changed something inside him forever.

"Let her nurse," Mrs. Wickenburg suggested. "It'll help start your milk."

Annie laughed. She had been so fascinated examining her daughter that she had forgotten to do what she had always told her patients to do. A little shyly she opened her nightgown and exposed one swollen breast. Mrs. Wickenburg discreetly turned away. Rafe reached out and cupped the warm, satiny mound, lifting it up as Annie settled the infant in the crook of her arm, then guided the turgid nipple to the birdlike mouth and rubbed the baby's lips. Annie jumped as the baby instinctively rooted at her breast and began sucking. Hot prickles spread through her breast.

Rafe laughed at the slurping sounds. His pale eyes were shining. "Hurry up with dinner," he advised his daughter. "You have an uncle who's wearing a rut in the floor waiting to meet you. Or maybe he'll be a grandpa to you. We'll have to work that out later."

Ten minutes later he carried the blanket-wrapped infant out to where Atwater was indeed pacing, his hat crushed to a shapeless mass where he had rolled it in his hands. "It's a girl," Rafe said. "They're both fine."

"A girl." Atwater peered at the tiny, sleeping face. He swallowed. "Well, I'll be damned. A girl." He swallowed again. "Jesus, Rafe, how in hell are we goin' to keep all those randy young bucks away from her? I got to think on this."

Rafe grinned as he pulled Atwater's arms out and placed the baby in them. Atwater looked totally panicked and his entire body stiffened. "Don't do that!" he yelped. "I might drop her."

"You'll get used to it," Rafe said, without any sympathy. "You've held puppies, haven't you? She's not much bigger."

Atwater scowled at him. "I ain't holdin' her by the

scruff, either." He cuddled the baby to him. "Damn shame, your own youngun and you wantin' to handle her like a puppy."

Rafe's grin grew bigger, and Atwater looked down at the sleeping baby lying so contentedly in his arms. After a minute he smiled, and made a rocking motion. "Guess it comes kinda natural, don't it? What's her name?"

Rafe's mind went blank. He and Annie had talked about it, choosing names for both a boy and a girl, but right offhand he couldn't remember either of them. "We haven't named her yet."

"Well, make up your minds. I gotta know what I'm gonna call this sweet little treasure. And next time you two decide to have a baby, let me know in plenty of time so I can be somewheres else. This is too hard on a man. I swear, I thought my old heart would give out."

Rafe took his daughter back, to return to Annie. Already he felt anxious at being away from her. "Grandfathers have to stay close," he said. "You aren't going anywhere."

Atwater gaped at his retreating back. Grandfather! Grandfather? Well, that did sound kinda nice. He was in his fifties, after all, though he prided himself on looking younger than his age. Never had a family before, except for Maggie, and no one since she had died. Scary as hell, but maybe he'd stick around, keep McCay out of trouble. This grandfather business sounded like a full-time job.

Rafe slipped back into their bedroom and found Annie sleeping peacefully. Mrs. Wickenberg smiled at him and held her finger to her lips. "Let her rest," she whispered. "She's worked hard and deserves it." With another smile, the woman let herself out of the room.

Rafe sat down in the chair beside the bed, still holding the baby. He was reluctant to put her down. She was asleep, too, as if being born had been as tiring for her as for her mother. He felt pretty wrung out himself, but had no inclination to sleep. He looked from Annie's face to that of their daughter, and his heart swelled so much that it pushed against his ribs and almost stopped his breath.

Nine months before he had held an Indian baby and helped Annie preserve her life. Now he held another baby, one to which he and Annie had also given life, but this time it was the life of their very bodies. From the minute he had first seen Annie she had turned his life around, given him something to live for, and if his remaining years gave him nothing else he was content, for this was enough.

EPILOGUE

*D*uring the next decade, the brilliant young banker J. P. Morgan arranged a financial coup that broke Commodore Vanderbilt's monopoly on the railroads. No hint of the Confederate papers ever came to light, but Rafe figured that Vanderbilt, knowing Morgan had them, didn't fight the banker as vigorously as he might have. It wasn't the justice Rafe would have chosen, the justice Atwater had meted out to Parker Winslow before resigning as marshal, but it was probably the justice that hurt Vanderbilt the most.

Somehow it didn't much matter anymore. He had Annie and their kids, and the ranch was prosperous. Sometimes when the kids had been rowdy, the two boys driving their sister into temper tantrums, when Annie had had a busy day with her patients and the cattle had been particularly stubborn, he and Annie would slip out to their place in the desert and make it all go away. He was a slave to her special magic and wouldn't have wanted it any other way.

AUTHOR'S NOTE

The story of the lost Confederate treasury happened pretty much as related in this book. The bulk of it was stolen, probably by a group of citizens, on its way back to Richmond from Washington, Georgia. It is also true that Tench Tilghman, a personable young man from Maryland, buried his share of the payroll, the Confederate government papers, and some of Jefferson Davis's personal papers. He kept a diary noting these facts, though the diary doesn't give the location of the buried treasure.

Tench Tilghman did indeed meet William Stone in New York in 1867 and divulge that he had buried the papers and money in Florida, and he did indeed die suddenly, four days later, without revealing the location, as far as is known. The rest of the story is from my imagination.

With apologies to Commodore Vanderbilt, I chose him because he was one of the richest, most powerful men of his day, and I needed such a man because only a very powerful man could have financed such a massive manhunt, or been so largely impervious to retaliation. This is a work of fiction, and except for the details of the Confederate treasury, it exists only in my head.

J. P. Morgan did break Vanderbilt's railroad monopoly.

The sources for my research are: *Southern Treasures*, by Nina and William Anderson; *Indeh, an Apache Odyssey*, by Eve Ball; *Magic and Medicine of Plants*, by Reader's Digest; and *Yesterday and Today in the Life of the Apaches*, by Irene Burlison.

POCKET BOOKS
PROUDLY PRESENTS

OPEN SEASON
by
LINDA HOWARD

**Now available in paperback
from
Pocket Books**

Turn the page for a preview of
Open Season. . . .

"Daisy! Breakfast is ready!"

Her mother's voice yodeled up the stairwell, the intonation exactly the same as it had been since Daisy was in first grade and had to be cajoled into getting out of bed.

Instead of getting up, Daisy Ann Minor continued to lie in bed, listening to the sound of steady rain pounding on the roof and dripping from the eaves. It was the morning of her thirty-fourth birthday, and she didn't want to get up. A gray mood as dreary as the rain pressed down on her. She was thirty-four years old, and there was nothing about this particular day to which she looked forward with anticipation.

The rain wasn't even a thunderstorm, which she enjoyed, with all the drama and sound effects. Nope, it was just rain, steady and miserable. The dreary day mirrored her mood. As she lay in bed watching the raindrops slide down her bedroom window, the unavoidable reality of her birthday settled on her like a wet quilt, heavy and clammy. She had been good all her life, and what had it gotten her? Nothing.

She had to face the facts, and they weren't pretty.

She was thirty-four, never been married, never even been engaged. She had never had a hot love affair—or even a tepid one. A brief fling in college, done mainly because everyone else was doing it and she hadn't wanted to be an oddball, didn't even quality as a relationship. She lived with her mother and aunt, both widowed. The last date she'd had was on September 13, 1993, with Aunt Joella's best friend's nephew, Wally—because *he* hadn't had a date since at least 1988. What a hot date *that* had been, the hopeless going on a mercy date with the pitiful. To her intense relief, he hadn't even tried to kiss her. It had been the most boring evening of her life.

Boring. The word hit home with unexpected force. If anyone had to pick one word to describe her, she had a sinking feeling she knew what that word would be. Her clothes were modest—and boring. Her hair was boring, her face was boring, her entire *life* was boring. She was a thirty-four-year-old, small-town, barely-been-kissed spinster librarian, and she might as well be eighty-four for all the action she saw.

Daisy switched her gaze from the window to the ceiling, too depressed to get up and go downstairs, where her mother and Aunt Joella would wish her a happy birthday and she would have to smile and pretend to be pleased. She knew she had to get up; she had to be at work at nine. She just couldn't make herself do it, not yet.

Last night, as she did every night, she had laid out the outfit she would wear the next day. She didn't have to look at the chair to envision the navy skirt, which hovered a couple of inches below her knee, both too long and too short to be either fashionable or flattering, or the white short-sleeved blouse. She could hardly have picked an outfit less exciting if she had tried—but then, she didn't have to try; her closet was full of clothes like that.

Abruptly she felt humiliated by her own lack of style. A woman should at least look a little sharper than usual on her birthday, shouldn't she? She would have to go shopping, then, because the word "sharp" didn't apply to anything in her entire wardrobe. She couldn't even take extra care with her makeup, because the only makeup she owned was a single tube of lipstick in an almost invisible shade called "Blush." Most of the time she didn't bother with it. Why should she? A woman who had no need to shave her legs certainly didn't need lipstick. How on earth had she let herself get in this predicament?

Scowling, she sat up in bed and stared directly across the small room into her dresser mirror. Her mousy, limp, straight-as-a-board brown hair hung in her face and she pushed it back so she could have a clear view of the loser in the mirror.

She didn't like what she saw. She looked like a lump, sitting there swathed in blue seersucker pajamas that were a size too big for her. Her mother had given her the pajamas for Christmas and it would have hurt her feelings if Daisy had exchanged them. In retrospect, Daisy's feelings were hurt because she was the sort of woman to whom anyone would give seersucker pajamas. Seersucker, for God's sake! It said a lot that she was a seersucker pajamas kind of woman. No Victoria's Secret sexy nighties for her, no sirree. Just give her seersucker.

Why not? Her hair was drab, her face was drab, *she* was drab.

The inescapable fact was that she was boring, she

was thirty-four years old, and her biological clock was ticking. No, it wasn't just *ticking*, it was doing a countdown, like a space shuttle about to be launched: *ten . . . nine . . . eight . . .*

She was in big trouble.

All she had ever wanted out of life was . . . a life. A normal, traditional life. She wanted a husband, a baby, a house of her own. She wanted *SEX*. Hot, sweaty, grunting, rolling-around-naked-in-the-middle-of-the-afternoon sex. She wanted her breasts to be good for something besides supporting the makers of bras. She had nice breasts, she thought: firm, upright, pretty C-cups, and she was the only one who knew it because no one else ever saw them to appreciate them. It was sad.

What was even sadder was that she wasn't going to have any of those things she wanted. Plain, mousy, boring, spinster librarians weren't likely to have their breasts admired and appreciated. She was simply going to get older, and plainer, and more boring; her breasts would sag, and eventually she would *die* without ever sitting astride a naked man in the middle of the afternoon—unless something drastic happened . . . something like a miracle.

Daisy flopped back on her pillows and once more stared at the ceiling. A miracle? She might as well hope lightning would strike.

She waited expectantly, but there was no boom, no blinding flash of light. Evidently no help was coming from on high. Despair curled in her stomach. Okay, so it was up to her. After all, the Good Lord helped those who helped themselves. *She* had to do something. But *what?*

Desperation sparked inspiration, which came in the form of a revelation:

She had to stop being a good girl.

Her stomach clenched, and her heart started pounding. She began to breathe rapidly. The Good Lord couldn't have had *that* idea in mind when He/She/It decided to let her handle this on her own. Not only was it a very un–Good Lord type of idea, but . . . she didn't know how. She had been a good girl her entire life; the rules and precepts were engraved on her DNA. Stop being a good girl? The idea was crazy. Logic dictated that if she wasn't going to be a good girl any longer, then she had to be a bad one, and that just wasn't in her. Bad girls smoked, drank, danced in bars, and slept around. She might be able to handle the dancing—she kind of liked the idea—but smoking was out, she didn't like the taste of alcohol, and as for sleeping around—no way. That would be monumentally stupid.

But—but bad girls get all the men! her subconscious whined, prodded by the urgency of her internal ticking clock.

"Not all of them," she said aloud. She knew plenty of good girls who had managed to marry and have kids: all her friends, in fact, plus her younger sister, Beth. It could be done. Unfortunately, they seemed to have taken all the men who were attracted to good girls in the first place.

So what was left?

Men who were attracted to bad girls, that's what.

The clenching in her stomach became a definite queasy feeling. Did she even *want* a man who liked bad girls?

Yeah! her hormones wailed, oblivious to common sense. They had a biological imperative going here, and nothing else mattered.

She, however, was a thinking woman. She definitely didn't want a man who spent more time in bars and honkytonks than he did on the job or at home. She didn't want a man who slept with any road whore who came along.

But a man with experience . . . well, that was different. There was just something about an experienced man, a look in his eyes, a confidence in his walk, that gave her goosebumps at the thought of having a man like that all to herself. He might be an ordinary guy with an ordinary life, but he could still have that slightly wicked twinkle in his eyes, couldn't he?

Yes, of course he could. And that was just the kind of man she wanted, and she refused to believe there wasn't one somewhere out there for her.

Daisy sat up once more to stare at the woman in the mirror. If she were ever going to have what she wanted, then she had to act. She had to do something. Time was slipping away fast.

Okay, being a bad girl was out.

But what if she gave the *appearance* of being a bad girl? Or at least a party girl? Yeah, that sounded better: party girl. Someone who laughed and had fun, someone who flirted and danced and wore short skirts—she could handle that. Maybe.

Big maybe.

"Daisy!" her mother yodeled once more, the sound echoing up the stairs. This time her voice was arch with the tone that said she knew something Daisy didn't, as if there was any way on earth Daisy could have forgotten her own birthday. "You're going to be late!"

Daisy had never been late to work a day in her life. She sighed. A normal person with a normal life would be late at least once a year, right? Her unblemished record at the library was just one more indicator of how hopeless she was.

"I'm up!" she yelled back, which wasn't quite a lie. She was at least *sitting* up, even if she wasn't out of bed.

The lump in the mirror caught her eye, and she glared at it. "I'm never going to wear seersucker again," she vowed. Okay, so it wasn't quite as dramatic as Scarlett O'Hara's vow never to be hungry again, but she meant it just the same.

How did one go about being a bad girl—no, a *party* girl, the distinction was important—she wondered as she stripped off the hated seersucker pajamas and wadded them up, then defiantly stuffed them in the waste basket. She hesitated a moment— what would she wear to bed tonight?—but forced herself to leave the pajamas in the trash. Thinking of her other sleepwear—seersucker for summer and flannel for winter—she had the wild thought of sleeping naked tonight. A little thrill ran through her. That was something a party girl would do, wasn't it? And there was nothing *wrong* with sleeping naked. She had never heard Reverend Bridges say anything at all about what one wore, or didn't wear, to bed.

She didn't have to shower, because she was one of those people who bathed at night. The world, she thought, was divided into two groups: those who showered at night, and those who showered in the morning. The latter group probably prided themselves on starting the day fresh and sparkling clean. She, on the other hand, didn't like the idea of crawling between sheets already dirtied by the previous day's accumulation of dust, germs, and dead skin cells. The only solution to that was to the change the sheets every day, and while she was sure there were some people obsessive enough to do just that, she wasn't one of them. Changing the sheets once a week was good enough for her, which meant she had to be clean when she went to bed. Besides, showering at night saved time in the morning.

Like she was ever rushed for time anyway, she thought gloomily.

She stared in the bathroom mirror, which confirmed what she had seen in the dresser mirror. Her hair was dull and shapeless, without style. It was healthy but limp, without any body at all. She pulled a long brown strand in front of her eyes to study it. The color wasn't golden brown, or red brown, or even a rich chocolate brown. It was just brown, as in mud. Maybe there was something she could put on it to give it a little bounce, a little oomph. God knows there were zillions of bottles and tubes and sprays in the Health and Beauty section of the WalMart over on the highway, but that was fifteen miles away and she usually just picked up a bottle of shampoo at the grocery store. She had no idea what the products in those zillions of bottles and tubes *did*, anyway.

But she could learn, couldn't she? She was a librarian, for heaven's sake. She was a champion researcher. The secrets of the earth were open books to those who knew where and how to dig. How difficult could hair products be?

Okay. Hair was number one on her list of improvements. Daisy went back into her bedroom and got a pad and pen from her purse. She wrote the number one at the top of a page, and beside it wrote: HAIR. Below that she quickly scrawled MAKEUP, and below that CLOTHES.

There, she thought with satisfaction. What she had was the blueprint for the making of a party girl.

Returning to the bathroom, she quickly washed her face, then did something she almost never did. Opening the jar of Oil of Olay that Aunt Joella had given her for her birthday last year, she moisturized her face. Maybe it didn't do any good, but it felt good, she decided. When she was finished, she thought that her face did look smoother, and a little brighter. Of course, anything that had been greased looked smoother, and all that rubbing was bound to have reddened her complexion, but one had to start somewhere.

Now what?

Nothing, that was what. She had nothing else to do, no other ointments, none of the mysterious and sexy little squares of color or dark-colored pencils with which other women lined their eyes and darkened their lids. She could put on her lipstick, but why bother? It was virtually the same shade as her lips; the only way she could tell she had it on was by licking her lips and tasting. It had a slight bubble gum flavor, just as it had when she was in junior high—"Oh, *God!*" she moaned aloud. She hadn't changed her shade of lipstick since junior high!

"You're pathetic," she told her reflection, and this time her tone was angry. Cosmetic changes weren't going to be enough.

She had to do something drastic.

Two gaily wrapped boxes were sitting on the kitchen table when Daisy went downstairs. Her mother had made Daisy's favorite breakfast, pecan pancakes; a cup of coffee gently steamed beside the plate, waiting for her, which meant her mother had listened for her footsteps on the stairs before pouring the coffee. Tears stung her eyes as she stared at her mother and aunt; they were really two of the sweetest people in the world, and she loved them dearly.

"Happy birthday!" they both chimed, beaming at her.

"Thank you," she said, managing a smile. At their

urging she sat down in her usual place and quickly opened the boxes. Please, God, not more seersucker, she silently prayed as she folded back the white tissue from her mother's gift. She was almost afraid to look, afraid she wouldn't be able to control her expression if it *was* seersucker—or flannel. Flannel was almost as bad.

It was . . . well, it wasn't seersucker. Relief escaped in a quiet little gasp. She pulled the garment out of the box and held it up. "It's a robe," said her mother, as if she couldn't see what it was.

"I . . . it's so pretty," Daisy said, getting teary-eyed again because it really was pretty—well, prettier than she had expected. It was just cotton, but it was a nice shade of pink, with a touch of lace around the collar and sleeves.

"I thought you needed something pretty," her mother said, folding her hands.

"Here," said Aunt Joella, pushing the other box toward Daisy. "Hurry up, or your pancakes will get cold."

"Thank you, Mama," Daisy said as she obediently opened the other box and peered at the contents. No seersucker here, either. She touched the fabric, lightly stroking her fingertips over the cool, sleek finish.

"Real silk," Aunt Joella said proudly as Daisy pulled out the full-length slip. "Like I saw Marilyn Monroe wear in a movie once."

The slip looked like something from the nineteen forties, both modest and sexy, the kind of thing daring young women wore as party dresses these days. Daisy had a mental image of herself sitting at a dressing table brushing her hair and wearing nothing but this elegant slip; a tall man came up behind her and put his hand on her bare shoulder. She tilted her head back and smiled at him, and he slowly moved his hand down under the silk, touching her breast as he bent to kiss her . . .

"Well, what do you think?" Aunt Joella asked, jerking Daisy out of her fantasy.

"It's beautiful," Daisy said, and one of the tears she had been blinking back escaped to slide down her cheek. "You two are so sweet—"

"Not *that* sweet," Aunt Joella interrupted, frowning at the tear. "Why are you crying?"

"Is something wrong?" her mother asked, reaching over to touch her hand.

Daisy drew a deep breath. "Not *wrong*. Just—I had an epiphany."

Aunt Jo, who was sharper than any tack, shot her a narrow-eyed look. "Boy, I bet that hurt."

"Jo." Sending her sister an admonishing glance, her mother took both of Daisy's hands in hers. "Tell us what's wrong, honey."

Daisy took a deep breath, both to work up her courage and to control her tears. "I want to get married."

They both blinked, and looked at each other, then back at her.

"Well, that's wonderful," her mother said. "To whom?"

"That's the problem," Daisy said. "No one wants to marry *me*." Then the deep breath stopped working and she had to bury her face in her hands to hide the way her unruly tear ducts were leaking.

There was a small silence, and she knew they were looking at each other again, communicating in that mental way sisters had.

Her mother cleared her throat. "I'm not quite certain I understand. Is there someone in particular to whom you're referring?"

Bless her mother's heart, she was an English teacher to the core. She was the only person Daisy knew who actually said *whom*—well, except for herself. The acorn hadn't fallen far from the mother oak. Even when her mother was upset, her phrasing remained exact.

Daisy shook her head, and wiped the tears away so she could face them again. "No, I'm not suffering from unrequited love. But I want to get married and have babies before I get too old, and the only way that's going to happen is if I make some major changes."

"What sort of major changes?" Aunt Jo asked warily.

"Look at me!" Daisy indicated herself from head to foot. "I'm boring, and I'm mousy. Who's going to look at me twice? Even poor Wally Herndon wasn't interested. I have to make some major changes to *me*."

She took a deep breath. "I need to spruce myself up. I need to make men look at me. I need to start going places where I'm likely to meet single men, such as nightclubs and dances." She paused, expecting objections, but was met with only silence. She took another deep breath and blurted out the biggie: "I need to get my own place to live." Then she waited.

Another sisterly glance was exchanged. The moment stretched out, and Daisy's nerves stretched along with it. What would she do if they strenuously objected? Could she hold out against them? The problem was that she loved them and wanted them happy, she didn't want to upset them or make them ashamed of her.

They both turned back to her with identical broad smiles on their faces.

"Well, it's about time," Aunt Jo said.

"We'll help," her mother said, beaming.